Chasing Elvis

By Glenn Marcel

The Invisible College Press, LLC

Arlington VA

Publisher's Note:
This is a work of fiction. Names, characters, places, and incidents are either the product of the author's imagination or are used fictitiously, and any resemblance to actual persons living or dead, events, entertainers, or locales is entirely coincidental.

ISBN: 1-931468-20-6

Cover Design by Jeff Carns
Second Printing

The Invisible College Press, LLC
P.O. Box 209
Woodbridge VA 22194-0209
http://www.invispress.com

Please send question and comments to:
editor@invispress.com

PART ONE

CHAPTER ONE
1982

The wannabe robber nervously fidgeted with the radio dial of the Coupe de Ville and cycled through several oldies stations until he finally found one playing an Elvis tune. Without thinking, he began harmonizing with the King. Soon his voice and the one coming from the radio were one. As he sang, his eyes turned to the rearview mirror and a Cheshire grin erupted on his dry lips. Other than the stretched out fabric where his potbelly strained the Elvis jumpsuit, the outfit clung to him as though it were sprayed on. The padding in the shoulders gave him the fake, in-shape appearance he desired. He ignored the double-chin and propelled his arms into a muscleman's pose, trying to highlight his biceps, but nothing happened when he flexed his arm. The fabric did not budge where muscle should be. Disappointed, his grin became a frown and he jerked his arms down, hitting the funny bone of his right elbow on the shifter. He involuntarily yelped and his eyes clouded with moisture as he stretched out the arm to relieve the numbness.

The mid-morning heat and humidity steamed off the street and sidewalk and the robber suddenly began to sweat. He tugged at the jumpsuit in a futile attempt to get air circulating against his clammy skin. He thought of starting the engine and running the air, but concluded that smoke belching out of the exhaust in front of a bank might arouse suspicion. He should have waited a few more minutes before pulling into the parking spot, but wanted to have a prime location from which to get away. He fanned his face with his hand and rolled the window down and the oven that was outside the Caddy quickly invaded the interior of the car. He wiped his brow with his sleeve and checked the mirror. Nothing happening behind him. Didn't want a cop pulling up. He inspected himself again.

He had always admired the cape because it was a truly original idea. The black cape of his jumpsuit flowed rearward from his padded shoulders and over the seat, its sequins throwing off diamond bullets of light into the roof of the Cadillac. Just his breathing caused the pinpoints of light to dance on the ceiling the way a mirror ball flooded with light in a dance hall made the hall's ceiling come alive. The laser-like lights flying off the sequins that flowed down the front of the jumpsuit glittered on the dashboard and his spit-shined, black, patent leather boots, causing the dash and shoes to also appear alive with movement.

The zipper on the front of the jumpsuit stopped twelve inches from his lower chin, leaving the graying wiry hairs on his chest exposed and causing him to frown even more. He routinely dyed his hair and wondered if the hair on his head was as gray as the hair on his chest. He plucked out a chest hair to examine it and winced at the sharp pain. He held the hair to his aging eyes and realized that he could not focus on the tiny follicle. He was too vain to wear much-needed glasses.

The Elvis-robber glanced at his watch for the fifth time in three minutes and then scanned the perfectly polished glass doors of the bank across the street. Disappointed to see that three customers were now at the locked door waiting for the bank to open, he curled his lips. It would be better if there were no civilians in the bank, but he accepted the slight setback. It would all go so quickly that only he and the one teller would even know anything was happening. It would be like the movie he had seen. He had played the movie over and over again on the Betamax to get the *feel* of how to rob the bank. Go in, make the demand, and come out with the money. It wasn't rocket science or brain surgery. There would be a problem only if he deviated from the checklist in his mind. "Just stick to the plan," he said out loud to himself, but then he panicked when he couldn't remember the first item on the list. *Oh, yeah, go in with the box,* he remembered. The quickly erupting panic attack subsided.

Two of the early bank customers were females waiting to make deposits to cover hot checks. In the vernacular of accounting, they had each made a withdrawal against a future deposit and the race was on to beat the presentation of the worthless check with a timely cash deposit. Neither customer was a stranger to the term, worthless check.

One of the female customers was plus-sized and wore a bright yellow tent that masqueraded as a size twenty-six dress. The woman held a tiny purse in her hand and a bag on a strap on her shoulder. Her round, ocean-blue eyes peered from under folds of flesh caked with pale blue eye shadow. The color of her eyes was striking. Perhaps an artist, or someone with a very vivid imagination, or someone good at squinting his eyes and interpreting shadows could envision the beauty hidden beneath the fat rolls.

The customer's brows were furrowed as she was frustrated. She was trying to dial the new-fangled thing, an experimental bag phone her father, a technician with the phone company, had given her. He had said the phones had proved successful in Chicago, Washington, D.C., Baltimore and Japan, and the phone company was trying it in Tennessee. He had said it would work only in the middle of town. Even though its numbers were slightly smaller than those on a regular telephone, she had trouble getting her stubby fingers to punch just one number a stab. On an epiphany, she plucked a pencil from her purse and used it to depress the numbers. The young woman had finally decided to tell her boyfriend that she was pregnant (actually seven and a half months pregnant) and would do it over the phone, rather than tell him in person. Someone, she couldn't remember who, had recently told her what a lovely telephone voice she had, and she needed to use whatever angle she could muster to her advantage. It would be a difficult call at best, as she and her boyfriend had not actually had intercourse yet, and although he had the I.Q of a boiled turnip, eventually he'd figure out that she couldn't get pregnant through oral sex and that he wasn't the *lucky* father. But the boyfriend was a few ounces shy of a full pint and there was an outside chance that he wouldn't put two and two together. Maybe she'd get lucky and the call would have static like the other occasions she'd used the phone. If things went badly she could claim a misunderstanding and disconnect the call. The phone could take the blame.

The actual father was a sailor on shore leave who woke up after downing enough gin to fill a bathtub, with three new tattoos and the ugliest woman he'd ever seen sharing his bed. The bewildered sailor managed to slip the clutches of his one-night stand and bolt for the door without having to divulge his name. But she would never tell her boyfriend the truth, or at least an unsanitized version of the truth.

The other woman customer was blonde, tall and slender and wore bell-bottom knit pants with a low waist and a ribbed blouse that stopped four inches from the top of the pants. She sported a wonderful tan and posed with a movie star's grace. Her hot check was made out to her plastic surgeon, and unfortunately, it wasn't the first bad check she had given him. The one for the boob job had also bounced. And since she simply had to have something done about her dimple-less chin, she didn't want to burn any bridges behind her. She struggled to make ends meet on the crummy eight thousand a month alimony she got from her ex-husband, who also happened to be a plastic surgeon and who had dumped her for his new nursing assistant.

The pretty lady looked familiar to the Elvis-robber, but he couldn't quite place her face. He thought hard about it for a few seconds, shrugged his shoulders and then peeked at his watch yet again. In two minutes the doors to the bank would be unlocked and he would do the craziest thing he had ever done. He pulled down the cover to the glove box, extracted a pair of rubber gloves, slipped one on his right hand, and then, using his teeth, slipped the other on his left hand. The latex popped his wrist when he released it with his teeth.

The third customer outside the bank was a male Puerto Rican teenager who needed to open a checking account to deposit his very first paycheck. He had *stolen* paychecks before and fenced them, but this check was the first he had actually earned. He would have simply cashed the thing at one of those neighborhood check-cashing places, the kind that require no identification and charge a premium, but his employer paid five percent more, in his case thirty cents per hour, if future checks were electronically deposited by the employer into a bank account. The employer thought he was teaching the underprivileged a valuable lesson in capitalism by making them use a checking account. But the teenager wouldn't even get any checks; he'd just open an account and withdraw the cash every payday. The teenager would play along for now with the pushy employer only because he needed the money and had no other prospects for a job. He was a bright kid, but his G.E.D. would not impress many prospective employers, especially with his juvenile record. The state of Tennessee had helped him get the job and if he lost this job he would have to go back to reform school. The kid would put up with the crap--for now.

The young man was dressed casually with a white tee shirt and baggy jeans that sagged from his waist almost all the way to his crotch, due to the weight of the pistol in his pocket. He had bought the gun from a guy he met on the street selling *genuine* Rolexes for twenty bucks apiece and .22 calibers for thirty. As a bonus the gun came loaded. He didn't know it yet, but this would prove to be the most important day of his life.

The bank's security guard squinted into glare coming off the bank's huge glass windows facing the street, as he rammed the index finger of his right hand up his nose, fishing for a booger that had annoyed him since he had awakened. The guard's mind drifted, as he twisted his finger, and he suddenly couldn't remember if it was Monday or Tuesday. This had been happening a lot lately, but it didn't matter. Each day was like the one that preceded it and the one to follow, except for Wednesday. His daughter visited at his assisted living place on Wednesday nights with his grandchild and brought him lasagna and soup to freeze for other nights. Wednesdays were special. The guard was pretty sure it was not Wednesday, as his daughter always called him early in the morning to remind him of her visit. She had not called this morning, or had she? He plucked his finger out of his nostril and mindlessly studied it. No success. The booger had escaped capture.

He rubbed his chin, trying to jump start his memory. Then he rubbed his forehead with the palm of his hand and adjusted his cap. His uniform was starched, which he took great pride in doing himself, and his shoes were highly polished. He had learned the secrets of a mirror-like shoeshine in his thirty years of military service. He marched to the front door and pivoted as though he were in drill or on a parade. He stood erect as though a steel rod ran through his spine. The two tellers nodded in unison to him, signaling that it was time to open the door. But Sergeant, as his friends called him, didn't budge. Sergeant couldn't see anything much beyond five feet in front of him, and certainly not the tellers who were thirty feet away. Cataract surgeries had left him just one more eye-exam from being declared legally blind. The tellers saw that Sergeant had not acknowledged their signal, so one of them smiled knowingly and said loudly, "It's time, Sergeant."

"No need to shout, I'm not deaf," Sergeant protested, passed his hand down his sleeve as though he were removing dust from it, patted the enormous pistol in the holster on his right hip, spun around, clicked his heels together and ceremoniously reached for the thumb latch. He had to feel for it several times before he managed to find it.

It would not be the first time that the bank had opened without an officer present in violation of company policy. The vice-president of customer relations, who was assigned the task of opening the bank that morning, was still fiddling with a flat tire in her driveway. She had picked up a nail from her neighbor's remodeling project and would miss the only truly exciting day of her banking career. Four thousand and eight hundred more consecutive days of uninterrupted thrilling bank business lay stretched before her. Later, she would reply, "Oh my goodness," and clutch her throat when told about the gunfire and blood.

But she couldn't complain to the neighbor about the nail in her tire because her complaint would fall on deaf ears. The neighbor had bitched for years about the banker's cat scratching his car. "Jerry," a grossly overweight, black, domestic short-hair liked the comfort of the heat of the engine block coming through the hood. Jerry slept on the car every night, and purred loudly, especially in the fall. It would take a hundred flats to catch up with the thousands of scratches her precious Jerry had inflicted on the neighbor's expensive Mercedes.

Sergeant flipped the latch and pried open the door. It seemed to him that the door was getting harder and harder to pull open, but he managed. The three early customers filed into the bank, Sergeant bowing to them from the waist and bidding them to enter with the gesturing of his arm.

The robber pulled an Elvis mask from the floorboard of the Caddy and started to slip it on, but stopped. He sneezed and suddenly began wheezing. He peeked into the mirror and recoiled in horror; his lips and eyes had suddenly become puffy. He inspected his hands; they had become swollen in an instant. He was having an allergic reaction to the latex! Of course, this realization precipitated a full-blown panic attack and his mind raced.

He considered calling off the bank heist, but decided that choice was not a viable option. They needed the money, and needed it now. He thought of waiting to see how bad the reaction to the latex would be, but didn't have the time. In half an hour the bank would have five more employees present and the lobby would be teeming with customers, making a robbery needlessly messy and more difficult. If he was going to rob the bank, this bank, it had to be now. Impulsively, as though he were in a race against the allergic reaction, he checked to make sure the water pistol was still in his pocket, slipped on the Elvis mask, grabbed the package wrapped in plain brown paper from the car seat and threw open the door to the Caddy. The door crunched a parking meter that he had parked too close to and he muttered a curse word through suddenly throbbing lips. He squeezed through the door that was jammed by the parking meter and heard a "rip" when he straightened his contorted body. He instantly straightened up and felt his rear, thinking he had torn the pants. Sure enough, he found a hole, but relaxed slightly when he realized that it would be covered by the cape. The hole felt yards wide to his exploring fingers, but was actually only a two inch slit.

He smoothed the cape down over the hole and managed to stumble across the street. As he approached the door of the bank he became aware that his rapidly swelling eye lids had become mere slits. Shapes, shadows and blurs were all he could make out. He continued because he had cased the bank many times and had the area pretty much memorized. He staggered over the curb on the other side of the street and bumped into the edge of the bank door, striking his nose. Blood gushed from under the mask and he wiped what was coming under the mask and down his neck and onto a sleeve. He couldn't see anything when he felt for the push bar to enter the bank, but groping, he managed to make it through the door without further injury.

Sergeant, who was still at the door, moved aside, nodded to Elvis and said, "Good morning, young man." Sergeant thought it odd that the man was wearing an Elvis mask, but then, kids these days did down right strange things. *Elvis had been dead five years and guys were still dressing up as him. When would it stop?* Sergeant wondered and shook his head. Or was it a Superman outfit. *This guy is wearing a cape. Is it Halloween?*

Elvis, mostly by memory, felt his way to the writing desk in the center of the lobby and placed the brown-papered package on it, next to a stack of deposit slips. The Puerto Rican kid fumbled at the desk with a checking account application that reminded him of the G.E.D test. He cursed in Spanish and mumbled under his breath. He pledged to himself that one day he'd rob his employer for revenge and the pure sport of it. How the hell was he supposed to remember his social security number? He conjured up a batch of numbers to fit the blanks and made up an address and phone number.

The plus-sized female customer stood midway between the desk and the teller window, whispering on her cell phone, "No sweetie, I think it was in that time you said it wasn't in." Her call was not going as planned. Her turnip-head boyfriend wasn't as slow as he appeared. She was having trouble getting him to swallow her tale. "I think it *was* that time you were so drunk that you didn't even remember we had gone out…right, between Christmas and New Year's." She blew her breath upward and her bangs parted.

The movie-star customer, hands on liposuctioned hips, obediently followed one of the tellers, heading to a back office to discuss the bank's worthless check policy yet another time. The customer knew the routine. When she strolled past Elvis, the movie star customer said good-naturedly, "Good morning, Elvis."

"Good morning to you, ma'am," the robber mumbled with numb lips.

The movie-star customer stopped, studied Elvis from top to bottom and shook her head. Elvis turned as she started to follow the clerk and his cape caught on the corner of the desk. The hole in his pants revealed red underwear. The customer started to say, "Nice underwear," but had gotten so far behind the clerk she had to forgo comment and catch up. She had a polite tongue lashing to attend.

Elvis felt a draft on his butt and swatted the cape down. He yanked his head around to see if anyone had seen his exposure. He then sucked in a deep breath, recognizing that the moment of truth had arrived, and headed for the opening in the counter where the other teller stood with a smile frozen on her face. The teller tilted her head, puzzled by the guy dressed like Elvis. *What did he want? Was there an Elvis impersonator convention in town? Seems like there is one every couple of months.*

Elvis awkwardly ambled toward the out-of-focus teller's cage.

"How can I help you, today?" the teller asked and smiled with her best customer relations smile. The guy could be a mystery customer used by the bank to test service, she immediately thought. She had heard a rumor that the bank was sending a mystery customer in that morning. *Pretty clever of management to send a guy dressed like Elvis.*

Elvis groped his way to the counter and stuck his hand in his left front pocket and pulled out a note and handed it to the teller.

"This is a gasoline receipt, sir." The teller shoveled the note back across the counter. Her face almost cracked in half from the wicked smile she forced.

"Oh, thank you very much, sorry," Elvis said. He quickly plunged his hand into his left-rear pocket, then his right-rear pocket. *No note!* He jammed his hand into his right-front pocket. *No note!* The water pistol fell to the floor when he pulled his hand from the pocket. He quickly groped and retrieved it and jammed it back in, squirting himself on the leg in the process, making it appear as though he had wet himself. *Must have left the typed note on the dresser of the hotel room. I'll have to go back to the room and get the note on the way out of town.*

"I need paper and a pen," he inarticulately said to the teller. She cheerfully produced a pad and pen and flashed her teeth. Of course, the robber couldn't see the details of her face.

Elvis probed with his hands for the pad and pen. His vision was now bat-like. He tried to write and actually moved the pen around, but then realized that it was upside down. He righted the pen, scrawled on the pad and handed it to the teller. Blood from his bleeding nose covered his neck and chest and he could barely breathe. His gasping and hissing made a gurgling, piercing, whistling sound every time he exhaled.

"Sir, we have a bathroom around the corner," the teller said, noticing the wet area at Elvis's crotch. She tried to frown while smiling and almost pulled a muscle in her face as spasms twitched her lips.

"I don't need to use the bathroom," Elvis protested, through thick lips, irritated. His wheezing and hissing as he tried to breathe now sounded like water chasing Drano down a drain.

"If you do, it's there," the teller said, grinned fiendishly and nodded towards the restroom. *This mystery customer thing is elaborate. I was always told the company made the customer a royal pain in the rump to really test you. This guy fits the description.*

The teller read the chicken-scratched note several times. Confusion clouded her eyes and she said, "Sir, I am *blonde*, but that doesn't mean you have the right to call me a nice *package* or a *mess*, and that I have to give you money." *The mystery customer is clearly testing me,* she reasoned.

"What?" Elvis asked, huffing and puffing. Now his ears had puffed up also and every sound appeared to come out of a drum located at the end of tunnel.

"I guess I don't understand your note," the teller apologized.

"It says, 'Give me your money, or I'll explode the *bomb* in the package on the writing desk,'" Elvis explained, slowly mouthing the words. His lips and cheeks had swollen so much that it was painful and almost impossible for him to talk.

"The *bond*?" the teller asked. "You're going to *show* me the *bond*?"

"No, the bomb, b-o-m-b. I'm going to *explode* the *bomb,*" Elvis tried to explain.

"Are you sure that's what this note says. Boy, is your handwriting bad, although I don't have much room to complain. Mrs. Franklin, my second grade teacher said my penmanship was like hieroglyphics."

"Look lady, if you don't give me the money now, I'll explode the package and everyone in here dies."

"What package?" the teller asked, slowly realizing that Elvis might not be a mystery customer.

"The one on the table in the lobby," Elvis hissed. He turned and pointed in the direction of the table, a table that he could not see.

"Oh, *that* package," the teller said.

"Yeah, lady. *That* package is a bomb."

"The Puerto Rican kid that came in the bank with you left a minute ago with *that* package under his arm."

"What?" Elvis said, stunned.

"Seems that your bomb is no longer here. Tisk. Tisk. Maybe the police can tidy all this up. I'll just have to call them now."

As the teller started to turn, Elvis yanked the pistol from his jumpsuit pocket. "Not so fast, lady."

The teller stumbled backwards and raised her hands.

"That's more like it," Elvis managed to blurt out between gasps. He pulled a small bag he had Velcroed to the underside of the cape and plopped it onto the counter. "Now put the money in the bag and do it quickly."

"Did you say, 'I'm a honey, but a hag?' Or 'Put the money in the bag?'"

"Lady, if you don't quit aking me these thilly questions, I'm going to shoop you."

"You're going to *shoe* me? Look buddy, it's very hard understanding anything you say. My Uncle Bruce was like that. Only person who understood him was his wife, Aunt Clem. After she died, Uncle Bruce had no one who could understand him. They put him in an old folk's home and he died from loneliness. He had nobody he could talk to, or at least no one who would answer him. You'll have to do a better job enunciating your words if you expect me to respond. I'm sorry for the inconvenience."

Exasperated, Elvis raised and then slammed the bag onto the counter.

The teller slowly came back to the window and began pulling bills from her drawer. *If this guy is the mystery customer, I'm filing a complaint with management. He doesn't have to be so rude.*

The plus-sized customer, not recognizing she was in the middle of a bank robbery, walked up behind Elvis and was talking on her phone when Elvis noticed her. He pivoted with the gun.

"Honey, I'll have to go," the woman calmly said into her phone, the gun inches from her nose. She stared cross-eyed at the pistol.

"Is that a phone?" Elvis asked.

"My father gave it to me to try," she said.

"Who's zat on the pone?" Elvis wheezed.

"My boyfriend."

Elvis pulled the gun from under her nose and her eyes refocused. He put his face next to hers and surveyed real close.

"Girl, a woman ike you needs all the hep you can get with men. Tell him you'll call him back in a few pinutes, that I hate to do anything to disrupt your love lipe, but you're in the piddle of a holdup right now."

"You got that, honey," the woman calmly said to the phone. "Yeah, on Main. Bye, sweetie." She turned off her phone by placing it back in the holster and closed the flap on the bag.

"Guy pays attention to a large woman like you, don't let him get away. What does your boyfriend do?" Elvis asked.

"Oh, he's a cop."

"Oh, God! And you told him Main Street!"

"Yep. He knows what bank is being robbed. My guess is the police will be here in less than two minutes."

Elvis whirled back towards the teller who was very slowly putting money into the sack. She was handling each bill as though she were putting eggs into a metal carton, making sure each bill faced the proper way. She smiled at him pleasantly. *I'm going to get a great write up if this guy is the mystery shopper.*

Elvis tried to jump onto the counter, but his foot caught the ledge and he fell onto the floor on his back. He split his pants even more and part of his red underwear protruded. He bounced up groaning and rubbing his back side, then crawled onto the counter and gingerly slid over to the other side. He nudged the reluctant teller away from the cash drawer and placed his pistol down on the counter. He hurriedly began shoving the rest of the money from the drawer into the sack. Errant bills floated to the floor.

"Your gun is leaking," the teller remarked. She put her hand to her mouth and giggled. *That settles it. This is the mystery shopper. Nobody would rob a bank with a leaking water pistol.*

"What?" Elvis said, concentrating on trying to stuff the fuzzy money into the fuzzy sack.

"Your water pistol is leaking," the plus-sized customer said.

Sirens wailed in the distance. Elvis jerked his face toward the door. Sergeant was ten feet away, with a look of cold determination on his ashen face. His gun was drawn and pointed at Elvis, or more accurately, in the general direction of Elvis. Sergeant's hand visibly shook. "Young man," Sergeant drawled, "put your hands up." Sergeant had waited his entire life to be a hero and here in the twilight of his life opportunity had finally come knocking. But then a frightening thought exploded into his mind. *Did I put the bullets back in the gun after I cleaned it last night?*

Elvis started to put his hands up, but in the same motion grabbed the teller around the waist and held her against him. He snatched a blurry object that he thought was a pen from the counter and put it against her throat. The pen was actually a thin blotter used to get fingerprints from customers who cashed checks. The ink smeared the teller's throat. "Put the gum down yold man," Elvis ordered, "or I'll spash her throat."

"Did you say, 'We're having fun, old man?'" Sergeant asked, perplexed. He drove his free index finger into his ear and reamed it out a little, twisted his jaw around and blew air out of his nose. This usually worked to improve his hearing. At that exact moment he realized that the booger he'd been chasing all morning had slipped out and was hanging from his nose as though it were affixed to a thread. It tickled his lips and he twisted them, trying to get the thing to fall.

"Gum, down!" Elvis shouted.

Sergeant's eyes narrowed. He'd seen Clint Eastwood movies enough to no that the good guy never put his gun down. *What would Clint say?* Sergeant's brows danced up. "Bullet's faster than the hand," Sergeant said with bravado. He felt like shifting the gun to his other hand to show the girls how he could handle it. He had practiced in front of the mirror a lot. But then his mind drifted to the thing brushing against his lips.

The teller rolled her eyes. "Old man, you'll probably shoot *me*. Do as Elvis says."

Sergeant seriously thought about pulling the trigger, but shrugged, lowered the gun to his side and then dropped it as instructed, but it caught his foot on the way down and fired. The errant bullet hit Elvis in the hand, passed through and impaled itself in the ceiling, hitting a sprinkler sensor. Water immediately rained down from the ceiling. Amid the mess and confusion Sergeant hyperventilated, his eyes fluttered and then he fainted dead away.

Elvis clutched the money bag in his bloodied hand, sprang over the counter and started for the door. The cape flowed at a right angle, exposing his red drawers hanging out of the ripped pants. As he was a few feet from the door, the movie star-like customer came around the corner from an office and ran into the lobby and shouted, "Elvis!"

Sirens were close now. The sprinklers had created a monsoon inside the bank and the bank's glass windows had quickly fogged. The makeup on the pregnant customer ran in rivulets of blue down her face. Her tent clung to her like cellophane. The teller with an ink-stained throat straightened her dress and passed her hand through her soaked hair; it appeared as though her neck were covered with mascara. Sergeant began to stir; his feet twitched and he reflexively swatted at the thing clinging to his lip.

Elvis stopped dead in his tracks and glanced back. He threw open the door, nodded and bolted through the opening, but the door closed on his cape, catching him at throat level; he was yanked from his feet. He landed with a thud on his rump on the sidewalk, quickly sprang up and tugged on the cape that was jammed in the door. A piece tore off and he was free.

He sprinted for the Caddy, but stumbled down and "ran" most of the way on his hands and knees, dragging the bag. He finally made it to the car, threw in the bag, squeezed through the door, hopped in and cranked the ignition. The engine raced and the Caddy glanced off the curb, sideswiping a Ford that was parallel parked in mid-block. The Caddy careened around the corner a split-second before a police cruiser with tires squealing slid onto Main Street.

The robber yanked off the mask, but couldn't see any better and miraculously made it the four blocks through town without wrecking or running anyone over. His heart began slowing to under a hundred beats per minute, but he felt more alive than at any time in his life. His senses, except for his eyesight, were on alert.

He was steering down a narrow country road when he felt the barrel of a gun pressed to his neck.

"What the hell?" the robber blurted.

"Man, you the worse bank robber I ever even heard of," the Puerto Rican kid said from the back seat in a thick accent. The kid then jumped into the front passenger seat. "I opened the package you left on the table and found the note threatening to blow up the bank in the box. I came back to see what you'd do and it looked like a Chinese fire drill in there. Man, what's wrong with your face? Looks like a scab."

"Allergic reaction, I think."

"Allergic to what? The smarts? You some kind of escapee from the loony bin? The FBI will be laughing at the bank's tape of the robbery for years to come. Probably be the lead on *Stupid Criminals*." The robber said nothing as he concentrated on steering. "You kind of look familiar. You been on television?" the kid asked, scratching stubble on his chin.

"Where did you get the gun?" the robber asked.

"On the street. I paid more for it than you paid for the water pistol."

"At least the water pistol wouldn't hurt anyone. Why does a young guy like you need a gun?"

"It keeps me always prepared for whatever pops up."

"Put it down before someone gets hurt."

"You'd love that, now wouldn't you."

"Look, kid. What do you want?"

"I don't want nothing," the kid said and grinned, as he moved the money bag from the floorboard to his lap. "I never believed in Santa Claus or the Easter Bunny growing up. But now I believe in a higher power." The kid clutched the bag to his chest. He felt like the luckiest person in the world.

Elvis turned the Caddy from the highway and down a narrow dirt lane to where he had hidden his getaway car. He drove under a thicket of pine trees and stopped the Caddy. "Maybe we can come to an arrangement," Elvis said. He pushed the shift lever from drive to park and set the parking break.

"Arrangement? I'm the one that got a gun, man. You got nothing. Let's see what's in this bag of goodies." The kid opened the moneybag to feast his eyes on the jackpot. He put his hand into the bag to feel the bills and pulled out a box the size of a pack of cigarettes. The kid, puzzled, looked at the wannabe robber and then back at the mysterious box. That's when the tiny bomb that the bank clerk had put in the bag exploded and red dye smashed into the kid's eyes and face. The gun fell from his hand and the bank robber picked it up.

"This bank robbing stuff is not as easy as it looks in the movies," the robber said and then straightened out the front of his jumpsuit. He looked into the rearview mirror, patted his double chin, and put the gun on the floor board.

"What the hell happened?" the kid blurted, blinking and trying to rub ink from his eyes.

The robber looked at the kid and laughed, thinking the boy looked like a sunburned raccoon wearing a red and tan mask.

"You just learned that a life of crime doesn't necessarily pay."

CHAPTER TWO

The basement of Adam Vaughn's Memphis bungalow was very large and seemed even more spacious because of its bright yellow walls and light-colored, pine-planked floors. A tubular skylight through a wall captured the last of the afternoon sunlight and sucked it into the basement, mixing with overhead fluorescent lighting and casting ethereal shadows. Each wall appeared as a textured, sepia-toned, black-and-white photograph snapped by a skilled artist. A sweet-smelling musk hung in the air, an odor similar to that found in grade school libraries--a mixture of mimeograph ink, dust, bleach and sweaty hair. A dehumidifier that Vaughn kept powered to protect the integrity of his valuables gently whirred in a corner of the room.

In addition to being a storage space for junk--Vaughn was a packrat--the space doubled as an incredible shrine to Elvis Presley. Keepsakes from every phase of the King's public life were jammed into the room. Original posters of all thirty-three of Elvis's movies worth several hundred dollars apiece were afixed in sleek metal frames and completely covered one of the walls. The poster collection altogether was probably worth ten thousand dollars, but Vaughn would never sell a single one of them for any price. He hadn't bought them to make a profit. They were part of his sanctum sanctorum. This was a place he could find peace and serenity. A glass trophy case held pristine original jackets and/or vinyls of Elvis's seventy-three albums, fifty-one singles and sixteen extended-play singles that had gone gold or platinum. These artifacts were deployed in chronological order, resting on six shelves. Although he had a state-of-the-art Bang & Olufsen phonograph, he would never play these pristine records on it. Instead, he played tapes of the songs and derived secondary satisfaction by just knowing the perfect records were available to play anytime he chose. This part of the collection was also worth thousands of dollars. The basement collection also contained memorabilia from concerts, autographs, personal effects, an Elvis jumpsuit, a bass guitar used by Ratz Adie, bassist in Elvis's band and a guitar that Elvis had used on tour in the mid-1960s.

Vaughn had bumped into a man from Louisiana who had been in the army with Elvis and the man had given him three private snapshots of Elvis and his mates in a pub. The pictures were not of great quality, but displayed the young Elvis with a guitar on his knees belting out a song. Vaughn had the pictures blown up to poster size and they were grouped on one wall.

However, Vaughn's most unique piece, though of no value, was an original letter from Joe Esposito, the King's road manager. Esposito allegedly found Elvis slumped in his bathroom that dreadful August 16, 1977 day at Graceland. In the letter Esposito politely tells Vaughn to go to hell and quit being so damned nosy. The story behind the letter was one Vaughn loved to tell, but had repercussions. Everyone who heard the story believed that Vaughn was certifiably mad.

Adam Vaughn's most *prized* piece, however, was an original letter from Gene Smith, Elvis's maternal cousin. Smith had viewed Elvis's body in the funeral coffin and stated in the letter to Vaughn that the person in Elvis's coffin was definitely not Elvis. The flattened nose on the imposter was a dead giveaway, according to Gene. Elvis's nose turned up; the stiff's nose did not. The coroner had argued that Elvis collapsed onto his face that horrible day and had broken his nose. Still, Gene Smith's opinion had gotten extensive coverage by the tabloids in the months after Elvis's death, stirring up the debate among loyal fans. The notion that Elvis had not died was fueled by the famous photograph taken after the alleged death in which Elvis is supposedly visible through the screen door of the porch of Graceland. This was followed by hundreds of alleged sightings, especially in and around Memphis. Vaughn had turned down three hundred dollars for the Smith letter back then and had not checked recently to see what it was now worth, but it was not unusual for such a letter to double in value each year. It could be worth thousands now, especially if Gene Smith were no longer living.

Vaughn relaxed in a navy leather recliner in the center of the basement amid his treasures with his five-year-old daughter, Melissa, on his lap. Her cup of overly-sweetened hot cocoa rested on a small nearby table. Even though the cup was full, the ritual was that she would only down a few sips. Melissa nestled her head against his neck and played with his shirt sleeve by twirling it in her fingers. Her pressure against him and her fragrance filling his nostrils dropped his blood pressure twenty points.

The *Blue Hawaii* album playing on quadraphonic speakers in each corner of the room acted as background for their quiet time, and for seemingly the millionth time he showed her the pictures and newspaper clippings of his scrapbook. The book had been lovingly pieced together over the years and included post-death clippings of sightings, benchmarks achieved and related stories. Vaughn was particularly interested in stories about the increasing wealth of the Presley estate.

Vaughn flipped a page near the beginning of the scrapbook. "Mel, this is the King when he was first on the *Louisiana Hayride*. See how everything in the picture seems to be alive and jumping. Fans at his concerts had a tough time sitting still. This was before he was a big star," he explained, tapping his finger on the picture.

"Before mommy went to heaven?" Mel asked in her innocent voice.

"That's right, sweetie. This is a picture of Graceland where he lived. And this is a picture of Baptist Memorial Hospital where they pronounced him dead on the day you were born."

"He died at the hospital?" Melissa asked, pressing her finger on the picture. She had asked the same question a hundred times.

"No. Remember? Daddy doesn't think Elvis is dead."

"Tell me the story again, daddy."

Adam Vaughn smiled and stroked his daughter's hair with his hand. "I was coming home from Baptist Memorial Hospital the day you were born and I heard them say on the radio that Elvis had died."

"Was mommy with you?"

"Mommy was at the hospital with you, sweetie." Melissa could never understand that her mother had died right after Mel's birth from an undiagnosed aneurysm. "I was driving home to shower and get some clothes. I wasn't paying very good attention when I pulled from my parking space near the corner of South Dunlap Street and Monroe Avenue and was grazed by a 1976 Lincoln. The impact wasn't severe. I wasn't hurt, but I was shook up. I got out of the car to inspect the damage, and this guy whom I had never seen before popped out of the Lincoln. I later came to realize that the man was Joe Esposito, Elvis's road manager. It was about three-thirty in the afternoon and the sun was bright and partially in my eyes, but I could see into the Lincoln. There was a lady seated in the front passenger seat and a man behind her in the back seat. The sunlight glinting off the chrome near the rear window of the Lincoln made it difficult to make out the features of the guy in the back seat. Esposito wasn't mad or anything, but he seemed extremely nervous. It was warm, but he was sweating much too much because it wasn't that hot. He met me at his hood and took out his wallet. He's got a fistful of hundreds and he offered them to me to just drive off and not call the cops. My car has very little damage to the left quarter panel, a couple hundred bucks at best. I'm in a hurry to get back to the hospital to see you. I'm about to tell the guy three or four hundred ought to do when the passenger rear door to the Lincoln opens and the guy in back steps out and leans on the top the car and asks, 'Everything alright, Joe?' Right then I looked at the guy leaning on the top of the car, but because of the sunlight I can only make out his general features. Joe then said, 'We'll be out of here in a minute.' I told Joe four hundred would be enough. He pealed off four crisp bills and handed then to me. I walked to my car and got in as the Lincoln pulled away and then it hit me. The voice of the guy leaning on top of the Lincoln; it was Elvis's. I jerked my head toward the Lincoln just as it passed me and the guy in the back is waving and smiling. I could only make out a portion of his face as the rest was in heavy shadow, but it looked to me to bc Elvis. A couple of days later I saw a picture of Esposito on television and I recognized him. I tried getting in touch with Esposito for weeks, but never could get him to return my calls. All I got was a crummy letter."

"Did mommy like this story?"

"Mommy went to heaven before I could get back to the hospital and tell her."

"That makes me sad. Was mommy pretty?" Melissa asked.

"You've seen her pictures, sweetie. Mommy was very pretty. Mel, it's past your bedtime. We need to get you upstairs, washed and tucked away."

This was the best part of Vaughn's day. He delighted in watching Mel splash in the bubbles in the tub and make submarines out of her two rubber duckies. The sound effects that came from her mouth were fabulous. When her hands looked like prunes and her eyes were glazed with sleep, Adam would pluck her from the tub. She was so cute running naked through the house with him in pursuit with a warm towel. This last burst of activity was really just her energy flaming out. He truly loved combing her thick curls as they dried and reading her stories while she drifted off to sleep. Tonight, when he reached down to kiss Mel's forehead as she snored lightly, he thought of Marie when the scent of Mel's freshly cleaned hair reached his nostrils. Marie always used baby shampoo to clean her hair. He closed his eyes and sighed, flipped the switch at the door and the lamp light went out and the night-light flicked on.

The phone rang as he walked into the kitchen.

"Adam, it's Ron."

"Evening, Ron."

"How's that lovely daughter of yours?" Detective Ron Wells asked warmly.

"She's in her toasty bed dreaming of angels."

"Adam, I called because of two things. My first cousin just moved back to town and she's very attractive and available."

"Now Ron, you know I'm not interested. I'm not ready yet."

"Adam, it's been five years. You know Marie would want you to get on with your life."

"I am getting on with my life. I'm raising Mel and I've got the investigation."

"Can I get you to at least come back to work? I checked with human resources and they said you could come back part-time."

"The mortgage cancellation insurance paid off the mortgage on the house. The settlement and Marie's life insurance will last until Mel starts school. As I've told you many times, her first day of first grade is when I go back to Memphis P.D."

"Adam, whenever you're ready to start seeing other people, let me know."

"You'll be the first to know. What's the second reason for the call?"

"I hate talking about it with you because it will only fuel that crazy idea of yours that you call an investigation."

"Alright, Ron, I've heard the disclaimer, now what is it?" Adam asked. All his friends on the force thought he was nuts, yet they kept him posted on anything remotely in line with his theory.

"There was a bank robbery this morning in Lafayette County."

"East of Memphis?"

"Yeah. Over near Macon, Tennessee, about twenty miles out. The robber was dressed up as Elvis."

"I can get my sister-in-law to keep Mel in the morning, if you've got a file that I can copy."

"Adam, it's just an impersonator. In the five years since his death, I think we've had a dozen robberies in Memphis with guys wearing an Elvis mask."

"Bank heists?"

"No, this is the first of those."

"Any physical evidence?" Adam asked.

"A video tape, some blood and a couple of witnesses."

"I'll be there at nine in the morning."

CHAPTER THREE

Adam Vaughn maneuvered his new 1982 Chevy Malibu into the driveway of the one-story 1950s ranch-style house on one of the few streets in Williston, Tennessee, a quiet hamlet of three hundred forty souls some forty scenic miles from Memphis. He opened his notebook, double-checked the address, got out of the car, padded along a brick walkway lined with daylilies, stopped at the porch and then hiked up cement stairs to a stained, oak front door. The air smelled of lilacs and ozone, a smell the makers of fragrances advertised as country fresh. A ceramic bulldog with peeling paint guarded the door. Vaughn pulled open the screen door and its rusty spring creaked. He started to knock, but the door opened before he had a chance. Abby Long greeted him with a wonderfully toothy, bleached-white smile and mischievous ocean green eyes. She wore such a light sheen of makeup that it appeared that she had none on at all. She had a fresh, clean look and only ruby-red lipstick hinted at anything unnatural.

Abby was an Amazon; she stood almost five foot ten inches tall and her tan was made to look even deeper by blonde, Farrah Fawcett-style hair. She wore a white, ribbed sweater, blue jeans and open-toe shoes with two-inch heels that caused her to tower over Adam. Her expertly manicured toenails matched her lipstick. The tape of the bank robbery had not done her justice. He thought she was the most classically beautiful woman he had ever met in person, and that she was extremely sexy.

Abby politely led Vaughn to a living room that was chock full of eclectic antiques from every corner of the world--England, France, China, even Australia. A carved Jade elephant from China topped with thick glass performed the duty of a beautiful coffee table. A tribesman carved from exotic African wood served as a floor lamp. Tanzanian tree bark was formed into a unique chair. There were dozens of such one-of-a-kind items that Abby had obtained in the divorce settlement. She wasn't overly fond of the antiques, but relished the idea that her ex didn't have them.

The walls were painted in a three-toned texture to look like ancient leather. A four-globed chandelier, each globe hand-blown by Italian artists, hung from the ten-foot ceiling in the center of the room. Oddly, what appeared to be almost a hundred shrunken heads dangled from the ceiling on thin strands of wire.

"I see you're interested in the witch doctor heads," Abby said, looking at the ceiling.

"Most unusual." Vaughn wanted to say something else that was clever, but couldn't think of anything. The heads were so bizarre.

"My father collected them from various tribes in Africa. He taught archeology at the University of Tennessee. Many of his friends sent him heads over the years."

"You mean they are real?" Vaughn asked, incredulous.

"All of them."

"What's that one?" Vaughn asked, pointing at a head that appeared to be white.

"That's my Uncle Charlie. If you'll look closely you'll see some other family members scattered about. Father had a sense of humor."

Vaughn involuntarily shuddered at the thought of relatives permanently staring at you and studying everything you did. Creepy. He then accepted Abby's offer of hot tea, which she fetched from the kitchen. Vaughn sat on a leather divan and morbidly studied the tiny faces suspended in air, wondering what stories these guys could spin. Uncle Charlie, whose face appeared to be grinning and trying to say something, really gave him the willies. He had the face of a huckster, the kind of guy who would cheat his kids in a game of Battleship.

"I used to drink coffee all during the day, but last year I read that too much caffeine can be harmful, so I switched to tea," Abby said, as she settled into a wing-backed chair that matched the sofa, casually folding her long legs under her. She patted back her hair with her hand and the long strands came to rest on her shoulders. She could have been a starlet giving an interview to a tabloid. She was truly radiant. She held her cup daintily with her pinkie exposed and sipped from the cup with a gentle sucking sound.

"I read last week that we should be drinking eight glasses of water a day. If I did that I'd never get off the toilet," Adam said. "Go figure." Abby smiled.

"Will this take long?" she asked. "Officer, I have an appointment with the doctor to discuss reshaping my eyes and putting in a dimple on my chin."

"Really? I am shocked that you would change anything about the way you look."

"The psychiatrist says I'm never going to be satisfied, but what does he know? He chain-smokes and has a gut the size of a Buddha. Will this take long? It took me a long time to get this appointment."

"This won't take too long, and I'm not here on official business, so please don't call me an *officer*." Vaughn held his cup with both his hands and slurped. He was embarrassed by the sound his tongue made and cringed; his face contorted.

Abby laughed, mock-saluted with her cup and sipped as properly as a debutante on review. "Of course, I didn't quite understand you on the phone. You are a policeman, but not on active duty?"

"Actually, I'm on extended leave. I have a hobby of investigating Elvis sightings. Some might say it's a perverted hobby." Vaughn mentally added, "ouch," and then glanced through the corner of his eye at the suspended heads.

"Sounds fairly harmless to me," she said and shrugged her shoulders. "Do you also chase UFOs and Bigfoot?" she teased.

"Just Elvis." Vaughn sighed. "That's my only addiction."

"Why do you do this?" she asked. She appeared to be genuinely interested. Vaughn thought that Abby should be a politician because at that moment the way she looked at him made him feel like they were the only people in the entire world. She also had a way of getting him to open up.

"My daughter was born the day Elvis supposedly died. My wife died shortly after giving birth; it was at the same hospital to which Elvis was taken and pronounced dead. I have this compulsion to find out if Elvis really died that day at the same hospital. I wasn't even a big Elvis fan then."

"I'm sorry about your wife, but I don't think I can help. I've already told the police everything I remember."

"The other witnesses said you called out, 'Elvis' to the robber and that he hesitated. Why did you call out like that?" Vaughn asked. The tea was a delicious change of pace, so he drank more and stole a quick glance at Uncle Charlie again. *Was he smiling now, whereas he was grinning before?*

"It'll sound crazy," she said, as she shifted in her chair to sitting on top of the other long leg. Her blouse inched up and exposed a sliver of her midriff. Adam was surprised that he was distracted by the beautiful tan skin juxtaposed against the white blouse.

"My guess is, you're as sane as I am," he said, trying not to look up at Uncle Charley again, or at Abby's exposed skin.

"I used to live in Memphis with my husband and daughter. I'm divorced now, but back then Amy, that's my daughter, she's now thirteen years old, went to school with Lisa Marie Presley. Elvis doted on his daughter. Every time there was a function involving Lisa Marie at the school, Elvis would attend. I met him quite often. That morning in the bank, the voice of the robber, the way he said, 'ma'am' and the way he carried himself, I thought it *was* Elvis. I got just a glimpse of his eyes through the mask he was wearing and it was as though I was looking into Elvis's eyes. But he's been dead five years, crazy, huh?" Adam was distracted, lost in thought. Many of the people who admitted to sightings of Elvis commented on the way the person carried himself. "What do you think, Officer Vaughn? Sorry, Mr. Vaughn?"

He didn't want to hurt her feelings, so he fibbed and answered, "I think what you're telling me will be useful in my investigation. Do you have a VCR? I want you to look at the tape of the robbery shot by the bank surveillance camera and tell me if you see anything else that causes you to believe the robber was Elvis."

"Yes, I have a VCR, but before we look at the tape, there was something else," Abby said. "I guess it just dawned on me."

"What?" he asked.

"Elvis always wore Aqua Velva. The robber had on a triple dose of the stuff, enough to choke a skunk."

CHAPTER FOUR

The Memphis police department didn't spend one penny more on office space and office décor than absolutely necessary, and most of the detectives did not take great pride in the appearance of the joint. Detective Ron Wells' cubicle was typical; it looked as though a tornado had rambled through. The top of his metal desk was a jumble of half-used notepads, torn pieces of paper with cryptic notes, smelly chunks of food droppings, empty containers of Chinese food, crumpled bags from fast food drive-thrus and half-eaten pencils. The metal walls didn't fare any better. Taped to one divider wall was a series of faded ten-year-old memos from the department's human resource section, most of them about nothing of importance. One memo referred to sexual harassment in bold type. Another wall sported a pin up from *Playboy Magazine*.

"Ron, looks like you need to get the city to issue a certificate of condemnation for your office," Adam Vaughn observed.

"Office? I've been in phone booths that were larger than this. I'll have more room in my coffin. Other than this crappy abode, low pay, long work days, ridicule from the public and the possibility of being shot and killed by a junkie, this job isn't half-bad," Ron deadpanned.

"I like your positive attitude, Ron. I'll call Zig Ziglar and tell him what a success story you are. I attended one of his seminars that featured a motivational speaker, Brian Flanagan. Guy could make the obituaries read like the funnies. I'll call Brian and get him to use you as a case study of how to fail in life without really trying. You'll be his don't-try-this-at-home poster boy. What else have you got on the Elvis bank robbery?"

"I hate to tell you." Wells swabbed the inside of his left ear with his car key. He pulled the key out and wiped it on his pants. Wells dreaded adding fuel to Vaughn's obsession.

"Ron, take the risk."

"The perp has type O blood."

"Same as Elvis," Adam noted. Ron rolled his eyes and let out a deep breath.

"So does one-third the population of the free world. We also got a partial shoe print from a mixture of water and blood. Size 11D."

"Same as Elvis."

"And about ten million other men in the United States," Wells said and shrugged.

"Anything else?" Vaughn asked.

"We got a piece of the perp's cape, but it won't help. Seems the fabric is pretty common."

"Could I get a sample of it?" At worst, the piece of cloth would make a nifty addition to his scrapbook.

"Yeah, I'll get it for you." Wells rose and started walking away. "Can I get you anything else while I'm up? Like a form to reactivate your butt with the department?"

The rundown three-story apartment building was in east Memphis amid a blighted area that had never had "better days." Even in the 1920s and '30s the neighborhood would have been one to avoid. The buildings in the area were of low bidder-quality and possessed zero architectural value. The neighborhood's current citizens had little, if any, lobbying power, as evidenced by the buckled streets and badly cracked sidewalks.

Vaughn knocked on the door of the second-floor apartment and heard something stirring behind it. He instinctively stepped back as the door started to open. An elderly woman with heavily wrinkled skin and stringy gray hair that fell on stooped shoulders peered at him from twinkling brown eyes. She had a gaping mouth devoid of teeth. She reminded him of Yoda, such was her skin and round face.

"You the guy that called?" the woman gruffly asked through a crack in the door.

"Yes."

"Like I said on the phone, It'll cost you a *hunred*," she said. Vaughn slipped a bill into her leathery, outstretched hand that barely made it through the crack. "If God had wanted you to keep it, he would have put handles on it," she said and laughed, and then hacked and coughed. The door closed and Vaughn heard the rattle of a safety chain. The old woman opened the door and waved him in. "Come on, you're letting out all the cool air."

Vaughn immediately choked on the stale air in the cramped apartment, air so thick with smoke that he could barely see the walls in the room. There were three ashtrays in the tiny living room and each of them contained a burning cigarette.

"Sorry the place is a mess. Maid doesn't come until next week," the woman said and then started to laugh again, but choked and began hacking the standard smoker's cough. The cigarette dangling from her lips almost fell out, but she hung on to it with the edge of her lips, as though it were an optical illusion. She swallowed the phlegm that came up from her throat into her mouth and gestured for Vaughn to sit on a tattered easy chair that sported a rusty, exposed spring. All of her furniture appeared as though it had been rescued from the dump.

"I'll just stand, if you don't mind." Vaughn did not want to explain to any emergency room attendants how he got his rear ripped open by a rusty spring at the home of a walking-and-talking human ashtray.

"Suit yourself, sonny." The woman deftly pulled a small flask from inside her bra and offered some to Vaughn, "Swig?" she asked, giggled when he said no, wrapped her lips around the flask's neck and sucked down. When she was finished, she flopped onto a dilapidated sofa as gracefully as a fish tossed onto concrete. Miraculously, she didn't crash through the decaying fabric. "I keep it in a flask so I don't forget where I put it. Probably don't swear either, eh sonny?" she asked. Vaughn noticed that the old woman's eyes sparkled with mischief. She clipped the cigarette between yellowed fingers and then wrapped her caked lips around the neck of the flask again and guzzled. "This is the good stuff, Mogen David."

"Mrs. Mangs, please look at this piece of cloth and tell me if it's from a jumpsuit you made for Elvis." She took the cloth into her hand. Vaughn noticed that her fingers were bloodless and creased. Tree branches in the dead of winter appeared more life-like.

"How did you find me?" she asked. "I crawled into this hole a long time ago and thought that I had brushed away my tracks, hee hee." She swallowed more Mogen David from the flask and caught some dribble on her chin with her hand.

"I found an old article in the newspaper about the making of Elvis's jumpsuits and it had your name and shop address. It was easy to track you to here."

"For the first couple of years after his death I used to get reporters calling all the time. After a while that eased to a trickle and then stopped. Nobody has wanted to talk to this old woman in years. I guess my fifteen minutes of fame only lasted five years, hee hee." She playfully shrugged her shoulders and bobbed her head from side to side. It was clear to Vaughn that she was lonely and missed the limelight.

"Mrs. Mangs, the cloth?" Vaughn gently urged.

She glanced at the tiny piece of material. "You know, I practically invented Elvis's jumpsuit. He had this vague idea and I turned it into what the world remembers. I understand that one of my jumpsuits is in the Smithsonian."

"The cloth, please."

"It's from a jumpsuit I made for him in 1975."

"You're sure?"

"I wouldn't say it if it wasn't so, sonny. He wanted this specific color. I dyed the thing myself. I remember each one as though they were my children."

"You made it in 1975; did you give it to him at that time?"

"Definitely. I remember it like it was yesterday. The final fitting was at Graceland and his kid was running around, playing." The old woman stared off and her eyes clouded, as if she were being transported back in time. A slight grin appeared on her tired mouth. "Kid had the run of the place. Always underfoot. Elvis used to play with her as though he himself was a kid."

"I'm curious about something," Vaughn said.

"Aren't we all?"

"Do you think he died in 1977?"

"Does a snake hiss? Do beer drinkers piss? Do you abbreviate Mississippi, 'M-i-s-s?'"

"I take that to mean that you think he died then."

"I sure do, sonny. Can't the astrologists let the poor man rest in peace?" She rubbed her chin with her hand and added, "Although there was one thing that happened that was kind of strange."

"What was that?" Vaughn asked.

"Let's see, he died in August…some time around June he ordered two jumpsuits and I measured him for them at my shop. That was the first time I ever measured him any place other than Graceland. He came there by hisself. He told me he was going to surprise someone and to keep the new suits a secret. You know, the papers said he weighed around two hunred sixty pounds when he died. That's not true. First jumpsuit I ever made for him, he had a thirty-two inch waist. That June his waist was thirty-eight. You show me a man who weighs two sixty with a thirty-eight inch waist and I'll show you a guy who is ten feet tall."

"Why was any of that strange?" Vaughn asked.

"Hold your horses, sonny. I ain't got to the strange part yet. On August 13, some three days before his death, I called up to go over to get a final measurement to tweak the outfit. His weight fluctuated tremendously. He'd get into these frenzies where he played racquetball for hours and hours and days and days on end and drop fifteen to twenty pounds in a month. Anyway, I called over there and Elvis himself answered the phone. He had given me this super-secret private line. He was very nice, as usual, but tells me not to worry about finishing the suits. He said he wasn't going to need them anyway. I told him they were finished and he said that he'd send over a check to pay for them, but cancel the order. Sonny, Elvis was a clothes hound. Those suits were beautiful and looked damn good on him, weight and all. There was room for them in his closet."

"Did you keep the jumpsuits?"

"I ain't got to the strange part yet."

"Sorry."

"The next week I get a check in the mail. It was Elvis's personal check and not one of those Elvis company checks. I had always been paid by the company check."

Vaughn's heart fluttered and the hair on his neck rose.

"The date on the check was August 18, 1977. How you like them apples?"

"The day *after* he supposedly died. That is strange," Vaughn said.

"Sonny, would you shut up. I'm just now getting to the interesting part." Vaughn nodded. The old woman enjoyed telling the story. It had been years since its last telling. She drank more from the flask that again disappeared into her blouse. "A month later, about ten at night there is a knock on my door at home and there stands this nervous-looking guy. He's twitching and shuffling and finally asks if he can come in. He looks harmless enough, so I let him in. He says he wants to pick up the two jumpsuits I made for Elvis. Well, I thought that was weird, being that Elvis has been dead a month and nobody but me and Elvis is supposed to even know about the jumpsuits in the first place. And what good are the jumpsuits to a d-e-a-d Elvis?"

"What did the guy look like?"

"It wasn't Elvis, you idiot, and it wasn't him wearing a disguise."

"Any distinguishing feature?"

"Had a big old scar over his right eye, just above the brow and that's all I remember about him." She really couldn't remember if he had a scar. She had told the story so many times that it had changed over the years, and somewhere along the way the scar had simply popped into the story and she couldn't remember when. Now, in her mind, the guy really did have a scar.

"You gave him the suits?"

The old lady rolled her eyes. "You ain't been listening too good. This guy comes to my *house* at ten at night. The suits are at the shop. The guy leaves me an address to mail them, which I did."

"He give you a name?" Vaughn asked excitedly.

"John Smith," she replied and giggled. She reached into her bra and drank from the flask yet again. Her cigarette appeared to be so close to her yellowed and wrinkled fingers that Vaughn thought she must be getting burned. She casually flicked the butt at an ashtray and missed. The pile of butts next to the ashtray spoke volumes about her aim. She didn't appear too concerned that this particular wayward cigarette was melting a hole in the floor tile.

"Do you remember the address?"

"No, of course not, but I can do better than that." The old lady swiftly moved through the door and into the next room as though she were a ghostly apparition. Her quickness caught Vaughn by surprise. Within seconds she was back with a mailing receipt, which she handed to Vaughn. It contained a delivery address and the signature of *John Smith.*

"Another *hunred*," the old lady said. Her eyes crinkled with the gigantic smile of an open, toothless mouth, cracking her face in half.

"What?" Vaughn asked.

"I can see it in your eyes, sonny. You've got to have that receipt, hee hee."

Vaughn reached for his wallet without hesitation.

CHAPTER FIVE

The apartment complex had received little or no maintenance for years and easily fit into the category of slum rental, although compared to Mangs's apartment, this place belonged on the cover of *House Beautiful.* Vaughn slowed as he made it up the last rung of stairs and rubbed his hand on his pant leg, leaving traces of dirt and rust. He glanced to the right and then at his note with the address and decided to turn left on the balcony. Four doors down he found apartment 409 and knocked. The balcony smelled of urine and stale whiskey.

A kid about seven years old materialized out of a door to his right and said, "She's home, but you'll have to knock loud. She watches the soaps and the TV's turned up." The kid then quickly sped down the steps.

Vaughn knocked again. In seconds he heard a female voice shout, "Hold your damned horses, I'm getting dressed!" After a minute passed, Marie Fulgar opened the door. She appeared even larger than she had in the video.

"I've already told you guys every thing I know," she said. She wore a blue and yellow printed muumuu. The shapeless dress flowed almost to her ankles, not quite covering up furry rabbit slippers.

"I appreciate your time, Ms. Fulgar."

"Aw, come on in, just don't expect anything new," she said as she held the door open.

Vaughn entered to find an impeccably kept living room. Framed pictures rested at forty-five degree angles on shiny table tops. Pictures on the walls were perfectly and evenly hung. A quick glance divulged not a speck of dust.

Marie slowly lowered herself onto the crushed velvet couch, and Vaughn took a seat in a matching chair that was set at a right angle to the couch. He noticed several boxes on a nearby entertainment center. One appeared to contain video tapes and had an index on its cover that read, A-K; another box's index read, L-S. He felt that T-Z was lurking somewhere out of sight. The entertainment center also had hundreds of albums that appeared to be arranged in alphabetical order on shelves. A single album rested on top of the entertainment center. Marie saw that Vaughn was looking at it and she got up, moved to it, put it into its cover and slid the album into its designated spot in the collection. "Sorry," she said, and then returned to her seat.

"Ms. Fulgar, as I explained on the phone, I'm not here on official business."

"My boyfriend told me about you. He's a cop. He says you're nuts about Elvis."

"I do have a theory, that's all."

"What is it?" she asked. She sat with her nubby hands folded across her belly, leaning back on the couch. She appeared to be very uncomfortable, but Vaughn somehow knew that this was how she always sat.

"I think Elvis faked his death and is living somewhere in Tennessee."

"Why would he do that?"

"His career was in a downward spiral; he had a drug problem and probably felt like he had to escape from all the pressure and scrutiny."

"It would have taken one hell of a conspiracy, don't you think?" she asked.

"Not really. All he had to do was wait until someone resembling him died and switch with the body. A couple insiders in the coroner's office is all it would have taken."

"How can I help you?" she asked. Vaughn could not tell whether or not she was judging his theory.

"Do you think it was Elvis who robbed the bank?" he asked.

"Off the record?"

Vaughn nodded.

"I've seen all of his movies. The guy in the bank *moved* like him. That's hard to describe or explain. Elvis had a unique way of carrying himself. The guy in the bank carried himself like he *was* Elvis."

CHAPTER SIX

Detective Wells guided the unmarked police cruiser off Highway 193, the Williston-Macon road, and onto a country dirt road, kicking up a cloud of red dust that swirled and mushroomed behind the car. He and his passenger, Vaughn, drove through a stand of poplars and were amazed when a deer scooted off from behind one, although neither said anything about the unusual sight.

Dust started to float into the car, so Vaughn rolled up the window. "Better put on the air," he observed, reached over and flipped the dial and the air conditioner kicked in. The blower initially pushed dust into the cab, but in seconds cool, clean air circulated throughout the cabin.

"They just found the car a couple of hours ago. I asked them not to move it until I could search it," Wells said. His eyes darted back and forth while peering at the road, adrenaline kicking in. The truth be told, for all of his bellyaching about budget cuts and long hours, the thrill of what he did for a living is what kept Wells going. Without his realizing it, his breathing quickened, his knuckles tightened on the steering wheel, and small veins popped out on his neck.

"Not real smart ditching the car without setting it on fire," Vaughn said. "Of course, what we saw on the tape showed that the perp was not exactly as experienced as Dillinger in the trade."

"It doesn't have plates and the V.I.N. has been filed off, but we checked in Mississippi, Kentucky, and Tennessee, and no such Cadillac has been reported as stolen," Wells said, as he pulled alongside two other cruisers. "At least that's what they said over the radio." He looked at the dust cloud and decided to wait a couple of seconds before getting out of the car. The officers who were already on the scene were yards away and milling about the abandoned Cadillac.

"Surely the robber wouldn't be stupid enough to use his own car to rob the bank and then leave it behind," Vaughn said.

"That's like robbing a bank and putting the demand for money on the back of your own deposit slip," Wells said.

"Guy in Georgia did that last month. Cops were waiting for him when he got home."

"No one ever said that criminals were smart. I read somewhere that the average I.Q. of prisoners is only eighty-three percent of that of the general population," Wells said. He turned off the ignition and they both hopped out and strode to the Cadillac. The other two officers nodded and went back to their cars without saying anything.

Vaughn and Wells stuck their heads inside the car. Ink covered the front seat and windshield.

"The perp's face is tattooed. The ink must have got him good," Wells said.

"Both perps," Vaughn said casually.

"Both?" Wells blurted out.

"Yeah. Look at the red dye on the seats. There were two people in the front seat when the dye bomb went off. Most of the driver's seat and most of the passenger's seat is not stained. Someone was sitting in each seat when the ink flew. The bulk of the ink caught the robber in the passenger seat."

"The witnesses in the bank all said that the Elvis guy drove off alone," Wells said.

"Could have picked up an accomplice later on, or the accomplice could have been hiding in the car," Vaughn said. "I forgot to ask. What did the handwriting analysis on the note the robber handed the teller show?"

"Adam, I was embarrassed to even ask for the analysis," Wells said, and his eyes turned away from Vaughn.

Vaughn sensed his friend was not divulging the entire story. "What did it show?" he pressed.

"Okay, the expert could not rule out that the handwriting was that of Elvis," Wells said and sighed. "Happy now?"

"Like the guy in *Dragnet* used to say, "Just the facts."

Vaughn slipped on latex gloves and deftly opened the glove box and found it empty. He then thoroughly checked under the seats. Nothing. "Let's look in the trunk," he suggested. Wells carefully opened the trunk with a pick lock. Nothing. He then opened the driver's side door and popped the hood latch and they scanned the engine compartment.

"When they lift for prints, have them do the fuses in the fuse box," Vaughn suggested.

"Good idea, but it looks pretty hopeless. We don't even know what state the car is registered in. Everything has been filed off the engine and the manufacturing plate has been removed."

"That's easy, Louisiana," Vaughn said.

"How in the hell do you know that?" Wells asked.

"Someone scraped off the inspection sticker, but some of the ink imprint is still on the glass," Vaughn explained, and then he leaned toward the windshield, his nose just inches from the glass. "Let's get on the radio and get dispatch to call Public Safety in Louisiana with the numbers we can read. Louisiana Department of Public Safety should be able to tell us what city the car was last inspected in."

"I know better than to doubt you, Adam, but how in the hell can they tell us that?"

"Watch and learn."

They returned to Wells's car and Vaughn got on the radio. He called the dispatcher and told her the numbers of the inspection certificate he had gleaned from the ink on the windshield glass and the make of the car. He also told her he was waiting.

"How is the number going to tell us where the car was inspected?" Wells asked.

"Specific numbers are assigned to specific inspection stations in Louisiana. The stations are accountable for the stickers and they keep a record of the name and license number of the owner. My guess is that the car is registered to someone in Transylvania, Louisiana; that's a wide spot in the road in extreme northeast Louisiana."

"How do you know that?" Wells asked, stupefied.

Vaughn did not want to tell Ron just yet about the mail receipt in his wallet that had cost him a hundred dollars. It just might be the piece of evidence that would set the world on its ear. Vaughn wanted to check out the address in Transylvania and what it might lead to before telling his friend that Elvis was alive and living in Transylvania. Ron thought he was crazy enough as it was, and there had been many wild goose chases.

The radio crackled and the dispatcher said, "Public Safety says the sticker was assigned to an inspection station in Transylvania, Louisiana and the vehicle was owned by John Smith. The sticker and the tags on the vehicle have not been renewed for a couple of years." Wells jotted down the name and address of John Smith that the dispatcher rattled off. They matched the address in Vaughn's wallet.

"Amazing," Wells commented. "I guess you're not going to tell me how you knew that."

"I discovered it in the ashes of an ashtray," Vaughn said coyly.

"I've got a court appearance this afternoon and in the morning day after tomorrow," Wells said. "What say we drive down to Louisiana in the afternoon day after tomorrow?"

Vaughn was too anxious to wait on Wells and decided to check out Transylvania on his own. He thought about bringing Mel with him, but decided to leave her with his sister-in-law. He would be getting back late, long past her bedtime. And routine was every thing to a five year old.

The Louisiana terrain was dotted with soybean and cotton fields and an occasional storage silo. The terrain was flat with occasional hills. The highway was mostly two-lane but had a wide paved shoulder, so he made excellent time, except when he had to slow down to go through one-horse towns.

He drove his Malibu along U.S. Highway 65 and chuckled when he saw the batwings on the water tower as he approached Transylvania. The town was nothing more than a small village that had adopted the name as a publicity stunt. And the stunt had worked. One of the main industries of the town was the sale of vampire tee shirts and trinkets. Vaughn stopped for directions at a mom-and-pop hardware store, bought a coffee mug with "I SURVIVED MY STOP IN TRANSYLVANIA" stamped on it, and eventually found the address on the Mangs mailing receipt.

A barn that had been cheaply converted into a house lay at the end of a dirt road that shot off of Highway 65. An old, wheelless Dodge truck was partially buried in the front yard among weeds that were five feet tall. A mangy dog stretched out on a rickety porch. Vaughn pulled onto a narrow lane carved through the weeds and drove up to the porch. A goose flew from the thicket, narrowly escaping the crush of Vaughn's tires.

He skidded to a stop and warily got out of the car, but the dog didn't seem to mind and didn't even move. Planks creaked under his feet as he crossed the porch to the bare door. He knocked on it, fearful that his knuckles might go right through the rotting pine wood.

"Just a minute," a voice called out. A minute went by, and then another. Finally the door opened and a shirtless, skinny, middle-aged man and the distinctive smell of marijuana greeted

Vaughn. "Yeah?" The man had a tattoo on his chest over his heart that read: DAGGER.

"I'm looking for a Mr. John Smith who used to stay here about five years ago." Vaughn attempted to peek through the door opening, but the man quickly shifted his body to block his view.

"I'm afraid I can't help you. I've been here four years next month and the place was vacant when I came." The guy looked over Vaughn's shoulder, clearly nervous.

"You own this place or you rent?" Adam asked.

"Neither. I stay here with permission of the owner for free, as long as I keep it up."

Vaughn looked around and almost laughed. *Keep it up?*

"Property is in a succession with a bunch of squabbling kids," the guy explained. "Look, you a cop or anything?"

"Maybe the owners know who was here before you," Vaughn suggested.

"I deal with the lawyer. Wait a minute and I'll get you his card." The shirtless guy disappeared and reappeared with a card that he gave to Vaughn. "Sorry I couldn't help."

Vaughn turned to walk away. "Wait a minute," the guy said. "The fellow that lived here moved to Moscow, Tennessee. I only know that because the mailman told me that once. Said the man's mail was being forwarded to Moscow. And how can you forget that name?"

"I know where that is," Vaughn said. "It's just outside of Memphis. Other than going to the post office, do you know how I could get in touch with the mailman?"

"You'd have to go to the cemetery. He died in a wreck last year. An old blue-hair shoved her Chrysler up his rear while he was putting a sample of deodorant into a mailbox just down the road."

Vaughn scribbled down *Moscow* on the back of the mailing receipt and placed it back into his wallet.

Vaughn could not control his excitement. There wasn't much to go on, but he had an idea. He was confident that there would be no one in Moscow named John Smith. He would go the city police in Moscow and find out who had moved to town five years ago. If that didn't work, he'd get Wells to make a request of the United States Postal Service to look into their records, although from experience he knew that forwarding information was usually kept by the postal service for only a year.

Excited, he started back for Memphis and made good time.

CHAPTER SEVEN

It was now four thirty in the afternoon and Moscow was only a few miles away. The sun was starting to go down and was at his back as he headed east on Highway 57. It was too late to get any investigation going today in Moscow. Besides, his sister-in-law mentioned something about a church function, so he needed to pick up Mel by six. He just wanted to see the town that might hold the key to his search. He would drive through quickly and head back for Memphis. *Who was this guy, John Smith? Why had he gotten the jumpsuits and why was his car used in a robbery? Was John Smith, Elvis?*

Vaughn smiled to himself as he drove along, passing fenced cattle and horses, mobile homes and rustic cabins. He passed an old diner and laughed at its name, then rounded a curve. He was admiring the scenery and almost didn't see the car veering across the center line at him. The car wove back into its lane, but then sharply came at him again. Vaughn hit the brakes and yanked the wheel. His Malibu plopped onto the grass shoulder as the oncoming car went past. He stayed parked on the shoulder for a few minutes trying to catch his breath. Finally, his nerves settled and he resumed his journey. He eased the car back onto the road, but kept his speed to about 50 MPH.

He relaxed his mind and thought about how excited Mel would be to see the cows and horses up close when he spied a beautiful Arabian stallion on its hind legs behind a fence on the left side of the road. The stallion's bridle was tethered to a candy-cane striped rope held by a gray-haired man who was flashing a training whip.

As Vaughn crested a hill, he turned his head to get a better look at the Arabian. When he turned his eyes back to the road he discovered a young boy riding a horse in the middle of his lane. He swerved the Malibu to the right, just missing the hind legs of the animal. The right tires of the car caught a rut on the edge of the road way and Vaughn instinctively tried to correct the path of the car as it jerked to the right. He over-corrected by turning the steering wheel to the left. The left front tire grabbed the pavement at a right angle, causing the car to shoot wildly to the left. It flipped over twice, crushing the roof and squeezing Vaughn between the seat and roof.

As he lay with blood oozing from his ears and mouth, his last thoughts were of Mel, Marie, and Elvis. Mel would be alright with his sister-in-law, but he felt sorry for her. She deserved better. Now she would have no mother or father. He wondered if Marie and Elvis were waiting for him in heaven. Would Marie be mad at him for not bringing Mel? If Elvis was in heaven, he'd punch him in the nose square away, or give him a hug. Vaughn wasn't sure which he would do, and would decide when he got there.

Four fuzzy hooves suddenly appeared next to his head, then two tiny, blurry feet, and then two more feet in a pair of cowboy boots. A butterfly landed on the window, inches from his nose, as he tried to read something on one of the boots. *Is that word, Elvis?*

He tried to mouth something, but nothing came out. One cowboy boot kicked in the windshield and then everything slowly went dark and quiet.

CHAPTER EIGHT
1999

Posters of dreadfully untalented musical groups lined the walls of Bennie San's bedroom: *The Crematorium of Death. The Nails of Death. The Deceased Pimples. The Vampires of Death. The Death Angels. Nine-inch Death. The Living Death. The Ultimate Death. Death After Death. Double Death.* Such were the typical groups admired by the mentally healthy young girls who roamed the San Fernando Valley in herds of stupor.

"Bennie, you don't have to have sex with every guy you date," Lannie Drees said to her best friend. "They're going to like you without the sex. You're funny, cute and like, totally smart. You've never made a B in your life, Miss four point oh." Lannie squatted on the edge of the bed with cotton balls stuffed between her toes and wet polish on her toenails. She wore a golden halo, as sunburst yellow headphones adorned her ears. The Sony radio seemed to be permanently attached to her head. She wore it everywhere. It was waterproof and she even listened to it while in the shower.

"I've told you before, Lannie, it's not that I'm smart. I've got a photographic memory. I look at it and it gets stuck in my head. I've got so much useless stuff in my head, if I could ever get on *Jeopardy*, I'd win a lot of money."

Bennie held a silver clip at the very end of a reefer and sucked through lips coated with shiny, black lipstick. Bennie's ears were stapled with silver, and she had a gold spike jutting from her chin. Counting the parts not visible when she had on clothes, Bennie had more precious metal implanted in her than that which passes through Fort Knox in a month. Airport metal detectors beeped their excitement when she appeared. Bennie's eyes were the color of, and as dead as, dishpan water. Streaks of purple, green and blue ran through her short hair. A haze of smoke snaked around her painted head.

Aluminum foil sheathed the windows of Bennie's room and sported pinpricks shaped like the moon, stars and crosses. Sunlight invaded the room through the tiny holes and cast laser-like figures on the room's satin, black walls. Light from an overhead lavender bulb caused Bennie's face to look like a druid Halloween mask. Creases of black and purple were carved in her cheeks and chin. Her eyes were hollow orbs. She would fit right in as a strung-out member of a deceased punk-rock band.

A poster of Lannie's talented mom, who had garnered five platinum albums, three television movies-of-the-week and two Grammy nominations, hung over the door. The artwork for the poster had been done when her mom was twenty-two, right after Bronk Allen had taken *You Change Your Feelings (Like Makeup On Your Face)* to Number One. The hit had stayed at the top of the Billboard charts for thirty-nine straight weeks, cementing Barbara Anne Drees' status as a major songwriter. Barbara Anne had the full package back then. Golden hair. Ruby, puffed lips. Glamorous. In the poster she was wearing a white Stetson, white boots and a calf-length dress that buttoned in the front. She was standing next to a not so youthful Elvis. He wasn't slender, but had not lost that marvelous sexy, sly smile. His cheeks were no longer sculpted, but he still had dreamy eyes. His hand was around Barbara Anne's slender waist and he had a look of fun and mischief in his eye. They had been captured in an exuberant moment at an awards show. Barbara Anne's body was sleek and fabulous. The poster framed the immortality of her magnetic, youthful beauty. But this was before the cancer came knocking on Barbara Anne's door with a decaying fist and vein-puffed tentacles for fingers, before chemotherapy and every kind of alternative therapy that money could find and buy.

"And what were you doing with Al Tautletub last Friday night in the backseat of his Mercedes in the parking lot of the bowling alley, Bennie? Looking for loose coins between the seats?" Lannie smugly asked. She smacked her gum and started to dab more clear lacquer on her toenails. She blew hard through pursed lips and her blonde bangs, the color of the week, fluttered.

"Al and I have been going steady for what, like four weeks now. It's almost like we're married. He is *sooo* cute. I just want to hug him and squeeze him. We're practically a married couple, you know," Bennie said and giggled. "Who told you about that, anyway?"

"Al told Josh, who told Lauren, who told Heather, who told Derrick, who made a poem of it and scribbled it on the boy's bathroom wall at school with your phone number."

"Like, is it good?" Bennie asked.

"Like, is what good?"

"The poem."

"Oh. Josh says it doesn't even rhyme," Lannie said.

"Like, now I see. I've been wondering why I've been getting so many calls for dates this week, you know. And from jerks I barely know," Bennie lamented. "I guess I'm now labeled the school slut." She passed her hand through her multicolored hair. "My personal trainer even made a move on me yesterday. After my workout, you know, I went to my room and popped in the shower. A minute later Denny, that's his name, he's naked and opening the shower door. Like, I told Denny, if and when I wanted him I'd let him know. Though he was *so* sweet. He offered to wash my hair. That's like my number one fantasy. A guy washing my hair, you know. So I let Denny wash my hair and like, I just had to, you know, pay him back." Bennie was doodling on an artist's pad with her free hand and doing an excellent job of drawing the Los Angeles skyline as viewed from the valley. She took one last drag from the roach, wet her fingers with her tongue and snuffed out the tip of the cigarette. She didn't offer the joint to Lannie because Lannie didn't do drugs. Bennie often wondered why Lannie remained her friend. They were as different as night and day.

"Tautletub's the quarterback, right?" Lannie said. "Too bad it's not October. You'd probably be elected homecoming queen."

"That would like, totally blow my mind. Linda Bishop got selected last year, but she had to go a few rounds with the entire offensive line. When she got like pregnant her parents sent her away to teenage-baby penitentiary. They're like Catholic."

"Yeah, I saw her last Christmas and she was fatter than the Goodyear blimp," Lannie said and rolled her eyes. "Duh!"

"Linda's back now. Saw her yesterday. She said the baby was living with her aunt in Santa Barbara."

"How did she look?" Lannie asked.

"Her dad bought her a new Mercedes convertible. I heard it was a present for not marrying the guy who knocked her up. Her hair looked awesome," Bennie said.

"She's such a loser. I hate those small pores. She tans so nicely and she's always so perky." Lannie said. "Her dad's got a new yard man from Mexico. He's real cool looking. Linda's taking personal gardening lessons, if you know what I mean."

"*She* told you that? It was their last gardener that poofed her up," Bennie said, although not as though she was surprised.

Linda's reputation would have qualified her for the All-Star Slut Team of any decade.

"No, our yard man told me," Lannie said.

"Have you seen the Mexican heartthrob?" Bennie asked.

"Looks like Ricky Martin, you know, before he started dressing totally Hispanic."

"Let's go out and celebrate," Bennie said.

"Like, what are we celebrating?"

"Duh? My new popularity. I won't have trouble getting a date for like the rest of high school."

"Want to go shopping?" Lannie asked.

Bennie frowned. "Dad took my cards away. Said I had overspent my allowance by three thousand dollars last month. Like, what am I, an accountant? Things are expensive. And with all the returns, it's impossible to keep track of how much I've spent in one month." Bennie had a habit of buying something on impulse, wearing it and then returning it a few days later. She struggled with keeping track of the credits her cards were due. Her closet was full of things she'd never even worn that she had forgotten to return.

"How cruel. Look, I still have all my cards and I don't have a limit," Lannie said perkily.

"Sweet. Your step-dad is so generous and he's a hottie. Saw him on Leno last week. That ponytail is just gorgeous. He was wearing jeans that must have been sprayed on. He was plugging his latest album, *Divorce, An Enema For My Wallet.* They showed the video and I got excited watching him ride that beautiful horse. I bet you're the only girl in school whose father is a fantasy object."

"My step-father doesn't ride. That's a stunt double on the horse. Richard has a bad back and couldn't even get *on* a horse. Wears a wig too, you know."

"Unh, unh."

"Oh yeah," Lannie sighed. "He's balder than a shaved bowling ball."

"Like, choke and barf," Bennie protested.

"Andre says Richard will be like in the Country Music Hall Of Fame one day."

"Who's Andre?" Bennie asked.

"He's this guy who teaches at the university. Tutors me in math on Wednesday nights. Mom like hired him to tutor me. Like what a waste of time. He just talks about the same things that the teacher at school does. But Johnny Rooks, you know, the tall guy with the mole on his cheek, looks a lot like Robert DiNiro, services my Porsche at the dealership, he says Richard's *just* a singer. Said Richard's never written a decent song. Said Richard just sings songs written by Rod Witherspoon, or some guy. Rooks said Richard doesn't *deserve* to be in the Hall of Fame. I told him I'd tell Richard the bad news and maybe Richard would like be buying me a Mercedes next year, instead of a Porsche, and from someone who appreciates country music, or at least knows how to kiss my butt just a little better."

"You ever see Richard, like, you know, undressed?" Bennie asked.

"Like gag me, Bennie. He's my step-father." Lannie put her finger down her throat and pretended to retch.

"Soon to be *ex*-step-father," Bennie correctly pointed out. The friendly divorce was wending its way through a myriad of accountants, consultants, lawyers and courthouses. The proposed settlement was thicker than the Los Angeles yellow pages.

"Saw *it* once. Mom had a birthday party for Richard. You know, their closest *two* hundred friends," Lannie said and rolled her eyes. "Garth, Allen, George. That television chef, what's his name? Yeah, Emeril. He catered the party. A lot of Cajun food that everybody thought was too spicy. Anyway, like after most of the famous people had gone home, the regular valley moochers decided to swim. Guess they wanted to be able to tell everyone they swam in Barbara Anne Drees' pool. As the night wore on, the number of people kept getting smaller. Finally, like at about three in the morning there were just seven or eight people left. Three guys and four women, I think. Anyway, I watched them from the third floor guest bathroom, which by the way has the ugliest wallpaper. Like puke, man. The colors are so last year. It's *so* embarrassing; I'll never let you go up there. Anyway, they stripped off their bathing suits and jumped into the hot tub. All seven, including mom."

"What did they do?" Bennie asked with her eyes fully opened. She was breathing hard.

"Nothing. They just drank wine, soaked and talked and laughed. After a while everybody toweled off, got dressed and went home."

"Well?"

"Well what?" Lannie asked. She plucked the cotton balls from her toes and stared at her toenails.

"How big was Richard?" Bennie asked.

"Oh, that. Looked like a half-inch prune."

"As if."

"Well, I *was* like thirty feet away," Lannie said. She tried to blow on her toes, but couldn't quite get her mouth close enough. She fell over onto her side trying to bend her body in half and laughed at herself.

"I'm like totally bored," Bennie said. "Let's go to Palmdale and shoplift at Dillard's."

"Bennie, you know I don't do that. We could go shop instead and use my cards, but bummer. My car is in the shop getting an upgraded stereo system."

"That's okay, I got the rental today, the Boxter," Bennie said.

"Thought you lost your license when you crashed your Vette into Federico's on Ventura Boulevard," Lannie said.

"Dad knows the judge. I got a temporary permit. Dad's also ordered me a new one, although I told him I really like the Boxter. He's thinking of letting me keep it when the new Vette comes in. After shopping, let's cruise on down to Long Beach and buy some weed. And tease Freddy, that new Chicano dealer."

"He thinks you're a babe, Bennie."

"Do you think he'd exchange some weed for sex?" Bennie asked and ran her fingers through her hair.

"Bennie, you've got enough money to buy not only his drugs, but to buy Freddy. Why mess with that guy?"

"He's *sooo* cute," she said and playfully swooned.

"Like, yeah," Lannie agreed. "Totally."

PART TWO

CHAPTER NINE
Present Day

Melissa Vaughn pressed her nose against the window of the Boeing 737 on final approach into Seattle. The mid-afternoon sun framed Mount Rainier and a few casual clouds cast shadows that made the mountain appear alive with movement. Melissa wished her assignment included exploring Rainier instead of a wilderness trip with yet another nut chasing Big Foot. But such was the life of a tabloid field reporter: tracking down the absurd to fill the pages of a rag. Actually, the standards at Melissa's rag, *Weird Magazine*, were set pretty low. No article from a salaried employee had ever been rejected--heavily edited, yes, but rejected, no.

"Are you going to call the office when we land?" Jeff Cloud, her photographer for the Big Foot hunt asked, as though he were asking the question as part of a long conversation. Jeff had finally awakened and turned down the volume on his iRiver player after four hours of in-flight snoring. The question constituted the first words out of his mouth since takeoff from LaGuardia. He wanted to be more sociable, but he was exhausted from his last assignment. He had cavorted all over the deserts of New Mexico trying to snap a picture of an alien from another galaxy that a professor at New Mexico State swore existed. The astronomy teacher claimed that the alien had impregnated his wife and absconded with her. At least that's what the alien's note said that the teacher found when he returned from a lecture. Jeff had wanted to tell the guy his slutty wife ran off with someone new, but didn't have the heart. Besides, the guy's story might sell a few magazines.

"I was going to wait until morning. It's after six at the office," Melissa replied, yawned and stretched her arms in the tiny space afforded her seat. She glanced out her window and again yearned to explore the mountain. She did a double take when it appeared that the shadows had cast the form of a face on Rainier. For an instant she thought of the story she did last year about the face of

Jesus being burned into a tree by lightning, or was it the face of the Virgin Mary? Religious miracles tended to meld together in the tabloids.

"You know what I mean. Are you going to call Jim?" Jeff asked. He strained his neck to get a better look at whatever it was that Melissa was studying outside the window.

"Why would I call Jim Bowen after hours?" she asked with a puzzled look on her face. She knew the answer, but was fishing to see what Jeff would say.

"Mel, *everyone* at *Weird Magazine* knows that you and Jim are doing it." Melissa blushed. "Although none of us can figure out why you're dating such a snake," Jeff said and shook his head.

"Why do you call Jim a snake?"

"That guy has completed more passes than Terry Bradshaw. Us peons that work in production call him the Silver Zipper," Jeff whispered, as though he were announcing a secret to a solitary deserving ear.

Melissa ignored the accusation about Jim. "If I do talk to him, what is it that you need from him?"

"I turned in an expense reimbursement sheet for our UFO trip to Spain over six weeks ago and accounting said he's holding it up. My rent is due and I'm a little short." Jeff fidgeted with the iRiver's earbuds, expertly twirling the wire with his fingers.

"Maybe accounting sitting on it has something to do with the marijuana you bought in Castille and hid on your expense account as *film*." Mel shot Jeff an I told you so look.

"Jim knows about that?" Jeff blurted, his forehead suddenly cratered with creases and worry lines. "I'm totally screwed." His pulse escalated and beads of sweat erupted on his brow.

"Of course not, how would he?" Mel asked. She wanted Jeff to know that if Jim knew about the false expense statement, she had nothing to do with it. Jeff was a little sloppy in his paperwork and would eventually get caught.

"Maybe I ought not call attention to the expense sheet," Jeff said, stared out the window at nothing in particular and shrugged his shoulders. He wiped his brow on his sleeve. "Forget about calling Jim."

"How much do you need to cover the rent?" Melissa offered.

"Thanks, but don't worry about it, I'll just sell a little weed to some friends," he said casually. Melissa knew that Jeff wasn't kidding about pushing a little weed. Office rumor was that Jeff could score whatever one wanted.

"So Jim and I are the scuttlebutt of the office," Mel said. Her eyes narrowed. They had been extra careful and had done nothing at the office to tip anyone off. What had gone wrong? Had Jim talked?

"Oh yeah, just thought you should know." Jeff beamed, as though he were doing Mel a favor.

"I thought they only talked about you," Mel said, grinning.

"Me?" Jeff asked surprised. He tilted his head and rubbed his tongue against the inside of his lips. "Talk about me? About what for crissakes?"

"Sometimes about drugs, but mostly about how deep you are into the closet," she said matter-of-factly and sighed. "You know, Jeff, I don't care if you prefer the weaker of the stronger sex."

"Oh, God! Everyone knows I'm gay?" Jeff cried out with anguish. His left hand subconsciously grabbed Mel's right arm. The male flight attendant that was walking in the aisle heard Jeff's exclamation and gave him a quick once over accompanied by a toothy, knowing smile. Jeff dismissed his new admirer with a flick of the wrist and a frown with the left side of his lips upturned in a sneer. The rebuffed flight attendant tossed his head back and darted off. Mel thought she heard the attendant mutter the word, *bitch*, under his breath, as he strutted away, clearly disappointed.

"I wouldn't lose any sleep over your outing," Mel said. "Half the guys in the office are waiting to ask you out. I think there may even be an office pool with the winner being the lucky first date."

"Oh, an office pool? I hope Gene, the guy in the mailroom, wins. For sure."

The flight was a couple of minutes late landing and there was a problem with their luggage. Jeff's clothes were lost somewhere over America. He reported the lost bag over a "service phone" to some chick employed offshore in India or Guatemala, whatever. The *customer service representative* was barely understandable and kept calling the suitcase American *Tourista* and pronounced California like Arnold Schwarzenegger, "*Caul e phone ya.*" Jeff kept his composure during the entire ordeal and successfully suppressed the urge to scream or beat the phone's receiver against the wall.

He and Mel clumsily rolled the rest of their luggage as they ran to the transportation section, thinking they were late. But they were wrong and spent several minutes debating what to do about their no show ride. It was a typical Washington afternoon, cool and breezy and they entertained themselves by watching the strange people come and go.

They were just about to retreat to the shuttle section and find a hotel when an ancient Volvo station wagon, plastered with patches of rust and belching puffs of thick, black smoke from its angry tailpipe, ran its right front tire onto the curb, forcing Mel and Jeff to jump back. The car scraped its underside on the concrete and clamored to a halt. Mel and Jeff were speechless as the driver's door flew open and a man wearing a white dust mask pulled up onto his forehead sprang from the door and sprinted around the car to the sidewalk.

Hatch Morgan did not look like anything that Mel or Jeff had expected. He was at least three-quarters of a century old, short, only five feet seven inches tall and at least sixty pounds overweight. Hatch was bald, except for sporadic patches of gray hair in a half-moon over his ears. He had more hair hanging out of his nose and ears than hair on his head. His skin was etched with spider webs of creases and his face was split in half by an enormous smile that revealed yellowed, crooked teeth. One eye was blue, the other green and they were not coordinated; the blue eye angled off from center. He had a chaw of tobacco the size of a baseball bulging against his right cheek. Brown spittle dribbled down his chin.

"*Weird Magazine*?" Hatch bellowed, grabbing for Mel's largest bag. He jerked the bag from her side and she was impressed by the old man's strength. He effortlessly lifted the bag.

"Mr. Morgan, I'm Mel Vaughn and this is Jeff Cloud." Hatch stuck out his free hand and Jeff reluctantly shook it. Hatch yanked his hand back, glanced at it and rubbed it on his pant leg when he surmised Jeff's grip was weak. *Feels like limp pasta, this one,* Hatch thought.

"Glad to meet you. Mama used to say that the only person you could trust in life died two thousand years ago on a cross. Friends, do you have the check?" he asked, getting right to the point, eyeballing Jeff from what he thought was a safe distance. Mel glanced at Jeff. "We sure do. Five thousand dollars," she said. "But you realize it's only payable if we get usable pictures of Big Foot?"

"That, I guarantee," Hatch boasted, as he tossed Mel's bag into the backseat of the Volvo and then spit brown saliva the consistency of molasses onto the poor sidewalk. He flipped the dust mask down over his mouth and climbed in through the driver's door. From their vantage point Mel and Jeff could not see the brown stain coating the exterior of the entire driver's side of car, the accumulation of years of spittle. The side of the car appeared as thought it was a giant, rolling piece of peanut brittle. Hatch turned the key and the Volvo sputtered to life.

The group was soon fighting airport traffic. Hatch hunched over the steering wheel and held it in a death grip. His knuckles turned white and the veins in his hands bulged. He drove as though he had never negotiated traffic before, but after a tangle of impossible turns the belching Volvo was merged into traffic heading north on I-5. It was only then that Hatch seemed to start breathing and he released his serious grip on the steering wheel.

"Where are we headed?" Mel asked a few minutes later, more to break the silence than anything else. If she was going to spend a couple of days with the nut, she might as well be friendly and get along.

"We'll get a plane at the Snohomish County Airport, Paine Field and fly up to Vancouver Island." Hatch kept his eyes glued on the roadway, as they were packed tightly in a sixty-mile-per-hour traffic jam. Any slight deviation from the exact center of the travel lane meant an adventure of metal and bones.

"Where on Vancouver Island?" Jeff asked. Mel had said nothing about leaving the country. He thought of his passport, but then quickly realized that he didn't need it for Canada.

"If I told you where, you might be able to get your pictures without paying my fee," Hatch said and smugly nodded to the mirror. Jeff, staring at Hatch's fried egg head decided to not say anything in response.

Twenty-five minutes of near misses and harrowing silence went by and then Hatch pulled the Volvo to an airport hangar. He squirted out of the creaking driver's door, pulled up the mask and spit on the ground, grabbed Jeff's bag and Mel's large suitcase from the back seat, handling them as though they contained Styrofoam and started from the car towards the gaping door of the hangar. Mel and Jeff stayed paralyzed in the car. A bag-of-bolts Cessna was the only plane visible in the hangar. It was a biplane; the pontoons were severely dented and the tiny tires were shiny and looked like maypops. The plane's windshield was cracked and the aircraft appeared to list to one side. The sides of the plane had been repeatedly repaired with Bondo or fiberglass filler, causing the plane to look like it was held together with bubble gum. The propeller had chunks missing along the edges. Mel started to tell Jeff to dial 911, but held off.

"Don't be a wasting, we're losing daylight! Landing on the lake in the dark can be damn tricky. Come on!" Hatch yelled. Mel and Jeff reluctantly exited the car and slowly made it into the hangar.

The hangar's concrete floor was slippery with oil and grime. Its windows had panes missing and parts of airplanes were strewn everywhere. The only light came from the open door.

Hatch threw Mel and Jeff's bags into the plane and ordered, "Saddle up, ponies." He rushed to the open doors of the hanger and slid one side all the way open, and then the other side.

"Where's the pilot?" Mel asked, looking about the hangar. A rat scurried across the floor and out the door. A gentle breeze ruffled some of the loose tins of the sheet metal walls. Mel felt as though she were in an oven constructed in a third world country.

"That would be me, young lady. Now, we really must be on our way," Hatch said and saluted with his right hand.

"Shouldn't you check out the engine, the tires, whatever needs checking?" Jeff nervously asked, as they climbed into the tiny cockpit. He sat on a board covered with cheap vinyl.

"Naw. Guy that owns the plane does that sort of stuff," Hatch explained, and then spattered the ground with a chunk of gunk from his mouth. "I wouldn't know what to look for, anyway. I'm lost around the infernal internal combustion engine."

Mel and Jeff looked at each other with worry in their eyes.

Hatch taxied the plane to a short runway and flared the engine a few times. Then he slowly revved the engine and the plane lurched down the runway. The tail of the plane seemed to dance back and forth as it picked up speed. After a few seconds, Hatch let out an *eeeehaaaaw*, pulled on the wheel and the Cessna leapt up from the runway. The ground receded quickly and the plane sputtered the way a lawnmower does in grass that's too tall, but then slowly clicked away from the airport. Mel and Jeff were finally able to breathe.

Minutes later the plane puttered over Puget Sound.

"Do you file a flight plan for a short trip like this?" Mel asked over the hum of the engine. She noticed with anguish light smoke spewing from the cowling of the engine and tiny black flecks appearing on the windshield. *Oil?*

"I couldn't do that if I had to," Hatch said and laughed easily. He sat at the wheel of the plane the way he sat at the Volvo; he was hunched over and his strong hands gripped the wheel as though her were trying to bend the metal.

"Why not?" Jeff asked, noticing for the first time that none of the instruments on the dash seemed to be functioning. They were analog, but there were no needles to peg the numbers on the dial.

"Only a licensed pilot can file a plan," Hatch said.

"You're not licensed?" Mel asked, her voice two octaves higher than normal. She passed a worried look at Jeff, whose skin appeared to be turning red in some parts and green in others at the same time.

"Never bothered to get one. Too much red tape," Hatch said matter-of-factly. He reached under his seat and pulled out an old Nibblets corn can and spat into it. Some of the spittle made it into the can, the rest dripped onto the floorboard.

"How long have you been flying planes?" Jeff asked, suddenly slightly nauseous.

Hatch looked at his watch and said, "Let's see."

"Oh my," Jeff squeaked.

"Just kidding," Hatch proclaimed and let out a belly laugh. "I learned in the Air Force during Nam."

"Had me scared there, Hatch. So you were a pilot in the war?" Mel asked, relaxing her own death grip on the seat. Jeff let out the air in his lungs and gulped in replacement air and then wiped his brow.

"Actually, I was just a mechanic. Me and some other grease monkeys learned how to fly on our own, joyriding what was left by the flyboys for us to fix."

Mel tried to say something but the words stuck in her throat. Jeff, now full-blown, about-to-puke nauseous, swallowed hard and tried to not throw up. He looked around but found that the window did not have a crank or handle. He tried to say something, but couldn't.

Within minutes they were floating over the Juan de Fuca Strait and had slipped into Canada.

"Those are the greenest trees I've ever seen," Mel commented as they flew over Sooke.

"And the water is a color I can't describe," Jeff observed, delighted that they hadn't crash yet, suddenly catching his second wind, believing they might just be able to make it. "Now can you tell us where we are going?"

"We're going to land on Cowichan Lake. That's a few miles north of Victoria."

"Cowichan? Isn't that the tribe that makes those wonderful wool sweaters that last a thousand years?" Mel asked.

"I don't know about a thousand years, but you do get a guarantee on them for life," Hatch said.

No one said anything else as they soaked in the sights of the Insular Mountains, flowing streams and stands of Douglas fir, hemlock, cedar, alder and maple. Several minutes later a shimmering, blue mirror that was the lake came into view. At first it was a sliver of blue, and then it grew.

"Looks big," Mel commented.

"Twenty-six miles long," Hatch said. "We're going to the northern part of the lake, just past Honeymoon Bay. I've got a cabin on the shore. We'll spend the night there and in the morning we'll take a hike to where the Big Guys will be." Mel arched an eyebrow and glanced at Jeff who was grinning.

Hatch pushed forward on the wheel and the plane swooped low across the water, dipping the wings to follow the shoreline. "There's the cabin," he announced, as he angled the plane in for a touchdown. Mel and Jeff braced for a jolt, but the pontoons feathered onto the water and the plane glided to an effortless stop. The motor of the Cessna alternately hummed and raced as Hatch taxied the bobbing plane to a wharf lined with the halves of automobile tires nailed to creosote posts jutting out of the water. A few birds squatting on the posts flew off as the plane approached.

Mel was stunned. What Hatch had described as a cabin was nothing more than a shack, a conglomeration of unpainted boards and disproportioned tin. "Is this the outhouse?" she inquired and grimaced.

"It'll grow on you," Hatch said, as the plane gently bumped the wharf.

"Along with mold," Jeff joked.

"I don't see any electrical lines," Mel said.

"That's because there is no electricity," Hatch explained.

"Guess you're going to tell me you don't have any running water either," she declared.

"Okay, I won't tell you," Hatch retorted. He killed the engine, but it fired and popped for an additional couple of seconds, the sound echoing off tall trees lining the shoreline. He quickly jumped out of the plane and tied a line to the dock. Dazed, Mel and

Jeff squeezed out of the pilot's door and took in the surroundings in stunned silence.

The shore appeared deserted with no other cabins in sight. Tall trees lined the lake, their upper branches trying to blot out the sky. Mel sensed that something was terribly wrong and then realized the problem. There was no noise, only soft and gentle sounds of the forest--leaves rustling, branches twisting, animals slithering and birds calling. The bustle of the city had been left behind.

The cabin was indeed cozy, although the sheer privacy curtains that isolated the two beds from each other didn't thrill Mel. You could read a newspaper through the curtain. She would definitely sleep in her clothes.

"Mel, you take the bed on the left, Jeff, the one on the right. I've got a sleeping bag and cushion to sleep on the floor by the fireplace," Hatch suggested.

Hatch kindled a fire in the fireplace just as the sun began to go down. In a minute it was roaring.

"Is it cool enough for a fire?" Mel asked.

"In a couple of hours, it'll be colder in here than a witch's tit on Halloween. Refrigerated air slips down from the mountains and the lake sucks all the heat away," Hatch explained and started for the door.

"Where are you going?" Jeff asked.

"I've got some smaller wood cut up and seasoned chips in a cart just up the trail. I need the wood for the stove. Be back in a couple of minutes to start supper. There's a bottle of wine with a real cork in it in the cabinet by the stove. Red I think. You can open it, if you like." And just like that Hatch disappeared through the door.

"Reckon ole Hatch is stirring up Big Foot?" Jeff asked and laughed.

"In a pond of strange ducks, Hatch would definitely stick out. I tried calling Jim a couple of minutes ago, but there's no reception on my phone here. Jeff, we're in the middle of nowhere with a guy right out of a ripper novel. Do you find this place creepy?"

"Not in the least. Besides, I've got my gun," Jeff said and patted his jacket.

"How did you get that through airport security?" she asked.

"I didn't, it was in my bag, the one the airline did not lose."

"Let's open the Lafitte Rothschild," Mel said. "That appears to be our only entertainment tonight here on mountain man's *Gilligan's Isle*."

Hatch was right. As darkness enveloped the cabin, the air quickly chilled. But the heat of the fireplace combined with the warmth of the Gallante Vinyards Cabernet Sauvignon to produce a perfectly purring tuning fork in Mel's head. The wine was exquisite and for some reason she felt more relaxed than she had in years.

The trio hungrily downed surprising Spam spaghetti that Hatch scrounged up in minutes, and then they sat around the fire and sipped more wine. Hatch, a lifelong bachelor, did not need encouragement to yap. He snuffed out two of the kerosene lamps, sat on the floor and studied the flames waltzing in the fireplace. As though he were in a trance, he began to talk.

"This place was built by Poppa. He barged all the tin and nails from the town of Cowichan Lake; it's across the lake and south of here. He cut the lumber from the clearing that surrounds the cabin and planed it himself." Hatched popped a new lump of tobacco into his mouth without missing a syllable. "We lived outside Seattle, but Poppa, who was a carpenter, used to come here for months at a time. One summer he brought me. We fished everyday and he taught me how to live in the wild, hunting for our food. We were out hunting one morning and stumbled into a Big Foot that was drinking from a natural spring. I was scared to death by that huge furry thing and could hardly breathe. Poppa acted as though seeing the animal wasn't a big deal. I swear I think they nodded to each other. We just continued on our way and when we were several hundred feet from the Big Foot he explained to me that the Big Foot had as much right to these woods as we did and that we must never tell anyone about the creature." Hatch leaned forward and expertly sent a stream of dark spittle into the fire. The fire hissed and flared up momentarily.

"If it's supposed to be kept a secret, why are you telling us now?" Mel asked.

"I'm in hot water with the IRS. They're disappointed that I haven't filed a return in twelve years. Government commie bastards. I need the money for back taxes. And if you read our letter agreement closely you'll note that you can't tell the readers exactly where the pictures are taken without my approval and you can't use my real name in the story. I'll only approve saying the pictures were taken on Vancouver Island."

"How many different Big Foots have you seen over the years?" Mel asked, playing along.

"Not many. There are three males and two females left."

"Odd man out must get testy," Jeff said and smirked. Hatch looked at Jeff, but didn't say anything.

"Left? Were there more?" Mel asked.

"There were as many as ten at one point. We don't think they died. We believe they just moved on. There have been reports of sightings a couple hundred miles north of her."

"What do they look like?" Mel asked quickly, trying to cover up Jeff's snootiness.

"You people can doubt all you want, but you'll see soon enough. Then you'll tell me if your eyes are lying."

Within minutes of the last lamp being turned off Hatch began snoring as loudly as a freight train chugging up a two mile low grade. The low vibration from his throat rattled and hurt Mel's ears. In between Hatch's sonorous belches, a blanket of night sounds filled the cabin. Chirping, rustling, hooting, flapping, scraping and brushing continued outside the cabin nonstop, only to be amplified by the cool, damp air. Light from a full moon drifted through the cabin's two windows and was just bright enough to cast shadows, when the occasional cloud did not block it. Gentle night breezes swayed the branches of the trees, causing hypnotic shadows to dance on the walls of the cabin.

The feather bed was very comfortable; the wine gave her a buzz and she was exhausted, but Mel could not sleep. Instead, she lay in the warm bed mesmerized by the playful shadows flickering on the walls and thought of Jim Bowen and their relationship. Jeff was right. Jim had a reputation for playing the field. But he had made it clear that his wandering eye was in the past. He was looking only to the future now and it was only Mel that he saw in it. She was emotionally involved with Jim, but if they broke it off, at least now, there would be minimal heartbreak. They had not yet gotten to the point where one indifferently brushed his or her teeth while the other squatted on the potty in the same bathroom.

Around midnight Mel reluctantly concluded that she had to pee, pronto. Ordinarily this would not be a big ordeal, but the cabin possessed no indoor plumbing. The outdoor necessary was a tin-covered lean to and it was, appropriately, outside, where it was presently darker than the inside of a sealed can. Mel threw back the covers, slipped on her sneakers and tip-toed to the door. The hinges squeaked as she slowly pried open the door to the roar of the night's bugs and such. She carefully shut the door behind her and then crept along the narrow porch to the side of the cabin on which the crapper was positioned. Gravel crunched under her feet as she walked the short distance to the outhouse's door. She opened it and reached in and felt for the candle and box of kitchen matches she had seen earlier and then, as she touched the box, she changed her mind and decided not to light the candle. Enough light poured through the half-moon cutout in the door to allow her to sit on the throne without mishap. She sat down gingerly and was relieved that nothing slithered away. As she started to tinkle, however, something brushed against the exterior wall with sufficient force to rumple the tin. The hair on the nape of Mel's neck rose.

"Jeff, that's not funny," she said, her heart beating so hard she thought she could hear it. "Jeff?" No answer. *Okay. Don't panic. Probably a branch scraping against the tin. I'll just finish, open the door and slowly walk to the porch.*

Mel started to stand and heard a grunt, or that's what she thought she heard. She froze. *My mind is playing tricks.* She reached for the candle, but it fell off the ledge of the plank it had been resting on. She then pulled up her pants, took in a deep breath and slowly pushed the door open. She waited for what seemed like minutes, but was only seconds, and stuck her head out of the door opening. Nothing.

A cloud floated over the cabin clearing and the moonlight streaming through the trees instantly evaporated. Mel put her hand to her nose and could not see it. *Oh, well, I'll just follow the wall of the cabin to the porch.* She put her left hand out and felt for the wall. *There it is!* She slowly began feeling her way to the porch. *Can't be more than four or five steps.* After four steps she bumped into something. She put her hand out and jerked it back. *Fur?!* She gasped. *Can't run in the dark.* She began to tremble. *What is that? Oh God! Is that breathing?* She put her hand out again and felt…nothing. *But I can sense whoever it is, whatever it is, is just inches away. No. It's moving away.* She heard the floor of the porch creak and then movement on the path to the woods.

The cloud moved off and moonlight lit part of the porch. Mel strained her eyes. *What is that walking across the clearing towards the woods?* Just as the thing made it to the woods a beam of moonlight hit the clearing. *It's a Big Foot?* What appeared to be a large ape-like creature turned towards her and then nonchalantly spun around and walked on its two legs into the woods. She took a step towards where the creature had disappeared, but was grabbed on the shoulder. The air rushed out of her lungs, she jerked her head and saw Jeff, who was staring at the clearing with his mouth hanging open, wearing only his drawers, boxers with smiley faces all over.

"Are you okay?" he asked.

"Did you see that?" she asked.

"Wish I had my camera."

"Nice undies, Jeff. Say, where's Hatch?" she asked as they both anxiously stepped to the cabin door and stopped when they heard the roar of Hatch's snoring. Hatch was bundled in his sleeping bag with his feet inches from the glowing embers of the fireplace. A grin painted his angelic face.

"I wish I was asleep and dreaming about whatever it is *he's* dreaming about," Mel said.

The smell of bacon crackling in the frying pan woke Mel from a deep sleep. She yawned and stretched and her first inclination was that it had all been a dream. But then she saw Jeff standing with his back to the fireplace. He was fully dressed and had two cameras strapped over his neck. He was definitely puckered and the look of anticipation in his eyes said it all; he was daydreaming about a Pulitzer.

Mel ate breakfast while Hatch and Jeff watched and tried to hide their eagerness. It was not easy gulping down the bacon and eggs and retaining the airs of a lady, but Mel semi-succeeded. She only got a little egg on her chin. She too was eager to find whatever it was she and Jeff had seen in the clearing.

With Hatch leading, they bobbed and wove through underbrush of ferns and berry bushes along a barely discernable path. Fronds bore the weight of condensation and mist, and when they brushed against the leaves, streaks of water soaked their clothes. A sheen of mist and fog clung to the ground and the sheets of sunlight that pierced through the towering trees formed what appeared to be shards of glass in the cool, damp air that smelled of berries, ozone and fresh rain.

Hatch stopped the troops at a broken tree felled by lightning. A large branch lay on the ground at its base. Hatch pulled off his knapsack that contained a thermos full of hot chocolate, candy bars and sweetbread wrapped in aluminum foil, and the adventurers rested on the fallen branch, using it as a bench. Hatch wiped his brow.

"Why are we stopping?" Mel asked. They had been underfoot for an hour.

"We're more than half way and this is a good spot to rest," Hatch said.

"I'm not tired" Jeff protested, barely hiding his heavy breathing that was caused more by excitement than by the exertion of the hike. The vision in the clearing by the cabin the night before fueled his expectation.

"Me neither," Mel said. Adrenaline pulsed through her veins.

Hatch pointed to the trunk of a nearby hemlock tree, "See that. That's most unusual." The tree bark was etched with claw marks and heavily stained with what appeared to be berry juice. "I don't know what to make of it. The creatures don't usually scratch up a tree like that. Lot of anger here."

Jeff crinkled his eyes at Mel and said, "Guess we'll have to risk it. Can we get this over with?" Jeff chuckled at what he perceived to be theatrics by Hatch,

"Okay, let's go," Hatch said. He hoisted his back pack on and shuffled off.

Mel and Jeff marveled at the pristine plants and flowers they discovered. They felt as thought they were walking through a *National Geographic* special on the History Channel. Everything was so green, colorful and crisp.

Forty-five minutes later they arrived at an area of dense growth with moss-covered trees. Hatch threaded the group through an invisible trail. The soothing sound of running water drew the threesome through lush vegetation. Suddenly and without warning they popped through the thickest of the plants and stepped into a small clearing dominated by a pond and a small, two-tiered waterfall. Immense trees acted as a light-filtering canopy and the overall effect was surreal. The pristine scene looked prehistoric; Mel half-expected a mechanical tyrannosaurus to burst through the trees. But other than a few birds and an occasional fish jumping, there was no nonhuman in sight.

Hatch appeared visibly shaken. "Damn, I've never been here without seeing a Big Foot." He twitched and stomped to and fro along the edge of the pond. His lips formed words he muttered and the veins in his neck popped out.

"Is there some other place to spot one?" Jeff asked in a tone that reflected skepticism.

"Not that I know of, but I tell you what, let's set up a day camp and rest here. We've got another eight hours before we have to head back to beat darkness. I'm telling you the things are always here. This is like their living room."

"Where's the television?" Jeff asked sarcastically.

"Our flight out of Seattle is not until tomorrow night," Mel said. "We've got all day."

"Good. You two pitch that tarp in Mel's backpack as a tent by the waterfall. It might rain this afternoon and we don't need to be getting wet with pneumonia. I'll rustle us up some wood to get a fire going and warm us up. A low-lying cloud drifts by and the temperature will drop twenty degrees. It'll be colder than summer in San Francisco."

Before Jeff or Mel could respond, Hatch was swallowed up by the dense growth. They began unfolding the tarp and untangling the lines.

"Hatch ought to go into show business as a magician. He disappears faster than the money in my checkbook," Mel quipped.

"Mel, I'm sorry what I said yesterday about Jim Bowen. I was putting my nose where it doesn't belong."

"That's okay. Shows you care. I'll be careful."

"We get a decent picture of a creature and we'll be famous," he said.

"Only in our own mind. If we can't tell anyone where we saw the beast and the sighting can't be verified, we'll be another piece of unbelievable hype in tabloid lore. There will be a hundred forensic photo examiners and half will say the photos are fake."

"Are you saying we need to capture one?" Jeff asked.

"Right. If these creatures exist, they've lived her for a millennium. What right would we have to destroy an entire race of whatever, just for cheap notoriety?"

"Damn, Mel, I'm getting all weepy inside listening to that drivel. You ought to write for the soaps."

"Seriously. If we told anyone where we saw such a creature, the place would be swarming with kooks. The creatures, no matter how many there are, would be captured and put in zoos and studied, or killed. Either way, it would be our fault. Wouldn't you be happy just knowing that their existence was true?"

A twig snapped behind them and they turned their heads. Jeff snatched his camera and quickly advanced the film. Branches moved and the sound of something advancing on them was undeniable. Jeff pulled his gun from his jacket.

Mel turned to Jeff. "Put that thing away, Jeff."

"I'm going to use it only as a last resort."

Foliage five feet away fluttered, and startled, Mel fell backwards, stumbling on a rock. Jeff thrust the gun up to waist level and his hand involuntarily tightened on the pistol grip.

Just as Jeff instructed, "Halt," in a raspy voice, a Vancouver marmot ambled into the clearing, and ignoring Jeff and Mel, moseyed to the pond to drink. The marmot had dark brown pelage with telltale white patches. The critter slipped its snout into the water for a few seconds and then turned and stared at Mel.

"These guys are some of the rarest critters in the world," Mel said, practically eye-level with the marmot. "Supposedly, there are only ten or so left in the wild."

"This little bugger must be oblivious," Jeff said, as he put the pistol back into his pant pocket.

"Unless this little guy thinks we're two Big Foots," Mel said. She raised her eyebrows.

"Would the *Manual of Style and Usage* of the New York Times require you to say, 'Unless this little guy thinks we're two Big *Feet*?'" Jeff joked.

"Seriously, maybe Mr. Marmot is used to sharing the jungle with two legged creatures that don't try to harm him. He sees us as his friends."

"Makes sense, I think….anyway, here comes one of his buddies," Jeff said, looking at swaying bushes and hearing twigs snap on the same path taken by the marmot.

But, instead of another marmot, suddenly a hunched over fury creature half-emerged from the thicket.

"Holy shit!" Mel exclaimed.

Jeff didn't move.

"Jeff, take a picture!"

Jeff threw himself to the ground, snapped his camera up and in one motion snapped off a picture. The creature threw up its hands and fell back into the blanket of vegetation.

"Let's go!" Jeff yelled as he followed the creature into the wall of foliage, but he soon tripped over vines and then Mel tripped over him. They sprang up and continued the chase, although they had no idea what direction to take. Jeff fell again and Mel dropped on top of him.

"I'm starting to think you're doing this on purpose," Mel teased as she got up and brushed herself off. They traipsed off again.

A minute later Jeff held out his hand to get Mel to stop. They strained their ears and heard branches being rustled nearby.

"That way!" Mel screamed, and off they went, tearing through the brush.

Seconds later Jeff stopped, held out his hand again and Mel froze. A moaning sound, close by, came to them from their right. They slowly stepped in that direction through a morass of bushes and were soon confronted by a huge hole at least ten feet across and five feet deep. The creature had fallen into it and was lying on its face.

Jeff handed Mel the camera. "Just point it and push this button," he instructed. She nodded, as her chest heaved. Jeff grabbed a vine from a nearby tree and lowered himself into the hole. He placed his hand on the creatures shoulder and started to flip it over. And that's when Hatch said in a muffled voice, through the ape suit, "Damn, I think my leg is broken."

Jeff managed to get a fire started and Mel made potted meat, wild greens and tomato sandwiches. The sun was almost gone and the water in Cowichan Lake was as black as used oil. The night noises of the forest began to crank up. Off in the distance an owl hooting dominated the early night air.

Mel handed Hatch a sandwich. "Thanks," he said. "Jeff, if you go down to the dock, the piling the plane is fastened to, I've got a basket tied to it under the water with a case of beer in it. Stays nice and cold."

"How about caviar and a hot shower?" Mel quipped.

"I'll get the beer later," Jeff said, accepting his cuisine sandwich from Mel.

"Hatch, why did you try to fake it?" she asked.

"Guys, I've never been to the waterfall and not seen at least one Big Foot. I panicked."

"So you keep an ape suit at the pond for such emergencies?" Jeff asked, facetiously.

"I put it there last week. Kind of my back-up parachute."

"You know I'll have to write the article exposing you as a fraud, Hatch," Mel said. "The agreement says if we prove you're a fake, we have the option of using your name and the location of this place in the exposé."

"I beg of you, don't do it. Even if you say I'm a fake, nuts will come out here and stumble onto the creatures and....it will get ugly."

"Guess I could use a beer," Mel said, suddenly thirsty.

"I'll be right back," Jeff said.

"Take a lamp," Hatch suggested.

"Moon's full, it'll do." Jeff said, slipped on his shoes and closed the door behind him.

"Jeff light in the loafers?" Hatch asked.

Mel shrugged.

"Doesn't matter to me."

"Then why did you ask?" Mel testily asked.

"Just curious."

"You know, Hatch, last night Jeff and I thought we saw a Big Foot out in the clearing."

"When?" he blurted.

"While you were snoring?"

"Oh God!" Hatch sighed.

"Oh God, what?"

"Once every seven years they come to the cabin looking for sweets," Hatch explained.

"Sweets?"

"Sugar specifically. Poppa said they go into heat every seven years and the only way to alleviate the horniness of the males is to have sex, or eat sugar. The wild berries they eat just will not do it. That stained tree we saw on the trail was a wild berry frenzy. There are two females and three males; that makes one male odd man out, so he's the one that needs sugar to satisfy his primal urge."

"Can't they share the females?" Mel asked.

"Would your husband want to share you with his friend? These are very intelligent, social animals."

A loud noise erupted on the porch and the door flew open. Jeff, caked with dirt, stumbled in with his pants at his ankles and collapsed onto the floor. "Quick, close the door and lock it!" he barked. Mel leapt up and quickly bolted the door.

"What the hell happened?" she asked.

"I needed to take a dump and I don't like that smelly outhouse. No offense, Hatch."

"None taken."

"I was crouching down in the woods by the dock, trying to do my business. A big fury thing attacked me and pinned me to the ground. I thought I'd choke to death on the dirt. Next thing I knew, the thing was licking my neck, and I swear it was trying to make love to me! I rolled over when it appeared that another Big Foot pulled the one attacking me off of me and yanked it away."

Mel grabbed one of Jeff's cameras and sprinted out the door into the darkness.

"I read an article in the paper last month about a judge who was disrobed because of comments he made in a rape case," Hatch said. "He implied to the victim, a well-built young blonde, maybe she deserved what she got by wearing a short, slinky dress, sweet perfume and a bra with enough padding in it she could play linebacker for the Bears. She was sending out signals she wanted sex and she got what she was secretly asking for, just not quite the kind of sex she really wanted."

"What's that got to do with me?" Jeff asked. He finally had his pants hiked up and was sitting on the floor panting.

"Maybe you're sending off the wrong kind of vibes? Just an idea, my boy. Just an idea."

"I'm afraid your flight is canceled, Miss Vaughn," the customer service representative said from behind the airline counter. "The best I can do is get you on a flight out first thing in the morning."

"Jeff, give me your ticket. We can get them both reissued at the same time." He placed his envelope on the counter.

The attendant fumbled with the envelopes. "I am putting in vouchers for the hotel and meals. Your flight leaves at 6:45," the attendant said in monotone; she was on customer service cruise control.

"Jeff, I'm going to call Jim," Mel said, "and tell him we won't be in until mid-afternoon," and plucked her phone from her purse. "You line us up transportation to the hotel and back to the airport in the morning."

He nodded and headed off towards a bank of phones.

Mel flipped her phone, punched the speed dial button and waited.

"Hey, Jim."

"Mel, where are you?"

"I'm stuck in Seattle. Our flight's been canceled. I won't be back until mid-afternoon tomorrow."

"That's disappointing. Tell you what; meet me at my place after four. I'll cut out of here early."

"Sounds great."

"I've got to go, got another call," Jim said.

Jeff ran up as Mel was hanging up. "I found us a red-eye on another airline. Gate closes in ten minutes. They'll send our luggage in the morning, and we will get home around three. But we've got to run."

They sprinted hard for the plane and arrived just as the doors were being closed. A frustrated attendant quickly corrected the tickets and the plane was off.

"Life on the side of a lake would not be a bad one," Jeff said, as the pilot awaited clearance for take off. "Life would be simple and besides, what could go wrong? There's nothing there to complicate life to death."

"My aunt used to tell me that the Vaughns had Murphy DNA in us," Mel said.

"What's Murphy DNA?"

"The story was that our ancestors go all the way straight back to the guy who wrote Murphy's Law. If it can go wrong, it will find the Vaughns."

Within minutes of take off, the cabin was quiet and most of the lights were off. Jeff slept with his head on a pillow and his iRiver's earbuds softly playing in his ears.

Mel peered at the twinkling dots of light far below and for some reason thought of her father. What would he think of her chasing Big Foot? From her memories of the stories he used to tell, he would probably wish she was chasing Elvis. She didn't want to get maudlin, so she pulled out her laptop and punched the story on her computer keys:

GAY BIG FOOT CREATURE ASSAULTS MAN

A family of Big Foot creatures has routinely visited the cabin of a native of Vancouver Island, Canada. Bill (not his real name) states that the clan has three males and two females and that the creatures have been coming around for years. "The animals are very social and friendly. Recently a gay, male acquaintance of mine was swimming naked in the lake next to the cabin and one of the male creatures tried to engage the acquaintance in amorous activity. I don't think the creature is gay. The female creatures of the clan were in heat and the male was worked into a tizzy by the situation and simply lost control," Bill said. Bill refuses to let Weird Magazine divulge his name or the location of his cabin. The acquaintance that was attacked also refuses to allow use of his name.

Weird Magazine apologizes for the quality of the photographs on the following pages.

CHAPTER TEN

Mel and Jeff flagged a cab right outside LaGuardia's terminal, threw their exhausted bodies into the back seat, gave the cabbie instructions to Jim Bowen's apartment and Jeff's walk-up, and off they went.

"Are you sure you want to share a cab? I really don't need a safety escort. This will pull you ten minutes out of your way," Mel said.

"It's four in the morning and all the crazies are milling about. If something happened to you I'd never forgive myself. Besides, I'm not going to the office tomorrow and ten minutes will not matter one way or the other."

"I appreciate the gesture," Mel said and surveyed the dazzling skyscraper lights of the city as the cab glided over the subtle bumps of the mostly empty streets. The only vehicles on the street were cabs. Neither Mel nor Jeff said anything for a couple of minutes.

"Mel, I think I should tell you something about my sex life," Jeff finally said.

The cabbie, a scruffy-looking Pakistani with a flowing red beard glanced in the mirror and arched an eyebrow. A smirk formed on his lips, his left eye half-closed; he nodded his head and leaned his head back to get his ear closer.

"Whoa there pardner," Mel protested and formed the index fingers of her hands into a mock cross. "I don't need that much information. That would be information overload."

"There is none," Jeff said.

Mel's eye lids closed partly and she tilted her head. "There is none, what?" She looked at Jeff's face that was covered in shadow, trying to see where this was going. Jeff appeared to have only half a face.

"I don't have any sex life, or more accurately, I have never had any sex life."

"Are you saying you are a gay virgin?" Mel fought off the urge to laugh.

The cabbie let out an audible sigh, disappointed that he would not hear anything that was worth repeating to his cab mates or the waitress that had just moved in with him.

"That would be one way of putting it."

"So the scuttlebutt at the office is wrong?" Mel asked, not sure how to respond.

"No, I'm gay, or at least I think I am. But I've never done anything."

"You *think* you're gay? But you really don't know?" Mel laughed out loud.

"I've never had urges for a female. I've had them for males." Jeff turned his head away from Mel and glanced out the window at a homeless man with no pants on pushing a shopping cart along the sidewalk. The basket overflowed with junk. The man was scratching his rear with an aluminum can.

"Jeff, *I've* admired the anatomy of other females, but that doesn't make me gay."

"Please don't say anything to anyone," he pleaded.

"We could stop the rumors. Invent you a girlfriend, an affair," Mel suggested.

"I really don't want to engage in deception."

Mel had nothing she felt like saying and silence filled the cab again.

The cabbie refocused on his driving, disappointed that the conversation had ended without any resolution.

"What's your next assignment?" Mel finally asked and yawned.

"It'll be fun. I get to capture on film an annual Elvis festival."

"I've never heard of such a thing, an *Elvis festival*? Mel asked.

"There's one every year in Tupelo, Mississippi; Collingwood, Canada; Liverpool, England; Hagerstown, Maryland; British Columbia; Kissimmee, Florida; and other cities. Kissimmee just had their twenty-fourth festival."

"How do you know this stuff?" she asked.

"I've been on the camera crew for many alleged Elvis sightings, some of which led me to such festivals."

"Who's the magazine's reporter for the article this time?" she asked.

"No one's been assigned yet. The festival goes on for a week. The reporter will be there from the beginning and I'll show up as usual towards the end to snap a few pictures. They're always a lot of fun."

"I've heard of Elvis impersonation contests. I'll bite. What goes on at an Elvis *festival* for an entire week?"

"There's a look-like-Elvis contest, an antique Cadillac show, a dance contest, a pie-baking contest, Elvis films are run twenty-four hours a day in a cinema and there's the obligatory Elvis impersonation contest. I understand the same guy has won the impersonation contest at this one for eleven straight years. There are usually co-stars from Elvis's movies present and his friends. Heck, at one festival in Florida, Elvis's nurse showed up one year and made over ten grand just signing autographs. And the promoters usually bring in a big star from country or pop radio who does a tribute concert. This year I think they're bringing in Richard Drees and the Prairie Dogs."

"Where's this festival being held?"

"Moscow, Tennessee."

"Oh," Mel groaned.

"Mel, what's wrong? You look upset."

"My father was killed in a car accident outside Moscow, Tennessee, when I was a little girl. Strangely enough, he thought he was tracking Elvis at the time."

Jeff decided not to upset Mel any more and ended the conversation about the festival.

The cab brushed the curb as it pulled up to a four-story brownstone whose steps were brilliantly lit by powerful flood lamps hung over the entrance. The ornate polished glass and metal door glistened under the glare of the light. The brownstone had been built in the late 1880s and was perfectly restored. A row of peculiar gargoyles stared from a cornice and classy etchings were carved in the walls. The twenty-four-hour-a-day doorman, however, was on break smoking a cigarette out back.

"Wow! Bowen gets paid more than I thought he would," Jeff commented and whistled. "A lot more."

"Rent's what I get paid in a month," Mel said. "Could feed a thousand starving Armenians for a year."

"Or ten thousand anorexic New York models. You want me to wait? If he's not in you'll have trouble getting a cab. I don't mind," Jeff offered.

"No, I have a key. If he's not in, I'll just crash here."

"A key? Sounds more serious than I thought," Jeff teased.

Mel realized her mistake. "He was out of town last week and gave me the key to feed the cat and water the plants. That's all."

She opened the cab door, said good-bye over her shoulder, bolted up the steps and was through the building's entrance before Jeff could respond.

Mel fumbled with the key to the penthouse apartment, managed to get the door open and quietly slipped into the darkened living room. She flipped the switch for the lamplight and it came on. She smiled; the cat was stretched on the sofa. *Jim would not approve. That damn cat is supposed to stay off the five thousand dollar sofa.* She scanned the room. She would never comprehend or accept how anal Jim was; everything was perfectly in its place. The room looked like a museum, with antique pieces tucked into every corner and original artwork crammed onto all available space on the walls.

She crept into the enormous industrial-sized kitchen and marveled at how antiseptic it appeared, Except for the stainless-steel appliances and stainless-steel work island in the center of the kitchen, everything was gleaming white: cabinets, glossy walls, marble floors and recessed light panels. She had joked with Jim that the kitchen island looked like the movie set for an autopsy room. She retrieved a crystal glass from the cabinet and bottled water from the refrigerator. After drinking most of the glass she began to head for the master bedroom and commenced stripping. She left a trail of clothes along the hall, taking off the final piece, her bra, just inside the door of the bedroom.

Soft light bathed the room through a large skylight. Mel's blonde hair softly cascaded to her shoulders, outlining her angular face, high cheekbones and perfect, dimpled chin. Her ocean-green eye appeared darker in the dim light and her marathoner's body seemed even thinner, making her ample breasts look out of place.

She studied the enormous Louis XIV bed and smiled. Jim was on his back under a satin sheet, but she could still see that he was naked. Mel moved to the side of the bed, pulled back the sheet and slid in, nestling against Jim's warm body. He smiled and stretched out his arm, cradling her head onto his shoulder.

Mel heard a strange sound and saw a blur at the foot of the bed. Then another body slid against her and she shot up and screamed. Jim Bowen quickly sat up and clapped his hands, causing the lamp to come on. His secretary pulled the cover over her breasts, looked at Mel and joined her in screaming.

Jim jumped out of bed. “Oh, god!” he said loudly.

Mel moved to the side of the bed Jim had just vacated and mimicked Bowen’s secretary in covering up with the sheet. The episode soon became a tug-of-war as to who would get the sheet, which the adrenalized Mel rapidly won. The secretary was left with trying to cover up three areas of her body with two hands, unsuccessfully. The secretary leaped from the bed, as though unseen high-voltage currents were shocking her.

“You bitch,” the secretary blurted, shooting eye-darts at Mel.

“You bastard,” Mel sneered at Bowen, trying to freeze-dry the naked Jim with her armor-piercing look.

“Who is this bitch?” the secretary demanded, then caught herself. “Oh, I’m sorry; you’re one of the reporters, aren’t you? I’ve seen you from afar.” The secretary fussed with her hair with her hand.

“Honey, what I do for a living is not important at the moment,” Mel retorted and turned up her nose.

“Mel, I can explain,” Jim stammered.

“This I have to hear,” the secretary said and quit trying to hide her body. She dropped her hands, finally realizing that Mel was not the enemy.

“Lolita, here…,” Jim began, blinking heavily and searching for words.

“Lolita? Lolita? You’ve got to be kidding me,” Mel said with a grin, her eyes darting back and forth between Lolita and Jim.

“Momma named me after a book. I never read it,” Lolita explained shamelessly and then shrugged her shoulders.

“Lolita just came over here unannounced,” Jim pleaded, as though the pronouncement would somehow get him off the hook. “Totally unannounced.” He glared at Lolita accusingly.

“So, Lolita, here, just *unannounced* jumped into your bed and raped you?” Mel growled.

“Mel, I don’t know any man who could turn her down, look at her,” Jim said accusingly and pointed at Lolita. Lolita took the comment as a compliment and sucked in her already smooth tummy, pushed out her chest and flashed a pearly white smile. Then suddenly the smile turned into a pout.

“Wait a minute buster,” Lolita said. “I had to give head at my interview to get the job as your secretary.” Lolita turned to Mel, “I can’t type worth a damn,” she explained apologetically. “I really wanted a job as a gofer so I could work my way up to a reporter position. I read all the trash magazines and I think I could write that stuff without breaking a nail." Lolita subconsciously looked at the nails on her right hand and said, "Oh well." She turned her eyes back to Jim. "And every day I've got to put up with your groping me." Lolita bent over, flashing her lovely derriere, and plucked up her purse that was in a heap of clothes in the corner of the room. "Just today he gave me this," she said, holding up a key to the apartment. "He said if I didn't come over tonight my job might be in jeopardy."

"That's crazy," Jim said, holding up his hands in protest. He shook his head back and forth.

"I guess every woman who works at the magazine has a key to this love nest," Mel sighed.

Lolita reached for the nightstand handle and jerked the drawer open. "While he was sleeping, I found this." She pulled the drawer out and dumped it onto the bed. Dozens of packaged condoms and keys spilled onto the sheet.

"I can explain," Jim said. He was now profusely perspiring; sweat poured from his forehead as though a spigot had been opened.

"Explain? Like Nixon explained Watergate?" Mel commented sarcastically.

"Who's Nixon?" Lolita asked, squinting her eyes in thought.

"Darling, he's a guy on Fifth Avenue who performs castrations on lying, cheating, double-dealing bosses--without anesthesia," Mel answered, spying Jim's private parts out of the corner of her eye.

Bowen involuntarily covered his testicles with his hands and grimaced.

Mel sprang up, found her purse, snapped open her camera phone and got off a couple of quick pictures before Bowen bolted from the room.

CHAPTER ELEVEN

Lannie Drees, wearing bleached-out jean overalls and a white tee shirt, slouched at her favorite table in the Beverly Hills Wilshire Hotel's dining room. Her blonde hair was short and spiked. She wore ruby lipstick and a light covering of makeup and sipped sparkling water with lemon in it, while thumping her fingers on the table.

"Miss Drees, are you sure that I can't get you something while you wait on your guest?" the waiter politely asked.

"Francois, thanks, but I really am fine right now." Francois was her favorite waiter, always one step ahead of her needs. Lannie dismissed Francois with her eyes when her phone rang. She retrieved it from her purse and noticed that practically every one in the restaurant was talking on their cell. She glanced at the caller ID and flipped open the cover.

"Hey, mom."

"Lannie, doll, I hope that I haven't caught you at a bad time."

"No, Bennie hasn't come yet, what's up?"

"Richard called and asked if you would like to join him in London. He's doing several concerts in Europe and thought you might have fun with the band."

"You know, mom, you and Richard get along better now that you're divorced. It would be a blast to join Richard in London. Could I could bring Bennie with me?"

"I don't know. Do you think her probation officer will allow it?" Barbara Anne Drees asked.

"We could go and not tell the dork, although it won't hurt to ask," Lannie said.

"Richard will send the jet for you tonight. The plane will be at the Hollywood-Burbank Airport at 11:00 p.m. Richard apologizes in advance. Seems Senator Musgrave is hitching a ride on the flight and he can be quite a pain. Oh, we don't have a thing in the house to eat. I'm ordering something from Federico's, would you mind picking it up."

"No problem, I'll get it on my way home. Mom, Bennie just came in. Squeak at you later."

Bennie San's hair was green and two inches in length. She had even more piercings than five years ago. Her nose alone had two diamonds and seven gold studs. Her long-sleeved, ribbed cotton top stopped three inches from her waist, exposing two silver studs in her navel. She had a tattoo over the navel stud that read: *Go Lower*. She was wearing an old pair of jeans that had slits at the knees and shiny, worn-out areas at her rear, rubber flip-flops and gloves with the fingers cut out.

"Hey dudette. What's up?" Bennie said.

"Girl, you look great. If I were a bush leaguer, I'd want some of you. That's what I'm saying," Lannie chirped back. It was a lie. Bennie looked like death. She was twenty-two years old but had the puffy eyes of a fifty year old. The skin on her fingers was wrinkled and her head jerked with a very slight, but noticeable tremor. She was ultra-thin. Her neck looked as slender as her wrists. She could almost put her hands around her waist and touch her fingers. Lannie was concerned about her friend who burned the candle from both ends and sometimes in the middle.

"Yeah? Must be that pure Columbian I got last week. Freddy, you know, says he's never seen anything so fine. Even Clinton would have to inhale."

"Would you ladies care for a menu?" Francois asked, seemingly materializing out of thin air. He held two large folded posters. Over a hundred items were featured on the menu, although he knew the young ladies would not need menus.

"Bennie, I know what I want," Lannie said.

"Order for both of us."

"Okay, Francois, we'll have a bowl of seafood chowder, Caesar salad with extra croutons, a filet with lump crab meat topping, medium-rare, a loaded baked potato with extra chives and for dessert, vanilla ice cream with Praline cream."

"And bring us a bottle of champagne," Lannie said. Francois glided away.

"Are we celebrating?" Bennie asked.

"Richard has asked us to go to London tonight. He's on tour."

"Fantastic!" Bennie squealed. "What's the weather like there? We'll have to hit the shops this afternoon. I need a new wardrobe."

"Will your probation officer let you go?" Lannie asked.

"If he doesn't, like I'm cutting him off."

"Bennie, you slut. Bopping your probation officer?"

"How else do you think I can avoid whizzing in the jar? Besides, he's kinda cute. Drives a Z3."

"We can shop tomorrow in London. I'd go this afternoon, but I've got a massage scheduled, an appointment with my therapist and mom wants me to pick up supper. She wants to have dinner with me. Quality time. She's gotten very clingy lately. Every time she looks at me she gets teary eyed."

"Ladies, here's your soup and I hope you don't mind, I brought out the salad also," Francois announced. He knew Bennie's soup would be gone in seconds. He placed the chowder and salads on the table, uncorked the champagne, poured two glasses, expertly placed the bottle in a silver bucket brimming with ice and iced water, clicked his heels together and withdrew from the table while still facing Lannie and Bennie.

"You ever *date* Francois?" Bennie asked. She put her finger in her champagne and then into her mouth. Champagne dribbled down her wrist and under the sleeve of her blouse.

"As if, Bennie! Really! I could never date the hired help." Lannie politely dipped her soup spoon into the chowder bowl and sipped the soup.

Bennie put both her hands on her bowl and raised it to her lips and then gulped the entire contents in seconds. She wiped her mouth with the linen napkin. "That's not true," Bennie said. "The summer between our junior and senior years in high school you *dated* Barbara Anne's chauffeur and the security guy. What was his name? Leon?"

"Nothing of that sort happened."

"Whatever. Francois like does you with his eyes every time he looks at you," Bennie said.

"He's just being sweet."

"Yeah, right," Bennie said. Bennie grabbed a handful of salad with her fingers and stuffed it into her mouth.

"You and Freddy still a pair of aces?" Lannie asked.

"Lannie, I'm trying something now that you've just got to try." Bennie swallowed a fistful of free-range greens, pecans, apricots and croutons and gulped champagne.

"What's that?" Lannie asked and sipped from her glass.

"Freddy's pimping me."

Lannie spit champagne out her mouth. "What?"

"It's so exciting. He arranges my date and I have sex with the guy for money. It's so thrilling. You wouldn't believe it."

"Bennie, that sounds dangerous."

"Freddy waits outside. All I have to do is scream, whatever, and he'll come in and straighten the guy out. And you know what? It's made our sex life that much better. Freddy's hard all the time. He affectionately calls me his little *ho*."

"Does Freddy sleep with other women?"

"Like, yeah. He has to. That's how he develops his clients. He sleeps with them and turns them onto drugs, but it's strictly business to him," Bennie said.

Lannie wanted to say, like, duh? Bennie, how do you think Freddy got you? Instead, she asked, "How many times have you done this?"

"Only about eight times. We just started day before yesterday."

"You've been with eight guys in three days?" Lannie squealed.

"Yeah, isn't it great! Actually, there was this set up with two guys and one woman, so it's not as often as you think."

"You've been with a woman?"

"I didn't do anything. It's what they call, passive bisexual."

"Did it turn you on?" Lannie asked.

"I didn't notice it too much. I was busy."

"How much do you charge?"

"That's the funniest part. It's a hundred for the bush probe and a hundred and twenty-five for the other. Gosh, Lannie. You know I've always preferred the other anyway. These idiots are paying more for something I'd probably give them for free."

"What are you doing with the money?" Lannie asked.

"What money?"

"You know, the sex money."

"Freddy's taking care of that. He handles the money. He's putting it in a savings account for me. He keeps twenty percent for himself. Expenses and all. Plus, he keeps me supplied with my medicinals for free. Say, when are you going to finish college? When you're on Medicare?"

"Don't start with me, child. Mom and I argued about that yesterday. I straightened her out but good. Told her she had no room to bitch since she had never even been to college. Her telling me about college is like a virgin writing a sex manual. Duh?"

"You've been in college, like what, four years now?"

"If I pass the two courses I'm taking now and go to summer school, I'll be a junior next year," Lannie said. "I start out every semester with the best of intentions, you know. I sign up for twelve hours, but there are so many asshole teachers. They want you to read this. Read that. Make reports. Whatever. Like, I drop those courses. I usually carry, you know, only three to five hours a semester. My overall is pretty good though. Two point one. Mom said I had to finish in the next five years, or else. Like I can't believe she told me that. She knows I don't handle pressure well. Anyway, she won't be around five years from now, right?" Lannie drank the rest of her glass of champagne and nibbled on her salad. She was such a picky eater.

"She's got really cute clothes," Bennie said. "Think I might get a shot at the closet when the time comes?"

"Bennie, that's crass. Like, where's Francois? I can't believe I'm going to have to pour my own champagne."

As if he knew it was the very last second he had to perform his duty, Francois sprinted around the corner and floated to the table. He poured the glasses full. "The entrée will be here presently, madams." And then, as if by magic, two tuxedoed assistants appeared with sizzling platters and butter, chive, and cheese-drenched potatoes. Francois supervised the placement of the plates and withdrew after being assured nothing else was needed at the table.

Bennie methodically sliced her petite filets into five pieces and popped a piece into her mouth. Lannie played with her salad, moving it around the plate with her fork.

"You're lucky your mom has a goal for you," Bennie said. "She's like Ricky's Lucy. My parents are like Fred and Ethel, second bananas to the world stuck in television reruns. They've played second banana so long they don't have any expectations. They just keep hoping I'll wake up one day and tell them I'm going to do *something* other than go shopping. If I told them that I was going to college, dad would croak. Gasp and croak. Speaking of which, how's your mom doing now?" Bennie popped the second chunk of filet into her mouth.

"The cancer has spread to her liver. They're telling her not to make plans for Christmas," Lannie explained and carved off a small piece of the steak and began chewing.

"Bummer, she gives such nice Christmas gifts. She in pain? I can get Freddy to get her something," Bennie offered. She finished off the filet, carved a huge piece of potato, and stuffed it into her mouth.

"Actually, she *is* smoking marijuana for nausea. She asked if I could get her some Columbian gold, the kind of stuff she used to get in the '80s. She says the stuff today is limp. She complains that the stuff she gets for her nausea would have to improve to be even called third rate."

"I'll ask Freddy."

"You see any of the old crowd?" Lannie asked. She was now playing with her potato. She wanted to eat with her mother later.

"Oh, yeah. Remember Al Tautletub? The quarterback. He's selling stocks and bonds. Works for Merrill Lynch. He called and wanted to sell me stock in a hot new startup. I told him, you know, Freddy was putting my money in a savings account. Al said cash was a good thing to be in right now, but when the market starts to move, you know, I should get into stocks. I told Freddy about what Al said and he just smiled. Freddy has a nice smile. I like the star in the gold covering on his front tooth. I think Freddy already knew about what Al said."

"What else did Al say?"

"Oh, yeah. He's going through a divorce. Said he married Emily Tompkins, head cheerleader. You remember her? She was like the fattest cheerleader ever. Weighed at least one hundred ten. What a blimp. Anyway, Emily decided she preferred the bush rather than Popsicles."

"Lesbian?"

"Caught her with her face in the cookie jar. Emily ran away with her aerobics instructor. They moved to Key West and opened a nude aerobics studio there just for gays and lesbians. Business is so good, Al said Emily is thinking of franchising. Guy in San Francisco is making inquiries."

"Poor Al."

"He asked me out," Bennie said.

"You going?"

"As if, Freddy would get jealous."

"You left it at that?" Lannie asked.

"No. I told Al I was seeing someone, but if he wanted some nookie to give me a call and I'd get him in touch with my pimp."

"What did Al say to that?"

"Nothing. I think we were disconnected."

Francois floated in and removed Bennie's empty plates. Lannie asked for a doggie bag. One of Francois' assistants showed up with two large plates of ice cream swimming in praline sauce. "Would madams like the usual, decaf coffee and Kahlua?"

"Yeah, like way sure," Lannie answered.

"Francois you're so sweet. If you ever need a little on the side, call me and I'll hook you up with Freddy," Bennie said.

"Who's Freddy?" Francois asked.

"Never mind," Lannie said. "Francois, make mine a double Kahlua."

Francois strutted from the table. *Oh, what I'd give to be twenty years younger. American women! So liberated!*

"Did you hear about Linda Bishop?" Bennie asked.

"No."

"She's opened a landscape-design business that caters strictly to the stars."

"She always had a thing for guys who work with dirt," Lannie said.

"One of her clients is Enrique Iglasias."

"Don't tell me she's doing him."

"Actually, she's doing Iglasias's gardener," Bennie said. "*Dating* would be more the word, since both of them are single."

"I thought she was married to a doctor. Guy did boob jobs twenty-four-seven at a clinic in the Hills," Lannie said. "He was on Good Morning America last year raving about Botox injections making nipples bigger."

"That was *so* stupid. You make the nipples look *bigger*, that makes the rest look *smaller*, duh? Anyway, Linda *was* married to him. But he got arrested for income tax evasion and like the feds levied a six million dollar lien on everything Linda and he had. Most of her jewelry, you know, was taken."

"He go to jail?" Lannie asked.

"No. He jumped bail and ran off to Mexico with a nurse and money he'd squirreled away in an offshore account. He's performing breast enhancements at bargain prices in Tijuana. My dad says the fugitive doctor is pouring money into the National Republican Committee. He's pushing for a pardon. Wants to come back to America. Seems Mexican guys are more ass men than tits. And he never learned how to do asses. The tit business is slow in Mexico."

The coffee and Kahlua arrived at the same time. Francois gently placed the saucer and cups on the table, and a large glass next to each cup and retreated.

The girls poured the ice cream and coffee into the glass and stirred it well. Then Bennie gulped down her Kahlua-coffee shake. Lannie sipped hers.

"I gotta pee," Bennie said and twittered, as she pushed herself from the table

Lannie winked at Bennie and followed her to the bathroom. A large mirror spanned the width of the room, hanging over three porcelain lavatories trimmed with gold fixtures. Bennie stepped into one of the four stalls, flipped up the toilet seat, rammed her finger down her throat and scoffed up the entire meal. When she came out, Lannie confronted her. "Bennie, that's not good for you."

"I've got it under control. Thanks for the concern."

They washed their faces with cold water and patted them with luxurious, complimentary hand towels. Bennie ran her fingers through her hair and broke out a small vial with a silver lid from her purse.

"You want some of this, Lannie girl. Make you beautiful and all-knowing."

"You know I don't do that stuff."

"You're sure? This is some good stuff."

"Positive."

Bennie cracked open the lid, held the vial to her nose and inhaled. She did the other nostril and pinched her nose. "Ah, sunshine," she proclaimed as she replaced the vial into her purse and swaggered toward the door. "I might be up for another dessert," she announced.

CHAPTER TWELVE

Alex Chalmers, the manager of the London Palladium, nibbling on a bagel coated with strawberry cream cheese, again read the dressing room requirements for Richard Drees and the Prairie Dogs:

50 pounds of ice
8 bottles of Crown Royal
12 cases of Coors Light
6 cans of Coke
50 eight-ounce clear tumblers with bumps in the plastic
17 rolls of toilet paper
3 number two aluminum wash tubs
125 Scott Deluxe napkins
2 dozen Trojan Warhorse Ribbed Condoms
1 tube of K-Y Jelly
4 bottles of Calamine Lotion
1 tube of Boudreaux's Butt Paste
1 Vicegrip pliers
6 dozen Chips Ahoy chocolate chip cookies (whole, not broken)
2 pounds of American sliced cheese
1 loaf of sliced whole wheat bread
1 bottle of Tabasco
1 fifty count bottle of Bayer Aspirin
13 family-sized bags of Zapp's potato chips
1 can of bean dip

"Dex, I think the Prairie Dogs are alcoholics in heat," Alex said to his assistant, who was thumbing through *Rock & Roll Magazine*, gazing at the pictures of guitars.

"I wonder what the pliers are for," Dex said, not looking up from the magazine.

"Probably some wild sexual ritual. The Dogs drink all this, they'll let Richard down and there won't be much of a concert. What band was it that had a giant penis come up through the floor in the middle of their act?" Alex asked.

"It was that punk rock band, The Steel Penises."

"Their dressing room requirement included sixty-three gallons of Ben & Jerry's Vanilla and Pecan," Alex said.

"Did they eat all of the ice cream?" Dex asked.

"Bloody bastards put it in a bathtub and the leader of the group, Crank Neuman took a bath in it," Alex said.

"Sounds harmless enough."

"Actually, mate, it was rather tragic," Alex said.

"What happened? I don't bloody remember."

"That was before you started working here. Crank's groupie friend hopped in the tub with him and she died."

"She bloody drowned in a vat of ice cream?" Dex asked, bewildered.

"Actually, mate, she succumbed to an allergic reaction to the pecans."

"Terrible, terrible. Bloody terrible," Dex exclaimed and shook his head. He peered at Alex to see if he bought his fake sympathy routine.

"Actually, mate, what was terrible was no one missed her. Housekeeping didn't find her body until they drained the tub the next afternoon. When the detective called Crank, who was on his bloody jet over Ireland, his only comment was, 'So that's where the little lass was.'"

Alex picked up an Ovation 1866 Legend guitar from a stand and started strumming the twelve-string and singing.

"I like that. What's that you're playing?" Dex asked.

"Another one of mine," Alex said and smoothly picked a catchy rift and belted out a line, "Vanilla and pecans, who would have thought, she would have bought…the farm…."

"How many songs have you written, Alex?"

"Hundreds."

"Ever sell any?" Dex asked.

"I'll never tell," Alex answered and grinned.

Lannie Drees' room at Two Hyde Park Square looked out onto the serene gardens of the square. The hotel was close to the Palladium, so the girls decided to walk to the concert rather than ride in the limo that Richard had sent for them. It didn't help that the limo driver looked like Jack the Ripper, cloak and all. Besides, it was a gorgeous night and they had been sitting on a plane forever. The idea of moving around was appealing.

A pair of hip hugging jeans and a white tee shirt that had been cut and sewn at a line just below her breasts clung to Lannie's thin body. If she tilted her head back, her breasts were visible. Or if a strong breeze blew. Or if anyone simply bent over in front of her and looked up.

Bennie wore black hip huggers and a black bra with Mardi Gras sequins pasted all around its perimeter. Her motif matched her black lipstick. Purple sandals tied with thick ribbon matched her hair.

"You're going to wear a bra to the concert?" Lannie asked.

"It's a decorative bra. Madonna used to wear this kind of thing on stage all the time."

"It was her *costume*. To you it's just a bra."

"Whatever. So, we just tell them like who we are and we get backstage?" Bennie asked as they walked east in the park. It was a warm summer evening and the lights strung through the trees appeared to add even more stars to the clear, twinkling sky.

"Richard says that if anyone gives us trouble, you know, just call him on his cell and he'll play the part of the spoiled irrational music star. I have his number in my pocket," Lannie said.

"Anybody gives us trouble and I'll claw their eyes out. These Londoners have never tangled with a California bitch before," the eighty-five pound Bennie warned. "What's Richard doing after the party?"

"We're going to some private club and meet the rest of the band and the road crew."

"Sounds like fun. I hope they have some good stuff, at least some weed. I could use a little pick-me-upper," Bennie said.

"Don't worry. Richard doesn't even call the road crew, *road crew*. He calls them the *Mary Jane,*" Lannie said.

"Does Richard mess with groupies?" Bennie asked. They passed a bench on which a man wrapped in garbage bags slept. Two empty gin bottles lay on the ground under his feet. He snored as though he were in a Three Stooges movie. A pigeon nibbled bread crumbs from his beard, hopping back every time he exhaled and hopping forward every time he inhaled.

"I don't know. I've never been on the road with him before, except when I was younger. Back then, mom and I went on the road with him all the time. Things were fairly tame as I remember.

The cops or an ambulance was usually only called a couple of times a night. Mostly drug overdoses and domestic violence."

"Must be fun being on the road. Every day's a new day," Bennie said. "Good sex with no strings attached."

"The strings would have letters, like S-T-D, Bennie."

"Whatever. I wish Freddy were here. I bet he could fake a British accent. The black dude at the airport today with the accent cracked me up. I wonder how you say, 'Yo' in British?" Bennie asked, serious. Lannie wanted to explain to Bennie that British and English were the same language, but dropped it.

The girls talked about some of the crazy things Bennie did in high school as they scurried along. When they got to the concert hall everything was a mess. Security people ran around as though they were chasing rabbits through a maze. Lannie and Bennie were stopped in the foyer and couldn't get in until Alex Chalmers happened by. He had talked to Richard Drees earlier and knew about the step-daughter. With Alex's help, the girls were soon being led backstage by Tim, the band's road manager.

Tim's beard was shaggy and he had really long hair that was held in a ponytail by a rubber band. He had a sharp nose on a delicate face and piercing blue eyes. He wore bleached-out jeans and a Prairie Dog sweatshirt. The artwork on the sweatshirt was a cartoon of two prairie dogs humping. The humpee grinned with a toothy smile. "I'm taking you to Richard's dressing room," Tim explained. "I'll introduce you to the Mary Jane after the concert."

Tim paid close attention to Lannie. Every time he and Lannie made a turn he gently guided her through the turn with his hand on her. And since her tee shirt stopped far up her back, his hand touched her skin often. Lannie liked the way his hand seemed to stay on her longer than necessary. Bennie waved at everyone the group met or chanted, "What's up?" She received a few hard looks at her sequined bra. After several twists, turns, and intimate touches Tim led the girls into Richard's dressing room.

"Hey, Lannie, Bennie," Richard cried out with a huge smile; a joint hung from his lips. He sat on a stool with a guitar on his lap. He had already threaded nine strings onto the twelve-string guitar. He held the tenth string in the Vicegrips and he was pulling the string through the hole in the tuning peg and wrapping it around the stem. Then he turned the peg to take up the slack and the string tightened. He plucked the string a few times while turning the peg and hit the correct note. One string was done in seconds.

Lannie and Bennie hugged him. “Richard, what’s that Butt Paste for?” Bennie asked, eyeing the tube resting on the counter.

“A pharmacist in Louisiana invented that to treat diaper rash. I put it on my left shoulder. It stops the strap of the guitar from chaffing. I change guitars almost twenty times during the show and the straps can rub me raw sometimes, even through my shirt. The paste stops me from chaffing.”

“What’s that K-Y Jelly for?” Lannie asked.

“I change strings on all my guitars before every show. I put a dab of that on the frets before I string the guitar. It helps my fingers slide over the frets. A trick of the trade. You girls need to get to your seats. I have to be out there in about fifteen minutes. We’ll have plenty of time to visit after the show.”

Tim led the girls through a warren of halls and passed a room where the Prairie Dogs were lounging around a large table. The Dogs were telling rowdy war stories about past concerts, arrests, trashed hotel rooms, smashed limos and other fond remembrances, and were drinking beer, passing a joint and munching on potato chips. Of the seven Dogs, six were bald and had potbellies. They had yet to put on their wigs. They all looked as though they could be young grandfathers.

“They look a lot older than I remember,” Lannie said.

“They’ll toss on their wigs and head bands, a last dab of makeup and they’ll look like kids for the show,” Tim explained. “Hollywood on guitars.”

“They look pretty loose,” Bennie said.

“They’re drunk and stoned and fairly nervous right now, but once they get into the first song and all the gear works, they’ll be fine.”

Tim escorted the girls to two seats in the front row. “Come backstage after the show. Richard says you can ride with me to the party. And for god’s sake, don’t throw your panties on stage. That’s really passé these days.”

“I’m not wearing any. Can I throw my bra?” Bennie asked. Lannie shook her head and Tim grinned and scurried off.

The concertgoers were a hodgepodge of oldies and newbies. Richard had been a major star for twenty years, so some of his earliest fans were in their fifties and sixties. His newer hits had recruited younger fans. None were disappointed in the show.

The group started with Richard’s first hit, *If You Were A Prairie Dog I’d Find Your Hole,* written by Rod Witherspoon, and then launched into their biggest international hit, *You Drive Me*

Nuts and Me Heart Nuts, also by Witherspoon. The song became a monster hit in the USA only after it was banned by the BBC, and after the American Civil Liberties Union filed suit in New York City to get it played on the local public broadcasting affiliate.

The band sang their latest and greatest, *The Iceman Just Came* and the crowd sang along:

Chorus
That cold, cold heart
Left an icicle in my vein
It stopped and went all frozen
When I heard you'd changed your name
That cold, cold heart
Feels like a ball and chain
It stopped a beating
When I heard the screen door slam
Oh damn, the iceman, just came
Oh damn, the iceman, just came

I wish I had a nickel
For every dime I've spent
I wouldn't be but half as broke
And maybe I could pay my rent

I wished I'd said I loved her
Every chance I had
Maybe she'd still remember me
And her kids would call me dad
They don't
She won't
I can't ignore
How she walked out the door
Without crying

Chorus repeated

I wish I were better looking
Or at least she'd think so
Maybe I'll reinvent myself
And become her big hero
I wish I were richer

Maybe win the lottery
Then she'd come crawling home
On two worn out knees
I won't
She won't
I can't ignore
How she walked out the door
Without crying

Chorus repeated

I wish I were the eyes
Inside her head
Then I could see
What she sees in me
And change what she's misread
I wish I'd just listened
To what it was she said
Maybe she'd still talk to me
We'd sleep in the same bed
We don't
She don't
I can't ignore
How she walked out the door
Without crying

Chorus repeated

The Prairie Dogs played for all of two hours to a boisterous and appreciative crowd, including three callbacks that the Dogs milked to perfection. By the end of the concert the crowd was exhausted and high, and the hall's air smelled of reefer and sweat.

The girls were hit on a dozen times as they made their way through a throng of wannabe groupies nestled backstage. The hitters ranged in age from nineteen to sixty-three: ten males, one semi-male (Lannie and Bennie couldn't tell if *it* was a he, a she, or a shim) and one female. Bennie enjoyed the attention. They eventually made it to Richard's dressing room and were let inside by Tim.

"Well, how'd you like the concert?" Richard asked. He sat on a stool and was sucking on a joint and wiping makeup from his face.

"That's as much fun as I can have with my clothes on and my mouth shut," Bennie said. Richard shook his head and started to same something in response to Bennie, but couldn't think of anything to say.

"I like your new songs, *I Gave Up Fishing and Football For You (It's The Least That I Could Do)* and *Sex With You (Is All It's Cracked Up To Be),* Lannie said.

"They will probably be the next singles we release," Richard said.

"Bennie, one of the members of the band would like to meet you," Tim announced.

"Cool," Bennie said. She was already bored out of her mind and wondering when the fun would begin. She felt like she was the bank in a game of Monopoly at an old folk's home.

"See you at the party," Richard said as he started to unbuckle his pants. "I've got a few things to finalize with Mr. Chalmers, the manager here. He's got a song he wants me to hear."

Tim led the girls out of Richard's dressing room and into a narrow hall, turned a corner and then into a large room. It was the same room they had seen the Prairie Dogs relaxing in prior to the concert. The bass player squatted on a low stool at the table. He was rolling flat American cheese into small balls and popping them into his mouth. He had his wig still on, but the frown lines and crows feet around his eyes indicated that he was at least fifty years old.

"Rat, this is Bennie and Lannie," Tim said to the bass player.

"Hello lasses," he said with a thick accent.

"You're from England?" Bennie asked.

"You've just insulted my Scottish ancestors," Rat said and smiled.

"How does someone from Scotland play country music?" Bennie asked.

"With my fingers and very carefully. Seriously, I've lived in Dallas for fifteen years and Memphis before that. I was in Elvis's road band when I was a wee laddie. You should have heard my accent back then. Elvis never understood what it was I was saying. He called me, Cuz. He said it was 'cuz he couldn't understand a thing I said."

"They call you Rat because of the cheese thing?" Bennie asked.

"My name is Ronin Ratz Adie. You can blame me mum for that."

"Ronin is a nice name," Bennie said. "I'll call you Ronin, unless you mind."

"As you like. Can I give you a lift to the party? I've got a rental."

"You can go with Rat and I'll take Lannie in the limo," Tim said. "And Rat, no detours."

Ronin cut a curve sharply and the tires of his tiny Ford squealed. Bennie was forced against the door until the Ford came out of the curve.

"You always drive like Ray Charles?" Bennie asked. She was enjoying his erratic steering.

"Only when the motor car's engine is running."

"This car is so tiny I bet it doubles as a coffin if you die in a wreck," Bennie noted.

"Wouldn't work as a commercial for the car," Ronin replied.

"Life on the road must be difficult, unless you have a regular dealer in each town. Do you have any weed?" she asked.

"You're awfully forward now, aren't you?" Ronin commented.

"And feisty and horny and other things," Bennie said.

"That bag on the back seat, it's my drug emporium and magic elixir trove. It's my American Express. I don't go anywhere without it."

"How do you get it past airport security and customs?" Bennie asked.

"I know it looks rather large, but it fits up the old wazoo rather nicely."

"Cool."

Bennie pulled the bag to the front seat and opened it. She held up a plastic bag. "Is this what I think it is?"

"Be careful with that. It's a mixture of heroin, cocaine and other creative things."

"You holding out on me, Rat? Next thing you're going to tell me is that you're hung like a porno star."

The limo meandered through the back streets of south London.

"Richard told me that Bennie is a trouble magnet," Tim said. Music played softly through speakers in the doors and overhead panel. Bottled water and ice, flavored with lemon twists, sloshed in their glasses. They sat closer than necessary in the wide seat, their arms touching. "Richard says she's been arrested twice for shoplifting and a couple of times for writing worthless checks."

"Bennie's a free spirit. A bit misguided sometimes and terribly naive. She hurts herself, but would never intentionally cause pain to anyone else. I guess you could call her a flake."

"And what about you, Lannie Drees?" Tim asked in a low hushed voice. "What's your biography?"

"What did Richard tell you about me? I'm curious."

"He said you were pretty and smart and still searching for your soul. I agree with the pretty and smart. I don't know about the soul part." He reached out and put his hand over hers. She surprised herself by not pulling it back.

"I'm surprised he didn't also say that I was a spoiled brat. I've been known to be rather demanding." His hand was warm and hers tingled when he rubbed the top of it with his fingers.

"Whatever puts flowers in your garden. Some guys watch soccer for sport, drink pints at the clubs. I like to spoil women. They are God's greatest gift to man. I am a confessed serial romanticizer."

"I don't know whether I should laugh at that line or feel flattered," Lannie said. She had a surprising urge to lean over and kiss him.

"You didn't laugh," Tim said. "You too are a hopeless romantic at heart."

They peered into the darkness as the limo stopped, started and swayed through the streets. The silence was not awkward. They were sending messages through their hands with gentle squeezes and electrical impulses.

"Do you know my mother?" Lannie asked.

"Very well. Best lyricist I've ever known. She could spin Shinola from manure. It was a shame she and Richard couldn't get along."

"They did a world-class job of hiding their problems from me, their spoiled kid. I never even saw them argue. What was their downfall?"

"Can you imagine one hundred soldiers with two Generals in charge? And no war in sight? Each had their own idea on how to drill the troops."

"Ego problems?"

"I'd prefer to say it was a collision of strong, capable wills."

The limo smoothly stopped in front of an enormous Victorian hotel. "Tim, this is the joint," the driver announced over the loudspeakers. The driver hopped out and scurried to the rear passenger door.

"Thanks for the nice conversation, Tim. I didn't mean for it to get so serious."

"Serious? Hell, I thought I was courting. This is my best foreplay to sparking."

He pressed his hand and arm against her back and helped her from the car. For the first time in her life, Lannie Drees' mind went blank and she lost her breath; she thought she was going to stumble and was relieved when she managed to walk.

Tim and Lannie strolled into the ballroom. It was sixty-five feet wide by one hundred feet long, had a fifteen-foot ceiling, 1850's reproduction wallpaper and antique gaslights with electrical bulbs. Buckets of iced beer rested on one table and opened bottles of Crown Royal and glasses on another in the center of the room. It appeared as though the circus had come to town. The cavernous room was packed with people in every mode of dress, from tuxedos and formal evening dresses to skimpy halter-tops and faded jeans. Some had small dogs in their arms; others stroked cats. Some were swigging free Crown Royal, others, Coors. Some were smoking marijuana. Others were snorting cocaine from a tray being passed around the room by a roadie dressed as a hotel waitress, complete with a white doily pinned on the top of her head. The waitress' skirt, however, stopped at her hips. You could see her fully exposed panties from a rear view, although no one seemed to notice. The partygoers were all chattering about mundane things. Small cocktail talk.

"I don't understand this. We came right over after the concert. I would have thought we would have beaten all these people here," Lannie said. She paid particular attention to a couple in the far corner. They were kissing and the man had his hand down his date's dress.

"These are groupies. They follow the band around. They seldom go to the concerts."

""Why do they do this?" she asked.

"They get free booze and drugs and get a chance to rub elbows with Richard and the Dogs and Richard's friends. There is a rumor that Elton John will be here tonight."

"The former Beatle?" she asked.

He laughed. "He's done a couple of their songs. Close enough."

"How long have you been with Richard?" she asked.

"I graduated from M.I.T. in 1996. Got my M.B.A from Princeton in 1998 and was hired by Richard at that time."

"One of the smart guys,"

"I had to study very hard to get smart," he said.

"What do you do for Richard?"

"I invest his money and run the concerts."

"Damn, and I thought you were a roadie."

"But I am. I'm an educated gofer."

"You're more than that," said the voice from behind them.

"Richard! This party looks like fun!" Lannie squealed and hugged her ex-stepfather.

"Unfortunately this spectacle will be a bore, I'm afraid. There are a few record label folks here and a few magazine whores, but most of this throng are freeloaders," Richard said.

"I had no idea," Lannie said. "Tim says the former Beatle, Elton John may be here."

A puzzled look took over Richard's face. Tim shrugged his shoulders. "That was a rumor started by my publicist," Richard said. "Say, where's Bennie?" he asked.

"She's coming with Rat," Tim said. Richard seemed to frown, and Tim sensed his displeasure with Rat.

A tall, waistless woman who looked like Mamma Cass bumped into Richard. "Richard, darling. It is so nice to see you." The woman wore an evening dress completely covered with silver and black sequins. She opened her purse that hung from a leather strap across her shoulder, pulled out an envelope containing a cassette, and handed it to Richard. "I think you'll just love the third tune. It's so you."

"Justine, you know any submittals have to go through TACKETT first," Richard said. He tried giving the envelope back to her, but Justine would have nothing of it. She crossed her arms over her chest and tucked her hands under her armpits.

"Richard, dear, I've been calling your people for weeks and cannot get through," Justine said. "I hope you're not trying to avoid me, darling." Justine pulled a lighter from her purse and lit a long, thin cigarette that dangled from her mouth.

Tim grabbed Richard's arm and tugged him away. "Richard, we are very late. You must come now."

Richard allowed himself to be dragged by Tim. "Justine, I'll call you later," Richard said over his shoulder.

"Promise, darling?" Justine shouted, as Richard was led away. Justine straightened out her dress and seemed to float toward the door. Mission accomplished. She left the party.

Tim, Richard and Lannie turned the corner and stepped into in a wide hall. Richard dropped the envelope in a trashcan. "Thanks, Tim."

"Who was that dreadful woman?" Lannie asked. "Some kind of alien being?"

"Worse. She used to be a lawyer. She shed her serpent skin and put on airs. Now she's an independent agent. Hawks songs," Tim said.

"And ruins parties," Richard said. "There's Bennie." Rat and Bennie had entered through a rear door and were coming up the hall. Bennie leaned on Rat, who supported her with his arm. Her eyes were half-opened and spittle drooled down her chin. It was obvious she had thrown up on herself.

"Damn, Rat," Richard said. "Is she okay?"

"She'll be fine. I'm taking her to my room to freshen up a bit."

"I think I want to take her to *her* room at our hotel," Lannie said. She moved to Bennie and put her hand on her arm to steady her. Bennie was so skinny and light that Lannie could have tossed her over her shoulder if she had chosen to do so. Tim also put his arm around Bennie and propped her up.

"I'll go with Lannie and make sure that Bennie gets tucked in," Tim said. Rat looked disappointed. Bennie had promised him a special treat for the hit and now he was going home alone, or with one of the dreadful road-scummers.

"I agree," Richard said and gave Rat a hard look.

At the sound of Richard's voice, Bennie struggled to fully open her eyes. When she focused on Richard she seemed surprised. "Oh, Richard, it's been way too long."

CHAPTER THIRTEEN

Lannie Drees snored under the covers of her bed at Two Hyde Park Square. Although it was ten in the morning, she had only been asleep a couple of hours. The heavy drapes locked out most of the sunlight, but it was still too bright in her room. She was dreaming of the concert last night, replaying it in her head. She remembered it perfectly, except that Bennie was playing guitar with the band, horsing around with Rat Adie. Bennie was dressed in a prairie dog outfit with her face showing through a cut out of the costume. They were playing Richard's mega-hit, *If I'd Only Known Then (It Wouldn't Hurt So Much Now.)* Bennie was jumping up and down to the beat of her strums and shaking her hair. She was dancing and bumping her prairie dog butt with Rat's. Rat was wiggling and gyrating. The crowd was going wild. But the drummer had it all wrong. The bass beat was definitely not in sync. It was most irregular.

Lannie's head began to move and she tried to open her eyes to tell the drummer he definitely sucked. One eye cracked open and its lid twitched violently. Lannie concluded that it wasn't the drummer who was out of rhythm. In fact, there was no drummer. The drumming sound was created by someone banging on her door. Wearing only her panties Lannie managed to crawl out of bed, stumble to the door and open it.

"Lannie, you need to get decent." Richard said and crossed the room to a chair, snatched Lannie's robe from it, and handed it to her. He placed the bag he was holding on the dresser and helped her get her arms into the robe's sleeves. He wrapped the robe around her and tied a bow in the belt.

"Richard, it's way too early for me. I had a long night." She yawned.

"I know, Tim told me." He got two cups of coffee from the bag, took the lids off and handed one to Lannie. She yawned again, put the coffee on the nightstand and made it to the dresser where she found her hairbrush and ran it through her hair.

"I've got to wee, I'll be right back." She stumbled towards the bathroom, made it through the door, and promptly urinated in the bidet. She ran water through the faucet, but failed to get her hands wet. Still, she dried them on a towel. She sleepwalked back to the bed and sat down with a thump.

"It was pretty ugly. She threw up most of the night," Lannie mumbled, retrieved the coffee from the nightstand and drank from the cup; the liquid singed her throat. She woke up completely. "Damn! This is hot! Richard, what are you doing here?" she asked, as though she noticed for the first time that he was there.

"Tim told me about the needle marks all over Bennie's arms and between her toes. Did you know?" Richard asked.

"No. I mean I know she smokes weed and has done some cocaine. But no heroin." Lannie stretched her arms and then shifted in the chair and crossed her legs.

"I've called her parents," Richard said.

"Is that wise?" Lannie asked.

"Why do you ask?"

"She's sure to tell them that you and she had an affair, which by the way I find disgusting and revolting. You and my best friend cheating on mom." She didn't sound angry. She said it matter-of-factly.

"It never happened, Lannie."

"*Never* is a long time, Richard."

"She made it up. I bet when you ask her after her head is clear she'll even be surprised she made the accusation."

"Richard, are you saying you did not screw around on mom?"

"That's between Barbara Anne and me."

Lannie placed a wet cloth on Bennie's forehead. The telly was on and a nattily dressed chap, replete with white shirt and bow-tie was doing a remote feed from Piccadilly Circus--something about the police trying to protect tourists from pick pockets and swindle artists. It seemed that London was having an outbreak of lame-brained tourists. All the smart tourists were going to Italy, the reporter joked.

"Hey you," Bennie said when she opened her eyes and glanced around. "We're still in London?"

"Yep. You've been sleeping for eighteen hours."

"Have I been a naughty girl?" Bennie asked.

"Not too much trouble."

"Shucks. I have a reputation to uphold, you know. I hope that I at least broke a heart or two. That was some bad stuff I got. I have a Hiroshima headache. Ronin said that stuff was purer than the Virgin Mary. Wow. Get the jackhammer out of my head."

"Bennie, Tim and I took care of you last night."

"Thanks, I'll leave a big tip when we go. He's hot for you, California girl. You guys play put the weenie in the bun?"

"We saw the needle marks in your arms and between your toes," Lannie said.

"It's not what you think and anyway, it's my body."

"Tim told Richard and he called your parents."

"Fred and Ethel are not going to care what their little girl does to herself. Trust me," Bennie said.

"Why are you doing this?" Lannie asked.

"You're the last person I thought would give me a hard time."

"Bennie, I care for you. That's why I'm concerned."

"If you care for me, then leave me alone. I've got everything under control."

"You're going to die, Bennie."

"Lannie, we're all going to die, sooner or later."

"It's the sooner I'm concerned about."

"Alright. I can see that I have to tell you. But you can't tell anyone. I can't die from vitamins."

"Vitamins?" Lannie asked. "What are you talking about?"

"I don't shoot up drugs, Lannie. I might be stupid, but I'm not an idiot, excepting last night, which was an obvious bummer. And I'm never doing that again. Did I play blow the hose with Rat? I hope so. He's such a nice guy. Anyway, I see an acupuncturist in Beverly Hills. Dr. Dat. He says I've got to take the vitamins because the high blood pressure pills I take bleed me of nutrients."

"I didn't know you took blood pressure pills."

"It's just a diuretic. I've been on them for years. As skinny as I am, who would have ever thought that I could have a blood pressure problem, You know, Freddy would never let me do something heavy like heroin. He's too protective. I have to sneak cocaine behind his back. He's worse than a parent."

"He's a regular guardian angel, ain't he?" Lannie said mockingly.

"He's taking night classes at Los Angeles Valley College."

"A real student of learning."

"He's taking business classes. Says he doesn't want to work the streets all his life and wake up at twenty-seven with no future. I'm going to take a couple of courses with him next semester," Bennie said. "Then I going to help him branch out into numbers."

"I can see the headlines now, Valley Girl Is Valedictorian and Becomes World's Most Successful Bookie's Assistant," Lannie commented.

Lannie and Bennie laughed hard and then had a good old fashion pillow fight. However, since the Two Hyde Park Square was chintzy with pillows, feathers did not fly. Only beads of foam flew from the split pillows, so it was not a Kodak moment. Nevertheless, it was a great girl-moment.

"Bennie, you said something last night."

"Like what, girl?"

"You said you and Richard were an item."

"Who did I tell *that* to?" Bennie asked.

"Richard, Tim and me."

"Oh, well."

"Well?" Lannie asked.

"Well what?" Bennie asked, evasively.

"Did you and Richard do, you know, *it*?"

"Depends on what the definition of *it*, is."

"When did you become a democrat?" Lannie asked.

"What's wrong with a guy getting some at work? Half of those Senators keep a nest full of little birdies in Washington."

"Seriously, did you and Richard have sex?"

"Only in my imagination, which is where all the best sex happens anyway, you know." Bennie wiped her hand across her face. "He turned me down."

"When?"

"Every time."

"When?"

"Every time I slept over at your place I offered myself to him. Even caught him in the tub one night, but it didn't work. Also, I went to his office once, thinking he felt uncomfortable at home and that's why he turned me down. But that wasn't it. He turned me down there too. I tried to blackmail him once. Told him that if he didn't let me do him, I was going to tell Barbara Anne we were doing it anyway. He said he had already told her about my advances. He was real sweet about it. Said that I would find the right guy one day, my soul mate. I wonder if he was talking about Freddy."

"Freddy may be your *cell mate* one day."

"Okay, my little California princess, tell me about Prince Tim. Is he cool, or what? I saw how he was stoking your back last night. Hands of *buttah*!"

"That was my first time," Lannie said.

"First time with a roadie? Is that what you mean?" Bennie asked. Bennie lived vicariously. Hearing about wild passionate love from Lannie was better than doing it herself.

"I was a virgin before last night."

"What are you talking about, girl? You've bedded dozens of guys."

"Not a one. I lied about all the others."

"Incredible! How did you get dates in high school?"

"I lived off *your* reputation. I was your best friend. Guys thought I was loose too."

"But you went steady with several guys. How did you hold them off?" Bennie asked. She was excited with this revelation. This was better than a month of Christmases.

"Since I was your best friend and therefore must have put out like a mink in heat--if I wasn't doing them--it must have been their fault. Of course, I strung some of them along with hand action," Lannie explained.

"Does Tim know he is *The* Man?"

"Even though I feared chasing him away, I told him."

"He must have thought he'd hit the Sex Powerball. Got himself a twenty-three year old virgin. Well, Miss First-timer, tell Aunt Bennie how the cherry popped."

"It was better than a hot fudge sundae," Lannie said with a coy look on her face and gleam in her eye. She ran her tongue over her lips and then smacked them loudly.

"Go girl. Start at the beginning and don't leave out one detail. I'm mushy just waiting. Tell me about Terrific Tim, The Cherry Buster. What is Terrific Tim's last name?"

Lannie's brow furrowed and she said, "I don't know."

CHAPTER FOURTEEN

The corporate offices of *Weird Magazine,* located on Fifth Avenue in Midtown Manhattan, were just awakening when Mel and Lolita exited the elevator with sleepy-eyed co-workers and stepped into the magazine's foyer. They steamed past posters of past monthly covers; mostly shots of freaky aliens, freaks, freaky celebrities, and outrageous headlines, and walked into a large, open space full of open-aired modular stalls. The staff calls the area the PIT. This is where the lifeblood of the paper pumps. Minions who had advanced degrees in fiction writing gathered the details of the minutiae relished by inquiring minds from all corners of the globe. They were paid yeoman's wage. Most of the little people worked at the magazine because it gave them an outlet for their creativity and they loved seeing their name in the by-line. Some were delusional and thought that a stint at the magazine on their resume would help them land a bigger and better job. In reality, most would slip-slide into something even less productive like a college English professorship.

The magazine suffered from tremendous turnover. There was only so much satisfaction one could draw from warning the world about impending attack by the warring denizens of Pluto. And the net of most paychecks would barely pay for subway fare to and from the office. The average length of employment was three years and the average age of the staff was well under thirty.

A large scheduling board draped one wall. It had six permanent headings imprinted over long vertical columns: ALIENS, SUPERNATURAL OCCURENCES, CELEBRITY DIRT, MIRACLES, SCIENCE NUTS and ELVIS. A grid flowed from under the headings to the floor. Each such square was topped by a month and in each square was the name of a reporter, cameraman and tentative headline. The magazine tried to have at least one story about all six of the super topics in each issue. And since the stories had to be in the can a minimum of forty-five days before the print and ship date, elbows were constantly flying. Every drawer contained antacid pills.

Currently, the headings had the following headlines penciled in for next month's issue:

ALIENS: These Men Really Are From Mars, Colony Of Martians Found In Iraqi Desert;

SUPERNATURAL OCCURENCES: Earth-Destroying Meteor Rapidly Approaches, May Be Here In Time For Christmas, Shopping Season In Jeopardy

CELEBRITY DIRT: Arnold Schwarzenegger May Be Adopted By Ted Kennedy, Claims It Legalizes Run For Presidency

MIRACLES: Mummy Dead For Five Hundred Years Now Teaches Egyptian History at Oxford University, His Wife Says She Always Knew Something Was Amiss

SCIENCE NUTS: New Herb Found In India Doubles Size Of Penis Overnight And Grows Hair

ELVIS: Elvis Has Secretly Worked As A Security Guard At Graceland For Twenty Years, And We Have His Paycheck Stubs To Prove It!

Mel and Lolita marched past the board, passed a cubicle where Jeff, his head buried in work, sat, waved at him when he looked up, all without a word being spoken. Then they took a right turn down a hall and barged into Jim Bowen's office. The carpet was so thick that they nearly stumbled when they sunk in it to ankle depth. Bowens' office reeked of testosterone. The sofa, two client chairs and the executive chair were covered in leopard skin. Dozens of stuffed and preserved snake heads hung from a wall. And even though Bowen had never been on safari and had never even fired a gun, an elephant head and that of a tiger hung from another wall on grass-cloth wallpaper.

Mel ignored all the tribal junk and, holding an official-looking manila folder under her arm, beat a path to Bowen's desk. A sinister sneer decorated her lips. Lolita followed in lock step, but didn't appear as confident as Mel. Bowen had a phone to his ear and gave a look of annoyance when he noticed the intruders.

"Hold on, I'll be with you in a second," he said to the phone's receiver and punched the hold button. "Good morning, ladies," as though absolutely nothing had happened the night before.

"Yes, it is a fine morning, boss," Mel said. She walked around Bowen's desk, plucked a fresh carnation from a vase on his windowsill and placed it in her hair behind her ear. Jim swiveled in his chair and cleared his throat.

"What can I do for you ladies this morning?" he asked, his eyes darting back and forth between the two women.

"I think it's promotion day," Mel announced.

"What are we promoting?" Jim asked, not fathoming what Mel meant and where all this was heading.

Mel adjusted the strap on her blouse and leaned close to Jim, causing him to rock back. She pressed forward to where her mouth was inches from his nose.

"Us, boss," Mel answered, her lips moving towards his ear.

"What are you talking about?" Bowen asked, grinning pathetically. He was trying to sink his head into the leopard skin of his chair, afraid that Mel was going to bite off his ear.

"I think I'm ready to be named head writer and Lolita has graciously agreed to be my assistant, doubling her current salary. I get a ten percent raise and can pick my stories. I pick the Elvis festival in Tennessee as my first assignment as head writer."

"Now see here, Mel. You can't come in here and tell…"

"Sexual harassment," Mel said and grinned.

"What?" Jim managed to get out of his rapidly constricting throat.

"It could cost the company millions. Even if we don't win, you'd be ruined," Mel explained and batted her eyelashes.

Cornered, Jim rallied. His initial defensiveness melted away and he took on an offensive posture. His back stiffened.

"You and the bimbo here can't prove anything. Those pictures you snapped don't mean a thing. Trick photography. I can get an expert to prove it. It's *he said, she said.* I've gotten my way with women around this office for years. Yeah, what I did was illegal, but you'll never prove it." A confident look masked his face. "Now get out before I have you thrown out by your ears." He thrust a finger at the doorway.

"Excuse me," Lolita said. "This bimbo just did."

"Did what?" he asked, even more annoyed at the intrusion. His pointing finger twitched, but he still awkwardly kept it suspended in mid-air, not knowing what to do with the digit next.

Lolita pulled a small tape recorder from inside her bra, waved it under his nose and shrugged her shoulders. "I guess I forgot to mention I had a tape recorder capturing all this wrangling."

"You devious bitches," Bowen blurted and reached for the recorder, but Lolita had anticipated the move and easily yanked her hand away and giggled.

"No, no. No can touch," Lolita teased as she protected the recorder.

"Calling us bitches is like a snake calling a rabbit a serpent, you viper," Mel said, glancing at the snakes on the wall.

Bowen tugged at his tie's knot and wiped perspiration from his brow. "Let's be reasonable. Ladies, I'm not without means. Maybe we could quietly settle this disagreement amongst ourselves." He reached for his checkbook in the desk drawer to his right. But Mel tapped his hand with the folder she had been clutching and Bowen quickly withdrew his hand from the drawer's knob. Mel dropped it onto Bowen's desk. "That's our new promotions. If you don't sign it now we go straight to our lawyer's office."

"Bunch of ball busters," Bowen proclaimed, as he opened the folder and began to hurriedly sign the two pieces of human resource paper.

Mel shoveled the papers into the folder and started for the door with Lolita triumphantly in tow. Mel turned back towards Jim, stopped and warned, "And Jim, you mess with any more office stock and we'll blow the lid off of your career. It'll take you longer to find a job than the feds have taken to find Hoffa."

The new head writer and her new assistant strutted out of Bowen's office, but stopped at the end of the hall before turning the corner to enter the PIT. They held each other's hands and heartily laughed at their deed.

"That went as expected," Mel said.

"Are you sure you want me to do this?" Lolita asked.

"It's our duty to womankind, or some kind of gibberish like that."

Lolita unbuttoned the top three buttons of her blouse, pulled her compact mirror from her purse and rubbed a finger over one of her eyebrows. She smeared on fresh lipstick. "Lolita, that's enough. Hell, you look fine enough to make *me* want to go muff diving. Let's don't overdo it."

Lolita smirked, turned the corner and made a beeline for Jeff's cubicle, then entered it, and he looked up. "Can I help you?" he asked innocently. He had never noticed this young, attractive woman before and had no clue what she was doing in his office area.

"You bastard!" she yelled at the top of her lungs and peeked out of the corner of her eyes to see that there were at least ten people within twenty feet paying attention. She stepped up to Jeff and bitch-slapped him. The crack reverberated throughout the PIT. Keyboards stopped clicking and hold buttons were pushed. "You two-timing monster! You get me pregnant and then after the abortion, I find that you're doing Molly, my best friend! I'll never forgive you. You cunt-happy slut!" Lolita pretended to start crying, put her hands to her face, pivoted and then quickly walked away; she made it through the PIT and onto the elevator without laughing out loud.

Jeff rubbed his hand on his face, stunned. Mel floated into his cubicle. "You okay?" she whispered.

"What the hell was that?" he whispered back.

"That's Lolita, your ex-girlfriend and my new assistant. You can thank me later, Big Stud." She winked at him, and waltzed out of his office humming, leaving Jeff in shock and sucking air through his mouth like a guppy out of water. However, groups of women seemed to come together instantly and the room filled with a buzz of chatter about Jeff's ruthlessness with women. Many of the women gave him a sexy smile.

The packed Manhattan bar bustled with the din of a young, fashionable after-work crowd, all climbing the slippery ladder of success to better titles and bigger paychecks. Most would stab their mothers in the back for an office with a window. They toiled in places where ethics was something one preached, not put into practice. The men in the bar were looking to score and the women were there to keep score. Both sexes (and a couple of tweeners with perfect doctor breasts waiting for a snip job) were enjoying their Friday unwinding from the coil of weeklong stress. Pickup lines were being practiced and honed for closing time.

Mel and Lolita, wearing designer outfits and perfectly coifed hair, melded right in with the pretentious crowd, and occupied a booth in the rear. Mel, as was her usual practice, sat with her back to the wall and her face to the door. A psychiatrist once told her it was an issue of trust. She had unsuccessfully argued that she always did this because she was merely interested in seeing who came in.

"I haven't had that much fun since high school when I slipped a frog down the back of Julie Pine's dress in Biology lab," Mel crowed. She sipped from her second glass of Chivas on the rocks.

"I've never had that much fun with my clothes *on*," Lolita joked. She reflected after she made the comment and determined that it was a truthful statement. She raised her daiquiri to her mouth.

"Julie Pine had to unzip her dress to extricate the little froggy, and when she did, tissue from her bra flew out. Little Miss Playboy-tits suddenly became flatter than a west Texas road," Mel said and grinned. "She got dropped from the guys' speed dials faster than a teenage boy drops his pants when his first date says, *yes*."

"That's pretty fast, but do you really think Bowen will let us get away with this?" Lolita asked, still worried about losing her job.

"He's got no choice. He's as ambitious as a first-term politician. His career would go in the tank if we spilled the beans. His confession on your tape is better insurance than Prudential's. Besides, I deserve to be head reporter and you earned your stripes on your knees."

"Truth be known, I feel that I'm preaching to the choir here, Bowen's actually a lot of fun," Lolita admitted and tried to suppress a devious grin.

"That will be our little secret," Mel said, and patted Lolita's hand resting on the table. "Let's toast our new positions with *Weird Magazine*." They clinked their glasses and drank in unison.

"I've been in the tabloid business less than a week and I've already been promoted. What's next?" Lolita asked. She stared at Mel blankly.

"You're going to have to work. On Monday I'm catching a flight into Memphis. I'm going to visit an old friend and then drive to the Elvis festival in Moscow, Tennessee. I'll snoop together some stories and then you and Jeff can join me on Thursday. Spend the first part of the week putting together an office for us and thumbing your nose at Bowen. The festival ends Sunday afternoon, so we can fly back to New York that evening. We'll be back at work on Monday."

"I'm a little nervous about flying down to Memphis," Lolita said.

"Afraid of flying?"

"No. I've never been an assistant to a reporter before. Hell, for that matter I've never been an assistant to anyone. Mel, I danced at a girlie club until recently and I have no clue what's expected of me."

"I expect you to have fun," Mel said, raised her glass in a mock-salute and then drained the remainder of the Chivas.

CHAPTER FIFTEEN

Freddy waited in front of the entrance to the parking garage trying to look cool and he was doing a good job of it. His hands were tucked into his pockets and he sucked on a self-rolled cigarette and expertly blew rings into the air without taking the cigarette out of his mouth. He was especially proud of the three rings simultaneously wafting in the breeze, but quickly tired of the game just as he was getting damn tired of his life. He changed gears more often than a race car driver on a quarter mile oval. One day he's a street-tough pimp working five girls, fighting to maintain his territory. He's cutting deals, recruiting customers, negotiating room rates, keeping everything in his head, as though he had a computer for a brain. He could instantly recall the home and business phone numbers of his regular clients. He remembered what the maximum rate each client was willing to pay and their personal preferences. But to his clients he was just a pimp.

But he wasn't a bad pimp. He treated the girls right. Hardly ever hit one, unless the bitch really asked for it. He even bought the girls birthday cards and presents whenever he could remember the dates and he gave them the day off at Christmas. None of them ever had to stay in jail overnight. He put up their bail quickly and only charged them twenty per cent interest per week until they repaid it. That was five percent cheaper than a loan shark would charge. Yes, he treated his girls very nicely.

But then there was his other life. The next day he's a college student studying some hard-ass stuff surrounded by silver-spooners and candy-asses. Community college was hard, except the classes with numbers. The classes with numbers were easy. He could add three columns of numbers in his head as fast as any spooner could enter the numbers in a calculator. That thing called Algebra, he could figure out in seconds the amount that the letter in the formula represented, just by looking. The teacher asked him one time how he did that. Freddy told the teacher it was none of his damn business. But who was going to pay you for just being able to do numbers fast? He'd never seen an ad in the papers seeking some one who could do numbers. And the stupid college wouldn't give you a degree in just numbers. You had to take that English and history shit. And he hated that stuff. Who cares who the twenty-third President of the United States was? All anyone cared about was whether they had a place to sleep and could they get enough clothes, food and sex.

However, college did open up a completely new territory. The spooners had a lot of money they were willing to give away in exchange for anything they couldn't get at home. Pussy. Drugs. Fake Rolexes. Styling shit. Freddy vowed he'd keep coming to college as long as he could, as long as the spooners gave him business. Easy money. These people spent money like there would be more tomorrow by just waking up.

But even though every day was downhill, Freddy was bored. It was time to branch out and it was his lucky week. Fingers Anderson had fallen (or gotten pushed) out of the back of a truck and cracked his head wide-open. Stained the sidewalk and died on the spot. Someone said Fingers' brains were as small as a large order of French fries, and this made Freddy wonder: Was that super-sized or not?

Fingers ran a numbers racket in Ingleside for One-Eye Landon. One-Eye let it be known that the territory was now up for grabs. Twenty-five thousand down and forty-percent of the net take each week was One-Eye's franchise fee. It was the perfect setup. One-Eye handled the protection and payoffs. All the lucky bidder had to do was take bets, loan out and collect money and act as the bank. Of course, if you got caught with sticky fingers, lying about the receipts, One-Eye saw to it that your franchise and you were terminated.

One-Eye had explained that the operator had to put up the forty-percent of the weekly take until the remaining twenty-five thousand was paid. Thereafter, One-Eye got only twenty-five percent off the top for expenses. Just fifty thousand and you would be set up for life. Of course, nobody dwelled on the fact that life expectancy on the streets was only about two years and that sometimes legs and arms had to be broken to collect. Still, Freddy thought the deal was doable, but he didn't have that kind of money. His operation was small potatoes. Freddy didn't even have to pay anyone protection money or a franchise fee. Protect what? His was a one-man operation. He wasn't part of anything. The only reason he even got a meeting with One-Eye was through his uncle. Uncle Jonas was a bagman in Chinatown for One-Eye.

Freddy spent his money as fast as he made it. Everything cost serious money. He was a broke-dick punk and he (and One-Eye) knew it. His empire wasn't even a blip on the radar of a guy like One-Eye. One-Eye was offering him the deal of a lifetime.

Where was Bennie? He looked at his watch again, held it up to his ear but couldn't hear anything. He shook his wrist again. He was about to give up when Bennie's topless Boxter rounded the corner. It screeched to a halt at the curb and he hopped in over the door and squatted comfortably in the leather seat.

"Hey, baby," he said and kissed her on the neck. "You're looking awfully fine today. The foxiest fox in the fox house; that's what I'm saying."

"Keep that sweet talk up and I'll just have to pull over," she purred. "Sorry I'm late, but my idiot shrink just wouldn't shut up. She's worse than a lawyer. Uses five-dollar words to describe two-cent action. Says I'm suffering from *transference*. What the hell is that supposed to mean? I think *she's* the one who is nuts. She's suffering from shit-on-the-brain. Who could have a job like that? Listen to perverts all day. Daddy must like throwing his money into that furnace. Six years of analysis and that woman still doesn't know who I am. How does she expect me to figure out who I am when she can't and she's a damn expert?"

"Baby, I need to talk to you. Let's go get some food."

She drove them to their favorite steak place in the valley. It was a simple joint, but popular and the parking lot was full so she valet parked. Freddy told the kid that if he scratched the paint he'd die before the next sunrise. The kid grinned, not knowing how to respond to a death threat over paint, and drove off at a snail's pace.

Bennie and Freddy were lucky; there was no waiting line. They were immediately escorted to the last available table in the restaurant. The place was not classy, although it did have some nostalgia value. Metal building. Black and white tile floors. Plastic table covers. Old-time salt and pepper shakers. Butt ugly, but efficient waitresses. A one-page menu. All the food was prepared from time of the order; there wasn't a microwave in the place. The chef had a no-nonsense reputation. There were no pretentious titles to the food. A potato was called a potato, a steak a steak.

"I treat you good, huh baby?" Freddy asked as they waited for menus.

"The best," Bennie said, wondering where this was leading. Freddy was usually direct and came right out and said what he was thinking. She playfully squeezed his knee under the table, but got no visible reaction.

"I've got a favor to ask you." He flipped a cigarette from his pocket, clenched it between his lips and clicked his lighter.

"Anything, sweet pants," Bennie said.

"I need fifty thousand dollars right away," he casually said as though he was yawning. He lit the cigarette, sucked in a drag and coolly blew smoke to the ceiling.

The hostess who had seated them sprinted up out of breath. "Excuse me sir, you can't smoke in here. It's against the law," she said. "There's a huge fine."

"Alright, you damn Nazi bureaucrat," Freddy snarled, and stubbed out the cigarette into the tablecloth, burning a hole in the vinyl.

The woman's jaw dropped, but she was so grateful he had put out the cigarette she said nothing about the tablecloth. She turned and walked away. *I'll spit in his food,* she decided.

"And you want to like borrow from the kitty you've been collecting for me and investing?" Bennie asked.

"Baby, that ain't but a couple of hundred dollars. The futures market in heating oil hasn't taken off yet."

"Bummer. Then what do you want?" she asked.

"Maybe you could get the money from your parents."

"Borrow it?"

"You could just take it from them," Freddy said and shrugged his shoulder. He pulled another cigarette from his pocket.

"Steal it? Freddy, I wouldn't have a clue on how to do that."

"I could kidnap you and demand a ransom," he said, staring at the wall in serious thought, wondering if he should do that even if Bennie didn't want to go along. When it was over she wouldn't want to press charges anyway.

"They wouldn't pay it."

"Do you think they'd lend us the money?" he asked. *Scratch kidnapping.*

"Freddy, we did that, you know, your self-esteem would suffer. You'd need help eventually. My bitch shrink would like be buying another Mercedes."

"It would really be a loan and I could repay it in three months." He explained One-Eye's proposition in great detail, although he doubted she was following along. Her eyes clouded and she went someplace in her mind where he could never follow. He always considered her thinking to be as shallow as spilled beer.

“It would be great watching you like run your own minority-owned, small business, but I shouldn’t get any money from my parents. Besides, there is no way they would lend it to me or you anyway. It would be better if we did this on our own.”

“Baby, you’d have to get gang-banged by a stadium full of conventioneers from Dallas to make that much money.”

“I’d do every guy in L.A. for you, you know that.” She looked around and then leaned over. “Freddy, I know. Why don’t we just rob a bank?” She eagerly bobbed her head.

“What? What bank?” Freddy popped the cigarette into his mouth again, but then grabbed it with his hand and crushed in with his fingers. The tobacco fell onto the tablecloth.

“My dad’s got money at First Union. They should have at least fifty thousand dollars lying around. We get a gun. Do you have one Freddy? We’ll need two. One each. I want a big one. Big enough to scare the *beejesus* out of any old bank guard. It would feel deliciously perverted stealing dad’s money from his bank. The more I think about it, the more I think it would be fun.”

“It’s not that simple. You don’t just go into a bank and get a bag full of money and walk out free and clear,” Freddy said. “They’ve got cameras, guards, buttons they push to call the cops.”

“You tell them they can’t push any buttons, or else, and you wear a mask, you know, so they can’t see who you are,” she said.

“Believe me, they catch you.”

“My Boxter is fast.”

“We get caught; your daddy can’t get you out of trouble.”

“I get wet when you say the word *trouble.* And the thing to do is not get caught.”

The bar in the Beverly Hills Wilshire Hotel was almost empty; the afternoon crowd had not yet arrived. There were only a few alkies seated at the bar, getting an early jump on the train to the gutter. A few guys were waiting for their mistresses; a few hookers were waiting for their tricks. In an ironic calamity the guys and hookers were overlooking each other.

Lannie drank cola from a frosted glass and Bennie, a gin on the rocks. Both were unintentionally dressed as Halloween sluts.

“Miss, oh miss,” a guy dressed in a starched shirt and business suit seated two stools down from Lannie called.

“Are you talking to me?” Lannie asked.

"You and your friend…," the guy started to say.

"Why don't you crawl back under the rock, or call your wife and tell *her* you're horny," Bennie said.

"Young lady, I was just trying to get your attention. Something fell out of your purse and is under your stool."

"Oh, sorry." Lannie reached under her stool and picked up her cell phone.

Francois, patting his handkerchief on his profusely sweating forehead, eagerly supervised the readying of Lannie's usual table. He told Lannie the table would be ready in a few short minutes.

After Francois departed, Bennie excitedly told Lannie about One-Eye's proposition and the plan to rob a bank. Lannie couldn't believe what she was hearing. "Bennie, you can't rob a bank. You and Freddy could be shot. Nobody gets away with that kind of thing."

"Then why do they have most-wanted posters at post offices? Those people got away with it, didn't they?"

"The robbers eventually get caught, Bennie, and then spend a lot of time in jail."

"We might just get away with it. Bet it would be a hell of a rush. Better than sex. And *if* I had to go to jail, maybe lesbianism diving isn't so bad. Except where do you get good drugs inside jail? Drugs inside jail are probably like, so weak."

"Is Freddy in favor of this hair-brained scheme?" Lannie asked and then swigged down the rest of her cola. She had tried for years to steer Bennie to a safer lifestyle and now Bennie was thinking of doing something just dreadful. Bennie had done some stupid things in her life, but this ridiculous scheme would be the worst.

"He says another opportunity will come along. He's only twenty-four."

"He's right, you know." Lannie plucked peanuts from a bowl on the bar, tossed one up and caught it with her mouth. The bartender placed another cola and frosted glass in front of her and then poured her glass full.

"I heard that people sell their body parts," Bennie said. "There's this like underground market, probably on the Internet. Get big bucks for a kidney."

"Bennie, you're really scaring me," Lannie said, as peanut caught her in the eye. "Damn," she blurted and then rubbed her eye.

"Sisters donate a kidney to brothers all the time. And those are for free."

"They do that because it's life and death and they do it out of love," Lannie said. She rubbed her eye that now stung from salt.

"I love Freddy," Bennie said.

This frightened Lannie even more than the thought of Bennie robbing a bank, but she couldn't think of anything to say. If she said something negative, Bennie would be mad at her. If she said something positive, then Bennie would take it as approval. "I know you think you do, Bennie, but Freddy might just be a daughter's way of rebelling against her parents. Besides, getting money to set up a loan-sharking operation and bookie racket ain't exactly life and death."

Bennie ignored Lannie's accusation and said, "I've got two kidneys and could easily, you know, get by with just one."

Lannie decided to try shock. "Suppose you got sick and your remaining kidney stopped working?"

"Someone would like give me one."

"Okay. What if you sell a kidney and then you and Freddy break up. What's in it for you?" Lannie asked, sure she had finally scored.

"I'm providing the money and will be Freddy's partner. He'd have to buy me out if we spit up. Anyway, we're not splitting up. I'm about to ask him if I can move in."

Lannie tried not to panic. "You move in with Freddy and daddy's wallet shuts down." A practical assault on this lunacy.

"I don't care. Freddy and I will make a lot of money in his new deal. Anyway, Freddy says I've gotten so good at whoring he's going up on my rates. I'm going to be his highest-priced girl. Isn't that sweet? A few holiday gatherings and dad will be Freddy's best friend. They'll be swapping Christmas cards and carving turkey together before you know it. There's not that much difference between being a rock promoter and being a pimp." Bennie put her finger to her chin. "In fact, there is no difference. Everybody gets screwed in the end. Say, is that a pun?"

Lannie sighed.

CHAPTER SIXTEEN

Freddy examined the dilemma from every angle and reluctantly agreed that robbing a bank was the only quick way they could get the money to buy One-Eye's numbers franchise. Once the decision was made, they began training and planning.

"I didn't realize this would like get so complicated," Bennie complained. She wore mink designer earmuffs over her ears, a Prairie Dog tee shirt, pink Capri pants and Gucci shoes. She definitely was not dressed like your average shooting-range patron.

"Now what's the problem?" Freddy asked. Bennie was bitching more often than his sisters ever did and he had to really struggle to keep from slapping the little rich bitch. He had never struck Bennie and he didn't know why.

"Could we find a gun that will *not* break my nails? Paaaaleeese ? I've already cracked one nail slipping my finger into the trigger area." She squeezed the gun handle in her palm and it felt surprisingly good. *Maybe, happiness is a warm gun,* she thought. She raised her arms and clamped her hands around the pistol's handle. Last time, when she shot the thing, she accidentally shot the carpet shelf two feet in front of her. She kept her eyes *open* this time, pointed the barrel at the paper target and pulled the trigger. The explosion made her hands jerk and her ears tingle. She rocked back, savoring the rush that flowed through her body.

"Forget about your precious nails and worry about where you're shooting," Freddy advised.

"Are these the biggest bullets that will work in my gun?"

"Bennie, only one size bullet works in any gun."

"How do you know that?" she asked, amazed that Freddy had figured out the bullet issue before she had even asked him.

"Bennie girl, the details are what get you. You can't put too much planning into a thing like this," Freddy explained. He emptied the spent cylinder of his pistol, dropping the empty casings onto the floor. "You've got to anticipate everything that could go wrong." He started squeezing new shells into the pistol, but fumbled and dropped the gun onto the floor. Shells ran everywhere. He tried to act cool as he slipped on the bullets and caught himself from falling by grabbing the shelf, the way a novice ice skater awkwardly grabs a wall.

"What's going to go wrong?" she asked, stepping on a bullet herself and slipping down. Luckily, her gun did not fire. Freddy helped her up by her arm.

"Do I look like Miss Clairvoyant? I don't know," he said.

"If you don't know what's going to go wrong, how can you anticipate it?" she asked, a confused look on her face.

"Bennie, don't take everything I say so literally," Freddy answered. He shook his head side to side and reached into his pocket. His pockets were crammed with enough empty casings and bullets to have fought for the Mexicans at the Alamo. His fingers were numb from holding the gun through so many firings, and he had a hard time remembering which pockets held live shells and which held spent shells.

"What does *literally* mean?" Bennie asked.

"It means let *me* do the thinking and planning," Freddy fussed. He tried to reload his pistol with fingers he could not feel, and kept dropping the bullets. He had to keep bending over and pluck out casings from the cuffs in his trousers and the floor.

"Whatever, but if the guns will not be loaded, why are we having target practice?" Bennie asked. She placed her gun on the carpeted shelf, pushed the retrieval button, and a wire pulled the paper target towards her.

"Bennie girl, did I say the guns would not be loaded?"

"You said we wouldn't like shoot anybody." She inspected the target. She had fired over thirty times but had hit the target only once. The mark was on the tip of the right shoulder of the cutout. She hoped that any body she had to shoot at was really big and tall, at least larger than the paper target.

"The guns can be loaded and nobody gets shot," Freddy explained. "Unless you pull the trigger nobody gets shot, right?"

"But, if we're not going to shoot anybody, why have loaded guns?" She blew on the smoke still coming out of the barrel of her pistol, twisted the gun in her hands and peered into the barrel. Her right eye was half an inch from the barrel opening and her eyes crossed.

Freddy slowly lifted the gun from her hand. "Bennie girl, don't ever point a gun at your face again. It could go off."

"I just wanted to see, you know, what it looked like in there."

"We're bringing loaded guns because of *what if*," Freddy explained, on the cusp of some smelly, deep bullshit.

"What if *what*?" The excitement of shooting the gun had finally worn off and Bennie, as was often the case, was beginning to be bored. She wanted to file her damaged nail and her ears were too hot. *What will I wear for the robbery? Where will I shop for the outfit? Dress or pants?*

"What if the bank teller refuses to put the money in the bag?" Freddy asked. "What would you do?"

"I'd... shoot her?" Bennie answered with a confused look on her face.

"No, if yelling some *F* words doesn't get her to do it, then you pop a shot into the ceiling. She'll fill her drawers with poop and the bag with money." Freddy finally got a bullet into his pistol. He spun the barrel and enjoyed hearing the rapid clicking.

"I get it. The gun is to *scare* people." Bennie said, relieved.

"That's right, Bennie girl. Let them know we mean business. What if the money is still in the safe and the manager will not open it? What would we do?" Freddie asked, looking into the holes in the cartridge cylinder.

"Shoot a round into the ceiling?" Bennie replied tentatively.

"We probably already did that. I plan to shoot one in the ceiling right up front. That way they think we're desperados. If the manager will not open the vault, I'll slap his face with the barrel. I saw that in a movie once. Manager bled all over the bank robber, but he damn well opened the vault door."

"That wouldn't hurt him too much, would it?" Bennie asked. She was now furiously filing her nail.

"Just a couple of stitches. You've never been to the movies? People get pistol whipped all the time. The next scene, hell, they're just fine. Can't even see the scratch on their faces. What if the cops showed up and we had to take hostages?" he asked. He finally got all six bullets into his pistol and twirled it like a cowboy before a duel.

"Freddy, that wouldn't be the thing to do. We can't take hostages. They might get hurt."

"You *have* to take hostages, Bennie girl. It's like an unwritten code. Hostages were invented at the same time they invented banks. If the cops show up, you yell out that you've got hostages and you fire a round into the ceiling to show the cops that you mean business."

"We keep shooting into the ceiling and we're liable to get a chunk of plaster on the head. Be my luck you're knocked out and I have to do everything myself. Maybe we should wear helmets Freddy, just in case."

Freddy sighed. He twirled the gun on his left hand, and as he started to change it back to his right hand, it went off. The bullet impaled the carpeted shelf. Freddy looked around to make sure nobody saw the accident.

"Freddy, be careful."

"Bennie, I did that on purpose." Sweat was streaming off his brow. His hands were shaking. "What if we walk in, start the robbery and the guard shoots at you?" he asked.

"I've been in the bank with my father. The guard is a sweet old man. He'd never shoot at anyone. He always smiles and has the shiniest shoes."

"Bennie, *what if* he starts shooting?" Freddy asked, his voice raising.

"I drop my gun and put my hands up?"

Freddy dropped into a crouch and fired at his paper target, emptying his pistol. Then he said, macho-like, "You cap his ass until he falls."

"I couldn't do that. He's such a sweet old man. He once gave me a lollipop. Freddy, would it be alright if *my* gun is not loaded?"

"Yeah, baby. I'll just carry two."

"Bennie, you can't do this," Lannie pleaded. They were sitting in Bennie's car across the street from First Union Bank. Bennie was studying the bank, getting her game face on. Actually, she had no idea what she was doing there. Freddy had told her to stake out the bank, and she had no clue as to what that meant.

"I get like so confused sometimes," Bennie said. "I can't remember if we yell, 'This is a stick up, nobody move,' or 'Nobody move, this is a stick up.' I can't remember when Freddy shoots into the ceiling or what to do if the manager will not open the safe. Maybe Freddy will let me write it down. That's it. I could like have a cheat sheet on my wrist just like I used to do in high school. There's way too much to remember. I don't know how people ever remember it all. Bank robbing is complicated."

"Where *is* Freddy?" Lannie asked. She was sipping a Slim Fast and munching on a Snickers.

"He's at the library researching how to hotwire a car."

"You're going to steal a car?" Lannie asked. "I'll let you borrow mine if you need one. No need committing two crimes."

"Like, yeah. We have to have a getaway car. I wanted to use mine, but Freddy said my car is too recognizable. I told him that there are *hundreds* of Boxers in the L.A. area, but he said there are *thousands* of Honda Accords. He read a magazine article that said the Accord was the most stolen car in America. Freddy said it must be easy to steal one. That was good enough for him. Freddy said any fool bought an Accord, fool *expected* it to be stolen."

"You guys don't sound very.... organized," Lannie said. She tore open the wrapper of another Snickers.

"We will be. Freddy's a detail person. He's even practicing talking like someone from Boston. That way the bank's employees will think he's from out of town. He said he really wanted to speak French, make them think he was from France. But he didn't know how to speak French. I told him that I could get Francois to teach him the words necessary to rob the bank, but Freddy said the bank's employees probably didn't know how to speak French anyway. He would yell, *this is a bank robbery* in French and half the employees, seeing that Freddy is Hispanic, might think he was delivering pizza, or asking them if they wanted their cars washed. See how he figured that out?" Bennie asked and commenced filing her nails.

"Are you guys going to hide out after the robbery?"

"Like, yeah. I wanted to take a vacation. Like go to Europe, but Freddy said that would call attention to us. I told Freddy that no one in Europe would recognize us."

"I think he meant that using your passport here and buying tickets here would call attention to the two of you," Lannie said.

"Oh. I get it now. Whatever. We decided to hide out in Disneyland. We could have some fun, and who ever heard of bank robbers going to Disneyland, right?" "Damn!" she said, as she broke a nail.

"But Bennie, Disneyland isn't open twenty-four hours a day. You'll have to travel on the roads to go home at night. There may be roadblocks. That defeats the purpose of hiding out."

"Silly you. That's why we're buying a three day Disney pass and sleeping in the bathroom of the service station just outside the parking lot entrance," Bennie explained.

"They have security that patrols the parking areas. They won't let you spend the night," Lannie said. "They clear the lots every night."

"Freddy has a cousin who slept in the Disney parking lot an entire summer. He slept in the service station bathroom at night and broke into cars in the daytime. He made enough money to bring his sister and brother from Mexico. His brother's first child born here is called Goofy. Freddy and I will sleep in the bathroom and move to the car when the coast is clear. Don't worry about it. We're wearing clown masks during the job. No one will know *we* are the robbers. The bank camera will only get a picture of two clowns."

Lannie started to say something, but decided it would be useless. She chomped on her candy bar.

Richard Drees and the Prairie Dogs' new single, penned by Rod Witherspoon, *I Liked You More (When I Knew You Less)* bolted up the charts, streaking from number eighteen to number one in just one week. Fat residual checks streamed into Tim Reed's office so fast the postman joked that he was germinating a hernia carrying them up the steep, terraced walkway to Drees' house.

Drees' mansion sat nestled on two wooded acres and gripped a sheer hill outside of Denver that had a spectacular view of the city and painted mountains. A scenic herd of buffalo roamed the hillside of his neighbor, although when the wind was out of the east, the smell was not patriotic.

The home's modernistic exterior was a hodgepodge of steel and glass and its interior was dominated by wood and fur. Every room had at least one exterior wall of solid glass and at least two dead, mounted animals. The structure soared three stories above a table of slanted rock. The lower floor functioned as the office complex, while the second and third floors held the living quarters' six bedrooms and eight baths. The complex had been designed by an architect with an ego and a blank check. Drees' home had been featured on the cover of numerous magazines.

Tim held his cell phone to his ear, as he watched clouds slip over the faraway purple and blue-green mountains. The view was so stunning that he often slept on the couch at night instead of driving to his place in Aurora. Watching moon shadows dance across the mountains fascinated him. It was better at putting him to sleep after a stressful day than counting sheep or buffalo.

"Hello, Lannie."

She recognized his voice instantaneously. "Who is this?" she played, excited he had finally called. She stood up in her bedroom, trying to make herself more alert.

"It's Tim."

"Tim who?" She fought a snigger.

"Tim Reed, you remember, London?"

"Of course, the guy in the subway." She giggled.

He sensed her game and played along. "What guy in the subway?"

"The guy with the fury legs," she said,

"That wasn't me. That was me mum, a gigantic Leprechaun. Dad liked to sit and twirl the fur with his wee fingers till the coat was so shiny he could comb his hair in its sheen. Mum braided her legs on Easter, and we hid eggs in there. She did such a terrific job of hiding the eggs we often didn't find them for weeks. I'm not like that. Actually, there isn't a hair on me body. Found out I was adopted from a hairless clan of nomadic Gypsies."

She laughed carelessly. "I was wondering if you were a slam-bam-thank-you-ma'am guy who never called his virginal conquests."

"Richard's had me busier than a one-armed referee trying to signal a touchdown. Would it help if I apologized profusely?"

"Only after flowers, candy and Jewish foreplay, you know, two hours of non-stop begging."

"If I can put the begging on my credit card, you'll have it at your doorstep tomorrow, fair maiden."

"That would be sweet, but I do think it's something you have to do in person for the proper effect, you silver-tongued devil."

"Richard has a meeting in L.A. with his record label genius in the next couple of days, and I'm coming. Could we get together then, Lannie?"

"I don't know, I was really trying to make it a month without shaving my legs or brushing my teeth."

"I don't do teeth, darling, but I would love to sit in a hot bubble bath and shave your legs. Bottom to top. I used to practice on mama."

"That sounds *so* nice. Do you wash hair too?" she asked, thinking of Bennie and her personal trainer's delectable nooner.

"What hair do you have in mind?" he teased.

"Why, Tim Reed, I do believe you've got me blushing."

"Us country boys know how to rile our women."

"Being an uneducated woman, master Tim, I'm not sure what *rile* means, but is it scrumptious?"

"Ouch, you're doing ninety in a thirty-five zone there, darling."

"Are you going to arrest me?"
"Among other things."
"Use handcuffs?"

CHAPTER SEVENTEEN

"I thought we were going to steal the car at night," Bennie said, confused, and then flipped through the pages of a copy of *Weird Magazine.* "Says here that Egyptian mummies are really aliens and will come to life when the next comet approaches earth."

"Bennie, we're robbing the bank today. We need the car now. Besides, I'm having enough trouble seeing the wires in the daylight," Freddy said, frustrated. His feet jutted in the air over the driver's seat and his head was squeezed under the dash. The wires didn't look like the wires in the library book when you're looking at them upside down. He separated a strand of wires with his shaking fingers and tried to snip a wire with a cutter, but caught his finger. "Shit!" Blood squirted onto the floorboard. He twisted around, sat in the seat and compressed the wound with the handkerchief he plucked from his back pocket.

"I hope robbing the bank will be easier than stealing a car," Bennie said, wishing she had used the bathroom before they began the adventure. She now had to tinkle in the worst way.

"It'll be a piece of cake," Freddy assured her as the bleeding slowed to a trickle.

"Did you check under the mat for a key? The doors weren't locked and a lot of women just throw them under the mat instead of fighting with their purse."

"Why do you think this is a woman's car?" Freddy asked, more humoring her than interested in her answer. The pain in his finger worsened by the second.

"Like, duh? The driver's seat was scrunched all the way up. I can smell White Diamonds perfume, and there's an Enya disc in the player."

Maybe she ain't dumber than dirt after all. Freddy probed under the mat with his good hand and found the key. He inserted it and cranked the engine. "Alright! We're on our way."

"Freddy, will it be alright if I use the bathroom at the bank? I gotta pee so bad my teeth are floating."

Francois carted off the uneaten balance of broiled Pacific trout, sautéed range vegetables and twice-baked potatoes stuffed with avocado, Bavarian goat cheese and garlic shrimp.

"Lannie, these past couple of days have been the best," Tim Reed remarked, then hoisted his glass for a toast. They clinked their stems, and he drank from his glass of champagne.

"Am I glowing? And I don't mean from a champagne buzz," she asked, beaming.

"Western Edison will have to put a meter on you to check for wattage usage."

"This has been much too fast for me. I might not look like it, but I've got a lot of balls in the air. Mom's about gone. Bennie's about to get into bottomless trouble. I'm desperately trying to make a decision on school, and now I'm involved with a dashing man of the world. Whew!" She rubbed the back of her hand across her brow, faking a swoon.

Francois appeared with two plates of Bananas Foster, expertly placed them on the table, asked if they needed anything and disappeared when they said no.

"How is Barbara Anne?" Tim asked. He tasted a spoonful of creamy dessert.

"She's bed ridden, gets round the clock care and has oxygen tubes down her nose. Doctors give her less than a month. She's happier than a tick at a dog show. Go figure."

"Happy?" he asked, surprised.

"She's having a blast. She's writing the script to a testimonial banquet she wants Richard to host a year after she's gone, and she's getting off writing all of our roles."

"That sounds macabre."

"I read my part. It's all a bunch of crap. Makes her out to be Super Mom and Mother Theresa all rolled into one."

"Has it been tough having world famous parents?" Tim asked.

"Richard's not my father. I don't know who my father is. Mom never spilled that bean."

"Oh," he said and nodded.

"I guess I've never really done anything with my life. Why try? I'll never be able to stack up to their achievements. Kids born to famous mothers have no uphill. Everything is downhill starting with the slap on the rear."

"You seem to be treading water very nicely now," Tim remarked.

"Until now I've just drifted where ever the current has taken me. I've been very lucky not to run into any land sharks. Closest I've come is Bennie and I think I've failed at trying to get her straightened out."

"God gave us free will and it seems like he gave her more than one human needs," Tim commented.

"I don't know how *I* survived her teenage years."

"Lannie, you don't seem any worse for wear. I asked Richard if I could date you."

"How Victorian, but what if he had said no?" She asked and arched a brow.

"I would have had to quit working for him, I guess," Tim said and tilted his head.

"Great answer, but you didn't even know me."

"I knew enough," he said.

"I don't know what to say."

"You don't have to say anything, really. Richard said you've never had a serious beau before."

"I've never met anyone I wanted to be serious with--before now."

He leaned slightly forward and cupped his hands over hers. "The feeling is mutual."

Lannie sipped her champagne, but started to gag, as the liquid went down the wrong pipe. She retched and then threw up onto the table.

"Are you alright?" Tim asked, suddenly with his arm around Lannie's shoulders.

"Yes. In fact, lunch tasted better the second time around."

Freddy skidded the Honda to the curb in front of the bank, grazing the tires.

"Why did we steal a standard shift, like if you don't know how to drive a standard?" Bennie asked. She nervously rapped her fingers on the dash.

"Did you take a bitch pill this morning?" he sarcastically asked. *What an attitude!* he thought.

"What's going to happen, you know, when we have to get out of here in a hurry, and you like stall this thing?"

"I've got it under control. Trust me. Everything's cool." He pulled out the short checklist and went over it. "I've got the car gassed, two guns, the wigs, the gloves, the clown masks and bullets. I think that does it. Shit! I forgot the bullets!"

"Are we going back to your place to get some?" Bennie asked, not eager to go into the bank just yet. "I still gotta pee."

"No, we'll just do this without bullets."

"How are you going to shoot a round into the ceiling if you don't have any bullets?"

"I won't. I'll improvise. I'll just yell real loud."

Bennie was grateful Freddy had forgotten the bullets. "Freddy, assuming they give you the money, what are we going to put the money in?"

"Shit. We need a bag, don't we?" Freddy started taking his shirt off.

"Freddy, do we have time to get it on in the car right now?" Bennie asked.

He rolled his eyes, pulled his shirt and then tee shirt off and tied the sleeves and neck opening of the tee shirt into knots, making a bag out of it. He pulled his shirt back on.

"Bennie girl, you let me do all the talking, okay. Just like we planned."

"I think we should rehearse some more, especially now that we don't have any bullets. That changes everything."

"I'm rehearsed out. We have to go now. In one hour there will be *two* guards on duty instead of one. We're ready. Now let's put on our clown masks. There might be a surveillance camera on the front door."

Freddy put on a black wig and was about to put on his mask.

"Can I have the black wig? Here's the blonde one," Bennie said, holding out the blonde wig.

"What difference does it make?"

"My face looks fat with blonde hair," she whined.

"No one is going to see your face, Bennie."

"Well, I don't want to *feel* that my face is fat." She pouted.

Freddy closed his eyes and silently counted to ten. "Okay, here's the black wig."

They put on their wigs and masks.

"I can't see too well. The eye-holes are not wide enough," Bennie complained.

Freddy pulled her mask off, angrily ripped larger eyes with his fingers and placed the mask back on Bennie.

"Anything else?" he groaned. Sweat cascaded off his face. His shirt was already soaked.

"Don't have a cow," she said. "I'm just making sure everything is right."

"Let's go," he said, slipping a pistol into each pocket of his jeans.

Freddy stepped out of the driver's door onto the sidewalk. He moved to the other side of the car, took hold of Bennie's arm, looked both ways and they crossed the street. They stopped twenty feet outside the swinging-glass doors of the bank.

"Remember, don't say my name and don't say anything unless you have to. Got that?" Freddy asked.

"Sure, Freddy. Just like we planned. I wish you'd let me bring in a cheat sheet."

He tugged on her arm and got a good head of steam to explode into the bank, almost dragging her as he raced along. They were going to fly into the bank running. Once in the door Freddy would pull a gun from each pocket--one in each hand--and yell, *Freeze, this is a stickup!*

Freddy pumped his legs faster. He held out his hand to push the door open as they charged. The camera would record only a blur of clowns. But the door didn't move. It was stuck solid and Bennie's momentum caused her to bump hard into Freddy. His head smacked against the door. He was knocked out instantly and fell to the sidewalk on top of Bennie.

CHAPTER EIGHTEEN

Freddy groaned and slowly began to stir. The web inside his head was thick with spiders.

"You're okay, sweetie," Bennie said. "I've brought you back to your apartment. After you were knocked out I pulled the car around and like dragged you onto the seat. Then I drove you here, although I don't mind telling you that the Honda doesn't drive nearly as nicely as my Porsche. Shifter is a tad bit sluggish, you know. That guy lives under you helped me get you in bed, although he like kept one of your pistols. He said he'd return it later, although I suspect you'll have to like *take* it from him. I didn't like the look on his face when he took it. Whatever. I parked the car around the block, you know, in case the cops come by, although I don't know why. I wore the clown mask all the way here. The opening you put in the eyes was super! The door to the bank door was locked because it's a banking holiday. Seems they have one every couple of months. Really. Can you believe that? The bank wasn't even open. I'm like totally bummed out. The sign said it would be open tomorrow. If you're feeling up to it, we could go back tomorrow. I put the bullets in my purse so we wouldn't forget them again."

Freddy shook his head to clear it, but the fog bank didn't lift. "Who *are* you?" he asked the human parrot.

"Freddy, it's Bennie. You hit your head hard on the bank door and even harder when you hit the concrete. You've been knocked out for hours."

"But who *are* you?" Freddy repeated.

"I'm your girlfriend, Freddy."

"There's no way I would have a girlfriend as ditzy as you. And why do you keep calling me Freddy?"

"You don't know who you are?"

"Bitch, if I knew who I was I surely wouldn't be asking an idiot like you." He rubbed his head.

The gleam in Bennie's eyes dissolved and she looked at him the way a puppy looks at its owner after a rocker goes over its tail.

The press release was issued within an hour of her death.

"Barbara Anne Drees, noted songwriter, divorced from Richard Dress, died today after a long bout with cancer. She is best known for penning the mega cross-over hit, *You Change Your Feelings (Like Makeup On Your Face)* that reached Number One on the Billboard charts three different times with three different artists, Bronk Allen, Cowboy Jones and the Hung Heifers, and Richard Drees and the Prairie Dogs. Ms. Drees had five Platinum albums and earned two Grammy nominations. She was a television star, appearing in three movies of the week, one opposite James Brolin. She is survived by a daughter, Lannie. Ms. Drees was forty-two. Funeral arrangements are incomplete, although it is known that Richard Drees and the Prairie Dogs will be performing a memorial tribute concert at the burial service."

"Lannie, I'm so sorry," Tim said into his cell phone. "If there is anything that I can do, please let me know. Richard's plane is having mechanical problems so he and I are catching the next commercial flight into L.A."

"Let me know the flight information and I'll meet you at the airport."

"Don't you have a million details to take care of?" he asked.

"Not really. Mom had months to plan her funeral. She left an eight-page list. And her lawyer is taking care of everything anyway. I meet with him tomorrow at three in the afternoon. Will you be here by then?"

"We'll be in late tonight."

"Great. Would you come with me to meet with the lawyer?"

"Sure," he said, but felt awkward not telling her what he knew and what was going to happen to her next.

Bennie let herself into Freddy's apartment even though she knew he'd be upset. He had said the extra key was only for emergencies, but if he didn't want her in his apartment when he wasn't there, why give her a key? She tossed her purse onto a coffee table in the living room and noticed that Freddy's black book was on the table. She picked it up and rummaged through it. She liked the way he wrote her down as *Ben. That is sooo cute.* She was about to close the calendar, but decided to check today's date. Oh boy. There was an entry for "*B*." She reasoned that she was "B" and was to meet "Ed" in room 308 of the Radisson Midtown Hotel at six o'clock.

She opened the journal under *E* and found "Ed". She had not met "Ed," but he was apparently a regular client of Freddy, as he had three stars scribbled next to his name. "Ed" liked the woman to be waiting naked in the bathroom with the television on. "Ed" would slip into the room, get naked and wait for the woman to come out of the bathroom. "Ed" liked to give and receive oral and loved to be spanked. He brought his own paddle.

Bennie looked at her watch. She had time to run home and bathe before she was to meet "Ed." *Freddy will be impressed that I took care of the business when he forgot and that I did this without him.*

"Where have you been, Bennie? Your mother and I have been worried sick." her father asked. He was your typical southern California, fortyish, rock promoter. He had a pot belly, ponytail and three-day-old stubble that masqueraded as a beard. He wore an open-collared silk shirt, tight jeans and had a thick gold chain around his neck.

"Dad, not now. I'm in a hurry," she said as she walked past him and into the hall leading to her bedroom.

"Tonight! You, me and your mom are going to talk." He padded over to the bar and poured himself a scotch. The boom was about to be lowered on Bennie and the plug pulled.

Bennie's face held a pound of makeup as she rode the elevator. *Why did Freddy call me an idiot? Does he appreciate all I do for him? Does he love me? He's never used that word. I'm going to ask him if he loves me, and if he doesn't say yes, I'm breaking up with him.*

She exited the elevator, found the room and entered. She flipped on the television, sauntered into the bathroom and undressed. She studied herself in the mirror, really noticing herself for the first time in years; she didn't like what she saw. The image in the mirror showed the ravages of drugs and bulimia. Her bones stuck out. She easily counted her ribs. There were dark sacks hanging from under her eyes. She got even more makeup from her purse and packed it under her eyes. She still did not like the image she saw in the mirror and almost started crying. She heard the door to the room open and then slam loudly. She heard "Ed" throwing his clothes against the wall and then heard the bed springs creak when he threw himself onto the bed. "Ed" grunted loudly, which was her cue. He was ready.

She opened the door. The lamps were turned off. Only the glow from the television lighted the room. She couldn't see "Ed," but could hear his breathing as she approached the bed.

"I want your willie," she said in a husky voice, playing the role. She climbed into the bed and slid down to where her head was even with his waist. "Ed" said, "I've only got thirty minutes, so let's hustle it up."

Bennie bolted upright and her hands jerked to her head.

"What's wrong?" "Ed" asked.

"Dad?"

"Oh shit! Bennie?"

Bennie screamed and screamed and saw herself being swallowed by her own mouth. Soon there was nothing. She was inside herself. And there was nothing there. She howled at the emptiness.

CHAPTER NINETEEN

In a bit of irony, Mel's route from Memphis International Airport to Ron Wells's apartment brought her by Graceland. As she drove by and wistfully eyed the gate, she overcame the urge to stop and pressed on in her claustrophobic, seemingly rubber band-powered rental car. Within minutes her car choked to a stop amid luxury imports and SUVs in the parking lot of a handsome condominium complex. Following Wells's faxed map and directions, she left the car and walked by wonderful water fountains and trellises thick with climbing jasmine, the sweet smell of which filled the air. She passed a uniformed gardener on his knees, concentrating on pulling even the tiniest weed from a flower bed of roses. She went by three freshly painted doors, stopped at number 137 and knocked.

The door opened quickly and Ron Wells engulfed her in a bear hug. "You're right on time. I can't tell you how happy I am to see you again," he said, as he led her through the door and into the living room. Wells had aged gracefully. He still carried his college weight, and his two-hour-a-day workouts were reflected in his strong shoulders and bulging shirt sleeves. His gray hair was as thick and silky as always.

Mel's attention turned to a small framed picture on the wall next to a stone fireplace. It was a black-and-white of her, her dad, and Uncle Ron. She was only three or four years old. Dad was holding her on his lap and Uncle Ron kneeled next to Dad on one knee, smiling lovingly at the little princess. She turned from the picture and caught Ron looking at her in the same prideful way.

"It's been only three years, Uncle Ron," Mel said. She took a chair opposite the fluffy sofa, where Ron eased down.

"Would you like some hot tea?" he offered. A steaming porcelain tea pot rested on a trivet in the center of the coffee table, surrounded by decorative cups, a creamer and a sugar dish.

"That would be great, but you didn't have to go through the trouble."

"No trouble for family. Any sugar?" he asked.

She nodded, "One."

"You always had a sweet tooth. It's amazing you've maintained such a lithe figure. Mel, it's great to see you, but what are you doing in Memphis?"

"I'm passing through. I have an assignment nearby, covering the Elvis festival in Moscow."

The spoon slipped from Ron's fingers and clamored onto the table. "Oh, I… see," he stammered.

"Does that upset you?" she asked.

"You dad wasted a lot of his life pursuing Elvis. He was killed near Moscow."

"Uncle Ron, I'm going to Moscow because I was assigned the job. I don't share Dad's obsession with finding the King." She wasn't being entirely truthful. She had always wondered what the area where her father had been killed looked like. She needed to see the spot as part of an explanation she knew she'd never understand. "You never did tell me exactly why he was going to Moscow that day," she said.

Ron took in a huge breath, let it out and then walked out of the room. Mel rose and went to other framed pictures on the wall. One brought a tear to her eye. Aunt Bessie, her dad's sister, who raised her after his death, Uncle Casey, Bessie's husband, now deceased, Uncle Ron and Mel were captured in a springtime pose at a country fair. Mel, eleven years old, had more cotton candy on her face than on the stick. The adults appeared giddy and childlike in their happiness. It struck Mel for the first time where she had learned to enjoy life and have fun. She had been engulfed by joy in her formative years. She wished that she had hugged Aunt Bessie and Uncle Casey more.

Ron came back into the living room carrying a wooden box about the size of a toaster. He placed it on the coffee table and they retook their seats.

"Mel, I want to apologize to you for not giving this to you earlier."

"What is it?" she asked, her eyes riveted on the box.

"It's your father's notes from his investigation of a bank robbery that he thought was perpetrated by Elvis. The investigation led him to Moscow the day he was killed."

"Why did you hold this information back?" she asked.

"I didn't think the investigation was headed anywhere."

"Okay."

"And I thought you'd figure out why he was fixated on finding Elvis."

"Uncle Ron, he told me the story hundreds of times."

"I know, but….." Ron said; his voice trailed of and his head drooped. He stared at the floor.

"But what?"

"He never told you the true story. He told you only what he thought you should hear."

"I don't understand."

"Mel, you were just a little girl. You had to be sheltered."

"I'm not a little girl anymore. Sheltered from what?"

"Everything he told you about supposedly seeing Elvis when he left the hospital right after you were born is true. But the story you've been told about the way your mother died isn't."

Mel's back stiffened and the air rushed from her lungs.

"I need to know," she whispered hoarsely.

"When Adam left the hospital after you were born your mother was the picture of perfect health. She was so happy. Aunt Bessie, Uncle Casey and I left so she could get some well-deserved rest. Shortly after we left, something went terribly wrong and Marie started bleeding profusely. An artery or vein had been nicked and nobody had noticed. No one was with Marie, so she pressed the button to summon a nurse. Elvis had been wheeled into the hospital shortly before, and the whole place was nuts. The nurse assigned to Marie's floor snuck over to the emergency room to get a view of Elvis. No one saw Marie's light flashing at the nurses' station. Marie, weak from the delivery and loss of blood, tried to get up and get help. She passed out and was later found at the foot of her bed. The bleeding was such a shock to her system that she went into cardiac arrest. A claim was made against the hospital. The settlement is what allowed Adam to stay at home with you all those years."

Tears streamed down Mel's face. "Was dad looking for Elvis to extract revenge?"

"Oh, sweetie, you know better than that. Your father would have never hurt *anyone*. Adam wanted to look Elvis in the eye and *tell* him what had happened. He wanted Elvis to know the grief that had been caused by his faking his death."

"So, indirectly, Elvis caused the death of *both* my mother and my father?"

"I was afraid you would look at it that way."

"Do *you* think Elvis faked his death and is still alive?" she asked.

Ron turned his eyes away from Mel, stared at the teapot for almost a minute, carefully measuring his words, and then looked back at Mel. "I don't know."

"Did you ever try to see what Dad was on to, or ever conduct any investigation yourself?" she asked.

"I didn't have the heart for it. Part of the reason I never told you any of this is I was afraid you'd waste your life chasing Elvis."

"Why have you changed you mind now?" she asked.

"You're a grown woman now and I finally realized that it's not my decision to make regarding what's in that box; it's yours."

"Any trail in that old box would be very cold and almost impossible to follow," she said. "I'm not going to be in the area very long, I'll take the box to my hotel and start reading."

"You're going to stay with me. I insist."

The aroma of fresh Virginia ham sizzling in a skillet roused Mel from her feather bed in the guest bedroom. She sat up, thumbed through a phone book on the dresser, made a couple of calls and then quickly picked fresh clothes from her suitcase and hopped into the shower. Minutes later she popped into the kitchen just as Ron was plucking a sheet of fresh homemade drop biscuits from the oven. Over-sized eggs bubbled in the frying pan.

"Smells wonderful, Uncle Ron, but you shouldn't have gone through so much trouble."

"Trouble? Trouble's what the IRS gets you into. Believe it or not, I fix a big breakfast every morning and eat leftovers for lunch. You slept like Sleeping Beauty. I was about to send troops up the stairs to rescue you from Mr. Sleep's clutches."

Mel yawned. "I stayed up until four reading Dad's notes."

"I figured you'd do as much."

"Do you think the Memphis Police Department still has the blood collected from the bank robbery scene?"

"I knew you'd ask that. Seems most of the stuff from the old files was scanned into computers years ago and tangible evidence on unsolved cases was tossed out."

"That's a shame, given technology today."

"It's possible the sample was misfiled and kept. I'll call an old friend who is still in the department."

"Whatever happened to the old Cadillac that was abandoned?" Mel asked.

"Went into the forfeiture compound. It may have been used by the department for a while and I assume it was eventually auctioned off to the public."

"It would really be an antique, but do you suppose you could try to find out who owns it now?"

Wells took the phone receiver from the wall and dialed one of his old friends in the MPD. A couple of minutes later he told Mel, "I've got a fax machine in the computer room. My buddy said he would fax me a list of the owners of the car from the time it was auctioned off until now. If the car was ever surrendered to a junk yard, we'll even have the name and address of the yard." He began piling slabs of ham, perfectly cooked eggs-over-easy and fluffy biscuits onto a platter. "We'll eat from the family plate."

Mel grinned at Ron. When she was a little girl, Aunt Bessie would conjure up delectable and obscene portions of breakfast food every Saturday morning. The victuals would be piled high on a giant platter. The family would stab at the plate with their forks and the tasty morsels would go straight into hungry mouths. Aunt Bessie called the platter the family plate.

Mel and Ron polished off a sizeable portion of the fare while chit-chatting about Mel's childhood. The ritual soon digressed into the same pattern established at Aunt Bessie's table. Fill a fork, eat its cargo, and then tell a tale and laugh. Mel was transported back to the easy and comfortable time of her youth.

The spell was interrupted when a loud beeping sound came from down the hall. "That's the fax machine," Ron said. He left the table, went to the machine and was back within seconds. He handed the printout to Mel.

"This is interesting," Mel said. "The car's had only one owner since the auction."

"Nothing unusual about that, Mel. A lot of people love those old cars. Could be a collector," Ron commented.

"What's interesting is that the owner of the car lives in Moscow, Tennessee."

CHAPTER TWENTY

Mel Vaughn guided the rental into the driveway of the Williston, Tennessee address. She turned off the ignition, but the car sputtered on and belched for a few seconds. It was the same house but looked nothing like Adam Vaughn had described in his notes. Weeds lined the walkway; chips of paint peeled away from the walls and gutters dangled. The sun was shinning brightly, but when Mel climbed the blistered steps to the porch, she half-expected bolts of lightning to fill the sky, as though the house was a movie set for a haunted mansion. The button for the door bell dangled from a thin line protruding from the wall next to the door. She nervously pushed the button, expecting to get shocked, and was relieved when she didn't.

The door opened and Mel almost recoiled.

"Yes?" the old woman asked, seemingly confused.

"I'm looking for Abby Long," Mel said.

"That would be me and you must be Melissa. Come on in."

Mel was shocked. Her father had described a stunningly beautiful woman. This woman's appearance was almost hideous. Abby Long's eye lids drooped, her face was severely wrinkled, her nose seemed as though it was about to fall from her face, her skin was weather-beaten and her breasts sagged tremendously.

Abby led Mel into the living room where the shrunken heads still hung from the ceiling. They were now caked with dust and tangled with spider webs.

"Your father must have described me to you. You seemed surprised to see that I look like this."

"I apologize if I was rude," Mel offered.

"I wasn't insulted. I've gotten used to the way I look."

"What happened? Dad said you were the most beautiful woman he'd ever met."

"I didn't know when to stop. I had more than one too many plastic surgeries. There's very little left to keep my nose on my face and the muscles to which breasts attach are gone. I spent too much time in the tanning booth." Abby shrugged her shoulders. "What can I do for you?"

"I read dad's notes carefully, but had some follow-up questions."

"Honey, it's been over twenty years since that bank robbery."

"You mentioned the distinctive voice and the cologne the robber had; is there anything else you can remember?"

"And the ring."

"What ring?" Mel asked, surprised.

"The robber had on latex gloves, but a ring on his right ring finger bulged under the latex."

"Did you recognize the ring?"

"Not at the time."

"What do you mean?" Mel asked.

"I'll show you. I'll be right back," Abby said and walked out of the room.

Mel studied the heads and thought that a couple of them were moving slightly. She spied Uncle Charlie, looked away and then jerked her head back at Uncle Charlie. *Had he blinked?*

"Here," Abby said, as she pushed an old *Life* magazine at Mel that was opened to a picture in its middle.

Elvis was playing his guitar and he had a whopper of a ring on his hand. It had a giant E formed by a mass of diamonds set in yellow gold.

"Do you think that was the ring?" Mel asked.

"Could have been," Abby answered. "It was that size and had bumps that may have formed an E. Remember it was hidden under latex gloves."

"Abby, have you ever been to Moscow?"

"I go to the Elvis festival every year. It's just down the road from here."

"Have you ever seen anyone there you thought was Elvis?"

"Honey, most of those impersonators do Elvis better than Elvis did Elvis."

"Have you ever met any one there who you thought might be the bank robber?"

"Come to think of it, a couple of years ago I bumped into this old guy who was working in one of the booths. It made me smile just seeing him. He had a beard and an old hat pulled over his ears. Hearing him talk turned my head."

CHAPTER TWENTY-ONE

Mel reviewed her father's notes on Marie Fulgar yet again and still remained totally confused. She got out of the car and approached the entrance gate to the mansion and was swiftly met by a congenial, but armed guard; an Uzi hung from his shoulder. Mel explained that she had an appointment with Miss Fulgar and was cheerfully led by the guard past a bountiful garden teeming with flowering plants into a courtyard dominated by a magnificent Italian water fountain and a marble and quartzite waterfall. The fountain brimmed with exotic strains of fish that looked prehistoric. The courtyard held numerous pieces of bronze and marble sculpture from around the world. A butler dressed in tails met them at the door and escorted Mel through a great hall with an arched ceiling. The walls of the hall bore original art from the great masters and famous modern artists. The butler deposited Mel in the study, which was really a cavernous room with antique books filling shelves on three of the four walls. The fourth wall looked out on an indoor pool. The pool was Olympic-sized and appeared to be trimmed in gold filigree.

Mel was taking in the view when a voice from behind her interrupted her trance, "Miss Vaughn, so nice to see you." Mel turned around and her eyes took in a truly gorgeous woman who was in her early forties. The woman approached and extended her hand, "Marie Fulgar Kamall."

Mel shook Marie's hand and could not hide the look of shock on her face.

"I see you were expecting the person your father met years ago."

"I don't understand," Mel said.

"Several years ago I was referred to a medical clinic in England that was doing experimental weight reduction surgery. They performed their miracle and I soon lost over two hundred pounds. I later trained for a flight attendant's job with Pan Am and on a flight from New York to Istanbul, I met the sheik. It was, as they say, love at first sight and within the year we were married. As you may have read, I was unfortunately widowed two years later when Sheik Kamall's private jet crashed on takeoff from Oman. I got over seven hundred million dollars in my settlement with his other wife."

"I apologize for my reaction," Mel said.

"It's quite natural and I've experienced it before."

"So you run the famous Kamall Foundation?" Mel asked. She had read about its vast endeavors and was impressed.

"Yes. We try to help unwed mothers all over the world. We provide health care, food and shelter and job training. We donated over fifty million dollars last year."

"You could live anywhere in the world, why here in Memphis?"

"I have other homes in California, Florida, France, Turkey and Saudi Arabia. I travel to each of them at least once a year, but I stay here a lot because I love the chicken fried steak," Marie said and laughed.

"Have you had occasion to think about what we discussed on the phone?" Mel asked.

"Miss Vaughn, I don't think there is anything I can add that I didn't tell your father. I'm sorry.

"Well, thank you for your time," Mel said and started for the door. "I think I can find my way out."

"Wait a second," Marie said. There is one thing, but it had nothing to do with the bank robbery. A couple of years ago I went to an Elvis festival outside of Memphis."

"In Moscow?"

"Yes, and there was a guy there that was working one of the booths. His hair was short and gray and he had a beard, but he reminded me of the bank robber, the way he moved."

"Did you get his name?" Mel asked.

"I'm afraid not."

Mel decided to go straight to Moscow when she left Fulgar's estate. She had been on the road less than an hour when she realized she had not eaten. She felt hungry so she decided to take pot luck and turned into the gravel parking lot of a diner a few miles out of Moscow. A large neon sign announced that the Elvis Diner was open. She chuckled at the name of the diner, extricated herself from the expense-account-compliant piece of rolling turd she was droving, avoided muddy puddles dotting the grass-covered parking lot, ambled past a Jaguar convertible and made it through the yellowed, glass front door of the diner.

She quickly surmised that the Elvis Diner deserved to be featured in a *National Geographic* foldout; it was a classic 1950s diner. A bar counter covered with white, spotless Formica spanned the entire width of the long narrow room. Behind the bar and against the wall was a stainless steel counter on which rested gleaming mixers, dispensers, fountains and shelves full of plates, bowls and cups and glasses. An opening in the wall allowed passage of food from the kitchen. Chromed barstools with red vinyl seat covers stood at attention along the bar, spaced out like well-trained sentinels. Clear, round glass pie and cake covers presided over enormous, multi-layered apple, blueberry and banana pies with flaky crust and spilling with stuffing. A huge, gleaming Wurlitzer jukebox anchored one side-wall. A string of small, red vinyl booths surrounded white Formica tables and lined the wall opposite the bar.

Mel ambled to the bar and tossed her purse on it. A waitress with blonde curls dropping from under her baseball cap sporting a large orange "T" finished folding a dish cloth and approached. The waitress produced a hand-written, laminated menu from under the counter and plopped in front of Mel. The menu was brief; it listed less than ten items.

"Meat loaf ain't turned green, yet, though the train is nearing the station. The other daily special, the 'tater stew will make your tummy smile. You need some time, hon?" the waitress asked.

Mel pushed the menu across the counter to the waitress. "I'll have the stew."

"Good choice." The waitress pivoted and hollered to the opening to the kitchen, "One stew, and make sure it's kilt!"

Just then the phone in Mel's purse rang, so she grabbed the bag and yanked out the phone. "Mel Vaughn, here."

"Mel, it's Lolita."

"Hey, Lo. You find out anything about that name I gave you?"

"Do puppies like they's momma? Migel Matranga, the guy you wanted me to check out is a doctor who graduated from Vanderbilt University. Practices general medicine in Moscow, Tennessee. A real motor in Moscow. He's been president of the Chamber of Commerce for five years and is active in all the usual rural rah rah stuff: Elks, Kiwanis, Knights and American Legion. His funeral will be a six-copper. No record. A clean, All-American citizen. Probably pays his taxes early. Why did you want me to check this guy out?"

"He owns an old Cadillac."

"Oh, okay, girlfriend, if you run across a guy who owns an old Edsel, has a million in the bank and one foot on a banana peel next to a grave, let me know," Lolita purred.

"Bye, Lo." Mel smiled and snapped her phone back and noticed that the waitress was leaning over the bar, practically hovering over Mel's head.

"What was that?" the waitress asked, with a bewildered look on her face.

"Beg your pardon."

"What was that?" the waitress repeated, with the same astonished look on her face.

"That's between me and my assistant."

"Not the conversation, hon, that thing you had by your ear."

Mel almost laughed. Even in rural Tennessee people surely had cell phones. "My… phone."

"I thought that was one," the waitress said and then pulled her hand up by her head, pointing her thumb over her shoulder to a sign that read: NO CELL PHONES ALLOWED!

"Sorry," Mel said.

"If I thought you had seen the sign and used the phone, I'd have to do something drastic, like get the police to issue you a citation or worse, change your order to the meatloaf."

"Thanks. Actually, it's a good policy."

"I know, I invented it," the waitress said.

"The owner must have gotten a lot of complaints to establish such a policy," Mel said.

"Just one."

"What?" Mel asked.

"Just one complaint."

"Oh."

"From my mother."

"Well, that *one* would be enough."

"Darn right. She said she didn't need the distraction when she was chowing down. Besides, she holds the mortgage. Giving her the red-ass wouldn't be smart."

"So you're the owner?"

"Me and the mother-bank. The joint has been in the family almost sixty years. I thought about selling it a couple years ago. But what would I do then? I can't type and hooking's still illegal."

A bowl of steaming potato stew appeared in the opening and the waitress brought it to Mel.

"Pretty clever naming the diner after the festival," Mel said.

"Heck, that ain't how it got named. Elvis used to come fishing in the area all the time. He ate here every morning. When he answered the roll up yonder we put his name out front. We like to think that the festival got named after the diner. What'll you have to drink? We make the best tea this side of Buckingham Palace."

"Tea's fine."

"You drink that and if you get in the mood, we'll sing God Save the Queen and go find us a crumpet to…., ah, whatever it is you do with a crumpet," the waitress said.

She then reached under the counter and a glass and pitcher appeared and she expertly poured. A pay phone on the wall at the far end of the diner began ringing and she sped off, almost leaving a vapor trail.

Mel tasted the stew and found it terrific. Onions, bell pepper, garlic and parsley swam in the savory gravy. She picked up the glass of tea, brought it to her mouth and her eyes wandered. She noticed for the first time that two other people were in the restaurant. A handsome, clean-cut man about twenty-five years old sat at the bar only three stools from her. He wore a denim shirt and jeans and topsider shoes. He would have fit right in on the campus of Amherst at a Young Republican's Club social. He too was enjoying the stew.

An old gentleman occupied a booth in the corner, near the jukebox. He had long, gray hair and a scraggly beard. His clothes were ragged, but clean. He was enjoying a coffee and a plate of chicken fried steak and a mountain of mashed potatoes, smothered with white gravy. He wore a metal collar and was reading an old and battered magazine.

"Lot's of atmosphere, huh?" The question came at Mel from her side. She turned her head back. The young man seated at the bar grinned. He had a model's smile with blonde hair and piercing dark eyes. Mel was instantly attracted to him.

"Takes you back a few years," Mel said, searching for more words, but none could be found. An uneasy silence ensued.

"I read about the festival and decided to see what all the fuss was about," the man said. His smile showed perfectly straight, gleaming white teeth.

"If the festival is a bust, it was worth it coming here just for the stew," Mel said.

"This place isn't quite perfect. I can't find the easel," he said.

"A what?" Mel asked.

"The easel on which Norman Rockwell surely painted this place," he said. "I swear I saw this place on the cover of an old *Saturday Evening Post*."

Mel popped a spoonful of stew towards her mouth, but mostly missed. Sauce dripped down her chin onto the counter. She noticeably blushed and looked back at the young man, but he was not looking at her and hadn't seen her clumsy moment.

The waitress hung up the phone and stepped to the guy's spot. "Anything else, hon? Rolaids? A quarter to call 9-1-1?"

The man glanced at Mel. "I'm afraid this is my second bowl." He bore a sheepish grin.

"Hon, you are so far off the record that no local would be impressed," the waitress said. "There's a guy who comes in here for breakfast and eats two bowls *and* grits *and* eggs. A ginsling like you needs to stoke it up a bit to achieve any level of notoriety."

"What's a ginsling?" he asked.

The waitress put her hands on her hips and blew air through her bangs with pursed lips. "It's a word you can say out loud in front of your momma and without having to go to confession, but if there were ginslings in the military, they'd have to salute privates. They're the bottom of the totem pole of life. Slightly above amoeba status."

"Ouch," he playfully retorted. Mel laughed.

"All visitors to the area start out as ginslings," the waitress explained.

Mel had the feeling that the waitress had similarly toyed with many a visitor.

"What do I have to do to graduate to the next level?" the man asked.

"Used to be you had to marry your first cousin, you know, when in Rome do as the Romans, but since most ginslings don't travel with their first cousins, we lowered the bar. All you've got to do is spend fifty bucks in town, or buy a festival pin. You then get automatically promoted to honorary local status.

The guy beamed. "My first cousin is so ugly, when she was a baby, her parents used her as a hood ornament on a rusted out Edsel. Won first prize in an ugliest car contest, three years running."

The waitress chuckled. “Pie’s from a seventy-five-year-old recipe. It’s free today to all blonde-haired ginslings.”

He patted his taut belly. “Thanks, but the only thing I could handle now is the check.”

The waitress produced a bill from her pocket whereupon the guy planted a ten dollar bill on the counter and got up to leave.

“Debra Ann, could you get me a refill on the tea?” the old guy at the booth called out in a metallic voice. A piercing, screeching sound rang out loudly from the old guy’s voice box. The strange noise came at them from behind, causing the young guy and Mel to turn in unison. The old man held a finger to a metal box affixed to his throat and thumped the box. The noise stopped.

“Sorry to interrupt,” the metallic voice boomed in monotone. “It just goes off sometimes.”

“No problem,” the young guy said. He nodded to Mel and headed out the door.

The waitress strolled over to the old guy’s booth carrying a pitcher. “Jessie, you be careful now. Too much of this stuff and you’ll blow out that antique prostate of yours that the doctor loves to shake hands with.”

“Debra Ann, I love it when you talk dirty, but mind your own damn business,” the old guy retorted through his voice box.

The waitress poured his glass full and slipped back to the counter.

“Hon,” the waitress said, “if you and that young hunk who just left here ever meet in a dry forest, call the Forest Service immediately.”

“Why?”

“The sparks you two set off would start a fire on wet grass.”

“Debra Ann? My name is Mel Vaughn.”

“Damn, girl. I thought you’d changed your name since that time a long time ago in a far away age when you answered that phone in violation of diner rules with that very same name.”

“Debra Ann, there’s not much gets by you.”

“Nothing I can smoke, eat, drink or chew and what’s inedible.”

“I’m in town for the festival and I’m a writer.”

“A writer? Hell, hon, nobody’s perfect. Even I made a mistake a few years ago, or so I’m told.”

“I’m going to be doing a story on the festival. It wouldn’t hurt for the diner and you to be featured in the story. You seem colorful enough,” Mel said.

"A story, huh? What if the diner gets all famous and groupies start hanging out. Next thing you'll know, Visa will be wanting to do a commercial. You know, 'Come to the Elvis Diner hungry, but bring your Visa card, because the Elvis Diner don't take no American Express,' or some kind of babble like that. Course, I don't take no kind of plastic here. I want that stuff what's got a dead person's picture on it and the full backing of the government. They can print the stuff as long as they got paper."

"I take that to mean that you'll be interviewed for a story. Maybe a few pictures," Mel said.

"Heck, I ain't due to the beauty parlor until after the festival is over," the waitress said and patted her hair.

"Debra Ann, take it from a city girl, you look good enough now to go shopping on Fifth Avenue."

"That where the hookers hang out?" Debra Ann asked.

"The ladies of the night hang out a few blocks off Times Square."

"Ladies? Who said anything about ladies? I meant boys of the night. Sometimes a woman's gotta do what a woman's gotta do, if you get my drift."

"Oh."

"Just kidding, hon. Debra Ann's got a local fan club. And of course, I'll give an interview and all." She plucked at her side and pulled on the waistband of her hose that had bunched up.

"Where's a good hotel?" Mel asked.

"There ain't none in town. Mom has a few rooms she lets out, but she's full. People that stay with her have been staying with her for years. Everyone stays in Memphis, Germantown or at the mom-and-pop on Highway 57. I recommend staying in Memphis."

"I'll take the check, Debra Ann."

"There's no charge for big city reporters. It's a special today." Debra Ann plucked the check from her apron pocket and tore it in half.

A pan crashed to the floor in the kitchen and clanging reverberated through out the diner. Debra Ann didn't jump or react in any way.

"Who's in the kitchen?" Mel asked, twisting her neck to get a look into the kitchen.

"That's Nestor. He's been dropping pans here for over thirty years. Another ten and he'll be an expert."

"Will we be able to talk to him for the article?"

"Suit yourself, although Nestor's a pint short of making a gallon. Some of our horses have more brains than he does."

"I appreciate the information, Debra Ann," Mel said as she pushed herself from the counter. "I'm going to use the bathroom on my way out. I'll be back in a few days."

"Mel, even though this is Tennessee, we don't normally announce we're going to the potty, especially an indoor potty and in mixed company," she said as she nodded at the old guy in the booth.

"Sorry."

Debra Ann laughed loudly as she picked up Mel's plate.

The old guy at the booth shook his head and buried his head in the newspaper that he was now reading.

CHAPTER TWENTY-TWO

Mel switched on her cell phone as she stepped towards her car and the phone chirped, indicating a message in her voice mail. She speed-dialed her message service and punched in the number that Uncle Ron had left. She pressed SEND and Ron's phone rang within seconds.

"Uncle Ron, it's Mel."

"How are things out in the country?" he asked.

"Different, for sure. I just had lunch at this absolutely fabulous diner outside of Moscow."

"The Elvis Diner."

"Yeah."

"That place is legendary for its stew," he said.

"I know you didn't call me to talk about my lunch, Uncle Ron."

"Mel, I've got some great news about the evidence file in that old bank robbery. A friend of mine found the file stuck to another old file. The evidence had not been thrown away."

"Great! What was in it?" Mel asked. She unlocked the door and slid behind the wheel.

"There is a blood sample collected from the bank and a partial print from the car. Actually, the partial print was collected from the passenger door handle. I guess I forgot about that."

"Is there anyone who could run the partial print to see if it picks up a match?" she asked.

"Mel, I'm afraid there's not enough of the print to run against the data base."

"Is there enough of a print to compare against a suspected print?"

"I don't follow you," Ron said.

"Could you see if you can find a print of Migel Matranga and get someone to compare it to the passenger door print? He's the guy who bought the car used in the robbery at police auction. He lives in Moscow, Tennessee. And by the way, humor me. If I remember right, there is a famous fingerprint of Elvis that was taken when he registered for a gun in Tennessee. Could you get hold of that print and check it also with the partial found on the door?"

"I'll try," Ron said. He was concerned that Mel would become obsessed with finding Elvis the way her father had. "Do you want me to do anything with the blood sample?"

"Let's see how the print comes back. If it's a positive, I'll try to get a DNA sample from Matranga, or find a hair from Elvis. What the heck, Uncle Ron, could you try to get a hair sample of Elvis from a dealer and run a DNA check between it and the blood?"

"Mel, even though the robbery happened a long time ago, what you're doing could be dangerous."

"I'll be careful, I promise. Call me when you get some information about the print."

Looking into the car's mirror, Mel spread on fresh lipstick and then cranked the engine and got the lame thing moving. She nursed the car over and through ruts and out of the parking lot and steamed onto the state highway.

It was a magnificent Tennessee day. Sun-drenched, open fields blanketed with the greenest grass Mel had ever seen seemed to vibrate under dancing shadows etched by high-flying, wispy clouds. Trees strained under the weight of thickly packed leaves that swayed in a gentle breeze. She rolled down her window and took in a deep breath. The air smelled of freshly cut grass and hints of manure and lilacs. She fumbled with the radio dial but gave up when all she could find were country stations.

As she rounded a sharp curve she was surprised by a procession of a tractor pulling a lo-boy trailer followed by a line of pickup trucks coming in the other lane towards her. She hit the brakes, skidded to a stop and then pulled off onto the shoulder. As the tractor came along side of her, its driver stopped and pulled off his cowboy hat and nodded to her.

"Howdy, ma'am."

"What's going on?" Mel asked, as she glanced at the trailer the man was pulling. In the middle of the trailer was a large, horned bull. The animal seemed frozen, as none of its parts appeared to be moving.

"It's a funeral."

"For the cow?"

"Bull. He's a bull. Old Thunderbolt succumbed to a jealous rival two days ago. The other bull didn't want to share his missus. There was a ruckus and Thunderbolt took a horn in the scrotum and bled to death."

"How can he stand up like that without falling?"

"The taxidermist stuffed him and he's bolted to the floor of the trailer."

"I see."

"Got metal rods through his legs. He ain't going anywhere I don't take him."

"Where are you taking him?"

"There's a rodeo this side of Memphis tonight. Thunderbolt is usually the star in the show. I get an appearance fee with the bull and the contract doesn't say one way or the other that he's got to be alive."

"I see."

"After the show, we'll have a service and Thunderbolt will become a permanent display in the arena's restaurant, being famous and all. I'm getting a thousand dollars for him." The driver of the truck behind Thunderbolt blew its horn.

"Gotta go," the cowboy said, and just like that the tractor pulled off.

The headlights on the trucks were illuminated, so Mel paid her respects by waiting until the last truck had passed her before continuing on.

About a mile down the road she came upon a truly different sight. On the opposite side of the road were two enormous tents erected in a rolling field of shimmering green grass and atop the tents were spires. Atop the spires were large, white flags flapping in the breeze. One flag was emblazoned with red letters spelling ELVIS FESTIVAL; the other read ELVIS LIVES. A couple of pickup trucks were parked at the open ends of the tents and several people were milling about lowering kegs out of one truck.

On the right side of the road, across from the tented area, about twenty booths had been set up in a clearing. The flaps of the booths were lowered, except that the flap of one booth was up. A makeup-covered clown wearing a large cowboy hat with a two-foot brim fought with helium-filled balloons that were being pushed about by a stiffening breeze.

Mel noticed that a red, heart-shaped balloon had come free and was rapidly ascending against the cerulean sky. She pulled into the grassy parking lot of the booths, got out of the car and started towards the clown. The air smelled alive with scents of flowers as grass crunched under her feet.

"Hi there," Mel said. The clown was crouching and facing away from her with his face close to the valve of the container. The clown, surprised, turned quickly.

"Hello, young lady," the clown said in a high-pitched, helium voice.

"Didn't mean to surprise you," Mel apologized.

"That's okay, but I'm not open yet. We don't actually start until tomorrow, although there's a reception at the town hall tonight."

"I don't want to buy anything just yet. I stopped because I was curious. Why are you dressed in your outfit if the festival doesn't start until tomorrow?"

"I'll sell a few of these at the reception in town, but mostly I'll blow up balloons by mouth and make them into dogs, hats, animals, that sort of thing. You're a tourist?"

"Kinda. I'm a reporter for one of the tabloids. I'm covering the festival."

"You didn't look familiar. Ever been in these parts before?"

"It's my first festival."

"Look, I'd love to chat," the clown said, "but I'm sort of rushed right now. I've got to finish up here and get set up in town."

"I understand. Thanks for the conversation," Mel said and started for her car, but then decided to walk across the road to visit the tent area. As she made her way to the road through the booths' parking area, she angled toward the closest tent. When she got to the shoulder, she noticed something in the weeds on her side of the road a few yards down. Curious, she walked along the shoulder toward the object. As she was almost to the thing, she was startled by the horn and wind of an eighteen wheeler passing on the road within inches of her. She lost her balance and fell to the ground onto her buttocks. When she realized what had happened she was embarrassed. She shook her head and started to get up, but saw that she was almost on top of the thing in the weeds. She brushed away the weeds with her hand and immediately gasped. She recoiled and tried to get up to run, but all she could manage was to claw backwards in the grass. She somehow made it to her feet and turned, stumbling onto the roadway. A horn blared and tires screeched. She froze.

A car swerved and missed her, again by inches. Stunned, Mel aimlessly made her way back to the clown's stand. He saw Mel as she stumbled up and he vaulted over the counter.

"Are you okay, lady?"

"I need to sit."

The clown put his hands on her hips and set her on top of the counter.

"You look like you've just seen a ghost," he said.

"I did."

"Can I get you a cold drink?"

"That's alright. I'm fine now." Mel pointed to the shoulder of the road. "That thing on the shoulder, what is that?"

"That's a cross. When people lose a loved one to a car accident they sometimes put up a cross with the loved one's name on it and the date of the accident."

"Who put that one up?" Mel asked.

"Why do you ask?"

"The cross has my father's name and the date he died on it."

Fifteen minutes later, Mel's nerves had settled and she steered her car out of the grass parking area and onto the road. But no sooner had she done so, she heard a flop, flop and the steering of the car pulled to the right. She pulled onto the shoulder and got out of the car to investigate. The right front tire was flat.

"What next?" she asked, frustrated. She then made her way to the trunk and opened it. She was angry to see that the spare was also flat. She slammed the trunk and heard something behind her. She turned to see a sleek Jaguar convertible with its top down slowly come to a stop on the shoulder.

The young man from the Elvis Diner grinned from behind the wheel. The sun bounced off his thick blonde hair and the sunglasses perched on top of his head glistened. He turned off the Jag's engine and smoothly hopped out of the convertible.

"My specialty, a lady in need," he said as he approached Mel.

"I'm afraid the spare is also flat. I got this from the rental car company from hell."

Mel opened the trunk and the young man peered in.

"Flatter than a dime," he noted. It looks like we've got limited options here. We can take off the right front tire and run it into town, which is only a mile down the road according to that sign." Mel glanced at where he was pointing and a sign read: MOSCOW 1 MILE.

"Or, I can take you into town and drop you at a service station and you can give the grease monkey your keys and he can come out here and get the tire and fix it. Some places have the equipment to fix it with a plug while it's still on the car."

"No use getting all sweaty taking the tire off if it may not even be necessary. Let's just go into town and drop me at a station. I would appreciate the lift."

They turned towards the Jag when the clown stopped his dated El Camino on the road nest to them. "You need any help?" the clown offered.

"No thanks. We've got it under control," Mel answered back. The clown nodded and went on.

The young man walked Mel to the passenger side and opened the door for her. She slid onto the supple leather seat. "Thanks," she said as he gently closed the door.

He scooted around the front of the car and eased behind the steering wheel. "My name's Mark," he said, as he cranked the powerful engine. He shifted into drive and pulled from the soft shoulder; the tires squealed when they hit the pavement.

"I'm Melissa." The freshening wind from around the windshield felt marvelous against her face and the sense of speed gave her a rush. She blinked into the wind, as her hair whipped over the seat rest.

"What are you doing in these parts?" he asked, stealing a glance at Mel.

"I'm a tabloid reporter covering the festival."

"Looking for flying saucers?" he asked.

"If I could find one being flown by Elvis, now that would be perfect."

He laughed and Mel liked the way he did it, unreservedly. They rounded a corner and were at the city limits of Moscow where an old-fashioned service station stood on the right side of the road. Mark pulled in and ran over a small rubber hose which caused a bell to ding, ding. He stopped the car at a full-service pump.

"I saw a restroom sign on the side of the station. I'll go there first," Mel announced and then realized that maybe she indeed had a problem of announcing in the presence of men that she needed to use the bathroom.

"I'll line up someone to help with the tire and fill my tank," Mark said.

Mel got out of the car, walked across the concrete pad and around the corner of the station building. She entered the door of the restroom and was relieved to find that it was clean. She locked the door behind her, hiked down her pants and perched on the toilet. She then noticed and read unflattering, rhyming verses referring to someone named Lillie, complete with a phone number. She finished her business and washed at the lavatory. She started out the door, but decided she needed to freshen her makeup. She pulled a small compact from her purse and then put the purse on the lavatory counter. Two minutes later she checked her face in the mirror, zipped the purse, threw its strap over her shoulder and opened the door. She looked down for her first two steps, but a blur grabbed her attention. She glanced up to find a gun at her nose, a gun being held by the clown she had seen at the balloon booth. Startled, she stumbled backwards through the open door of the restroom, tripped and then fell. She reached out to grab something, anything, but missed the lavatory. She hit her head on the toilet on the way down. She saw a red, bulbous nose, rouge-colored cheeks and a painted smile right before she lost consciousness.

CHAPTER TWENTY-THREE

The five-hundred-dollar-per-hour lawyer's office was nestled in the San Fernando Valley, just off Van Nuys Boulevard, not far from the Van Nuys Airport. The lawyer liked the location because of its proximity to the Lear Jet 60 that he kept at the airport. Of course, like most adult males with expensive toys, even though he had a pilot's license, he hardly ever used the plane. Mostly, he loaned it out to the various television, movie and recording stars he represented, who in turn hired their own pilots. The jet was a marketing tool, an effective magnet for new clients.

The sleek building had cream-colored, stucco walls, a slate roof and fifty-thousand dollar bronze front doors on which were etched the faces of long dead famous actors and actresses. The building had no sign, but did have a redwood board with the number of the street address etched in it in tasteful gold lettering. The structure was one-story, approximately six thousand square feet and had three conference rooms, four secretarial offices, a spa room, a workout room, a juice room and two waiting rooms. One waiting room was for those whom the lawyer tagged, screen media clients. The other waiting room was for music clients. The designations, however, sometimes confused the receptionist. She didn't know what to do with first-time clients who were both active in the movies and had singing careers. Barbara Drees, who had fallen into the bi-career category was simply brought in through a private rear entrance and went straight to one of the conference rooms. The lawyer's office was two thousand square feet and had a netted driving range, three putting holes, a soundproofed gunshot range and a basketball goal. He never met clients in his office; he always met them in one of the conference rooms.

Tim Reed and Lannie Drees parked in the private lot behind the structure, between a Rolls and a Ferrari. They nodded to the two chauffeurs who were waiting, and then passed between two rows of colorful planters, ablaze with flowers, lining the walkway to the private rear entrance. Tim pressed the buzzer for the door that was really Buster Keaton's nose. The bronze door opened and a very pretty young lady wearing a designer dress and high-heels escorted them over continuous-pile, wool carpet straight to the Jungle Room, conference room number two, where they each took a seat at an enormous table.

The walls of the conference room were covered in aggressive, hand-painted fabric with various shades of yellow, orange, brown and green, arranged in lines heading in every direction over a tan base. Museum-quality paintings hung from the walls, as did the heads of exotic animals that had been bagged by the lawyer's friends. An original Rodin rested in one corner. The jungle colors of the wall were matched by yellow and green, checkered fabric on walnut chairs that had ivory arm rails and various forged, brass animal heads as feet. Eighteen-karat pencil holders and coasters dotted a single, oversized slab of carved granite that functioned as the conference table. Two crystal telephones sat on the tables. A waterfall cascaded out of one wall over genuine lava rock from Hawaii. Butterfly Koi swam in pools at its base. The falling water's soothing sounds were complimented by new age elevator music coming from speakers hidden behind the fabric on the walls. A ten-foot movie screen hung unrolled from the ceiling; a hand-built Japanese projector hidden under a multicolored floral arrangement made of blown glass by an artist in Italy.

"Can I get you a latte, imported water, anything?" the receptionist asked.

"We're fine," Lannie replied.

No sooner had the receptionist cleared the door, than the tornado hit. Stephen Greenbaum, wearing a crisp Armani suit and tie, custom shirt and Gucci shoes floated into the room. He had come a long way from anchoring his night school class at Cal Northern School of Law. He had on a futuristic headset and was talking into the microphone. "What do you mean he says the song is too *feminine*? Nusbaum, I don't give a shit if he has to have a sex change operation, tell the bastard he's under contract to record the song....Okay, I understand....Okay, kiss his ass if you have to, baby, blow him if you have to, but get him to the studio. Bye, I've got another call..... Hello, Caleb....No, I didn't get the paperwork...What do you mean it's in the mail? You dumb schmuck, ever hear of a fax machine, email, FedEx? I don't care.

If I don't have the paperwork within the hour, Ringo's signing with Arista, baby. Bye, I've got another call."

Greenbaum clicked off his phone with a switch on his belt and turned to Lannie. He gave her a half-hearted hug, as though she had some unmentionable disease that he wanted to avoid, and gave her a peck on the cheek that was more sound and show than kiss. "Lannie, sweetie, it's *so* nice to see you. Terrible, terrible thing about Barb. The world has lost its poet."

The receptionist stuck her head in the door. "Stephen, Cher's on the line and she says she just has to talk to you now, or she'll die."

"Princess, tell her that I'm tied up and will call her within the hour. If she complains, joke with her and tell her we know the name of a great mortuary."

"Mr. Greenbaum...," Lannie said.

"Lannie, Lannie. I'm practically family; sweetie, call me Stephen."

"Stephen, this is my friend, Tim Reed, I hope it's okay for him to be here."

The receptionist stuck her head in the door again. "Stephen, Arnold is on the phone and says he's just read the most fantastic script for an action piece and needs to talk to you. Says he's interested in *zec* producing with Sly as the lead."

"Princess, please hold my calls, except if the vet calls about my cat, and bring me the Drees file on my desk. Tell Arnold I'll get back with him within the hour, and that I read the script and its more Van Dam than Sly. Now, Lannie, sweetie, let's see. Oh, yeah, if you consent to Tim being here, it's fine with me. He should probably be here, anyway."

Lannie turned to Tim, who shrugged his shoulders.

Princess walked in with the Drees file and placed it on the conference room table in front of Greenbaum.

"Lannie, sweetie, as you know, I've represented Barb for twelve years. Handled all her affairs. She looked lovely, by the way. Thought they laid her out splendidly and Richard's band never sounded better. Anyway, sweetie, I've got some news you will probably thinks is great, and then some not so great news. Two pieces of bad news, actually."

"Stephen, can we just get to it," Lannie said. She was still looking at Tim and wondering why Greenbaum said Tim should be there.

Greenbaum opened the file folder and fumbled with some of the papers. “Barb left an estate of one hundred and eighty-three million dollars.”

“Holy crap!” Lannie exclaimed.

“That’s net after all taxes and debts, except for the one item I’ll explain in a minute.

“I knew mom had money, but I never dreamed it would be that much.”

“It’s not all cash, sweetie. Some of it is the value of the houses. Some of it is stock. Most of it is the value of future royalties on songs in her record label. There’s only four and a half million cash on hand.”

“So I can’t tip the pizza guy?” Lannie said sarcastically. “What’s this about a record label? Mom’s songs are on the TACKETT label.”

“Barb owns one hundred percent of TACKET. Over the years TACKETT bought the rights to hundreds of songs. The label owns the rights to all of Barb’s songs, of course, but also most of the early rock and rollers, including over fifty Elvis titles. Every time someone puts one of the old songs in a commercial or movie the royalty meter spins and spins.”

“Who runs the company?” Lannie asked. Her head was spinning.

“Well, Barb did with the help of a board of directors which includes me, your stepfather Richard, and a fellow by the name of J. Dee Hood.”

“Who’s he?” Lannie asked.

“I don’t know him well,” Greenbaum said and shrugged his shoulders “He flies in once a year for the board meeting and then leaves the next day. I don’t even have his social security number. Barb made arrangements to make sure he got paid.”

“How much did mom pay him?” Lannie asked.

“Fifty thousand.”

“For a one-day meeting?”

“That’s the way she wanted it. We actually have a board meeting in a couple of days. You’ll get to meet Dee.”

“You mentioned two pieces of bad news. What is it?”

“Under the will, you become CEO of the record label and can vote her share on the board, but I’m sorry to tell you that until your thirtieth birthday, you get only five hundred thou a year, use of the houses and your medical and educational expenses paid. The rest of the estate is in a trust fund.”

"What happens when I'm thirty?"

"You get it all."

"Who is the trustee?" Lannie asked.

"Richard."

Lannie turned to Tim. "Did you know this?" Tim didn't have to answer out loud. Guilt painted his face. "Why didn't you tell me?" she asked gently.

"I'm employed by the trustee. Up until this moment, the trust was confidential."

"Will you be handling the affairs of the trust now?" Lannie asked Tim.

"Only minor administrative things. The bank will be investing the corpus and interest and cutting the checks to debtors and you."

Lannie turned to Greenbaum. "What's the second not so good news?"

"There is a sticky problem with one of the potential creditors of the estate, whom it could owe as much as two million dollars. One of the artists with TACKETT is owed for some old songs. We performed an audit on receivables from ASCAP and BMI and it seems that we've underpaid Rod Witherspoon."

"Gee, that only leaves one hundred eighty-one million after taxes," Lannie said.

"Actually, the payment of two million to the creditor would leave one hundred eighty-one *point three* million, as taxes are reduced," Greenbaum said.

"Stephen, I hate to see what you call *really* bad news," Lannie said.

Princess came in again. "Stephen, I know you told me not interrupt you, but Spielberg is on the line and he says he's about to lose the rights to Michael's new germ destruction book. Stephen looked at Lannie, sighed and flipped on his phone, "Steve, baby, what's up? Nothing, baby, just sitting in the spa." Greenbaum winked at Lannie, who glanced at Tim and gestured with a nod of her head. Lannie and Tim were out the door before Greenbaum even knew it.

CHAPTER TWENTY-FOUR

Mel drifted in and out of consciousness, but even when she was awake, nothing seemed real--and every thing was fuzzy. She opened her eyes and the old man with no teeth and a stethoscope draped over his neck was back. He was holding her wrist and appeared to be looking at his watch.

"Ah 'em," he grunted. "I've sent for the priest."

Mel tried to say, What on earth for? But only a groan came out.

A terrible screeching sound erupted and the old man clawed at his head. He rammed the butt of his hand against his ear, as though his head were a bottle of ketchup and he was trying to bump out the last, reluctant remains of the bottle.

"This is the worst case I've ever seen, I'm afraid," the old man mumbled, as he again struck his head. The screeching ascended to a higher pitch, not unlike the sound that fingernails make when dragged over a chalk board.

Mel tried to ask the old man who he was, but again, only a groan came out. The high-pitched sound exploded in her brain.

"Scalpel," the old man said to no one Mel could see, and then his hands were fumbling at her neck and a chill swept over her chest.

Mel's eyes opened fully and she saw a nest of hair dangling from the old man's nostrils. Her lids collapsed back down in a blink.

"I don't think we'll need any anesthesia," he said, again to no one Mel could see. "It's two small incisions and she's asleep." The screeching pounded harder inside Mel's head. She struggled and managed to fully open her eyes.

The old guy swatted at his ear and a piece of it fell onto Mel. She opened her mouth to scream and did. The face of the old man froze in fear and his eyes rolled back into his head. He fainted dead away on top of Mel. His breath smelled of decay and the aroma from under his arms caused her to retch. She bucked her hips and thrashed her head back and forth trying to get the old man off of her. His weight made it difficult for her to breathe.

Two fuzzy hands materialized and pulled the old man off of her and she gasped when she saw it was the clown.

"I'm sorry," the clown said and dragged the old man from the room. But as soon as the door shut behind the clown, a tall man wearing a white coat came into the room. Mel shrank back into the mattress when she saw that he also had a stethoscope around his neck.

"Good to see you've fully awakened," he said as he approached the bed.

"Who are you?" she said with fear in her voice.

"Dr. Matranga."

"The Cadillac guy?" she asked hesitantly.

"The what?"

"There's a piece of that old man's ear that fell into my gown. It's on my breast and it seems to be moving or crawling around. Could you get it out?"

Matranga immediately pivoted and stepped out through the door, but was back in seconds with a nurse wearing a scrub outfit.

"There is something under her gown. I can see it moving and I can hear it emitting a high pitched sound," Dr. Matranga said. The nurse nodded, gently put her hand down Mel's gown and pulled out the culprit.

"That's old man Wilson's hearing aide. I hope he didn't bother you too much. He wandered from his exam room and apparently into yours. He's got a touch of the old timer's. I can assure that he is harmless," the doctor said,

"I think he was saying the last rites and was about to operate. May have copped a feel. "

The doctor flashed a pen light into Mel's eyes. "Probably not. He's been gay over seventy years. Follow the light with your eyes." Her left eye moved with the light as he dragged it. "Now, the other." Mel obliged.

"That's good. You have only a minor concussion."

"Feels like a rocking combo with bass drum is having a concert inside my head. Where am I? Am I in the hospital?"

"This is my clinic. You're in Moscow. There is no hospital here."

"Who's the clown?" Mel asked.

"That's Billy Motts. He's an honorary sheriff's deputy. He's the one who was trying to arrest you."

"I remember. Arrest me for what?"

"The fellow you were with, the guy driving the Jaguar, he robbed the service station while you were in the bathroom and stole the attendant's car."

"I had nothing to do with him," Mel said.

A voice came from the door. "While you were out we figured out that you just happened to be in the wrong place at the right time," a dark haired man with dancing brown eyes said. The man entered the room and came to her bedside.

"How long have I been here?" Mel asked.

"About four hours," Dr. Matranga said.

"How did you determine I was not an accomplice?" she asked the brown-eyed man. He had an angular chin, high cheekbones, piercing eyes and a perfectly proportioned nose. From her skewed angle, Mel thought he was handsome.

"Motts saw you get picked up when you had a flat tire. The rental car company told us your employer. We called and they confirmed the information in your purse."

"Who are you?" she asked.

"Please excuse my rudeness; I'm the mayor of Moscow, Obediah Felton."

"Are you the agent for service of process?" Mel asked.

"The what, for what?"

"I've got to have someone on which to serve my million dollar lawsuit for false arrest."

"I don't know what to say," Obediah Felton said, his Adam's apple bobbing.

"Don't say anything. Just laugh. I was kidding. I'm sure the metropolis of Moscow's pocket is a deep as a contact lens."

"I'd like to apologize on behalf of the town," Felton said. "The guy driving the Jag had just put a gun to the attendant's nose. The situation appeared to be rife with danger."

"Apology accepted. Doc, when can I leave here?"

"Miss Vaughn, you can go whenever you feel up to it, but you will not be able to drive for twenty-four hours and when you sleep tonight, someone should wake you every couple of hours. This is to make sure there is no bleeding in the lining of the brain, although I don't expect a problem."

"Is there a cab I can catch?" Mel asked.

"I'm afraid not," Dr. Matranga said. "Moscow is a small village."

"Miss Vaughn," Obediah said, "I can take you wherever you want."

"I understand there is no hotel in town," Mel said.

"I tell you what, why don't you stay at my place," Felton said.

"I don't know," Mel said.

"I live in a garage apartment behind my mother's house," Obediah explained. "You can stay in the apartment and I'll sleep at mother's. It's the least we could do."

Mel started to sit up, but a pain shot from her hip, up her back and into her neck, causing her to groan.

"You bruised your hip in the fall," Dr. Matranga said.

Mel rubbed her neck. "Maybe a half-million dollar lawsuit will do. How big a lawsuit could Moscow afford?"

CHAPTER TWENTY-FIVE

"So this is where you live?" Mel asked Felton, as they turned onto a drive lined with tall pine trees.

"Disappointed?" he asked.

Mel studied the house, which was really nothing more than a small clapboard two bedroom that had been efficiently added on to by a rough carpenter. However, fresh daylilies, daffodils and roses hugged the entire perimeter of the house and fresh paint gave it a warm and cheerful disposition.

"I would have expected something a little more, how shall I say, presidential," she said.

"Moscow only has about four hundred residents. My position is unpaid. I actually own the service station where you were arrested."

"Ah, another target in my tangle of lawsuits."

"If you're disappointed in the house, you'll gasp when you see the garage I call home." Obediah guided the car along the curve around the house and pulled up to a garage that was hidden from passersby on the street.

"It's kind of cute, actually." The garage was a triple and the blue apartment above it was smartly trimmed in white. Covered stairs outlined with white rails led to a side entrance. Frilly curtains framed two large windows overhanging the front of the garage.

"It's almost a thousand square feet."

"So it's large enough to hold a bed and a toilet. That's all I'll need."

Just then, a little girl about five years old came padding from around the corner of the garage. She was beautiful, wearing a starched white dress and with a white rose in her hair over her ear. Her blonde curls jostled on her neck and a light breeze pushed her bangs to the side. The girl barely glanced up and continued walking to the house. She went up a short string of steps and into a door that seem to magically open before her.

"Who was that?" Mel asked.

"That's Maggie, my daughter."

"I thought you said you lived alone, Obediah."

"I do. Maggie stays with my mother."

"Where does your wife stay?"

"She's gone," he answered with a vacant look in his eyes as he looked off at a distant tree line.

"Where did she go?" Mel asked, not understanding.

He turned his head directly at Mel. His fierce eyes burned a hole in her face. "I tell Maggie that mom went to heaven."

"I'm sorry."

"Look, it's getting late. Let's get you situated. Mother will have dinner on the table in a half and hour. If you don't feel like coming down to dinner, I'll bring you a plate."

The face of an older woman appeared in the small window of the door through which the little girl had entered.

Obediah opened the trunk, got Mel's suitcase and led her up the stairs and into the apartment. He walked through the living room and showed her the bedroom and its bathroom.

"Everything is so clean," Mel said.

"It's a health hazard created by living so close to mother. She can't help herself. She comes over every morning and cleans. I tell her she's going to rub the veneer off the furniture, but she insists. Here is the key. There is a flip deadbolt on the door that cannot be opened from the outside. You'll have one hundred percent privacy. See you at dinner."

Mel surveyed the bachelor pad's Berber carpet, low ceiling, country furniture and small entertainment center. She giggled when she saw the television had rabbit ears. No cable or satellite for Mr. Mayor. She proceeded into the bedroom to change her clothes. The bed was king-sized and covered by a thick feather-stuffed comforter. The only other furniture in the room was an antique oak four-drawer dresser. On top of the dresser rested a medium-sized teak jewelry box. Mel's eyes were drawn to a large photograph on the wall near the door to the bathroom. It was a picture of Obediah Felton in jeans with the sleeves of his flannel shirt rolled up and his face cracked with a smile. He was sitting on a rustic bench apparently in a park, and a much younger Maggie was perched on his lap. Her long curly hair floated in an unseen breeze. Maggie leaned into her father the way a cat rubs against its owner showing affection. An attractive dark-haired woman whose face seemed to glow stood behind Obediah with her arms draped over his shoulders; her chin rested on top of his head. Her smile oozed love.

Mel entered the bathroom. She was not surprised that it was simple, a shower, toilet and lavatory. She looked in the mirror and noted for the first time that grime was smeared on her face and had apparently been there since her tumble in the bathroom. She washed her face and decided not to replace her makeup. She opened the medicine cabinet and found it mostly empty, except for two prescription bottles of pills. She vaguely recognized the pills as possibly heart medication of some type.

She went back into the bedroom and picked up her suitcase from the floor, tossed it on the bed, clicked the release tabs and it snapped open. She selected a pair of jeans and a designer tee shirt and changed into her new outfit. She started to go around the bed and towards the door to the living room to leave, when curiosity grabbed her and she got the urge to look in the jewelry box. Subconsciously she glanced at the bedroom door as though she was checking to make sure no one was looking and she approached the box. The dresser was so tall she could not see into the box, so she removed it from the top of the dresser and placed it on the bed. She noted that there was no dust on or under the box. Feeling guilty, she hesitated opening it. She was violating Felton's privacy. But she gave into the mischievous urge to see what was in the box, and she carefully lifted the lid. Her eyes immediately widened and her jaw dropped. The only thing in the box was an enormous gold ring with an *E* formed by diamonds.

Jan Felton had a faint smile on her face as she pulled dishes from the cabinet in her dining room and began setting them on the table. She was still very attractive for a woman her age. She couldn't wear a bikini, but slacks and knit tops exposed no flaws in her figure. A monthly trip to the beauty parlor kept her abreast of the town gossip and her hair a lovely auburn hue. She looked at least twenty years younger than her age. "So, let me get this straight, Obediah, you've got a pretty young woman in you apartment that you suspect is a robber?" Obediah sat in an arm chair staring out of the picture window, admiring the sunset. A parfait of blue, gold, red and yellow spread across the darkening sky. A poplar stand was silhouetted, creating a jagged black hole in the landscape.

"Mother, she's not a robber. Her car had broken down and a guy driving a stolen car picked her up. That guy was the robber. Besides, who said she was pretty?"

"I saw her going up the steps. I also notice that you've changed your shirt to the one I got you last Christmas and you've combed you hair." This was the first time the shirt was worn. The half-smile on Jan's face became a full-toothed grin. She was happy to see her son show some kind of interest in a woman.

"I'd gotten dirty at work, that's all." A squirrel scurrying across the lawn caught Obediah's attention. The squirrel was soon followed by old Frank, Maggie's hound dog. Old Frank wouldn't catch the squirrel; he never had, even in his younger days. Now, when Old Frank slept, sometimes in the twenty-three hours a day he snoozed, one could see that he was dreaming of chasing a rabbit or squirrel. He would jerk and make half-barking sounds and his feet would pedal as though he were running.

"I'll be full up by tomorrow, serving two shifts of breakfast," Jan said.

There was a knock at the kitchen door. Jan stepped through the kitchen and opened the door. "Hi, I'm Mel." Mel was immediately overwhelmed by the best kitchen-aromas she had ever experienced.

"Please come in Mel, I'm Jan." Jan led her into the dining room. Obediah stood up and awkwardly nodded and smiled. He started to sit down, but stopped midway.

"I hope I'm not an imposition," Mel said, not knowing whether to sit down at one of the chairs surrounding the dining room table or remain standing.

"Mel, why don't you have a seat," Jan said.

"The kitchen smells wonderful," Mel commented.

"My mother always said that the way you make a house smell like good food is to throw some onions in a skillet."

"Smells like more than onions," Mel said and took in a deep breath through her nostrils.

"Mother is being modest. She's won the cake baking contest and the pickling contest at the county fair eight years running," Obediah said.

"Big fish in a small pond," Jan said. "I'll finish up in the kitchen and have the food out in a minute. Why don't you two kids entertain yourselves?" She shot Obediah a smirk and pranced into the kitchen with a crinkle in her eyes.

Silent, awkward seconds seemed like minutes. Obediah looked at Mel and she at him, but no words passed. Finally, Mel asked, "How long has Moscow hosted the festival?"

"It started in 1980, three years after Elvis died. Actually, it's not hosted by the town. An out-of-state corporation owns the land and a local group puts the thing on and donates all the money to county charities. It started off small but has gotten quite popular. We'll get almost fifteen thousand visitors between tomorrow and the end of the week. What kind of story are you doing on the festival? The magazine you work for is not known for doing serious pieces."

"Are you a connoisseur of our rag?" Mel asked and laughed.

"Hardly, although don't take that as me being rude." He fidgeted with the collar of his shirt.

"I'm here to do a lighthearted, fun story."

Maggie materialized in the doorway between the kitchen and the living room. "Hey, Maggie, come in and meet Miss Mel," Obediah said. Maggie slowly moved towards Obediah, but shied away from passing too closely to Mel.

"Hi, Maggie, please just call me, Mel. Miss Mel will make me think you're talking to someone else.

Maggie took a seat at the table next to Obediah and appeared to be intently studying Mel.

"Maggie, how old are you?"

"Maggie doesn't talk, Mel," Obediah apologized.

"Oh, I see."

Jan came into the dining room holding a huge platter topped with carved roast, potatoes and carrots and placed it on the table. "I'll be right back with the vegetable platter and tea."

"Jan, can I help in any way?' Mel asked.

Maggie quickly got up from the table and went into the kitchen.

"Thanks for the offer Mel, but you just relax. I've got it all under control." She patted down her apron, turned and went back into the kitchen.

"I'm sorry about Maggie," Mel said.

"She's okay. There is nothing physically wrong with her. It's a reaction from the trauma of seeing her mother die."

"That's terrible."

"I take her into Memphis once a week for therapy, but the results have been slow going."

"How long has she been this way?"

"It will be three years this Christmas."

"Oh, God. Your wife died on Christmas."

"She and Maggie were walking to the car after church service and a drunk veered off the road and hit Darlene. A witness said Darlene pushed Maggie out of the path of the car."

"Were you there?"

"I was still in the church. Someone had stopped me to talk about town business. I often wonder if I could have done anything had I been with Darlene and Maggie." Obediah's sad eyes looked away from Mel and towards the window. Mel started to say something, but didn't know what the say.

Maggie and Jan came back into the room, Maggie carrying a tray on which rested four glasses of tea and Jan a small platter spilling with broccoli, cheese and rice casserole.

"Hope everybody is hungry," Jan said cheerily. "I cooked for the Russian army. And save room for dessert."

"And what would that be, mother?"

"Peach cobbler and hand-turned vanilla ice cream."

"That sounds wonderful," Mel said. She looked at Maggie, who again appeared to be intently studying Mel. Mel smiled at Maggie and she grinned back.

"Honey, you're as skinny as a rail," Jan said to Mel. "You look like you haven't had a decent meal in a while.

"I ate like a pig at lunch. Had the special at the Elvis Diner."

Jan looked at Obediah strangely, who glanced at Mel and then back at Jan.

"So you've met my daughter?" Jan asked.

"Your daughter?" Mel asked, not getting it.

"I owned and ran the diner for years. My daughter, Debra Ann has it now."

"I feel so stupid. She told me her mom had the only bed and breakfast in town. I should have put two and two together. Your daughter's a hoot."

"We think so too," Jan said.

Then suddenly everyone was staring at Maggie. She was nodding her head in assent. Stunned, Jan glanced at Obediah with a tear in her eye. "And so does Maggie," Jan said.

CHAPTER TWENTY-SIX

Tim and Lannie drove through the gate of the Bellhausen Clinic and stopped at the guard-post. “We’re visitors,” Tim said through the rolled-down window.

The puffy guard, whose uniform was three sizes too small, which caused his belly button to push through an opening in his shirt, handed Tim a placard. “Put that on your dash and park in the lot up ahead on your right,” the guard instructed. Tim pulled off slowly.

“You see any nuts? Doesn’t look like I thought a nuthouse would look,” Lannie said. The Bellhausen Clinic, which in years gone by would have been called an asylum, was a thirty thousand square foot, sixty bed psychiatric haven for the ritzy kooks of the City of Angels. Most of its patients were there on sabbatical from the stress of stardom. Others were there to kick one of the countless addictions claimed by people nowadays. None of the patients were there to lose weight. In fact, it was impossible to stay at Bellhausen and not *gain* weight. The most talented chefs in California manned the Bellhausen’s twenty-four-hour-a-day kitchen. The Bellhausen was legendary for its cuisine. It’s “restaurant” (dining hall) was written up in *Gourmet* as one of the top five places to eat in California.

The grounds were also impressive. The structure was a peach, two-story, stucco rambling edifice with a bright orange, Spanish-tiled roof. The grounds were dotted with towering palm trees and flowering shrubs of innumerable variety. Fountains, rock gardens and perfectly coifed bushes lined marble-covered pathways. The Bellhausen’s rambling grounds sported no fences.

Tim and Lannie found their way to the reception area and were soon led by a clinic volunteer to Bennie’s room. The volunteer knocked, opened the door and announced them.

Lannie was shocked at Bennie’s appearance, but in a good way. Bennie looked good. Her face actually had color; her hair was clean and neatly combed. It took a couple of seconds, but Lannie realized what else was so different--all of Bennie's piercings were gone.

Bennie was sitting on the bed, which was some sort of antique poster bed. When she saw Lannie she sprang up and ran to her. They hugged and squeezed each other and cried for a full minute.

Bennie finally opened her eyes and said, "Oh, hi Tim, snatcher of virgins."

"Good to see that you're still your old self, Bennie," Tim said.

"Girl, you look good," Lannie said.

"I feel good, although I've got the shakes big time. I haven't had any medicinals for almost three days. Doctor says it will take at least thirty days for me to stop shaking. Why don't you guys take a seat," Bennie offered and nodded towards two leather chairs in front of a large screen television. Lannie and Tim sat in the chairs and Bennie took a seat on an ottoman.

"I'm sorry I couldn't make the funeral. Was it fun?" Bennie asked.

"I'm not sure that's the word I'd use to describe a funeral, but it was interesting," Lannie said. "Richard played. Everybody who is anybody was there. The Rat asked about you."

"I'm sure *Entertainment Tonight* got a lot of film," Bennie said.

"Has Freddy been around?" Lannie asked.

"No and I don't think he will."

"Did Freddy know that your father was one of his customers?" Lannie asked.

"Best we could tell, no. Turns out I misread Freddy's little black book. I wasn't "B," anyway. Freddy's got this weird code. Doctor says someday I'll think of my Freddy-period as one hell of a rebellious time. Dad says he had a heart-to-heart with Freddy. I think Dad bought him off."

"*Dad*? Is it no longer Fred and Ethel?"

"Apparently he's a pretty cool dude. I've decided to call him Dad, for now."

"Bennie, you're not going to believe the latest. I'm now a record label mogul. Mom had this big deal thing and I'm going to be one of the people running it."

"Cool, but I think I'm through with the groupie thing. At least for awhile."

"How long will you be here?" Tim asked.

"There are no bars on the windows. I can leave anytime I like. The guy who cleans up is kind of cute. I might stay awhile."

Lannie and Tim waited patiently in Stephen Greenbaum's conference room number one, the Sports Room. The conference table was made of planks from seats in Yankee Stadium that were removed in a renovation. The seats were stools taken from an old bar in Fenway Park and the lighting fixtures had been salvaged from the old media room in Three Rivers Stadium. One wall was part of Fenway's Green Monster removed in a renovation.

Memorabilia adorned the other walls. Autographed pictures of Lombardi, Namath, Cobb, Chamberlain, Maravich and others were mixed amongst artifacts of sport. A chunk of the Roman Coliseum hung in a glass box. Bats used by Mantle, Rose, Aaron and Ruth filled a display. All of this was lost on Lannie who had no clue as to who or what these people or things were.

"You look nice, Lannie," Tim said. She wore a suit for the first time in her life, and her hair was pinned back. Her hair was natural blonde and she had on a light covering of makeup. She looked like a bastion of corporate America.

"I'm nervous," Lannie said. Her stomach churned.

"Don't worry, nothing can go wrong," Tim assured her.

The door flew open and Stephen Greenbaum waltzed in with his ear-held microphone at his cheek. He nodded at Lannie and Tim.

"Julia, honey, I know you've already done one of Grisham's books, but darling this one's got Coppola doing the script and directing." Greenbaum paused, looked at Lannie and shrugged his shoulders. "No, not *him*, darling, Sofia's doing it. Look, Julia I think you've got to do this thing even though you don't want to, honey. Your last picture tanked. I've got to go." Greenbaum pushed a button on his belt and said, "Hey, Sofia, babe, what's up? Look, Julia is dying to do the piece, although the money might be a little low. You caught me right in the middle of a meeting, studio brass. I can't talk, get back to you babe." He pushed a button and pulled the earpiece from his ear. "Break time. You guys need any tea? Say, where's Dee?"

"We haven't met him yet," Lannie said.

Greenbaum punched a button on the phone on the table and said, "Princess, bring us some tea and caviar, if you don't mind." He pressed the button again. "Dee was here a few minutes ago."

The door opened and Princess entered with a tray carrying hand-blown glass cups, a pitcher of tea and a serving dish of caviar and an assortment of exotic crackers. A man followed her into the door.

"Here's Dee," Greenbaum said.

"Sorry, the flight this morning upset my stomach," Dee said.

"Dee Hood, this is Lannie Drees and Tim Reed."

"Nice to meet you," Dee said and shook Lannie and Tim's hand. Dee did not look like what Lannie had expected. He was rough looking, older than she thought he would be. He had dark hair that appeared too dark for his age and a gray beard. The hair looked like an expensive wig. But Dee had a friendly smile and Lannie instantly felt comfortable with him, although she couldn't quite make out the once-over Dee was giving her. He was looking at her as though he were drinking in her soul with his eyes.

"Mom never once mentioned you, Dee," Lannie said.

"I probably have never been much a part of her goings on. In the great big universe of her life, I'd be a footnote, I guess."

"Stephen tells me you've always been on the board. Mom thought enough of you to rely on your counsel."

"My input hasn't been much. Your mom was a talented woman."

"First things first," Greenbaum announced, "Lannie has recommended that we maintain the remuneration Dee receives for being on the board." Dee nodded at Lannie and she acknowledged it with a return nod.

Greenbaum gave a glowing report on finances and a summary of the artists under contract. He reported on a squabble TACKETT had with ASCAP and BMI, but said a non-cash settlement was close at hand. He stated that an audit had been completed and it appeared that one of the artists under contract had been underpaid in royalties. Rod Witherspoon was owed almost two million dollars. Greenbaum was efficient in outlining the projects on the table for the following year. The label would pump out almost sixty albums. After only thirty minutes Stephen asked if anyone had any questions or new business.

Dee cleared his throat and spoke. "I discovered a new group I think the label should sign."

"Dee, I think Lannie should know that you have an incredible history of picking winning new talent."

"This group is out of Austin. They call themselves Bee Swarm. They're a cross between the Eagles and the Soft

Spaghettis. Johnny Rivers' nephew is the drummer." Dee shoved a piece of paper to the center of the table. "That's the name and number of their manager."

"Dee, we'll hop on it right away, thanks."

"I have a question," Lannie said. "Who is Rod Witherspoon?"

"He's a songwriter," Greenbaum said.

"I know that," Lannie said. "He wrote, or co-wrote at least ten songs for mom and he's written or co-written over a hundred songs performed by various artists signed by the label. I asked Richard, my step-father about Witherspoon and Richard said he had never met him, nor had he met anyone else who had ever met Witherspoon. Seems kind of spooky."

Lannie happened to glance at Dee Hood and the expression on his face surprised her. Was he worried? Bored?

"Lannie, sweetie, Rod Witherspoon is a huge money-maker for the label," Greenbaum said. "I'm sure in due time we'll all meet him now that Barbara Anne is not around."

CHAPTER TWENTY-SEVEN

All alone in the massive house, Lannie had trouble sleeping. Tim had flown off to the east coast to take care of the business angles of one of Richard's tours, and with Bennie in the psycho jail, she had no one to play with. She munched on pretzels and drank diet soda and checked her watch on average every five minutes. She listened to a few songs on the Prairie Dogs' new CD, but grew tired of it and switched off the player. She thumbed through *People Magazine* but threw it down when she stumbled on an article about her mother. The media seemed to never get anything right.

Lannie trudged into the den, flipped on the television and watched a couple of the shopping channels, but quickly got bored with that when she didn't see anything she wanted to buy, so she turned off the television. She thought of calling Tim, but he was on the right coast and it was too late for that. She then decided to snoop through her mother's things and made her way across the house and into Barbara Anne's bedroom. She was going to put this off for a few more weeks, not knowing if she would get upset going through her mother's belongings, but the idea of looking through the things got her adrenaline going and she perked up.

Barbara Drees' bedroom was located in the east wing of the mansion and it was the size of an average two-bedroom house. Actually, it was a suite of rooms with large sitting, makeup and sleeping areas, a small media area (with four televisions, a state-of-the-art CD player and custom speakers), a story and a half, one thousand square foot closet and a his and her bathroom, each with a Jacuzzi, shower, tub, and dressing area. The dressing areas had music piped into the ceiling and walls and also had a television built into a cut out of the mirror over Barbara Anne's lavatory. Lannie went straight for the closet.

She rummaged through box after box of shoes and clothes. Barb had been a packrat and Lannie soon grew tired. All the shoes seemed to look alike, new and unworn. She had just about lost interest when the door bell rang. It took Lannie a couple of minutes to make her way through the warren of rooms and halls and stairs to the front door, and the door bell rang a couple more times while she was on her way. She opened the door out of breath.

"Hey, Lannie. Looks like I interruptus a little coitus."

"Bennie, what the hell are you doing here?" Bennie wore a robe and was barefooted. "How did you get here?"

"A cab. I called one of my old tricks and told him he had better send a cab for me or I was going to call his wife. Apparently I'm a pretty powerful girl at this time."

"Come in girl," Lannie said. Bennie stepped in and Lannie closed the door behind them.

"What have you been doing? You're out of breath, Are you and Tim playing?" Bennie asked. She raised her eyebrows and smirked.

"No, I was going through stuff in mom's closet, and it's a long haul from there to here."

"That sounds like fun," Bennie said. Let's do that. I've always had a thing for Barb's stuff. They stopped in the kitchen, got fresh sodas from the industrial refrigerator and went straight to the closet.

"I feel like I died and went to Imelda Marcos heaven," Bennie soon said.

"I didn't know mom was such a shoe pig."

"Find anything interesting yet?" Bennie asked, tossing aside box after box, making a mess.

"The shoes are three sizes, seven, seven and a half and eight."

"Maybe different manufacturers shoes are sized differently," Bennie said.

"Each shoe is in triplicate, one of each size," Lannie said.

"Barb had a fetish, or couldn't remember what size she wore. She's got some cute stuff here," Bennie said as she started to fondle fur coats and ten thousand dollar gowns.

"You'll be able to take what you like. In fact, why don't you move in with me?" Lannie said.

"I've got to finish my tour at the asylum first. I just got out tonight because the cute guy who cleans up didn't show up tonight. Some old lady with no teeth came in his place and it freaked me out. Thinking about the guy gets me through the day," Bennie said and started looking at clothes hanging on what seemed like miles of racks. “Some of these could be worn to the Academy Awards, especially if you wore them backwards,” Bennie quipped.

“Mom went to all that stuff. She said she never declined an invitation to anything involving a red carpet.”

Bennie had made her way along one of the walls to a corner when something caught her eye. “Lannie, come look at this.”

Lannie popped up and sprang to where Bennie was pointing. Lannie pushed aside several dresses and a wall safe was revealed. “I never thought about whether mom had one of these before, but it makes sense.”

“It’s a shame we don’t know the code.”

“We do,” Lannie said. “Look, mom left the number on a piece of paper scotch taped to the key pad.” Lannie entered the code in sequence, a series of beeps occurred and then the door to the safe popped open. An envelope with Lannie’s name on it was propped up in front so it would be the first thing seen. Lannie reached in and got it. “Bennie, this is kind of scary. Why would mom leave me a note? She was never bashful about telling me anything. I’m scared.”

“Do you want me to go in the other room while you read it?”

“I want you right here.” They looked at the envelope in Lannie’s shaking hands.

“You’ve got the shakes as bad as I have them,” Bennie said. She held up her hands and showed how they were trembling.

Bennie followed Lannie to the area in the suite where the bed was and they sat on it. Lannie nervously opened the envelope and read it:

Dear Lannie,

If you are reading this letter, the cancer must have eaten my mind before I could talk to you. This letter is insurance that you will know the truth about your father. I never married him, but it was not because we didn't love each other. The situation was untenable. I never told you about him because it would have served no purpose. But as I know I am dying, I have decided to tell you that your father is Rod Witherspoon. Stephen Greenbaum will be able to help you find him, if you choose to do so.

Love,
Mom

```
P.S. I never had time to add a codicil to my will, but I want Bennie to have all my old clothes and shoes. I don't know what size shoe she wears, so I bought three sizes of each one I purchased the last couple of years. Her feet look to be the same size as mine.
```

They ran back to the safe. Lannie pulled out a bundle of loose sheets. "These look like lyrics to songs," Lannie said.

"Anything Barb did?" Bennie asked.

"None that I can recall."

"Let me see them," Bennie said as she took them from Lannie's hand. Bennie flipped though the pages, her eyes darting over the words.

"It's amazing how fast you can read that stuff," Lannie said.

"You're right; there is nothing in here that even resembles any of Barb's songs, or any songs I've ever heard. But all of them do have that funny mark that's handwritten, that copyright mark, and they all have Rod Witherspoon's name printed on them."

"My father wrote these," Lannie said.

They hurriedly searched the rest of the things in the safe, but found nothing else of importance. They tossed everything else back in, except Barb's letter.

Lannie drove as though she was being chased by kidnappers. The tires of the Porsche squealed on every turn as the car slid all over the road. The only reason no one was killed was because of the late hour; the streets were empty.

"Lannie, why do you think she didn't tell you before?"

"We'll find out."

"I wish your mom was still alive," Bennie said.

"I do, too."

"Now I can't send her a thank you note for the shoes."

Lannie pushed the intercom button at the Belair gate of Greenbaum's mansion. O. J. had lived a few blocks away at one time. Greenbaum's estate was hidden behind a tangle of landscaping and fencing. Amazingly, in seconds, Stephen's voice came back, "Lannie, what on earth are you doing here at this hour?"

"How did you know it was me?"

"Look up, sweetie, there are cameras everywhere."

"Can we come in?" Lannie asked.

The gate began to swing open. "Come to the side entrance on the right. The alarm system is easier for me to disarm for that door. The front door takes a surgeon's nimble fingers and an Act of Congress."

Stephen greeted them at the door. He wore a satin robe and had on Armani slippers. He led Lannie and Bennie to a large office off a long hall lined with glamour shots of Greenbaum's celebrity clients. The wall was a who's who of Hollywood. Stephen took a seat in a partner's chair behind a massive Louis XIV desk. The girls perched in exquisitely upholstered bishop's chairs, circa 1790.

"Can I get you ladies anything?"

"No, thanks, but how do you do that?" Lannie asked.

"Do what?"

"Every hair on your head is perfectly in place. Don't you sleep?" Bennie asked.

Stephen rolled his eyes and put his hand on his head and pulled. The toupee slid off revealing a hairless head. "Any more tricks you need to know? Why are you here?"

Lannie handed the letter to Stephen who quickly read it.

"I didn't know," Stephen said.

"Where is Rod Witherspoon, Stephen?"

"Lannie, I really don't know. Your mother had all communication with him. I never met him. We never had to send him anything because Barb took care of sending him his royalty payments."

"How can I find him?"

"Are you sure you want to find him? Surely he must know that you are his daughter. Yet, all these years he's chosen to not reveal himself to you," Stephen said.

"Stephen, I want to meet him."

"In the morning we'll hire an investigator to try and find him. I hope that Rod Witherspoon is his real name. Otherwise it could be difficult finding him."

CHAPTER TWENTY-EIGHT

The early morning fog had burned off by the time Mel and Obediah left for the festival grounds. The sun was topping the trees surrounding the Felton homestead and it appeared that it would be a marvelous, sun-drenched day. Old Frank lay in the sun napping and didn't even budge as the car slowly drove by crunching gravel.

Mel's rental was parked on the side of the drive.

"Thanks for getting my car fixed," she said.

"That's the least I could do."

Obediah maneuvered the car from the driveway and onto the road with the windows down. The air smelled of ozone and freshly mown grass. Mel sucked in a lung full and remembered that was the way air was supposed to smell. Living in the city robbed one's memory of something so simple.

"Last night was something special," Obediah said.

"What?" Mel blurted. She jerked her head and looked at Obediah.

"The way Maggie acknowledged what you were saying at the dinner table."

"Oh."

"That's the first time in years she's even hinted that she's listening to conversation. Her doctor will be excited."

"What do you think caused her to interact?" Mel said.

"I racked my brains out last night. Only thing I could think of was that it was the first time mother, Maggie, me and another female had been at the table at the same time. Maybe it brought back good memories of her mom, the way we used to talk around the table about our day."

"You haven't brought home any women to meet your mom in three years?" Mel asked.

"Not yet."

"I don't count?" Mel playfully asked.

"You know what I mean," Obediah said, not sure if he should apologize.

"So, I'm the first female to sleep in your bed since your wife... left?"

"Technically, I guess so."

Just like that they were turning off the highway and into the pasture where the two huge tents were set up.

"What's on tap today?" Mel asked, shifting her mind into reporter-mode.

"There's a large screen and projector set up at the elementary school gym in town and they will be showing Elvis movies all day until ten o'clock tonight. This afternoon at the tent on the right, the east tent, there will be an ex-housekeeper from Graceland, two guys who used to play in Elvis's band and several extras from the movies. They'll have movie stills showing where they appeared in the movie. All of these folks will be signing autographs. In the west tent there is an Elvis sound-alike contest. Qualifying starts in fifteen minutes with the final eight competing tonight for the championship. The winner gets to play an original song with the headliner guest band later in the week.

"What kind of nut would waste their time trying to impersonate someone who is dead?"

"You'd be surprised," Obediah said.

"Obediah, you go on in. There is something across the road I need to look at again. I'll catch up to you in a few minutes."

Mel carefully looked both ways and waited for the building traffic to turn into the tented area. When an opening occurred, she zipped across the road.

Almost all of the booths were opened, including the balloon booth. She walked to it and was warmly greeted by Billy Motts, the clown and erstwhile honorary deputy sheriff. "Hello, Miss Vaughn,"

"Billy, please call me Mel. Not much of a crowd today."

"This evening it will be packed. Everybody comes for the sing-off."

"Billy, is there anything you can tell me about that cross on the side of the road?"

"Mel, I really can't say anything about that. But maybe you could ask Obediah."

"Obediah? Why him?"

"Like I said, ask him."

"Have you known Obediah long?"

"All his life?"

"What was his wife like?"

"Sweet woman."

"Obediah took her death hard," Mel said.

"You wouldn't know."

"I've got a photographer coming in a few days. Can he take pictures of your booth and you?"

"Sure."

Mel walked back to the cross and pulled weeds away from it. She made a mental note to get Obediah to drive her back with some cleaning supplies and maybe a weed eater. She carefully made her way back across the road and saw that over a hundred cars had entered the tent parking lot in the few minutes she had been visiting with Billy and working on the cross.

She paid her two dollars to the gatekeeper and entered the west tent. A stage had been set up and it was awash with microphones, amplifiers, a piano, drums and guitar stands. There were chairs for about three hundred people. A funny looking man was talking into one of the microphones about the celebrity judges. The man was wearing a Porter Waggoner suit, but had on an Elvis wig that was too big for his smallish head. The wig drooped over where the man's eyebrows should be. Mel listened.

"And now, our fourth and final judge is a very special visitor. He played in Elvis's band off and on for four years and is now one of Richard Drees's Prairie Dogs. Let's hear it for Ratz Adie."

There was an enthusiastic applause as Rat stood and waved at the crowd.

"And now, without further ado, let's bring out our first contestant, the winner of this contest the last twelve years, our own Mayor Obediah Felton."

Mel peered at the stage as Obediah, two guitar players a keyboardist and drummer came from around a curtain. As Obediah approached the microphone his eyes and Mel's met. He smiled and she started laughing and then joined the crowd in clapping. As soon as everyone in the band was in place, the group started into *Suspicion.*

Mel couldn't believe her ears. She closed her eyes and the voice *was* Elvis's. Obediah was that good.

The crowd was mesmerized. Some of the older women cried in happiness. Everyone stood, grinned and swayed. Mel got caught up in the moment and forgot that she was there for a story and forgot about how skeptical she had been about all the Elvis hoopla. She had also forgotten how fantastic Elvis sounded. She had never heard him in person, but these people had, and they believed Obediah was Elvis on stage.

The contestants were allowed two songs in this session and Obediah did a version of *Love Me Tender* where it was just him and his guitar. It was incredible and gave Mel goose bumps. The crowd went crazy and it was obvious who the favorite was. The judges gave Obediah forty points, the maximum score. Mel made her way backstage and found Obediah being congratulated by musicians and other contestants.

"You are full of surprises," Mel said.

"Yeah, I'm one of those nuts who wastes his time."

"That was amazing," she commented.

"Let's go get a cup of coffee," Obediah said and then led Mel to a set of tables on the far side of the tent and a booth that sold coffee. A young man selling coffee didn't charge Obediah for two cups. Obediah found a cleared table and they sat at it.

"You ever think of cutting records?" Mel asked.

"I don't think I could do his songs any better than Elvis ever did them. I don't think there would be a market for rehashing what's already been done."

"I agree, but today, old is new. I bet that most of Elvis's songs could be rearranged into a *now* sound and they would sell millions with you singing them."

"Are you starting to have fun?" Obediah asked.

"I guess it shows. There are a couple of things I have to ask you?"

"Fire away."

"One of them is embarrassing."

"Did you try on my underwear last night?" Obediah teased.

"Actually you're not that far off."

"Well, you see, sometimes I like boxers and sometimes briefs."

Mel laughed until it almost hurt. "No, Obediah, it's not your underwear I'm interested in."

"I'm not sure how to take that," he said and laughed. Then suddenly he stopped laughing.

"What's wrong?" Mel asked.

"I can't remember the last time I laughed like that," Obediah said and his eyes clouded.

Mel reached across the table and squeezed his hand. He looked down at her hand and then into her eyes. “Thanks, Mel. I didn’t know if I would ever laugh again. But let’s not let this conversation get so serious. You wanted to ask me something.”

“I violated your privacy last night. I looked in your jewelry box and saw that magnificent ring. Where did you get it?”

“Why do you want to know?”

“I think it belonged to Elvis and may have been worn by a bank robber back in 1982.”

“Mother gave it to me in 1998 for my birthday. When I protested getting something so expensive, she said she got it at a pawn shop in Memphis for almost nothing.”

“Do you think she’d remember what pawnshop it was?”

“Maybe, but why are you interested?”

“It’s personal.”

“You said you had a couple of things to ask me, what’s the next?”

“Yesterday, where I had my flat, right across the road, there is a cross with a name and date on it. Billy Motts said you would know who put up the cross?”

“Why do you want to know that?” Obediah stared into her eyes and then looked away.

“The name on the cross is my father’s and the date on it is the date he died.”

The color drained from Obediah’s face and his mouth dropped open.

“You okay?” Mel asked.

“No, I’m not.”

“What’s wrong?” she asked.

“Give me a minute.”

Mel drank from her cup and noticed for the first time that another Elvis impersonator was singing. His rendition of *Blue Hawaii* was awful. She glanced back at Obediah. He appeared to be lost in thought, soul searching.

“Mel, I don’t know if you really want to hear this.”

“I won’t know until I hear it.”

“All this land belongs to some fancy corporation owned by an outfit out of California. When I was a kid, my Uncle Jess, who is not my real uncle, we just call him Uncle Jess…”

“I think I saw him at the Elvis Diner. He’s got a voice box?”

"That's him. Uncle Jess had a lease on this land, or at least the right to use it to keep cattle and horses on it. The day your father was killed, I was out here with Uncle Jess."

"You saw my father get killed?"

"Uncle Jess had a horse he was training. In fact, he was standing just about where we are sitting now, maybe a couple of yards west of here. I was riding old Butch, one of Uncle Jess's horses that he used to let me ride regularly. This is open livestock area and I was riding on the edge of the road, when old Butch sort of stumbled. I think he caught a hoof on the edge of the road. Anyway, next thing I knew, we were in the travel lane. Then I heard this horrible sound. A car…your father had come upon me and he hit his brakes and swerved. I don't know how he missed me, but he did. His tire caught the drop off of the pavement and he lost control and flipped. Uncle Jess and I got to the car, but it was too late."

Tears were streaming down Mel's face. "Did he say anything at the end?" she asked, barely audible.

"No, but he wasn't screaming or hollering or anything like that. I don't think he ever felt any pain."

"Who put up the cross?"

"Uncle Jess and mother."

"Why didn't you contact me and tell me what had happened?" she asked softly.

"I was just a kid. I'm probably your age, a little older. I heard Uncle Jess tell mother that the man, your father, had no wife and that his little girl was too young to understand that it was an accident."

"So they did try to find out about my family?"

"Apparently so." Obediah's head went down, his chin inches from his chest. "Mel, do you think in time you could forgive me?"

Mel wiped the moisture from her cheeks. "I came to grips a long time ago with my father dying in an accident, Obediah, an accident. I didn't know who you were, but you were forgiven a long time ago." Obediah lowered his eyes and a lump formed in his throat. He was about to say something.

Just then Mel's phone rang and startled, she jumped. She answered, "Hello," in a husky voice.

"Mel, it's Uncle Ron."

"Hey, Uncle Ron."

"Are you okay? You don't sound too good."

"I'm alright."

"I've got some crazy news on that fingerprint and that blood DNA."

"Well, it's my day for the crazies, Uncle Ron," she said glancing at Obediah. "What did you find out?"

"It seems that Migel Matranga got into a little juvenile trouble. Nothing serious, mind you, but there was a fingerprint of him available. I broke about thirty privacy laws that apply to juveniles to get it. There's an eighty-five percent chance that the print from the door of the Cadillac is that of Migel Matranga."

"Amazing," Mel said and looked at Obediah. She didn't want to say anything in front of him.

"I tracked down a hair sample of Elvis from a collector and was able to buy some. The blood had degraded considerably and the testing lab I used would never withstand the scrutiny of a good defense lawyer. They cut a lot of corners, but the owner is an old friend and he is very trustworthy. There is a ninety-five percent probability that the robber of the bank in 1982 was Elvis."

Mel dropped her phone and fainted dead away. Obediah was not able to get across the table in time to catch her before she fell, and she hit her head on the bench next to the table.

CHAPTER TWENTY-NINE

The lights were all fuzzy and the room spun as Mel tried to open her eyes. She heard Obediah's voice. "Mel, wake up. Mel, wake up. Do you think this is serious?"

Another voice answered, "We'll know when she awakes, but I don't think so."

"Doc, do we just wait?"

Mel managed to get her eyes half-opened and started to speak. The words slurred. "Grrrrrraaaa…"

"Take it easy," Dr. Matranga said. He felt her forehead with the palm of his hand.

Mel shook her head and a few cobwebs fell out. She stared into Matranga's face. "It's you."

"You're turning into one of my best patients, Miss Vaughn." He put his fingers on her wrist to time her pulse. "We're at my clinic again."

"It's all your fault, doctor," Mel said.

"Pardon me?" Matranga said.

Obediah stepped to the edge of the bed.

"Obediah, if you could leave Dr. Matranga and me alone for a second, I have something to talk to him about."

"Okay," Obediah said and reluctantly left the room.

"Miss Vaughn, you may be feeling lightheaded, even delirious. You fainted and hit your head again."

"In 1982 a man wearing an Elvis costume and mask robbed a bank and got away in a Cadillac convertible."

"I know, I bought the car used in that robbery at police auction. It's a nice car. I still have it."

"The car was abandoned by the robber and thoroughly searched by the police. It was lifted for fingerprints. One of your fingerprints was found on the passenger door."

"That's not possible," Dr. Matranga protested.

"You had a juvenile record and your prints are on record. They match the prints found on the car."

"Are you accusing me of robbing a bank?" Matranga asked, although not angry with the accusation.

"No. I'm not accusing you of anything."

"Miss Vaughn, stirring up the past could ruin people's lives, and maybe have serious consequences."

"Are you threatening me?" Mel asked.

"Of course not, it's just that some things are best left alone, that's all."

"Doctor, I have no interest in causing you any trouble. My father died trying to track down a lead on that car. I'm curious as to what part you play in this."

"I don't remember meeting anyone named Vaughn. Do you have any evidence that I did?"

"No."

"Miss Vaughn, believe me when I tell you that I did not rob any bank."

"I don't know why, but I believe you."

Obediah helped a shaken Mel up the stairs and through the door of the apartment. She leaned on him heavily.

Jan Vaughn was waiting in the living room. "You poor darling," Jan said, as she took over from Obediah the job of getting Mel to the divan. "There, that's better," Jan said as Mel collapsed onto the sofa.

"Thanks, Jan. I didn't realize how queasy I was until we started up the stairs."

"Obediah, why don't you run along. I'm going to help Mel get into her jammies and robe. She can spend the afternoon resting."

"Seems that I'm always getting shooed off," Obediah protested and then retreated out the door, muttering to himself.

"Jan, how do you put up living in such a small town? I bet everyone knows your business."

"They would, if I had any business to know," she said and giggled.

"What happened to Mr. Felton?" Mel asked.

"There is no Mr. Felton," Jan said with a voice devoid of emotion.

"But Obediah and Debra Ann?"

"I'm afraid I'm a marked woman. I've given birth to two children and raised them fatherless."

"The last immaculate conception ended in crucifixion," Mel noted.

"There was a lot of talk back then, but since my whole family was trailer trash before big hair was even associated with trailer trash, expectations were low. I didn't let anyone down."

"You've done well," Mel observed.

"I'm proud of my kids. Did Obediah tell you he graduated with honors from Vanderbilt?"

"He what?" Mel was surprised by the revelation.

"He's got a degree in biology and was accepted to medical school. Closest thing he comes to his degree in biology these days is an oil change at the filling station. At one time he was a researcher at St. Jude."

"Before his wife died?"

"Yes. That changed him."

"And Debra Ann?" Mel asked.

"Barely finished high school. She got her single-mindedness from her mother. She's wearing my genes; that's genes with a *g*. Ever since she turned thirteen, only thing on her mind has been boys, boys, boys."

"She's got her mother's good looks too."

"Thanks."

"Obediah and Debra Ann have a relationship with their father?"

"They don't know who their father is," Jan said politely, but the look she gave Mel warned Mel that she was close to crossing over the line.

"Sorry I brought that up. It's the magazine reporter in me asking probing questions without thinking."

"Obediah says you asked about the ring," Jan said and then looked away.

"I didn't mean to upset anyone."

"The ring came from a pawn shop in Memphis many years ago."

"Do you remember what year you got it?"

"Must have been in the early 1980's, probably '83 or '84, something like that. Why do your ask?"

"I think it once belonged to Elvis."

"The guy in the pawn shop said the same thing, but I thought he was saying it to jack up the price."

"Obediah says that Maggie goes to Memphis once a week for therapy, maybe I could go and we could find the pawn shop and try and track down whoever it was that pawned it."

"Mel, I don't know what's going on here. Obediah told me you're the daughter of the man who got killed trying to avoid running him over all those years ago. I'm sorry for your father." Jan's eyes moistened. "Maggie and Obediah are my life. Maggie is this fragile flower and Obediah's heart is as pure as gold, but barely holding together. Maggie's behavior at the dinner table the other night was just short of a miracle. And Obediah, well he's strutting around like a rooster with a new hen in the yard. We're just simple folk. When you leave here, Mel, make sure there are no regrets. Please be careful with the people I love."

Mel found her cell phone in the suitcase and the battery and the signal indicator were low. She speed-dialed her office and after being put through an electronic maize, the line rang and Lolita answered.

"Lo, it's Mel."

"Meet Elvis yet?"

"We're having lunch tomorrow."

"Really?"

"Lolita, any one ever tell you how gullible you are?"

"Not today."

"Something's come up and I need you and Jeff down here sooner than planned."

"Is there a problem?" Lolita asked, eager to get involved.

"Just tell Jeff that I'm guaranteeing him a Pulitzer if this is heading where I think it is."

"Does it play CD's, or only those old 45's? The old 45's are expensive."

"Lolita, what the hell are you talking about?" Mel asked.

"You said Jeff would get a Pulitzer."

"A *Pulitzer*, not a *Wurlitzer*. A *Pulitzer*, Lolita."

"Oh, anyway, Jeff's not here. He's on assignment. He said to tell you if you called that he'd fly straight to Memphis with the story he's covering and meet you in Moscow."

"What story is that?"

"He's with Richard Drees and the Prairie Dogs. They've just sold their one hundred millionth album. It's a big story. They're on tour and he's going to follow them to the Elvis Festival. They're the headliner act this year."

"I never heard of them. Lo, get down here as soon as you can. We'll join up with Jeff when he gets here. I have something for you to investigate before you come down."

"Will I get mentioned in the byline of the story?" Lo asked, begging.

"No, Lo, but you will get to keep your job as my assistant."

"Okay. Thanks omnipotent and all-knowing one," Lolita said.

"The festival is held on several hundred acres a couple of miles west of Moscow. See if you can find out who owns the land. I understand it's an out of town corporation. Get someone to run a title check to determine the current and previous owners."

There was a knock on the apartment's door.

"Lo, I've got to go." Mel pushed the button on her phone. "Come in, it's not locked," she shouted out and gathered the top of her robe together.

Obediah and Maggie popped into the room. "How are you feeling?" he asked.

"Better than I was when I hit my head this morning."

"What caused you to faint?" he asked.

"It was brain overload and shock. Mostly shock. I'm better now."

"Maggie and I are going out to the festival. I've got to sing in about an hour and we were wondering if you wanted to tag along?" Maggie was staring at the floor and shuffling her feet.

"Give me a couple of minutes and I'll be right down."

Ten minutes later Mel easily traversed the stairs and met Obediah and Maggie who were waiting at the car. Maggie had tossed on a knit top, jeans and sneakers. She had her hair pulled back in a ponytail and wore light makeup. She looked pinup-fabulous.

"I don't think I've ever seen a female get ready for anything so fast," Obediah said.

"It's not every day that a girl gets asked out on a date by a dashing mayor and his first lady. Besides, I've got cabin fever. The walls of that apartment are starting to fold inwards." Maggie lifted her eyes and blankly looked at Mel.

"A… date?" Obediah stammered.

"That's what we call it in New York City. Don't worry, I won't tell anyone that Obediah Felton went on a date. We can tell anyone who asks that I'm baby-sitting Maggie."

There were hundreds of pickups and cars in the tent parking lot, but none of them seemed to be parked in any organized fashion; there were no straight lines.

"The finals are a big deal. One year we got some footage on CNN," Obediah said, as he helped Maggie and Mel from the car. He took Maggie's hand. "Let's be careful, Mag, there are cars everywhere."

The trio bobbed and wove through the sea of cars. Right before they got to the tent there was only a narrow area to squeeze by. Mel and Obediah awkwardly started through at the same time and brushed up against one another. They stopped with their chests touching, their faces inches apart.

"Sorry, Mel." He was breathing hard and his breath smelled of Juicy Fruit.

"We have to quit meeting this way. Someone might think we're Siamese twins," Mel joked and laughed. Obediah pulled away, grinning.

A guy pranced by and Mel jerked her head. "That's the biggest wig I've ever seen."

"The look-alike contest is being held in the other tent," Obediah said.

"If Elvis were alive, I bet he'd settle for royalties on those wigs. That would net a fortune," Mel said.

They entered the tent and Obediah put Mel and Maggie in the VIP seating area. "Maggie, just stay here with Mel and I'll come get you after my performance."

"Is Jan going to be here?" Mel asked.

"Mom never comes to these things. She says they're silly." He hugged Maggie and kissed her on the cheek and scurried off.

An army of people was marching all over the stage area in organized confusion moving equipment around. Obediah was the first singer of the night, but from what Mel could tell all the seats were taken; it was a packed house.

"Maggie, why don't you come with me and get cold drinks? I think we have time."

Mel took Maggie by the hand and started to stand up, but froze when Maggie said, "I'm not a baby."

Stunned, Mel sat back down. "Maggie, I never… said… you were."

"At the house, you said you would tell everybody you were baby-sitting me."

"You're right. I'm sorry for using that choice of words. I was just joking."

"I'd love a Coke, Mel."

"Well then, let's get this big girl a cold drink." Mel wanted to rush backstage and tell Obediah that Maggie had talked, but decided to wait until after the show.

CHAPTER THIRTY

Obediah Felton finished his performance to a rousing ovation from the standing room only crowd. He jumped off the front of the stage and made his way to the VIP section.

"That was terrific, Obediah," Mel warmly said.

Billy Motts rushed up still wearing his clown outfit and a few balloons tethered to his belt. He handed Maggie a large red one. "Obediah, after the rest of the pretenders perform it's just a formality crowning you the King again."

"We'll see, Billy." Billy slapped Obediah on the back and headed for a group of kids at the festival with their scout troop.

"Maggie, wasn't your dad great?" Mel asked.

Maggie ignored her and played with her balloon.

"Maggie, do you have something to say to your father?" Mel asked.

A look of puzzlement came over Obediah's face as he looked at Mel.

"We'll talk about it later," Mel said.

Maggie yawned. "Mel, would it be alright if I left you here and ran Maggie on home and came back in about a half an hour?" Obediah asked.

"That would be fine. It will give me the chance to work on my story some more. The program says that in addition to the look-alike contest in the east tent, there are Elvis groupies who tell stories and allow you to take their picture. I think I need to interview some of them for the magazine article."

Obediah picked up Maggie into his arms. She was now visibly tired and nestled her head against his neck. "I won't be long," he said and was headed for the exit before Mel could say anything.

Mel wove her way through the throng of Elvis-worshipers and marveled at what an eclectic group they were. Some were obviously well-to-do and others were poor, simple folk.

Surprisingly, there were many young people, even some who were very young.

She eventually made her way into the other tent. There were small stages set up and each stage had a stool and about twenty chairs arranged around it in a semicircle. There were about ten stages scattered throughout the tent. Mel spied a sign on poster paper that proclaimed, *TRICIA BANKS, ELVIS'S NURSE*, and so that's where she went. Tricia was just wrapping up a forty-five minute presentation when Mel approached. Tricia was smartly dressed in a nurse's uniform, down to her white nurse's shoes. The audience began dispersing and Mel waited until two autograph seekers had gotten Ms. Banks to sign baseball caps with THE KING emblazoned on the crown.

"Hi, Ms. Banks, I'm Mel Vaughn with *Weird Magazine*. Could I ask you some questions?"

"I enjoyed your article on the lady married to an alien from Mars. You have quite an imagination."

"Thank you, Ms. Banks."

"Please call me Tricia."

"Tricia, I'm not very familiar with how these festivals work. Do you get an appearance fee for being here?"

"Lord heavens no. I live less than an hour's drive from here. When I go to other festivals they still don't even pay my traveling expenses. None of us get any money from the promoters of the festival, although I did get two hundred dollars for being on Jerry Springer."

"Why do you do this, then?"

"Honey, look at all these people. They're here because they loved the man. Me and the others come here because we loved him too."

"I'm confused. I didn't hear your speech, but how could you talk so long. Elvis was dead when he got to the hospital. What kind of nursing could you give him?"

"Elvis checked into the hospital several times in the few years before his death. He was in and out to kick the drugs that had a grip on him. I worked for a while on the floor where there was a private suite of rooms and Elvis stayed there to dry out. I spent a lot of time with him the last years of his life."

"What is your story?" Mel asked.

"Elvis was the kindest person. He loved everyone. We'd play rummy for hours on end to pass the time. We talked about a lot of things."

"Sounds like you should write a book," Mel said.

"Most of what we said was private. A book wouldn't be right."

"Did you see him the day he died?" Mel asked.

"I was working that day. As soon as they brought him in, word buzzed through the hospital. I had just finished my rounds so I decided to take a quick peek."

"You went to the emergency room?"

"It was crazy. Half the hospital staff raced into the room to see him. It wasn't morbid, or anything like that. Mostly curiosity."

"Did you get to see his face?" Mel asked.

"Sure did."

"Was it Elvis?"

"As I said on the Jerry Springer show, the nose wasn't right."

"So you don't think it was him?"

"I *know* it wasn't Elvis. The guy on the table was slimmer and he had a couple of streaks of gray in his hair."

"Did Elvis have gray hair?"

"Even when he was in the hospital Elvis had a personal groomer come around and do his hair every week."

"Tricia, will you be here later in the week?"

"Sure."

"I have a photographer who's coming down. Would it be alright if he got a picture of you?"

"Of course, but let me get you something." Tricia Banks went to a satchel that was under the stool on the stage and plucked out a large envelope and handed it to Mel.

"What's this?" Mel asked.

"It's my biography, a glamour shot-photograph and the phone number of my agent."

"You have an agent?"

"I stay booked for these things and other occasions about one-hundred days a year."

"If you get no money for travel and appearances, how so you afford to go to all of those?"

"I charge five dollars each for autographs. I'll gross about fifteen hundred dollars at this festival alone."

Mel did the math in her head. Tricia pulled in over a hundred and fifty thousand dollars a year in autograph fees. "I appreciate the conversation. If I need to get in touch with you about the story, should I do that through your agent?" Mel asked.

"I live out of a camper that I travel the country in, and I don't have a cell phone. I call my agent once a week to work out details. If you miss me later in the week here, just call my agent."

Mel said thanks and started to walk off when a terrible dread gripped her. She didn't know why, but she suddenly felt chilled to the bone and perspiration coated her forehead. She turned and stepped back to Tricia Banks.

"Tricia, the day Elvis was brought in, what floor were you working on?"

"The fourth floor, but why do you want to know?"

"Was that the maternity floor?"

"Yes."

"Did one of your patients fall out of bed and bleed to death while you were sneaking a peak at the dead guy in the emergency room?"

Tricia's face went serious. "A claim was filed and the hospital settled, but how would you know that?"

"I didn't know you were the nurse on duty until just now. The woman who died was my mother and I'm the baby that she had just delivered."

Tricia's hand went to her mouth and she gasped.

Mel was finally able to compose herself twenty minutes after Tricia Banks had left. She walked around bouncing off people looking for Obediah Felton but didn't see him. She didn't know why she felt compelled to see him; she wouldn't share her story with him. Her mind raced. Within twenty-four hours she had met the two people who had played major roles in the deaths of her parents. She had not been prepared for the encounters. She had not gone looking for answers; they had seemingly come to her. Why was this happening? She was lost in thought when a hand tugged at her shoulder and she turned.

"Maggie woke up as mom and I were tucking her in and she wrapped her arms around my neck and wouldn't let go. I had to wait until she fell back asleep. Mel, are you okay? You look like you've seen a ghost," Obediah said.

""I'm fine, actually."

"At the risk of boring you to tears, I see someone over there you might want to meet." Obediah reached down and gently took Mel's hand into his and led her to a fellow who had just finished his presentation. His hand felt soft and warm and it felt perfectly natural for his to hold hers.

"Whip Sanders, this is Mel Vaughn,"

"Mel, nice to meet you." Whip stood about six foot three inches tall and was slender with an angular face. His nose would be more properly described as a beak and he had a twinkle in his hazel eyes. Whip wore a denim shirt, well-worn blue jeans and a ranger-set belt and snakeskin cowboy boots.

"Whip lives just outside of Moscow now. He used to work for an ambulance company in Memphis in the mid to late 1970s."

"I was part of the emergency crew that picked up Elvis from Graceland the day he died."

"I'm with *Weird Magazine*."

"Then you must know about me," Whip said.

"I haven't paid attention to much of the Elvis stuff, Whip."

"The magazine did an article on me about ten years ago. I'm the guy who said the stiff at Graceland wasn't Elvis."

"Why is that?" Mel asked.

"We were dispatched to Graceland and pulled in front. The housekeeper met us at the front door and led us to the upstairs bathroom. The person was wrapped in a blanket. I was the lead technician, so I pulled the blanket back to check for a pulse on the neck. When I drew my hand back it was covered with makeup."

"Elvis had makeup on his neck?" Mel asked.

"The guy on the floor had makeup on his face and neck, but that wasn't the strangest thing that day."

"What else?" Mel asked.

"When I walked into the bathroom I could smell death."

"What do you mean?" she asked.

"Before I became an emergency tech I drove hearses. After a funeral I used to have to air out the hearse because of the smell. Death smells like .... well, death. The guy on the floor had been dead at least twelve hours."

"And you could tell that by your nose?"

"My nose may be big, but it works normal. Besides, hanging around funeral homes, I learned how to embalm. The guy on the floor had already been embalmed."

"How could you tell that?" Mel asked, fascinated.

"He had the puncture wounds on him and some of the fluid had leaked out. I could smell that also."

"Did you follow the body all the way to the emergency room?" Mel asked.

"That was another thing. Elvis was not pronounced dead at the house, yet there was a guy there that wouldn't let us ride in the back of the ambulance with the body to the hospital. We argued for a minute or so, but the guy had us put Elvis on oxygen and then shut the door."

"Who was the guy?"

"Said he was a doctor. We pulled into the emergency room drop-off area and the guy jumped out and scurried off. I never saw him again. I was afraid to say we didn't ride in the back with Elvis for fear of getting fired, so the report was written up normal."

Obediah's car slowly rolled out of the tent parking lot.

"Obediah, Maggie talked to me tonight."

"That's not something to joke about, Mel."

"I'm serious. Right before you started your performance we talked."

Obediah pulled the car onto the shoulder.

"What did she say?"

"She told me she wasn't a baby and that she wanted a cola."

"Amazing. I'll call the doctor in the morning."

"Congratulations on winning the contest. Those other contestants didn't look too disappointed. They knew you were unbeatable," she said.

He maneuvered the car back onto the road.

"The real fun part will be doing an original song with Richard Drees and the Prairie Dogs."

"I think I want to talk to your Uncle Jess about what happened the day my father got killed," Mel said.

"I told Jess you'd be wanting to talk to him."

"What did he say?"

"He didn't say anything one way or the other."

"Obediah, you were a kid. A little older than me. He was an adult. Maybe he can tell me something you didn't."

"What is it you want to know?" he asked.

"I'm not looking for anything specific. I just want to know the entire story."

"Do you want to talk to him now? He lives just on the other side of where the festival is?"

"Is it too late?" she asked.

"Uncle Jess is a night owl. He goes to sleep around four in the morning and is up and at 'em by eight."

"Let's do it."

Obediah slowed, drove onto the right shoulder and made a sharp U turn. He drove back past the festival and turned onto a narrow drive that cut through a row of pine trees. A hand-painted sign said, 17 MPH.

"He get a lot of visitors?" Mel asked.

"None."

They came upon a small clapboard house set on short piers. A porch with a plank floor ran the width of the house and an old hound dog with large, droopy ears slept on the front door mat. The dog didn't even lift an eyebrow when Obediah and Mel pulled up.

Lights under the porch were bug lights and on; they cast a yellow glow. If one squinted one's eyes, or looked at the scene from a distance, the house looked like a space ship about to lift off.

The screen door opened and the dog moved aside as Mel and Obediah got out of the car. Uncle Jess greeted them at the steps and welcomed them into the house in his metallic voice.

The living room was not what Mel expected. The sheetrocked walls were painted a Williamsburg blue and bordered by eight inch high wood trim painted white. The room had several designer lamps and very nice furniture of the sort sold by Ethan Alan. A ceiling fan whirred from the ten-foot high, tinned ceiling. The room had felt a designer's touch. Mel and Obediah took a seat on the Italian leather sofa.

"Any one want any coffee? Only take a minute," Jess offered.

Mel declined and Obediah shook his head.

"I'm sorry about your father," Jess said.

"Did you put up the cross?" she asked.

"I tried to find out something about your father's family, but the only thing I could determine was that he had you. I didn't find anyone to ask about the cross. I hope you don't mind."

"I approve very much. Obediah has told me what happened, but would you mind telling me what you remember?"

Jess told her pretty much the same thing that Obediah had. It sounded so clinical in the metallic voice, but Mel detected the sadness in Jess' eyes.

"Did my father say anything before he died?"

"Not that I heard. Are you really down here to cover the festival, or did your father's death bring you here?" Jess asked.

"Both of those," Mel admitted and then she looked at Obediah. "And more."

"What then?" Obediah asked.

"The reason my father was driving on that road also brought me to Moscow."

Jess and Obediah stared at Mel knowing she would tell them more.

"I was born the day Elvis was pronounced dead, at the same hospital. My mother's nurse skipped out to rubberneck at Elvis's body and my mother bled to death as a result. I met the nurse for the first time tonight, Tricia Banks."

"Oh God. I'm so sorry," Jess said.

"Mel, I didn't know," Obediah said. He felt her pain.

"My father was headed from the hospital when his car got brushed by another car. My father thought Elvis was in the car. Later, when he found out about my mother's dying, I think my father blamed Elvis in some way for her death and he became fixated on finding him. In 1982 a certain Cadillac was used in a bank robbery carried out by a man wearing an Elvis mask and one of Elvis's costumes. My father thought that the owner of the car had moved to Moscow and was heading to Moscow to track down the owner when he was killed.

"In a fashion," Obediah said, "your mother and father died as result of Elvis."

"There's more. The bank robber lost some blood in the robbery. The blood sample was lost for many years. Very recently the blood sample was checked against a strand of Elvis's hair and the DNA matched."

"Are you saying that you have proof that Elvis committed a bank robbery in 1982, some five years after he died?" Obediah asked.

"That's what the lab says."

"That's incredible," Jess said.

"The car used in the bank robbery was driven around by the sheriff's office for several years and then sold at auction in 1986 and bought by Dr. Matranga."

"He's real fond of that car," Obediah said.

"In 1982 fingerprints were lifted off the car," Mel said.

"Elvis's prints were found on the car?" Jess asked. "I would have read such a thing in the tabloids years ago."

"Elvis's prints were not found," Mel said. "But Dr. Matranga's prints were found."

"In 1982?" Obediah inquired.

"Yes."

"Before he bought the car?" Obediah asked.

"They were found right after the bank robbery," Mel answered.

"Maybe there's a logical reason Dr. Matranga's prints were found on the car," Obediah said.

"I asked him about that," Mel said.

"You've talked to Dr. Matranga?" Jess asked. Mel nodded. "What did he say?"

"He had no explanation. I thought he was going to say he had been around such a car, or had been near the bank and touched it, or something, but he offered no explanation."

"Is Dr. Matranga going to be accused of the bank robbery?" Jess asked.

"Of course not. His prints only show he touched the car at sometime before the robbery. It doesn't show he was in the bank. And…," Mel stopped in mid-sentence.

"And what?" Jess asked.

"Nothing," Mel said. Her mind raced and her eyes went blank.

"Mel, do you think Elvis is living here in Moscow?" Jess asked.

"Right now, the only thing I think is that a car used in a robbery by Elvis five years after his death ended up here in Moscow."

"Could there be another explanation why the blood and hair that were tested matched?" Jess asked.

"I can't think of any," Mel said.

CHAPTER THIRTY-ONE

"Lannie, honey, I'm afraid there is nothing more we can do," Stephen Greenbaum said.

"That's nuts. We have unlimited resources and we can't find Rod Witherspoon?" Lannie frowned at Bennie, who was sitting next to her in Greenbaum's crazily decorated conference room. Bennie was studying the stuffed elephant head hanging on the wall next to the waterfall. She was thinking that it would have been cool to have a fountain coming out of the snout of the elephant.

"Mr. Witherspoon never had contact with anyone except Barb," Stephen said.

"I've heard that song before," Lannie said.

"Look, I had *two* detective agencies on this," Greenbaum explained. There are one hundred and twenty-six Rodney Witherspoons in the United States. All but sixteen are white. The agencies followed up on all one hundred and ten. The agencies compiled a dossier on all of them and contacted all of those even remotely close to the age Witherspoon should be. "

"Why did they eliminate the nonwhites?" Bennie asked.

Stephen looked at Lannie and said, "That's rather obvious, isn't it?"

"I read once that the baby of one black and one white parent can appear to be white in all regards," Bennie informed them.

"Alright, I'll have the remaining sixteen checked out," Greenbaum said, reluctantly.

The door to the conference room opened and Princess entered carrying a sterling silver tray of appetizers.

"Sweetie, just put them on the table," Stephen said.

"I hate to ask him since we've kind of broken up, and dad would kill him if he knew I were even talking to him, but maybe Freddy can help. He has contacts that go deep underground," Bennie said.

"Who's Freddy?" Stephen asked.

"You don't want to know," Lannie replied. "Stephen, how hard can it be to find the right Rod Witherspoon?"

"You're looking for Mr. Witherspoon?" Princess asked. All eyes were on her in a heartbeat.

"Yes, Princess, we're looking for a person named Rod Witherspoon," Stephen said.

"He called the other day for you," she said.

"When?"

"It was the day you had that meeting with Lannie, Tim and Dee."

"Why didn't you tell me this earlier?" Stephen asked, incredulous.

"Mr. Greenbaum, I put the message where I put all the other messages from people who need their calls returned. It's impaled on the message spindle on your desk. Oh, wait, it's not there. That thing fills up every two days and I throw the messages away. As long as I've worked here, you've never returned a call."

"Princess, where did you throw it?" Stephen asked.

"It went out with the cleaning service this morning."

"Great, finding the guy is as simple as returning his call and we can't find his phone number," Lannie said.

"Is that all you want?" Princess asked. "He called from his room at the Hacienda Hotel on Sepulveda Boulevard in El Segundo; at least that's where he told me he was calling from."

"Are you sure?" Stephen asked.

"That's where he called from the first time," Princess said.

"He called again?!" Stephen shouted.

"The second time he called he said he was at a pay phone," Princess said.

"We'll have to go to the Hacienda Hotel," Bennie said and Lannie nodded.

"Why not let the agencies handle it?" Stephen asked.

"I want to find my father before he dies of old age," Lannie said sarcastically.

"Don't you want to know what he wanted?" Princess asked.

"Please," an exasperated Stephen pleaded.

"The second message was along these lines: 'I'll send you a letter to tell you how to deposit royalty checks.'"

The clerk at the Hacienda Hotel played a game on her cell phone while chewing her gum ferociously. The "pop" reverberated throughout the lobby whenever she smacked or burst a bubble. She kept the phone hidden under the counter and out of sight in case the manager appeared; she had been written up twice already this month. He had caught her smoking in the bathroom and she had cussed out a customer. The customer had wanted his bill reduced because of noise from street traffic. She had told the customer that she had received noise complaints *on his ass,* and he must have some big cojones to be bitching about other people's noise. Luckily, the altercation had not come to blows being exchanged. The clerk was almost to the Nirvana level of the game, the second highest level when the entrance door opened. She glanced up and did a double-take.

Lannie, Bennie and Freddy marched up to the counter. They were dressed as though they were about to dig a ditch. Each had on old jeans and rumpled and torn tee shirts. A cigarette dangled from Freddy's mouth and when he bellied up to the counter ashes fell onto the counter and onto a sign that read: For The Convenience Of Our Guests, No Smoking Permitted.

"What's up? Baby doll," Freddy said, blinking through the smoke rising directly into his eyes.

"Sir, our guests are not permitted to smoke in this area," the clerk said.

"That's great. If I see any of them smoking, I'll tell them about the rule," Freddy said. "I need some information, my lady."

"Sir, but you're smoking."

"Baby doll, I'm not a guest, so it's alright. Can you hop on your computer and fish out some telephone records and personal information on one of your guests?"

"Oh, my. That would be a breach of confidentiality. We couldn't do that without a court order or something like that."

"Something like that? I get it. You want to negotiate," Freddy said, excited.

"Negotiate?" the confused clerk asked.

Freddy slipped a twenty dollar bill onto the counter. "I think we can do a little business here."

The clerk eyes locked on the twenty. "Really, sir. I couldn't do that."

"I see. You're not motivated by the worldly things in life." Freddy reached into his back pocket and pulled out a stash of marijuana in a plastic bag and plopped it onto the counter.

"What's that?" the clerk asked, her eyes riveted on the bag.

"It's what you think it is, baby doll." Freddy flashed a toothy smile.

"I'll be right back," the clerk said and disappeared through a door behind the counter.

"Freddy, maybe we should leave. She could be calling the cops," Bennie said.

"Freddy is a good judge of character. She was trying to smoke the stuff in the bag with her eyes. We'll just wait," Freddy said.

Seconds later the clerk returned, grabbed the bag from off the counter, stuffed it into the pocket of a jacket she was wearing and replaced it with a sheet of paper.

"You forgot to ask the name of the guest and the period that we need the information for," Lannie said.

"That's the information, including passwords, to get into the hotel's computer."

"Thanks, baby doll." Freddy slid the paper off the marble, folded it and stuffed it into his pocket. He, Bennie and Lannie turned to leave.

"How can I get in touch with you for future needs?" the clerk asked Freddy.

He hiked out his wallet, pulled his card from it and pushed it to the clerk.

"Hey, while you're in there, the computer, could you give Brittany Corbin a fifty-cent an hour raise?" the clerk asked.

"I'll make it an even buck," Freddy said over his shoulder. "The shit I sell ain't cheap."

The information on Rod Witherspoon in the computer records of the Hacienda Hotel was a bust. Witherspoon had made no other phone calls besides the one to Greenbaum, although there had been four calls and not two as Princess had indicated. Witherspoon had paid in cash and left the car registration information empty. The trail stopped there at the hotel.

Freddy stretched back with his hands behind his head. The fine fabric of the sofa in the Drees's den felt good.

"That wasn't much fun," Bennie said.

"Fun? Bennie girl, you want some shit to make you feel better?" Freddy asked.

"Freddy, I'm supposed to be in drug rehab right now."

"Ain't no doctors here," Freddy observed, waving his arms.

"What do we do next?" Lannie asked.

"I've been thinking about that," Freddy said. I'll get my Uncle Jonas to talk to One-Eye Landon. One-Eye's part of an organization that is nationwide."

"So we put out an A.P.B. with the mafia?" Bennie asked and laughed.

"One-Eye's got a woman on the payroll who works at the IRS. She might be able to turn something up."

"Freddy, we don't have Witherspoon's social security number," Lannie said.

"We can find out from the greaseball lawyer how much money this Witherspoon guy was given. My guess is the guy uses the name Witherspoon for only this song writing gig and that he files a return for only the amount he receives from Barbara Drees. He's got a legitimate business writing songs and will want to keep it legit. Also, the IRS lady will be able to get us the tax returns of all the Rodney Witherspoons. We'll match up the money Barbara Drees gave him with the returns the IRS lady gives us. Right now, Lannie, we need to get at your mother's checking account records to try and figure out how much Witherspoon's been given. Even if the checks are for cash, they'll be large and stick out. We also need to talk to her accountant. The accountant might be able to find an IRS Form 1099 from your mother to the guy for the payments he's received. I'm guessing that Barbara's CPA would have insisted that a 1099 be given to Witherspoon, so that the payments to him could be documented and legitimately deducted as an expense off of her taxable income."

Impressed, Lannie asked, "Freddy, how do you know that?"

"I go to college, girl. I'm thinking of becoming a CPA, a Certified Pompous Ass."

Freddy moved over to the computer. "Now what are you doing?" Lannie asked.

"Brittany Corbin's about to get a promotion, at least on her pay stub," Freddy said. "She needs a raise to be able to afford doing business with me."

CHAPTER THIRTY-TWO

Mel threw on a tee shirt and jeans and decided to skip the Felton breakfast table and head over to the Elvis Diner. She felt a twinge of guilt as she hurried past the rear of the house and climbed into her car. She needed some more filler on the festival story and the diner seemed like the place to get it.

The rental car sprang to life and puttered out of the drive. Soon she was passing the festival and she noted that very little was happening so early in the morning. A few campers dotted the parking area and a couple of those had occupants out stirring up breakfast. Her window was rolled down and she smelled a whiff of bacon frying.

A light cloud of fog clung to the ground amidst the poplar and pine trees lining the road. And as the pavement droned a pleasant hum from the rental's churning tires, the fog swirled and a surreal landscape was painted. The fog made everything appear soft and subdued. A sense of calm pervaded Mel's body. She let out a deep breath. Almost as if by magic, off in the pasture just past the festival, on the opposite side of the road from where Obediah's Uncle Jess lived, a magnificent tan and brown stallion sprinted. Its mane flapped rhythmically and its tail jutted as though on a wire. Its legs and hooves were in sync as though they were the pistons of a powerful engine in an expensive foreign car. The beautiful animal seemed indestructible as its shoulder muscles rippled on the stroke of each gallop. Mel thought of stopping and studying the animal, but her rumbling tummy convinced her to continue on.

A minute later she came to the diner. The parking lot was jammed with cars bearing out-of-state plates and pickups with in-state plates. She parked on the shoulder of the road.

The noise stung her ears when she went through the diner's door. Dishes and utensils clanged and everyone seemed to be talking at the same time. Mel quickly observed that the only open seat was at the counter, so that's where she went. As soon as she sat down, Debra Ann appeared and started pouring coffee in a cup.

"Well, if it isn't Miss New York City in the flesh," Debra Ann said and smiled.

"Hello, Debra Ann. I guess you know I'm staying with your mother?"

"Way I hear it, you're staying in my brother's bed." Debra Ann said, grinned slyly and gently pushed the cup in front of Mel.

"Technically, as he says, that's true."

"Hon, I'm just razzing you. Sorry I ain't got time to chit chat, what can I get you?"

"Why don't you surprise me?"

"Good, it'll be the Special."

"What's that?" Mel asked.

"If I told you, it wouldn't be much of a surprise, now would it?" Debra Ann said, peeled off and penned a small sheet on a rotating metal wheel. She hollered, "Nestor, another fat and skinny pig, two ropes, taters and megs!"

The man next to Mel said, "Good choice," in a metallic voice. She turned and saw it was Jess. He wore overalls and a white, starched, long-sleeved shirt. He could have been anyone's grandfather.

"What did I order?" she asked and smiled.

"Fat and skinny pigs, those are a piece of flat sausage and a piece of bacon. The two ropes are grilled pork links. The taters are hash browns and the megs are messed-up eggs."

"Scrambled eggs," she chimed in.

"You got it," he said. "I hope your story on the festival is positive. We raise a lot of money for area charities."

"Jess, I haven't seen anything would cause me to write anything negative."

"Big city folk like yourself don't appreciate our way of life."

"Actually, I'm starting to understand what is so appealing about the area."

Mel heard a voice she recognized from the corner of the diner, turned and was surprised to see Jan Felton seated at a booth with Dr. Matranga.

Mel flagged down Debra Ann, who was working in a gear known by few mortals, "Debra Ann, would you mind if I got you to bring my food to your mother's table?"

"Okay, hon."

"Jess, I hope you don't mind," Mel said.

"Not at all girl."

Mel padded across the diner to Jan's table. Matranga looked up, and to Mel's chagrin, he grinned and said, "Mel, good to see you. Why don't you take a seat and join us?"

"That would be delightful, Mel," Jan said

Mel slid into the booth next to Jan

"Migel and I were just talking about you."

"My ears weren't burning," Mel said. "Must not have been too bad."

Matranga laughed out loud and Jan joined in.

"It's pretty silly that you think Migel robbed a bank years ago."

Mel's eye locked onto Matranga's, but his eyes were soft, kind and friendly. She expected fire and brimstone.

"I was surprised to see you here, Jan. What about all your bed & breakfast guests?" Mel asked.

"I have someone come in on Fridays and weekends. Those are my days off."

"Did Obediah tell you that Maggie talked to me? Mel asked.

"He did."

"He didn't believe me, do you?" Mel asked.

"Mel, I believe you. Maggie talks to me too."

"Does Obediah know that?"

"No. I don't tell him because it would upset him. Until now, I was the only person she talked to. She doesn't even talk to her doctor."

Debra Ann arrived with a platter of food and eating utensils for Mel.

"That's way too much food," Mel protested.

"Eat what you can and the rest just stuff in your face," Debra Ann retorted. "Mom, I hate to ask, but could you give Nestor a hand in the kitchen. He's about to have a cow. He's flipping the eggs and hard-boiling the flapjacks."

"Mel, you'll have to let me out," Jan sighed. "Seems a mother's work is never done."

Mel slid off the cushion and Jan made a bee-line for the kitchen.

"Dr. Matranga, you look a little tired," Mel said.

"I got in late last night. I was in Atlanta for business."

"Several years ago I was watching CNN and a professor from Louisiana State University was being interviewed," Mel said and cut off a piece of sausage and popped it in her mouth. "She was a forensic archeologist, or something of the sort. She specialized in helping the police find missing children. She could take a photograph of a child and with the miracle of a computer, she could age the photograph and produce a fairly accurate photograph of what the child should look like now."

"I'm not bored, but if you're going to make a point, please make it," Matranga said.

"The 1982 bank robbery was videotaped. And the tape shows a Hispanic adolescent in the bank right before the robbery. The tape is fairly clear."

"And?" Matranga asked.

"I looked at it again last night. You were in the bank right before the robbery."

"What do you want me to say?" Matranga asked.

"I don't think you were part of the robbery."

"Thanks."

"The tape shows you stealing Elvis's box that was supposed to contain a bomb."

"I really don't have anything to say."

Just then, Mel's phone beeped and she opened it and answered, "Hold on." She told Matranga she'd be right back, slid from the booth and went outside.

"Hey, Lo."

"Mel, I'm on my way to the airport and I'll get to Moscow early this afternoon."

"Stop in Memphis and get a room at a hotel right off the Interstate. There is nothing available in Moscow," Mel said.

"Got it. Look, I couldn't find out much about the tract of land other than it's owned by TACKETT Corporation, whose principal owner was Barbara Anne Drees."

"The ex-wife of Richard Drees?" Mel asked.

"That's her."

"The Prairie Dogs are playing tomorrow night. Is that a coincidence?" Mel said, more than asked.

"The TACKETT Corporation leases the property to a nonprofit group whose president is Migel Matranga," Lolita explained.

"I'm having breakfast with him now."

"Now *that's* a coincidence," Lo said.

"Keep digging on TACKETT. See you this afternoon, Lo."

Mel went back into the diner and started for her table, but Matranga was gone and so was her plate. She started to pivot and was tapped on the shoulder. She turned.

"I guessed you were here," Obediah Felton said. "I've got to ride into Memphis to get a few things for my guitar, do you want to come?"

"Another date?"

"I guess so."

"I think I need permission from your mother first," Mel teased.

"What?"

Mel walked behind the counter and into the kitchen. Nestor was fussing over an omelet and Jan was grating cheese over a bowl of grits.

"What's that?" Mel asked.

"Grits. Have you ever tried them?" Jan asked.

"Lord no, and I don't won't to."

"It'll improve your love life," Jan said.

"Can't improve what I don't have," Mel quipped.

Jan looked over Mel's shoulder and saw Obediah standing in the opening.

"Maybe that will change soon."

"Jan, I'm going into Memphis with Obediah and I was wondering if you could give me the name of the pawn shop where you got the ring that is in Obediah's apartment."

"It's E-Z Money Pawn and it's on Lamar Avenue."

"Thanks," Mel said and began walking away.

"Tell Obediah to quit grinding his teeth. He looks nervous," Jan said with a mischievous grin on her face.

"Jan says you've got quite an education," Mel commented. They were cruising on I-240, Obediah trying to stay in the left lane to exit at Lamar. Traffic going into Memphis was light for mid-morning.

"I saw the Commodores lose a lot of football games, that's all."

"What are you going to do when you grow up?" Mel asked.

"Haven't gotten there yet."

"You can stop me when I cross the line, Obediah. Maggie is never going to be a normal little girl. She will always be special, or at least look at herself as being special."

"Sounds like you're speaking from experience."

"I had a marvelous childhood, as well as I could have considering I was orphaned at such a young age."

"Here's our exit," Obediah announced and veered the car off the ramp. "I think the pawn shop is just off the Interstate. Didn't mean to interrupt."

"One thing I know, Maggie will not even begin to think of herself as being normal if you aren't."

"You think there is something wrong with me?" Obediah asked.

"You're afraid of women."

Obediah laughed nervously as he steered the car into the E-Z Money parking lot and killed the engine. "To be real to the point, I've lost my confidence," he said.

Mel reached across the short distance between them and cupped Obediah's right hand in her left. "I know, Obediah." She moved across the seat and held his head with her free hand and kissed him gently on the lips.

"I don't need pity, Mel," he said when she pulled her head back.

"Pity? I wanted to do that when I was lying on my deathbed in Matranga's office."

Obediah grinned. "Which time?" he asked.

"Both."

"We could stay in the car and make out like teenagers, or we could go into this pawn shop," Obediah said.

"It wouldn't look good in the Memphis newspaper that an area mayor was arrested for indecency."

"This isn't New York. They don't arrest people for kissing in public."

"My thinking is we've been there, done that. What's next?" Mel asked and ran her hand along the back of Obediah's neck, twirling her fingers in his hair.

"Are you making a pass at me, Mel Vaughn?" Obediah was surprised at the words that had just popped out of his mouth.

"We could get a room at that last motel we passed on I-240 and find out?" Mel suddenly realized that it was difficult to breathe and her heart was racing.

Following their better judgment, Obediah and Mel reluctantly decided to first finish business at the E-Z.

The E-Z would have benefited from a starring role in a vacuum commercial; dust and grime covered everything. Light was sheltered from the windows by metal bars, painted advertisements on the glass and a coating of reflective film. The weak rays that managed to cut through the windows showcased dust particles suspended in the air. As Obediah closed the door behind Mel, a tornado of suspended dust particles swirled to their left.

The walls were covered with every type of junk imaginable and run-down lawn mowers, bicycles, leaf blowers and chain saws littered the scratched and uneven linoleum floor. "Indiana Jones must shop here," Mel said.

"Hope you got your tetanus shot recently," Obediah retorted.

A curtain of beads parted and a portly man wearing rumpled tan slacks and a white undershirt came into the shop. His shirt sported the leavings of breakfast spaghetti.

"You guys look around. Got any questions, let me know."

"We're actually here trying to track someone down," Mel said.

"Cops?"

"No," Obediah said.

"I'm not in the tracking business, but let's hear you out."

"Do you keep a list of who buys your stuff?" Mel asked. "Back in the early 1980s a lady by the name of Jan Felton bought a ring here. Would it be possible to figure out who originally pawned the ring?"

"I don't have those records here, but I do have them at my house. They're in a storage room. It would be a lot of trouble finding such a receipt. What's it to you?"

"It could be important," Mel said.

"I like *important*. How much?" The man rubbed his fingers together on his right hand.

"Fifty dollars," Mel said.

"Important research goes for a hundred around here."

Mel opened her purse and then wallet and fished out five, twenty dollar bills and gave them to the funny looking little man. "How do I know you'll call me?" Mel asked, as she drifted over to a rack of magazines.

"What? You want I should give you a receipt?" the guy said as he stuffed the bills into his pocket.

"I'll give you my card. What's this?" Mel asked. She held up a leather folder.

"That's a collector's item," he said, not too convincingly. "It's Elvis's family tree on parchment and gold leaf."

"How much?" Mel asked. She liked the leather folder.

"Twenty bucks."

Jan spied on Obediah and Mel though the back door curtain as they drove up to the garage apartment. She almost laughed when she saw Obediah spring from the car; she knew what would come next. Obediah opened the door for Mel and walked her to the back door steps, holding his hand on her back.

"I'll be back in a couple of hours," he said and then bent down and drew Mel into his arms. She arched her back and they kissed. Their lips lingered for a long time and Jan thought of opening the door to interrupt them, but giggled instead.

Finally, Obediah drove off as Mel waved. The door to the kitchen opened and she went in.

"I was wondering what was taking you two so long in Memphis," Jan said. "Why don't we have a seat here in the kitchen? I've got some tea that's brewed."

"That would be lovely, Jan." Jan fussed with some glasses, sugar and lemon and was soon seated at the table.

"What hotel did you go to?" Jan asked, as natural as if she were asking what time it was.

Mel blushed and then realized her cheeks were beet-red.

"I don't know what you're talking about," Mel protested.

"I saw the way Obediah pranced over to you when he got out of the car. The weight of the world has been lifted off his shoulders. And you have a glow about you. Where did you go?"

"I don't feel comfortable talking about that with you."

"Never mind, Obediah will tell me."

"He will?"

"He tells me everything. Most everything."

"We found the pawn shop."

"I'd have been disappointed if you hadn't."

"A guy at the shop is trying to find the record of who originally pawned the ring."

"What will that tell you?" Jan asked.

"I don't know."

"Migel Matranga is a good man," Jan said.

"Why do you bring that up?" Mel asked.

"Because of what you're accusing him of doing."

"Jan, I'm not accusing him of anything."

"Migel came here after medical school and his internship and opened that clinic. He's the only doctor in town. He barely meets his expenses. The festival foundation has donated over a million dollars to charity."

"Jan, I promise that Dr. Matranga will not be accused of any crime."

"Good. What's on tap for you and Obediah this afternoon?"

"I was going to lay around here and wait for Obediah to come pick me up and then meet my assistant at the festival, but I think I'll go to the apartment, clean up and meet Obediah at the festival. What's going on there this afternoon?"

"There's a tribute band out of Memphis, and a food contest."

"What kind of food?" Mel asked.

"Elvis food. Peanut butter and banana sandwiches, fried chicken, dumplings, onion rings, a lot of comfort food. And there is the Priscilla look-alike contest."

"Incredible."

"Tonight there is one of the most popular parts of the festival," Jan said. "They'll have a viewing area set up to show outtakes from movies. Some of the extras and several actors from the films will be there."

"Where is Maggie?" Mel asked.

"She's off somewhere."

"I'll go off to my room now to freshen up."

"What's that you're carrying?" Jan asked.

"Some junk I picked up at the pawn shop."

CHAPTER THIRTY-THREE

"You've got some nasty stuff in here, man," Freddy said to Stephen Greenbaum while looking about the room. "These are some expensive toys." They were sitting in the Jungle conference room. Freddy sucked in on his Marlboro and blew out a smoke ring while studying stuffed snakes hanging on the wall.

"I wish you wouldn't do that in here. Only person who has ever smoked in here was the Duke," Stephen said, hacking.

"The Duke of what?" Freddy asked.

"The Duke, John Wayne."

"Who's he?" Freddy asked. He looked at Bennie and they both shrugged their shoulders at the same time.

"Stephen, you called me down here, what for?" Lannie asked.

"We've got a lead on finding your father." Stephen retrieved a FedEx folder from an accordion manila folder. "This came yesterday."

"What is it?" Lannie asked.

"It's from Rod Witherspoon. It's instructions on where to wire his royalty payments. It lists a bank and routing number that is in Atlanta."

"So, you've got an address?" Lannie asked.

"It's not that easy. The bank will not release the name and address of the account holder. I've talked to my bank and they've said that short of a subpoena from the feds they don't give out such information."

"Not much of a lead, Mr. Lawyer," Freddy said and blew out another ring.

"FedEx requires a municipal address and a telephone number from the sender. It's written on the Bill of Lading. I've called the phone number that's listed and eventually found out that the number is not a working number. Our investigator hired one in Atlanta to check out the address. There is an apartment at the address and the Georgia investigator is snooping around as we speak. At the moment we know that the apartment is rented to someone name Rod Witherspoon, that he pays his rent in cash and that he is seldom there."

"Stephen, whatever it takes," Lannie said.

"I've ordered around-the-clock surveillance until someone shows up at the apartment."

Princess knocked on the conference room door and entered.

"Mr. Greenbaum, I know you said you did not want to be disturbed, but there is a lady on the line who works with *Weird Magazine* asking to talk to you."

"Lannie, I'm sorry, but there is no telling what she's calling about. Those tabloids are just like the television and newspaper reporters. They call about a story at the last minute and you don't talk to them, then they print that they tried to get a comment from you but could not. They make it look like you are avoiding them. Lord knows what client they are calling about."

"Everyone has a gimmick," Freddy said.

Stephen switched on his headset. "Hello, this is Stephen Greenbaum."

"Lolita Carter with *Weird Magazine*."

"I'm with clients, if this will not take too long I'll answer any questions you have, although I must say I doubt that I will have any comment on your story."

"I'm not calling about a story. You are the agent for service of process for a company called TACKETT Corporation?"

"Yes."

"We are researching an article on TACKETT and have discovered that the company owns several hundred acres in Moscow, Tennessee."

"What about it?" Stephen asked.

"The sole use of the property is to host a festival once a year."

"Yes, we lease the grounds out to a non-profit group out of Moscow. The lease is public information. The group is headed by Migel Matranga."

"Yes, I understand that. Our research has concluded that TACKETT is part of a conglomerate owned by Barbara Anne Drees. What we really want to know is, who else is involved in TACKETT?"

"I can't go into that. The information is protected by the attorney-client privilege and if there is nothing else you need, I'm afraid this conversation is over." Stephen clicked off the phone.

"She was calling about TACKETT?" Lannie asked.

"It was nothing," Stephen said.

Lannie grabbed her cell phone from the coffee table in Barbara Drees' living room and looked at the caller I.D. "Hi, Tim."

"Lannie, is this a good time to talk?"

Lannie winked at Bennie. "Yeah, I'm alone."

"Any news on finding your father?"

"We're getting close. Where are you calling from?" she asked.

"I'm in Atlanta. We have a concert here tonight and then night after next we're in a wide spot in the road called Moscow, Tennessee. It's right outside of Memphis."

"What on heavens for?"

"Richard said that about a year ago Barb insisted that he and Barb play at the Elvis festival that's located there, so he booked it. He's not even making enough for expenses."

"I'm going a little stir crazy over here. Would it be okay if I joined you in Memphis?" Lannie asked. Bennie rolled her eyes, made fake-kissing motions with her lips and then buried her nose in a magazine.

"Stir crazy?" he teased.

"Alright, you win. I miss you."

"Is the missing me physical?"

"Alright, Tim. I'm hornier than a stampeding herd of Texas longhorns. Satisfied?"

"Then I guess you could come to Memphis. I'll fax you the particulars, but we'll be in Memphis by tomorrow at 4 p.m."

"Tim, I've never been to Graceland. Do you think we could go?"

"I'll check to see if it will fit into the schedule."

Bennie jumped up and down on the sofa mouthing, Road Trip, Road Trip, Road Trip.

"Would it be okay if I brought Bennie?"

"Sure. Tell her that Rat is already in Moscow and will be there when we get there."

Lannie's phone clicked. "Tim, I'm sorry, but I've got another call coming in."

"See you in Memphis, bye."

"Hello," Lannie said.

"Lannie, this is Stephen. We got lucky in the Atlanta surveillance. A man showed up at the apartment. The guy stayed at the apartment for a few minutes and left. The investigator says the license plate is a specialty plate that indicates the owner of the car is a doctor. He took some photographs of the guy and the first chance he gets he's going to email them to me."

"Did the investigator follow the guy?"

"He thought it was best to stay at the apartment. He's checking the license plate now to get a name and address."

CHAPTER THIRTY-FOUR

The two chartered jets touched down through partly cloudy skies within minutes of each other on the same runway at Memphis International Airport. The two groups joined at a private hanger and were ferried in the same mini-bus to the transportation area. Three paparazzi hurriedly snapped photographs of Richard Drees and his entourage as they were whisked from the mini-bus.

Within minutes Lannie, Bennie, Tim, Jeff and Richard were in the limousine headed for the Peabody Hotel.

"Jeff, does *Weird Magazine* consider you to be paparazzi?" Richard asked.

"I never thought of it before. Why do you ask?" Jeff asked.

"If you are, then the paparazzi just took a picture of paparazzi," Richard noted and laughed.

"Am I going to be in a tabloid?" Bennie asked. Her nose was crinkled and she was frowning.

"Were any of your breasts exposed?" Richard asked.

Bennie looked down, then at Richard and then down again and noticed that she still had on her shirt and said, "No."

"Probably not then, but why do you ask?" Richard inquired.

"If my probation officer's supervisor saw that I had left California, there would be trouble," Bennie said. "My officer doesn't mind much of what I do, but he would catch hell from his supervisor."

"Are you still *dating* your probation officer?" Lannie asked.

Richard and Tim turned their heads and looked at Bennie, waiting for an answer to the silly question.

"That was so last week. A youthful indiscretion. I'm on emotionally solid ground now. At least since yesterday, I think. Not since I got in trouble with my parents. Although we haven't formally broken up."

Tim ignored Bennie's commentary, pulled a complimentary bottle of water from the limo refrigerator, offered it around and when everyone shook their heads no, cracked open the cap. He gulped down a large swig and said, "First thing I want to do when we get to the hotel is bathe."

"I guess Lannie will need a bath too," Bennie said and rolled her eyes. She poked Lannie in the ribs with her elbow.

"Am I missing something?" Richard asked. He had been looking out the window marveling at the number of pickup trucks in Tennessee. Lannie tensed her lips and glared at Bennie and shook her head from side to side, signaling Bennie not to talk about Lannie's and Tim's budding relationship. Lannie didn't know if Richard knew how far she and Richard's relationship had progressed.

"What are we doing tonight and at what time?" Lannie asked, hoping to redirect the conversation.

"I'm dropping you guys off at the hotel and then I'm headed for the Gibson Guitar Factory," Richard said. "Every time I come to Memphis I buy a dozen or so guitars. The manager and I are friends. In fact, he used to send Barb guitars all of the time."

"*Buy*? When's the last time you *bought* a guitar?" Tim asked and smiled at Richard.

"You're right. Gibson gives them to me. They're custom jobs with my name and the band's name on them. In return, Gibson gets free advertising. I feel as though I'm paying for them when I playing them up on stage."

"I thought we'd eat at the Rendezvous around 6:30 and then hit Beale Street. Listen to some authentic blues," Tim said.

"Don't forget that at five I've got to sign autographs at the Memphis Rock 'N' Soul Museum," Richard said. "Of course, that's just upstairs from Gibson Guitar."

"I've got that set up. Your signing gig is only an hour. The limo will get you at 6:00 in front of the building and get you back to the hotel by 6:05 or so. If you want, you can go straight to the Rendezvous. Don't worry; I've booked a private room at the restaurant and we can be a little late."

Lannie's phone vibrated in her pocket. She plucked it out and saw that it was Greenbaum. "Stephen."

"Lannie. The fellow that went to Witherspoon's apartment in Atlanta is Dr. Migel Matranga. He's the fellow in Moscow, Tennessee who heads an organization that leases some land that TACKETT owns. The investigator got his name from the license plate. The investigator emailed me a picture of him and I've never seen him in my life."

"I'm going to be in Moscow tomorrow. I'll look up Matranga and see what he knows about Witherspoon. Good work, Stephen."

"Thanks. By the way, that fellow you brought to the office the other day, Freddy, he came by today and asked me if I needed some investigative work, needed some sex, or needed some one hurt. He said he had some one who could break a leg real cheap, if I ever needed one broken. Lannie, is that guy for real?"

"We'll talk when I get back," Lannie said, closed her eyes, shook her head and flipped her phone shut.

"When are we going to see Graceland?" Bennie asked.

"I've arranged a private tour tomorrow night after the concert in Moscow," Tim replied.

"I read in a tabloid once that a disguised Elvis is one of the tour guides," Bennie said.

"That sounds like some of the crap you'd read in our magazine," Jeff said.

"I've arranged for Elvis to give us a personal tour of the joint," Tim said, "even his gravesite."

Lannie and Tim slouched in the over-sized tub with bubbles and lather dripping over the side. Tim sat on the end away from the faucet with his legs spread and Lannie lay back against his chest. Music from an MTV station wafted from the bedroom into the bathroom. An opened bottle of champagne nestled in an ice bucket rested next to the rumpled bed. Two half-empty champagne stems perched on the lip of the tub.

"Does Richard know involved we are?" Lannie asked. She made eddies in the suds by waving her hand back and forth under the water.

"He's very happy about it. Although, I have to be honest, if he had objected, I would have cut you off." Tim played with the bubbles in Lannie's hair by blowing on them. The air felt cool against the nape of her neck and it soon erupted in goose bumps. She shivered, even though the water was still hot.

"If you would have done that, I would have cut *it* off," Lannie said, arched her head back and nibbled on Tim's neck.

"How does it feel to be a big record mogul?" he asked. He collected his glass and sipped.

"Other than the fact that I haven't a clue what to do, I feel good. The only salvation is that I know that you, Richard and Dee will not let me screw things up."

"Richard and Dee have the Midas touch, especially Dee. That guy is uncanny. He could smell a hit through a lead wall."

"How did he and mom hook up?"

"I don't know. That was long before I started working for Richard. Rumor is that Dee was managing a dive in Memphis and your mother played there years ago."

"I think by tomorrow Greenbaum will have found Witherspoon. I have this gut feeling I'm going to meet my father soon."

"Lannie, I'm sure you've thought of this, but Witherspoon has chosen all these years to not reveal himself to you. He may not welcome you with open arms."

"I have a theory about that. I don't think mom ever told him I was his daughter. He doesn't know about me."

CHAPTER THIRTY-FIVE

Melissa Vaughn was almost giddy as she drove to the festival. Her senses were heightened and her mind was as sharp as though she were on a caffeine rush. She tapped her fingers on the steering wheel in time to the song on the radio. Life was great. She had a romantic interest in her life and she was on the verge of solving an incredible mystery involving Elvis. How could Elvis have robbed a bank five years after his death? And why? The story would make her famous and establish her as a serious writer.

Right before she got to the turnoff to get into the festival parking area her phone beeped.

"Hello, this is Mel Vaughn."

"This is Joe with E-Z Pawn."

"Yes, Joe. What have you found out?"

"The ring was pawned originally by Barbara Miner."

"Barbara Miner… That name sort of sounds familiar. Do you have any idea who she is?"

"The only Barbara Miner I ever heard of was a young woman who started out in the music business in Memphis years ago, moved on to Nashville and became a big country star. She died recently, Barbara Anne Drees, ex-wife of Richard Drees, that guy with the Prairie Dogs."

"Thanks for the information."

Mel pushed the speed dial button for Lolita, but got an out of service message. She made a mental note to call Lo later and ask her to get any information she could on Richard Drees from off the internet, but then she remembered that Jeff was on assignment on behalf of the magazine with the Prairie Dogs. Maybe he could give her insight on Drees.

Mel parked in the grass lot among hundreds of cars. As she dropped her phone into her purse and started to pull on the door handle when there was a tap on her window. She looked up and was surprised and opened the door.

"Lo, what are you doing here?"

"I just drove in and was walking to that tent when I saw you pull in. This Elvis stuff is big in these parts. I haven't seen so many pickup trucks in one spot since I went to the New York port authority and saw the trucks being offloaded by the hundreds from a tanker. Watch where you walk, I'm sure the ground is covered with tobacco spittle."

"Elvis is an industry in these parts. You're not going to believe the story I've stumbled on. I'll fill you in later. I'm bursting at the seams to tell someone. But first, let's go into the festival. I want you to meet someone."

"Does that someone have a rich, cute cousin?"

"Actually, I didn't ask," Mel said and laughed. "Come on, let's go in."

Mel and Lo wove their way through the maze of cars and were only fifty feet from the tent entrance when they started to squeeze between a Chevy coupe and a large Dodge van. As they inched along the van its door slid open, two arms sprang out, grabbed them each by the arm and yanked them into the van. The door slammed shut and the two women recoiled from the gun barrel shoved at them.

Bennie sat in an overstuffed chair in the lobby of the Peabody Hotel flipping through the latest edition of *People Magazine*. She was passing time while Lannie and Tim "bathed." She glanced at a story on Barbara Anne's funeral and smiled when she saw one of the pictures. Rat was in the background looking as regal as a middle-aged, burned out druggie can. Bennie peered over the pages of the magazine at the ducks marching single file. *Now that is weird.*

"Hey, Bennie," a voice called to her from her side, breaking her duck watching focus. "It is Bennie, right?"

"Hi Jeff, where's your camera?"

"Believe it or not, there are some things that I do without my camera."

"Is that a come on line?" Bennie asked.

"I've never used it before. Does it work?"

"I've heard better, but a good looking guy like you wouldn't need much of line."

"Mind if I join you?" he asked and sat in a chair when she nodded. "Being a roadie would be tough, filling all the down time."

"I used to think it would be great being on the road all the time. Good drugs and sex and all, but I think I may have been wrong."

"About what part?" Jeff asked.

"Since all sex is good, I guess the drug part. I'm A.W.O.L. from rehab as we sit here and flirt. I've read your magazine a few times. You must see some strange stuff, or is all of it fake?"

"Some of it's real.... We're flirting?"

"Are you gay or something?" Bennie asked.

"Actually, the jury's still out on that."

"Amazing, I've finally met someone as screwed up as me."

"I'll take that as a compliment," Jeff said, not sure of what Bennie meant.

"So Jeff, you can't make up your mind about whether sex with guys is better than sex with girls?"

"No experience in either."

"Jesus, what is it these days. Everywhere I turn I find nothing but virgins," Bennie said to herself, thinking of Lannie's maiden voyage of discovery with Tim.

"What?"

"Never mind. Say, I'd invite you up to my room for a romp, that's what I usually do whenever I get bored, but I'm also a sexaholic and I'm trying to stop all my bad habits at one time," Bennie said.

"I understand," he said, although he didn't really understand anything she was saying.

"Do you want to go for a walk and find out where those cute little duckies went?"

"That would be nice," Jeff said.

"Maybe later we'll romp, but I'll decide if and when."

"Okay."

"Or at least the when part," Bennie said.

"Huh?" Jeff said and jerked his head.

"Mom, have you seen Mel? I called the apartment and there was no answer." Obediah Felton said to his phone.

"She left an hour ago to go to the festival to meet you. She should be there by now." Jan straightened her apron.

"I haven't seen her. I'll check the parking lot. If I see her car, I'll check the other tent and the booths across the highway."

"If I see her I'll get her to call you on your cell," Jan said.

Obediah exited the tent, stood on top of a bench and surveyed the parking lot. The cars were parked so haphazardly that it was impossible to tell if Mel's rental was in the field. He began to meander through the lot.

"This is a step down from the Jag you were driving earlier," Mel said.

"Who is this guy?" Lolita asked.

"Lo, he's a robber and car thief," Mel said.

"And now a kidnapper," Lolita added.

"I thought you would be long gone from these parts by now. What do we call you?" Mel said.

Looking at Lo, he said, "You're kind of hot."

Lolita involuntarily smiled, caught herself and planted a frown on her face.

"What do you want?" Mel asked.

"Call me Andy."

"You used to be Mark," Mel said.

"I've turned over a new leaf."

"You've got the gun, I'll call you whatever you want. Andy, what are we doing here?" Mel asked.

"I figured the magazine you work for would pay a nice ransom."

Mel started laughing loudly and then Lolita joined in with her.

"What's so funny?" Andy asked.

"The magazine we work for is a cheapskate rag and couldn't scrounge up more than a few thousand dollars, but more important than that, *Weird Magazine* would rather run an article on how its reporters were kidnapped than the fact that the magazine paid a ransom."

"You're a reporter too?" he asked Lolita.

"Administrative assistant," Lo answered and frowned.

"So the magazine wouldn't negotiate?" Andy asked.

"The boss hates us both. He'd tell you that you were doing him a favor, he'd praise you and hang up the phone laughing."

"I kidnapped a couple of losers," he said.

"Andy, you're the one living in a stolen van with the cops after him."

"My mother had such high hopes for me. She still thinks I'm in graduate school studying to be a physicist," Andy said.

"A mother's dreams die slowly, but hard," Lolita said. "Mine thinks I'm a successful reporter."

"My brothers were so successful," Andy said.

"Are you the youngest?" Lolita asked.

"Out of five," he said.

"That's a lot to live up to, a lot of pressure," Lolita said.

"If you only knew," Andy said. His eyes moistened.

"Have you really hung around here to kidnap me?" Mel asked.

"To be honest, no. I was sitting here and saw you walking up. The other day I felt a connection with you. I opened the door and grabbed you on impulse."

"That's so sweet," Lolita said. Mel glanced at Lo and grimaced.

"What do we do now?" Mel asked.

"Heck, I haven't the foggiest idea. I've never kidnapped anyone before," Andy said.

"Suppose we just call this a date," Lolita said.

"A date?" Andy asked.

"Let's pretend we're all friends and that we've just been sitting here and talking," Lolita said.

"And then what?" Andy asked.

"Yeah, Lo, and then what?" Mel asked.

"The date's over and we just kiss and leave," Lolita said.

"And you girls run to the cops and I don't make it out of the parking lot?"

"Andy, do we look like the kind of girls that would kiss and tell?" Lolita asked as though her feelings were injured by the question.

"I…I guess not."

"I tell you what I'll do," Lolita said. She reached into her purse. "Here is my card. I've been waiting to give that to someone. It's the first time I've ever had a business card. It's really beautiful."

"What am I supposed to do with this?" Andy asked.

"I wouldn't give you my card with my phone number and work address if I thought there was the slightest chance you'd get mad at me for turning you in to the cops, right?"

"You girls wouldn't tell anyone about any of this?" he asked.

"Andy…," Lolita started to say.

"My real name is Anthony."

"Tony, you have my word as a…. as an administrative assistant," Lo said cheerfully.

"Thanks, Lo," Tony said.

"Tony, have you ever killed anyone?" Lolita asked him.

"Good heavens no. Worst thing I've ever done is boost cars and a couple of armed robberies. Heck, this gun ain't even loaded. I never use a loaded gun."

"Give me back my card," Lolita instructed and took the card from Tony when he held it out. She extracted a pen from her purse and wrote on the back of the card.

"What's that?" he asked.

"That's my home phone number. You make it up to New York, give me a call."

Tony took the card from Lo and shoved it into his pocket. He reached for the handle to slide the door back and Lo grabbed his hand. "I haven't had my kiss yet," she complained. They studied each other's eyes for almost a full minute and then leaned over in unison and kissed. Their eyes were closed and their lips lingered so long that Mel cleared her throat.

With a grin on his face, Andy pulled the handle and the girls hoped out of the van. As Lolita's and Andy' eyes were locked, he swung the door closed.

"What was that all about?" Mel asked.

"You mentioned he had a Jag?"

"A *stolen* Jag," Mel said.

"But at least he had one."

Just then Obediah came from behind a muddy Ford F-150. "Hi Mel, I've been looking for you."

"Obediah, I'd like you to meet my administrative assistant, Lo."

"Nice to meet you," Obediah said and shook her hand.

Tony cranked up the van and it belched fumes on them. Obediah, Mel and Lo stepped away from the smoke. The van inched off and slowly started meandering through the crowd.

"Do you have anything to say about that van, Lo?" Mel asked.

Lo shook her head no.

"Obediah, I got a call from that guy at the E-Z Pawn Shop," Mel said. "He said that your ring was originally pawned by Barbara Miner."

"When I was a kid there used to be a place that mom would take me to in Memphis," he said. " Back then kids used to go into bars. This honky tonk used to have music most nights. I remember one of the performers was this really pretty lady called Barbara Miner. She later made the big time as Barbara Anne Drees."

"That's what the guy with E-Z Pawn said," Mel said.

"There is a lot going on today. Tomorrow the festival ends," Obediah commented to Lo.

"You're going to sing with Richard Drees tomorrow?" Mel asked.

"The winner of the sound-alike contest performs original music with the showcase band at the end of the festival. Last year I sang with Toby Keith."

"I want to meet Drees," Mel said.

"I'll arrange it. What would you girls like to see today?"

"What are our options?" Lo asked.

"Right now there's an Elvis Jeopardy contest in the west tent, a display of Elvis dinnerware and a hairstyle contest."

"Hairstyle contest?" Lo asked.

"It's not what you think. The winner is the guy who can get the most tubes of Brylcream gel to stick to his head. Last year Reverend Beals got eighteen tubes piled on."

"Oh, I see. What's in the other tent?" Lo asked.

"The east tent has a Priscilla look-alike contest, photographs of old Cadillac convertibles and an autograph session by guys in the army with Elvis," Obediah explained.

"Obie, you don't mind if I call you Obie?" Lo asked.

"Not at all. That was my nickname in high school."

"I like that, Obie," Mel said.

"Obie, don't take this the wrong way," Lo said, "but the Elvis dude's been dead twenty-five years. All the stuff you're describing would bore a redneck and cause a scholar to go hair lip."

Obie grinned. "To most of the people that attend a festival such as this, this is a social happening. Elvis *was* the cultural *icon* of their youth. Coming here gives them a link back to their youth. Participating in these seemingly innocuous events grounds them to a time that was simpler."

Lo stared off at a cloud and squinted her eyes. The hand was a little fuzzy, but the cloud was definitely a pitcher, well, almost. The vessels in her eyes tightened and then she looked from the pitcher floating above and at Obie. Her head tilted and she asked,

"What's an icon?"

All seven galleries of the Memphis Rock 'N' Soul Museum were jammed with Prairie Dog fans and the line snaked past Ike Turner's piano and B.B. "Beale Street Blues Boy" King's guitar and meandered to the table set up for Richard Drees to sign autographs.

He leaned over and told Alex Chalmers who was sitting next to him, “I won’t be here long enough to sign something for all these people. Hope the museum has some security.”

“Across the pond we’d just run for the door at the appropriate moment,” Alex said.

“Alex, I’ve known you for how long?”

“Since I became manager of the Palladium?”

“Actually, since before then. You used to do the sound at pubs here in Memphis in the early 80s. I was jealous mostly that you knew Barb before I did. She told me you guys collaborated on some songs. In all the time I’ve know you I don’t think you’ve ever said anything that I would want to repeat to another reasonably intelligent adult,” Richard said and chuckled. “Barb told me that you guys once dated and I can’t for the life of me see what she saw in a scrawny flake like you.” Richard smiled and signed an album that a fan shoved in front of him and shoved it back.

“Flake? We Brits have our aloofness to uphold, old chap. We wear it as though it were the family crest.”

“In truth, if you weren’t the best damn lyricist on the face of the planet now that Barb is gone, I wouldn’t give a plugged nickel to spend any time with you. You’re so full of crap.” Richard shook his head back and forth.

“So you think Barb was better, huh?” Alex asked, fishing.

“Why do you do sell all your songs through TACKETT under pseudonym?” Richard asked.

“You know why. Most of the stuff I write is country. How many people would take seriously country music written by a Londoner? The Beatles caught lightning in a bottle once, but I can’t see the Red, White and Blue having a country music British invasion.”

“You may be right. Rednecks in the south might not dance to music written by a foreigner whose ancestors lost the war for independence.”

“Do you think Lannie will be able to run TACKETT?” Alex asked.

“The label’s loaded with a killer song list. She’ll do fine with help. Alex, would you mind doing something useful and get me a soda?”

“Damn. I went from being the best lyricist on the planet to being a gofer.”

"You're better than that. I won't call you a gofer, I'll call you a lackey," Richard joked.

"Thanks for the promotion," Alex said. He jutted his nose into the air and was off to get a soda.

CHAPTER THIRTY-SIX

Bennie glanced at Jeff and their eyes locked. She reached for a bottle of water from the nightstand and the sheet slid from her breasts. Jeff's eyes widened and followed it down.

"You act as though you've never seen a pair of tits before," Bennie said. She unscrewed the cap and gulped half the bottle. Water dribbled down her chin and onto one of her breasts.

"The lights were off last night," he explained, mesmerized at the trail of water as it flowed downhill along her creamy skin towards the nipple.

"Only because you insisted." She replaced the cap on the bottle and put it back on the nightstand. As she bent over, the sheet revealed more of her hip and part of her rear.

"I was intimidated and scared," Jeff admitted.

"You did pretty well for your first time," Bennie purred and grinned.

"You're an excellent teacher."

"It's easy to paint when the canvas is blank." She stared off at the wall. "I can't believe I just said that," she said and giggled like a schoolgirl.

"Is lovemaking always so exhausting?" Jeff asked, his eyes still riveted on the trickle of water.

"If it's done right, I suppose."

Jeff leaned over and cupped the wet breast in his hand. "Will you be going to the festival this afternoon?" he asked, with no hint in his voice as to what his hand was doing.

"That's the plan, but why do your ask?" She looked down at his hand.

"I'll be there."

"Jeff, we're not lovers you and I. This is just a one time thing. You do understand that? I look at it as slipping off the wagon. You're a cute guy and I thought I'd help you out with your journey to figure out if you're gay or not. Although I do admit I find you....interesting."

"I'm pretty sure that I like women... a lot," he said and his head bobbed.

"Well, in that case, are you just going to hold on to that thing, or do you want to play with it and see where it leads?"

"That's disgusting," Lannie complained. Tim kept shaking the bottle and ketchup dripped onto the mass of scrambled eggs in his plate.

"I thought so too, until I tried it," Tim said. He struck the back of the bottle and a blob fell on his plate.

Lannie glanced around the restaurant in the Peabody Hotel and was relieved that no one in the breakfast crowd was looking at their table. "You're not going to get me to try it." She subconsciously folded her hands across her chest in defensive posture.

"Hey, suit yourself," he said and stuffed a forkful of red egg into his mouth.

Lannie pretended to shiver at the sight. "I tried calling the Matranga guy in Moscow but only got an answering service," she said. "I left my number. I'm trying to arrange a meeting," she said and bit into her hotcakes that were drenched with Steen's Pure Cane Syrup.

"So you think he knows Witherspoon?"

"Stephen's private eye thinks so," she mumbled with her mouth full.

"We'll see, Lannie."

"I made a life-altering decision last night," she announced. Her face took on a very serious demeanor.

He put his fork down and sipped some orange juice. "Now you're scaring me."

"I've decided to become a full-time student."

"What brought that on?" Tim asked, relieved, half-expecting something that he was not ready for, like she wanted to get married.

"I'm also changing my major, or more accurately, finally declaring one. I want to study business management, now that I'm a record tycoon."

Jan Felton hated meeting her lover in secrecy, but that's the way it had always been. No need for scandal. And no need to hurt Maggie and Obediah. She felt guilty with her selfishness.

She adored his little two bedroom cottage hidden in the corner of a twenty-acre tract thick with poplar and pine trees. His home was simple yet lacked for nothing. The kitchen had gleaming, industrial-quality appliances and an enormous work island in its center. The spacious den had a state-of-the-art entertainment center with the latest satellite and television technology. His compact disc collection was probably the largest private collection in the world. The bathrooms were as large as bedrooms and had a therapeutic pool and bidet along with the usual necessities.

Jan pulled the toast from the toaster and started scraping butter onto the knife.

"Every time you spend the night, you make me the biggest breakfast," he said. "I hate for you to come here and work."

"I don't see it as work, I see it as love." She spread butter on a piece of toast.

He came from around the island, put his arms around her and pulled her close. "You're as special as the day I met you."

She lifted her head and kissed him on the lips. "Thanks for being you," she whispered.

"For the millionth time, why don't we get married and you move in?" he asked, stroking her hair with his fingers."

"You know I love you and have only loved you," she said hoarsely.

"I know."

"That should be enough."

The crowd at the Elvis Diner was as noisy as ever, but Mel tuned it out. This had to be done.

"Obie, you know I'm going to have to leave here tomorrow morning?" She nervously toyed with the sugar shaker, took in a deep breath to relax and sat back in their booth by the window.

"I'm trying not to think of that." He looked out of the window at nothing in particular. This had suddenly turned very awkward.

"I've got some leverage at work and I might be able to persuade the magazine to open up an office in Memphis," she said.

He turned back to her and reached across the table and took her hand. "Mel, I don't want you to take this the wrong way. I like you a lot, but I'm not sure I'm in love with you and I don't want you doing something drastic thinking there is more here than there is. I hope that didn't come out the wrong way."

A sense of relief and calmness overtook her. "I feel the same way you do, Obie. I'd move to Memphis for two reasons. One, I have a relative, well, sort of a relative, I call him Uncle Ron, who lives there. I saw him the other day and realized I really need what he represents in my life--that connection to my past. Two, I'd like to see where our feelings for each other lead."

"I'm a little afraid of you, you do know that?" he asked.

"Don't be."

"Maggie likes you. Mom thinks you invented the world. And I'm overwhelmed. This could take some time to sort through."

"I'm very patient, but I need to warn you about something."

"Oh…"

"If I can swing a move to Memphis, that doesn't mean I'd be here a lot. Aliens, Bigfoot and the bizarre require a lot of travel on my part."

"I might be busy too. I talked to Dr. Matranga and told him I was reapplying to med school. He's got connections at Vanderbilt and said I would have no trouble getting in. He also said the foundation has scholarship money available."

"I guess you'd join him in a country practice," she said.

"Probably, but why do you think so?"

"The city folk probably wouldn't go to doctor named Doctor Obie," she said, laughed and squeezed his hand.

"You two need to get a room," Debra Ann said loudly as she approached with their plates. "People are beginning to talk."

"This place ain't so high class that it can't use a little lover's rendezvous every now and then," Mel said. Obie tilted his head and grinned.

"High class? I was thinking of taking out all these vinyl table coverings and putting in classy linen stuff."

"Really? Mom wouldn't like that," Obie said.

"But then I changed my mind. If God had wanted me to use linen table cloths he wouldn't have invented plastic trees," Debra Ann said with conviction.

"Huh?" Mel asked.

"Or did I get that backwards?" Debra Ann said. "Aw, hell, enjoy breakfast and stop the groping above the table."

"So anything *under* the table is allowed under the rules of the house?" Mel asked.

"As long as the reverend ain't in the building," Debra Ann said and pranced off.

CHAPTER THIRTY-SEVEN

The festival tent was jam-packed for the concert and for good reason. Not only was the local favorite Obediah Felton going to perform, but Richard Drees and the Prairie Dogs were scheduled to do a two-hour set. And the price of admission was only five bucks a head.

Backstage, Richard looked over the song that Felton had chosen and liked it a lot. It was a shame that the Dogs had run through it only once in rehearsal, but the Dogs were pros and he was confident the song would be well-received. Richard was also impressed with Felton's voice; the guy could sing. After rehearsal, Richard had invited Felton to go to California and cut some records. Surprisingly, Felton had not jumped all over the offer and had only been lukewarm about the possibility. The two agreed to discuss the possibility later.

Richard was peering over the sheet music when Lannie and Bennie ran up.

"Hey, girls."

"I'm really looking forward to the Graceland tour tonight, Richard. Would it be okay if I brought a friend with me?" Bennie asked.

Lannie gave Bennie a puzzled look, wondering how Bennie could have a friend in Tennessee.

"Sure, Bennie. Lannie, have you spoken to Dr. Matranga yet?" Richard asked.

"He hasn't returned my call. I asked Obediah Felton if Matranga was here and he said he was sure he would be. Felton said I could just ask someone to point him out to me."

"I'll see you gals after the concert. We're about to go on."

Mel, Jeff and Lolita sat in the front row of the VIP section.

"Jeff, have you been laid?" Lo asked.

"It shows, huh?" Jeff asked.

"Oh yeah. Question is: be it a he or she, big boy?" she asked.

"Definitely a she. It was wonderful."

"You'll have to give us the details later," Mel said.

"I took notes," Jeff said.

"You didn't, did you?" Lo asked.

"Just kidding."

Bennie and Lannie came around from behind the stage and when Bennie saw Jeff she waved.

"Jeff," Lo said, "if that's your little filly, I hope you cinched the saddle tight."

"Hi, Bennie," Jeff said as Bennie and Lannie approached.

"Hi, yourself. Is this the VIP section?" Bennie asked.

"You can sit behind us," Jeff said.

Lolita cleared her throat.

"Oh, sorry… Bennie, Lannie, this is Mel, my boss, and Lolita, her assistant," Jeff said.

Pleasantries were exchanged and Bennie and Lannie took seats behind Jeff.

"Jeff, are you from around here?" Lannie asked.

"No, but why do you ask?"

"I need a local to point out a Dr. Matranga to me."

"I'm not from here, but I know who he is," Mel said. "I saw him a minute ago. When I see him again, I'll point him out."

"Thanks."

Before anything else could be said, the band started playing. The crowd cheered, especially when Richard was introduced and came on stage. The music was loud inside the tent and it was difficult to be heard by the person next to you.

The Dogs opened with their brand new single, *Loving Her Is Like Driving Around With No Spare* and ran through most of the new album. Rat waved to Bennie between one of the songs and she waved back. The crowd was really into the concert but cheered loudest when Richard finally brought Obediah on stage.

Obie appeared nervous, but took on a new persona when Richard announced Felton's original song, *Love In Your Heart*; the band started playing and he started singing.

I've spent forever
Looking for the answers
Questions always are, why?

Marcel

Promises are broken
Cruel words are spoken
Hearts always left high and dry

Happy in good times
But sad through the bad times
Looking for love
Through it all

If I'd ever find love
I'd never know it
When it comes to loving
I'm blind

Chorus part a

Sunshine will fade
Hard times will stay
Love's fires go dark
If you don't have
Love in your heart

I've spent eternity
Searching for the truth in me
Never ever knowing
What to do

Reflections in the mirror
Couldn't be clearer
I have not got a clue

Sitting on the sidelines
Sifting through alibis
Looking for me
Through it all

If I'd ever find me
I'd never know it
When it comes to mirrors
I'm blind

Chorus part a repeated

Chorus part b

Dreaming, believing
Seeing, then feeling
A good woman's love--
Is that wrong?

Yearning, burning
Taking, then giving
A good woman love-
Is that wrong?

I want what you want
You want what I want
They want what we want
Good love

I've spent a lifetime
Trying to find
A woman to ease my mind

One to believe me
And never deceive me
And never play games with my
mind

I've searched in barrooms
And lonely old pool rooms
Looking for a woman
Who's kind

If I ever find her
I'd never know it
When it comes to women
I'm blind

Chorus part a repeated

The crowd went wild. Every one was on their feet and cheering. Everyone except Bennie. She stayed in her chair with her eyes and mouth wide open.

Lannie turned to her and noticed that she had a shocked look on her face. “Bennie, are you alright?”

“Lannie, no I’m not alright.”

“What’s wrong?”

“That was one of the songs in Barb’s safe.”

“What are you saying,” Lannie asked, not understanding.

“That is one of Rod Witherspoon’s songs that we found in your mother’s safe.”

Lannie jerked her head toward Obie who was taking a bow and then back at Bennie. “Who was that guy singing?” Lannie asked, excited.

Mel turned around. “His name is Obie Felton; he’s the mayor of Moscow.”

“I need to meet him,” Lannie said.

“We could do that now, if you wish,” Mel offered.

“Yes,” Lannie said.

“Follow me, we’ll go back stage,” Mel said and started for the aisle. Lannie grabbed Bennie by the arm and drug her along.

Obie had just finished putting his guitar in its case when Mel walked up.

“That was incredible, Obie,” Mel said and kissed him on the cheek.

Obie blushed and said, “Thanks, the band is wonderful.”

“Obie, this is......” Mel began, but hesitated, trying to remember the young woman’s name.

“Obie, I’m Lannie Drees, Richard’s step-daughter and this is my friend Bennie.” Obie nodded. “That song you just sang, Obie, where did you get it?”

“It’s an original tune,” he said.

“Who wrote it?” Lannie asked. Mel somehow sensed that the answer was important. She edged closer to Obie.

“Oh… My Uncle Jess wrote it.”

“Can I meet him?” Lannie asked.

“I’ll take you to his house after the concert. He lives so close we could walk to beat after-concert traffic.”

“Could you take me now, please? It means a lot to me,” Lannie said.

"Richard said he was going to call me up to the stage in a couple of minutes to help him with one of his songs. I'll take you there after that."

Mel saw how disappointed that Lannie was. "Lannie, I know where Jess lives. I could take you there."

"Great idea," Obie said.

During the walk to Jess's house Lannie explained to Mel that she had never met her father, that Rod Witherspoon was her father, and that Jess was apparently Witherspoon. The story excited Mel, as it would make a terrific piece for the magazine. She planned the article in her head as they walked.

They shuffled up the steps to Jess' porch and Mel knocked on the door. The sounds of a country song could be heard from inside the house.

Lannie's knees weakened when she heard the footsteps of someone coming to the door.

The door opened.

"Oh….hi, Dr. Matranga," Mel said.

"This is Matranga?" Lannie asked.

"Yes, I am."

"Doctor, we are here to see Jess, I think," Mel said, seeing the strange way that Lannie looked at Matranga.

Matranga opened the door all the way and invited them in. "He's in the back, I'll get him." He led them to the den where they waited while Matranga slipped through a door.

Lannie fidgeted with her purse. Bennie studied art hung on the walls and several minutes later, Matranga came into the room, followed by Jess.

"Hello, Mel," Jess said in the metallic voice, but when he turned slightly and saw Lannie, he froze in his tracks.

"Dee!" Lannie cried out.

"Who?" Mel asked.

"Dee. This is Dee Hood. He's a consultant to TACKETT RECORDS."

Jess sighed and his shoulders slumped. His hands went to his throat and he quickly removed the collar that reproduced the metallic voice. "I guess the charade is up," he said in his normal voice.

"I'm confused," Mel said.

"Did you write the song that Felton sang tonight?" Lannie asked.

"Yes," Jess/Dee said.

"Then, you're not only Jess and Dee Hood, you're also Rod Witherspoon."

Jess and Matranga glanced at each other.

"What makes you think that I'm Rod Witherspoon?" Jess asked.

"Witherspoon called Stephen Greenbaum's office, that's my lawyer, from the Hacienda Hotel in El Segundo once and left a message. He also left a message from a pay phone. But there were *four* calls from Witherspoon's room to Greenbaum's office. The other calls you made to his office you made them as Dee Hood, didn't you?"

"Congratulations on figuring all that out," Jess said. "What does the song I gave Obediah have to do with anything?"

"I found the lyrics to the song Felton sang in my mother's safe. The song was signed by Rod Witherspoon."

"I told Barb to keep that stuff safe, and I guess putting it in her safe was not very…safe," Jess said.

"I found something else in the safe," Lannie said. Tears welled in her eyes.

"Mother left me a note telling me Rod Witherspoon is my father."

"What?" Jess said. "That can't be." Then he looked away from Lannie, as if he left the room. A few seconds later he made his way to the sofa and sat down.

"You didn't know?" Lannie asked. She was now crying.

Jess shook his head. "I worked in a dive in Memphis years ago and your mother, Barbara Miner was just starting out in the business. We hit it off and one thing led to another. Yes, the timing is right. I could be your father."

"Why the cloak and dagger stuff with the names Dee, Rod and Jess?" Bennie asked.

"My real name is John Smith…," Jess started to say.

"What?!" Mel blurted out. "John Smith?"

"Yes, John Smith. I got in some serious trouble years ago and was running from the law. I got Barb to record my songs by using the name Rod Witherspoon as the writer. Later, when she asked me to help out with TACKETT I didn't want any one to know who I was. Rod Witherspoon became so successful that I was afraid to call attention to him, me. As Dee I kept a real low profile. Dee only ever met with Barb and Greenbaum. By the way, he doesn't know that I'm also Witherspoon. Barb, about the time you were born, wanted me to go to California and live with her. But I couldn't risk living a public life."

"Why the thing around your neck?" Bennie asked.

"Paranoia. I'd sent demo tapes to Barb with some of my songs and she used a couple of the dubs out of them as backup in a few of her songs. A few years ago a guy I met at the festival said he recognized my voice from a Barbara Drees song. I denied it, but he was adamant. I was worried that there might be others who recognized my voice. I started wearing the collar."

"Lannie, how are you doing?" Bennie asked.

Lannie looked at Jess and asked, "What do I call you?"

"Please call me Jess."

"Jess, I'm not feeling so hot right now, can we meet tomorrow and talk?"

"Lannie, I'd love that."

There was a loud knock at the door. Some one was impatiently banging on it. "I'll get it," Matranga announced and walked away.

A few seconds later, Freddy waltzed into the room.

"Freddy, what the hell are you doing here?" Bennie asked.

"One-Eye's lady with the IRS might be a little slow, but she sure is good," Freddy said. "Which one of you is Witherspoon?"

"That's alright Freddy. Everything is cool. In fact, Bennie and I were just leaving," Lannie said.

"Why didn't you call us about finding Witherspoon?" Bennie asked Freddy.

"I wanted to make sure this was the right dude first." Freddy answered.

Lannie got up and Jess stood when she did. Lannie moved to him and they hugged. She turned to leave and said, "Mel I'd like it if you came back with us to our hotel and we could talk."

"I'd love to, Lannie. There are some things I need to talk to you about, but I need to talk to Matranga and Jess. I'll get Jeff to bring me by the hotel in the morning if that's okay."

CHAPTER THIRTY-EIGHT

Jess turned off the stereo and sat on an easy chair opposite the sofa, where Mel reclined. "Can I offer you any coffee, tea, cola?" he asked.

"You know what I know, don't you?" she asked.

Jess glanced at Matranga who sat in a Kennedy rocker. "We think we do."

"I know Elvis used your Cadillac to rob the bank," she said.

"I guess you do," Jess said.

"My father was killed tracking you down. You have to tell me the story," Mel said.

"Do I have to?" Jess asked.

"You have no choice. My magazine's going to print some thing. You might as well get your side in."

"I guess you're right. I got to know Elvis when I worked in Memphis. He used to sneak into the bar late at night and listened to the talent. We became good friends. He used to escape from all the hoopla by coming here."

"To this house?" Mel asked.

"There was a cabin here. One of his relatives, I don't remember which, owned the land. We'd hunt and fish. It was a great place for him to unwind. I really liked this place. One night I killed a man in the bar in a fight. I was drunk and in my mind it was self-defense. But the guy turned out to be an assistant district attorney. I called Elvis because he was the only one I knew with pull. He suggested I hide out here. You know how he got as the years rolled on? He was miserable and turned to food and prescription drugs. He came out here once and told me of this plot he and his manager had hatched up. They had a guy on the inside of the coroner's office and the guy was waiting for a look-alike to die. They would switch Elvis with the dead guy and Elvis would come here. This went on for a couple of years. Every time the coroner guy would find a look-alike Elvis would chicken out. He said he would miss seeing his daughter. Finally, one day he called and said this is it. They dropped him off that day."

"That's the day I was born." Mel said. Jess didn't understand and stole a glance at Matranga who shrugged his shoulders.

"Elvis had squirreled away some money, but in a few years it was gone. He met this kid who had serious heart trouble but had no insurance. Elvis was told that the kid would die if he didn't have surgery. That's when he pulled the crazy stunt of robbing the bank. He did it for the kid."

"And you were the Hispanic kid in the bank that day," Mel said, looking at Matranga.

"I stole his box and hid in his car. Elvis brought me to live here with Jess and he helped me in ways I could never repay. He got more money from the bank robbery than he had expected. He paid for the kid's operation and the rest of the money paid for my college education. I went to med school on scholarship," Matranga explained.

"Why did you buy the car at auction?" she asked.

"That was Elvis's idea," Jess said "He thought the car was the only evidence that could possibly tie him to the robbery, so he got me to buy it. It was pretty stupid of him to use my car in the robbery. I didn't know Elvis was going to do it. He was desperate and did it on impulse on his own."

"Who got the diamond ring pawned?" Mel asked.

"That was me," Jess said. "I got Barb to pawn it. She had no idea how I came to have the ring."

"I look around here and note that at some time you came into some money," Mel said.

"Elvis liked to watch a lot of television and had no hobbies. He pretty much stayed close to this place and had a lot of time on his hands. It was the first time in his life he was not under pressure to provide a living for his entourage. He started writing music and was actually quite prolific. He wrote hundreds of great songs."

"And you passed on the songs to Barbara Drees," Mel said.

"I know a good song or group when I hear it, but I couldn't write a decent song if my life depended on it."

"Did Barbara Drees know they were written by Elvis?"

"She thought they were all mine," Jess said. "I still have almost a hundred decent songs he wrote. They're back there in the library."

"You know what I think?" Mel asked. "I think you've had plastic surgery and that you're Elvis and that's why you started wearing the collar."

"What do you need from me for a DNA check?"

"A lock of hair will do."

"I'll give it to you."

"Where's Elvis?" Mel asked.

"He died seven years ago. Had a heart attack on the front porch. He refused to go to the hospital. Matranga did all he could."

"Where's he buried?" Mel asked.

"In a way, that's the most bizarre thing about all this. He's buried at Graceland," Matranga said. "A friend of mind helped us sneak his body in one night and we buried him there. It was where he always said he needed to be buried."

"What did he think about all the fuss over his death?" Mel asked, curious.

"He thought it was funny and was amazed at the way the value of his estate kept escalating. He used to joke that most people pushed up daisies from their grave and he pushed up cash," Jess said.

"He was worried for the longest time though about his fake death being exposed," Matranga said. "A lot of the conspiracy theorists were right on the money. He didn't stop worrying about exposure until the guy in the coroner's office died. He was really worried about the photograph that all the tabloids claimed showed him through the back door screen of Graceland. It really was him. Like a fool he had gone back to get something and the camera caught him."

"This is the story of the century," Mel said.

"I have a lot of money," Jess said. "Could you be persuaded to not write it?" Jess asked.

"All the money in Tennessee would not be enough to buy this story."

"Would you think about it? I could put together three, maybe four million," he said.

"I'd like that hair sample now," Mel said.

"You think I'm Elvis? You don't trust us?" Jess asked.

"Would you prefer I get a public order to exhume the body at Graceland?" she threatened.

"I guess not."

CHAPTER THIRTY-NINE

Mel's head was spinning as she drove her car into Obie's driveway. What an unbelievable story she had unraveled. Uncle Ron would want proof, old detective that he was. But at least her father's redemption was at hand. He had started the ball rolling toward piecing together the story and would be proud of her. She had enough tangible evidence, the blood in the bank, the finger prints, the hair samples, the ring, that the story would bear up to scrutiny.

She was surprised when she pulled to the garage apartment to see Obie sitting on the steps waiting for her. She wanted to tell him the story but thought better of it. After the article was in the can she'd tell him. There was a chance, although a billion to one, that if she told him and somehow the story got out, she could be scooped.

"Obie, you shouldn't have waited up."

"What was all that about back at the festival about Uncle Jess?"

"I think he should be the person to tell you that."

"I just wanted to tell you that mom's full up and I'm spending the night at Matranga's office."

"Ugh. Why don't you stay here with me," Mel offered.

"Maggie will be up early and I wouldn't feel comfortable if she saw me that way. There's actually a small apartment at Matranga's office and the bed isn't bad. I'll be around in the morning to take you to breakfast."

She kissed him and started up the stairs.

"About what we talked about this morning, Mel," "I'm glad we see eye to eye."

"Me too."

Mel stepped out of the hot bath and wrapped a towel around her. Steam clouded the mirror on the medicine cabinet so she wiped it with a hand towel. She studied her face in the reflection for a few seconds and started to cry.

Who am I kidding? I love the guy. And he wants to take it slow. I want him to know that I won't try to be Maggie's mother, but I will be her best friend.

Mel wiped the tears from her face and opened the cabinet to get her toothpaste. She squirted some on her brush and cleaned her teeth. She slipped on her nightgown and made it to her bed, exhausted.

But as is often the case, she was too hyper to fall immediately to sleep and decided to read. She crawled out of bed, found the old leather thing she had bought at the E-Z Pawn Shop on the dresser, and got back under the covers. She inspected the leather and smelled it and then opened the cover and in two seconds she gasped. She threw the book down and ran to the bathroom, opened the medicine cabinet, closed her eyes and cried again.

A few minutes later she threw on a pair of jeans and a shirt and headed downstairs.

She knocked several times and looked at her watch. It was after two in the morning. The curtain moved and then the door opened.

"Mel, are you okay?" Jan asked.

"We have to talk."

"I know you love Obie, but it can wait until the morning."

"I know who Obie's father is," Mel said.

"Oh my," Jan said, opened the door and Mel stepped in. "Have a seat at the table. I need some water. Can I get you anything?"

"No thanks."

"What's this nonsense about Obie's father?" Jan asked as she poured tap water from the sink into a glass.

"I'm going to tell you a tale, Jan."

"Okay."

"And you can interrupt me whenever you want."

"Okay."

"Many years ago Elvis used to come around and hide out in a cabin just up the road from here. He used to go to the diner to eat because he liked the food, but mostly because he was infatuated with a young, beautiful waitress who worked there. The waitress was shy, but after a while she became smitten with Elvis. He asked the waitress out and she eagerly responded to his attention. They were in love and one thing led to another and the waitress got pregnant and bore Elvis a son. My guess is that the pregnancy was planned from the perspective of the waitress. In any event, the son was sickly and a couple of years after Elvis faked his death and moved to the area the son needed a costly heart operation to save his life. The young woman didn't have the money for it and neither did Elvis because he had left all his fame and fortune in Graceland. Elvis robbed a bank with a friend's Cadillac, used the cash to pay for the operation and had the young woman go to the E-Z pawn shop to get his ring out of hock. For some reason Elvis and the woman never married, but had another child, a daughter. I believe that pregnancy was probably planned."

"How did you figure all that out?" Jan asked. She seemed calm.

"I confirmed that Elvis robbed the bank with DNA. And I confirmed tonight that he used Jess's car to rob the bank to get money for a sickly kid."

"How did you find out about Elvis and me?"

"The medicine in Obie's cabinet is for his heart."

"That's strictly preventative. He's healthy."

"And tonight I saw Elvis's family tree. His great grandmother on his mother's side was Martha Tackett. That's where the name of Barbara Drees' record company comes from. My guess is she got it from Jess. Elvis's great grandfather also on his mother's side…"

"Was Mileage Obediah Smith," Jan said.

"I know Elvis died of a heart attack and is buried at Graceland."

"Who told you that?" Jan asked.

"Jess and Matranga."

"What are you going to do with this information?" Jan asked. Her face was serene.

"Before I figured out who Obie's father was, I was sure that I was going to write an incredible story. I'm not sure now."

"Mel, it would ruin our lives."

"I know. Even if I just published the TACKETT part of the story, there's a good chance someone would figure out the rest like I did."

"So what are you going to do?" Jan asked.

"You don't seem too upset," Mel said.

"Deep down I always thought that the story would come out. I'm not worried about me. I can take anything. It's Maggie and Obediah I am concerned about."

"I have to go into Memphis in the morning early and when I get back we'll talk. If you hear from Obie in the morning tell him I'm sorry I missed breakfast." Mel felt like she had to discuss all this with someone or her chest would burst, and that person would be Uncle Ron. He was the only person she knew that she could truly trust. "Can we talk when I get back?"

"I'd like that."

CHAPTER FORTY

Mel tossed and turned all night and was happy when the sun finally came up. She called Uncle Ron to make sure he would be home and when asked why she had to see him, she simply said it was a matter that could not be discussed over the phone. Only after she assured him that she was not in any trouble did he hang up. She pulled on her jeans and a shirt and didn't even put on any makeup and was out the door within minutes of hanging up the phone.

Soon, headed for Memphis, she was driving by the festival tents and thought the site looked ghostly. There were no cars in the lot and the canvas was covered by a thick layer of mist. She glanced off to the left and when she saw the white cross her heart leapt and her eyes teared up. She also felt a tremendous sense of pride in her father.

As she approached the diner she saw Obie's car pull from the gravel lot of the diner and was surprised when it headed away from town. Instinctively and not knowing why, she slowed to maintain her distance from Obie's car. She felt a little ashamed of herself. Here she was *tailing* the man she loved.

A couple of miles from the diner the brake lights on Obie's car lit up and it pulled into a drive that was mostly hidden by dense bushes. If a passerby wasn't looking for the drive, odds were great it wouldn't even be noticed. Mel slowed and then pulled off the highway into the drive and onto a narrow gravel road that wound through dense underbrush and tall trees. After half a mile she came to a clearing and stopped abruptly. Obie's car was parked in front of a quaint house that had been invisible from the road.

Then Mel was surprised when the driver's door of Obie's car opened and Jan stepped out. Jan closed the door and started for the porch of the cottage. Before she got to it, however, a man came out of the house and met her. They hugged and he escorted her up the steps and in through the door. The man had short gray hair and a neatly trimmed gray beard. He appeared to be about five foot nine inches tall, was trim and well-tanned.

Mel backed the car up about fifty yards, pulled off of the gravel drive, and parked the car behind a growth of bushes. She got out of the car and started on foot through the woods. She made her way to the cottage and realized that she couldn't just walk across the clearing and up to the house. She would be easily exposed and seen. She determined that the rear of the house abutted the woods and that if she could circle around she could get closer to a window and be protected from discovery by the woods.

Somewhere along the way she quit feeling like a louse for snooping and felt a sense of adventure. The rush she had felt the night before again pulsed through her veins.

With great effort she made her way through the dense growth and finally came to the rear of the house. She pushed back a branch that was heavy with fronds and peered into a large window and saw Jan and the gentleman seated and talking at a table. Jan appeared to be crying and the gentleman often put his arm around her shoulder to reassure her. After a few minutes the gentleman got up and moved away from the room but came back in a few seconds with a glass of water for Jan. The gentleman and Jan talked for half and hour and then they both stood.

Mel panicked. It dawned on her that Jan would see the rental car, confront her and that this would make Obie upset. She had to do something, and fast.

Mel reasoned that since Jan was in the back of the house, it would be safe to run across the clearing. This would save time and in this way Mel could get to her car before Jan saw it.

Mel quickly backtracked and made her way through the woods to the side of the house. She hugged the corner and peeked around it. She couldn't see Jan and the gentleman, but she thought she could still hear them in the back of the house. Mel took a deep breath and started sprinting across the clearing. She had taken but a few steps when she stepped in a hole, heard a snapping sound and a terrible pain gripped her leg. She fell to the ground writhing in agony. She then realized she was screaming. Seconds crept by, then minutes and then the sky darkened.

She opened her eyes and Jan was standing over her. "Mel… Mel," Jan said.

Mel saw a shadow next to Jan and the distinctive smell of aftershave invaded her nostrils and she saw Charlie's shrunken head hanging from the ceiling. She blinked her eyes and wondered if she was conscious. She pulled her thoughts together and the searing pain now was just a numbness. She envisioned a beautiful stallion running freely in a gorgeous green meadow. The shadow lurking over her grew larger.

"I'm sorry," Mel said to the shadow.

"Mel, do you know who this is?" Jan asked in a voice that seemed far away.

Mel nodded and said, "Yes, I do," and passed out.

She awoke in Dr. Matranga's clinic with jelly fish swimming in her head. She pried open her eyes and was relieved that the silly man with the crumbling ears was not back.

The door flew open and Obie burst into the room and was soon followed by Dr. Matranga.

EPILOGUE

From the vantage point of her office desk at TACKETT RECORDS Lannie could see the taller buildings in Los Angeles popping through the canopy of smog that covered the city. The buildings looked like shiny steel and glass boxes stuck in an endless, flat cotton ball.

It was difficult for her to concentrate on studying geometry with such a beautiful view, so she only half-heartedly glanced at the text book every now and then. She was not overly concerned about the test tomorrow. Tonight she had a tutoring session with Freddy, who had worked her into the busy schedule of his new business tutoring college students in math. In forty-five minutes he would make sure she understood everything in the chapter.

The phone on her desk rang and startled her. “This is Lannie.”

“It’s just me.”

“Bennie, I was just thinking about you.”

“Hey, I have to go shopping this afternoon, do you wanna come?” Bennie asked.

“You don’t know how wonderful that offer is. I was hoping to be rescued from this ivory tower.”

“Good. I need to buy a whole new wardrobe. I’ve gotten way too big for any of my clothes. Goodyear is thinking of hiring me, putting a tether through my nose and flying me over sporting events,” Bennie said.

“Suppose I meet you at one at Federico’s for lunch; we can shop afterwards,” Lannie suggested.

“Great. They’ve got a new low-carb menu and I should be able to find something I like.”

As soon as Lannie hung up the receiver the phone rang again.

“Lannie, it’s Jess.”

“Where are you?”

“I got in early and I’m at your house,” he said.

“I just made a date for lunch, sorry,” Lannie said.

"I can't see you until tonight anyway," Jess explained. "I've got a meeting with Tim at Greenbaum's office to go over some record business. We're thinking of getting into hip hop. Can we meet at your house around eight? Or is that too late?"

"That'll work just fine," she said.

"See you then."

Lannie put the receiver down and stared off at the horizon and wondered how everything could appear so perfectly in place. She reached for the phone to call Tim, but then drew her hand back. She studied the friendship ring on her finger and a huge smile erupted on her lips.

The skin underneath the cast itched, so Mel ran the coat hanger under the plaster of Paris and rubbed it on her leg. It was the tool that Dr. Matranga had suggested to ease her torment, and it worked. She finished her scratching, pressed her back against the trunk of the tree and relished the warm breeze on her face. She raised her sunglasses, plucked a glass of lemonade from the blanket on which she sat, rubbed the cold glass on her forehead and then slurped a piece of ice into her mouth.

Jan and Maggie hunted for four leaf clovers a few yards away, and she could hear Maggie singing as she danced in the ankle-high grass. The child never shut up anymore. Seemed like since she started talking she never stopped, but no one complained.

Jan grabbed her grandchild and twirled her around in a circle and Maggie squealed in delight. After a few turns Jan, dizzy, collapsed onto the grass laughing with Maggie on top of her. They rolled in the clover.

The cloppity clop of hooves thundering on the ground in the distance could be heard, even though the horse and rider appeared to be only a foot or so tall. Mel marveled at how fast Obie was going on the horse. Obie's hair was pushed backwards by the rushing wind and he bobbed with each gallop so fluidly that he looked as if he were part of the animal. As Obie drew closer the sound of the hooves beating time grew louder and the magnificent straining muscles of the beast became better defined. The horse looked to be as powerful as the mightiest of stallions.

Obie waved and in a few seconds he was pulling on the reins and slowing down. He came to rest and jumped down a few feet from where Mel rested. He turned loose the reins and the horse wandered off.

"I've got it here," he said and pulled the magazine from his knapsack.

"Have you read it?" she asked.

"Nope. I wanted us to do that together." He dropped down on the blanket onto his belly and unfolded the paper. "Let's see. The story on the Elvis Festival is on page three. You must not have much pull at *Weird Magazine,*" he teased and then flipped the page.

"Go ahead, Obie, rub it in."

He laughed and began reading the article…

Elvis Pressley has been dead over twenty-five years, yet his fans refuse to let him go. In Moscow, Tennessee, which is a short drive from Memphis, a non-profit organization holds an Elvis Festival every year. Many of the fans swear they've seen Elvis at the festival and come back every year searching for him. Most of the participants go just to have fun and enjoy the sound-alike and look-alike contests, the comfort food, Elvis's movies--and to hobnob with fellow worshipers of the King. The most interesting part of the festival is meeting the many people who acted with Elvis, served in the military with him and even nursed him. They still have a deep love for the man. "For whatever reason people come here, they leave having touched a piece of their youth," Obie Felton, the Mayor of Moscow said. "Sometimes they find a little magic and discover a piece of themselves they've forgotten or lost."

The next festival is in April. The following three pages of pictures give you a sampling of what to expect at such a festival. Elvis festivals are held all over the world and can be located on the Internet.

ABOUT THE AUTHOR

Glenn P. Marcel grew up in rural, Cajun Louisiana in the sleepy 50s and turbulent 60s in a town where the doors to his parents' home were never locked. He enjoyed off-beat employment experiences while growing up, including picking okra, bailing hay, collecting bills, pumping gas, selling Greyhound bus tickets, building houses, waiting on tables, roughnecking and selling clothes. He is a graduate of Louisiana State University (B.S. '73 and J.D. '75), and is currently practicing law in Baton Rouge, where he lives with his wife, Kathy.

Chasing Elvis is Marcel's second novel to be published. *Juggling The Truth* (Charleston Press) was published in 1989. He recently completed his fifth novel.

Also Available from The Invisible College Press:

City of Pillars, by Dominic Peloso
Tattoo of a Naked Lady, by Randy Everhard
Weiland, by Charles Brockden Brown
The Third Day, by Mark Graham
Leeward, by D. Edward Bradley
Cold in the Light, by Charles Gramlich
The Practical Surveyor, by Samuel Wyld
UFO Politics and the White House, by Larry W. Bryant
Utopian Reality, by Cathrine Simone
Phase Two, by C. Scott Littleton
Marsface, by R.M. Pala
Treatise on Mathematical Instruments, by John Robertson
The Rosicrucian Manuscripts, by Benedict J. Williamson
Proof of the Illuminati, by Seth Payson
Evilution, by Shaun Jeffrey
The Phoenix Egg, by Richard Bamberg
Axis Mundi Sum, by D.A. Smith
Diverse Druids, by Robert Baird
Attac and Defence of Fortified Places, by John Muller
Strega, by Richard Bamberg
Chasing Elvis, by Glen Marcel
New England and the Bavarian Illuminati

Lightning Source UK Ltd.
Milton Keynes UK
11 January 2010

148444UK00001B/197/A